SAVAGE WILD HEARTS

THE SAVAGE WILDS
BOOK ONE

SEAN FLETCHER

NEVER MISS A RELEASE

Get notified about new releases, exclusive ARCs, cover reveals, giveaways, and more by **joining my author newsletter.**

To those wild stories that keep us up at night

"Maybe there is a beast…maybe it's only us."

—William Golding, *Lord of the Flies*

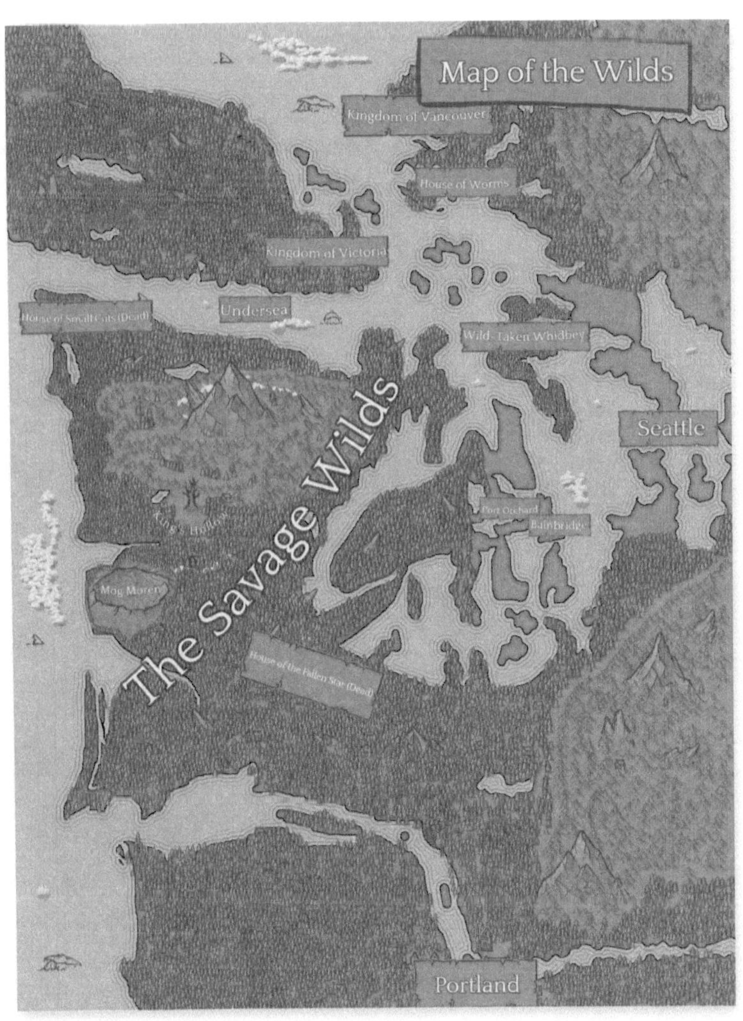

Map of the Wilds
Kingdom of Vancouver
House of Worms
Kingdom of Victoria
House of Small Cats (Dead)
Undersea
Wild-Taken Whidbey
Seattle
The Savage Wilds
King's Hollow
Port Orchard
Bainbridge
Mog Morey
House of the Fallen Star (Dead)
Portland

THE SURVIVOR

My first clear memory was of blood.

It covered me so entirely that when I moved it was like peeling off a layer of skin or tearing a scab. It stung the corners of my eyes and infused copper on my tongue.

I could remember little else. Certainly not who my parents were, nor how I, a helpless, nearly naked child had been the sole survivor of a town where the Wilds had killed everyone else. Or so Peyton told me later.

I *do* remember seeing her face for the first time. She'd emerged over the rubble, as vines curled green fingers around pieces of jagged stone and dragged them deeper into the trees. Her eyes met mine. Her jaw slacked.

"One's alive!" she shouted over her shoulder. "One's— Oh my god, oh my god."

She kicked at something—a red-eyed little beast that scurried out of sight—and cut around a sprouting fern growing inches in seconds.

She was nearly crying when she scooped me up.

"Are you hurt anywhere? I can't believe it; I can't *believe* it. Are your parents nearby, sweetie?"

Other memories came unbidden. Bodies in a dark mass on the ground. Someone holding me close as Peyton did, then screaming—ripped apart in a flash of blue.

Peyton took my silence as a negative. She stopped only once to turn back to the trees. They'd already encroached closer, just like the undergrowth.

"Damn you," she muttered. "Just leave us alone."

A flicker of movement in the trees, slipping between the trunks so fast I nearly missed it. A person? Another child, like me?

A boy's face?

Looking back, I must have imagined it. Everyone had died, Peyton assured me.

"Everyone except you," she'd murmur against the top of my head while she held me tight. "My little heart gem. My little piece of heaven."

I'd learn later that the forests had been normal once. Normal trees, normal plants, normal animals. That may have been two generations past or a hundred. It didn't matter. Anyone who remembered a time before the Wilds was long dead.

What mattered was what happened when the Wilds appeared. Its tainted magic sank its roots deep. Plants grew in a frenzy. Trees tripled in size. Beasts never before seen crawled from the night itself. It was said that in days, once-safe forests became full of teeth, and full of *them*.

Humans fought back as best we could. We expanded when we were able, and the Wilds pushed back. The Wilds devoured cities and we burned the green.

Eventually we reached an impasse. Humans retreated into a few pockets of safe cities and towns and tried to live peacefully surrounded by the Wilds. We harvested what we were able. The brave and stupid amongst us even turned to harvesting the Wilds' heart gems, stones found within chests of the beasts, filled with magic even we could use.

"Don't you ever go back there!" Peyton screamed when she discovered me returning home one night, holding a bloody fistful of heart gems I'd been eager to pawn off. Selling them would help her, I'd thought. Help *us*.

She'd squeezed me so tight I nearly choked.

"Never, ever go back there, Val. The Wilds lost you once. It won't lose you again, and it never forgets. *Promise* me you'll never go back."

"I promise," I'd said, terrified by her fear. "I promise."

If only I'd kept that promise.

CHAPTER
ONE

I crouched low in the undergrowth, berry juice and blood covering my face, and stared deep into the Wilds.

The Wilds stared back.

The blood wasn't mine. Not yet, though there were plenty of things out here that would spill it given half the chance. Some of those things were around me. Scurrying, scuttling, rustling, scampering. None of what I hunted had noticed me, but that could change in an instant, as could my luck.

For humans, nowhere in the Wilds was safe. Not even for a moment.

I tracked my quarry as it fluttered between the overhead branches. I slowly tilted my head. The twigs and berries I'd woven in the curls of my black hair caught on the brush, and I avoided wincing.

The bird paused, let out a throaty caw. Ever so slowly, I raised my bow and pulled—back muscles straining, scar on the inside of my arm stretching—until it was fully taut.

Breathe out. Hold. Center.

Times like this, the moment before the kill, everything else faded out. My vision funneled. Even the Wilds, which were never quiet, seemed to hold its breath, as though waiting to see what would happen.

I released the arrow.

A hissing flight followed by a meaty thwack. The bird dropped. I breathed again, and the Wilds came rushing back. The smell of churned dirt. The glistening, chilly mist on my skin. The distant crack as creatures disturbed the underbrush deeper within.

I hurried to grab the bird before something else did. The arrow had pierced right through. Its glassy eyes peered up at me, no longer tinged gold and red.

"Thank you for your sacrifice," I mumbled as I tugged the arrow out. "Or your clumsiness, or plain bad luck. Whatever it was, thanks."

I slung the bow on my back and pulled my hunting knife. My quiet and effective tools. Nothing loud and obnoxious like the pistols and assault rifles some hunters carried. I didn't need to draw more attention to myself.

I hovered the tip of the knife over the bird's heart. "Easy does it. Easy…"

I plunged it in. Warm blood ran down the blade and coated my fingers, but in no time I'd pulled out a misshapen, glowing gem. The heart gem.

My own heart fell. The bird had been small, but I'd hoped its heart gem would have been bigger than this. Along with the meager pickings I'd already collected today, selling it would barely cover the price of getting out here and back.

Grumbling, I stowed the gem in my pouch and used the blade of my knife to dig a shallow grave. The moment I'd removed the heart gem, the rot had begun. The bird's muscles and tendons turned to wet leaves and slender roots. Mushrooms sprang from the tips of its wings and its feathers changed to veiny leaves until I was lowering nothing but a collection of damp forest debris into the hole.

No matter how many heart gems I took, I never got used to that.

I stood and checked my watch. Three hours until the bus left, and I was stuck out here. To me, the Wilds and all their terrible beauty were like a drug: dangerous, but with a high that was even more alluring.

But even I didn't want to spend the night out here. That'd be a death sentence.

Still, I needed more heart gems. Bigger ones. That meant bigger, more dangerous prey, and that meant going deeper. I could risk it. I had to.

I found an open glen with a stream running through it. After checking that nothing was watching me, I washed the blood off my hands and refilled my Nalgene, the cold water turning the tips of my fingers numb. I didn't stop scanning the edges of the trees, pausing on every flicker of movement.

To me, who'd spent so much time here, there were patterns to my surroundings. Scars from past fires and magic run amok. The greenery was a map that a discerning eye could navigate, leading a person away from danger. Or, if read poorly, straight into it. I breathed in mist, and the faint ashen taste of magic came with it.

I was crouching among the reeds before I knew why.

Everything had gone quiet. Even the insects stopped humming. Then I heard it moving in the trees. Something bigger than any deer or bear, something that uprooted saplings and trembled the earth.

I focused on the lichen-consumed rock my hand rested on and thought small thoughts. *I am invisible. I am not here. You will pass me by.*

Whatever it was did just that and time started again. I

slowly stood and stared at where it'd gone. A delightful, terrible fear came over me.

A beast that big had to have a massive heart gem. If I could get it and sell it, that'd surely be enough get us by for a couple weeks. Maybe even a month. Danger be damned. I was going after it.

I double-tied my bootlaces, freed myself from the muck, and followed, easily finding the cleared trail the beast had left. I started to jog, senses on alert for the moment the Wilds hushed again.

I soon came across broken branches that told me the beast had gone left, deeper in than I'd anticipated. I pushed aside branches and slid down a hill into a small gulley, jeans soaking with mist.

A green shape loomed and I froze, certain the beast had snuck up on me.

It was a small prop plane, claimed by the forest. Vines grounded its wings, and half a tree burst from the carcass of its fuselage.

"Nothing to be scared of," I said to calm my rapidly beating heart.

I ran my hand along the rusted propeller, held fast by roots. Most people stayed safely within Seattle's city limits or the well-guarded suburbs surrounding it. Most relied on hunters like me for heart gems and protection. Maybe this pilot had wanted to find a lost loved one. Or uncover a town that the Wilds had long claimed. Or maybe they'd been stupid. Whatever the reason, they'd paid dearly for it.

I leapt inside the raggedly torn rear and checked for any remaining supplies. Finding none, I made my way around to the torn cockpit and my stomach dropped.

The pilot and their passenger had been dead long enough for their skin and muscles to rot away or to be stripped by scavengers. Slender vines of delicate white corpse flowers wreathed their arms and legs that remained. The missing limbs might have been lost in the crash or torn off.

I forced myself to look at them. No matter how many days I survived, no matter how much I learned and how beautiful and even comforting the Wilds could be, there were things within that would end me without a second's thought.

Something caught my eye at the bodies' feet. Someone had built a small house—a shrine—from bark-flaking branches. The coppery-gold leaf of a glint bush was nestled inside. An offering taken from one of the rarest plants in the Wilds.

I reached for my knife, turning slow in a circle. The few glint bush leaves I'd ever seen didn't last more than a few hours after being picked. Maybe this one had been left by a pilgrim from one of the numerous religions that'd cropped up around the Wilds. Maybe that was just my wishful thinking.

With an uncomfortable, tingling awareness of being watched, I kept moving, only stopping long enough to grab a handful of herb blooms for Peyton.

"You can't go," Peyton had said this morning. She'd managed to push herself out of bed and lean against the door frame, something she hadn't been well enough to do in a while. A thin, baggy nightgown draped her withering frame, and her hair stuck to the near-constant sheen of sweat coating her forehead. "You know how much I worry when you do. It's a gamble every time, and one day you'll lose."

I'd concentrated on cinching my knife tighter to my belt and thought carefully about how to make her understand something I didn't understand myself.

"You'd rather I watch the rot eat you alive?" I said. "That's less of a gamble and more of a certainty."

"I'm getting—"

She gave a thick, wet cough, lungs filled with wild rot just like thousands of others. She managed a wan smile when the coughing stopped. "I was going to say better."

I gently looped my arm around her and helped her hobble back to bed, where she'd stayed since the rot had entered its final stage. I hated this room, hated that it reminded me of how powerless I was against what tore her apart.

"I'll bring you more herb bloom to ease the pain. I almost have enough saved to visit the clinic in Seattle. I heard they've found a treatment that should be one hundred percent effective."

"Don't do this, Val," Peyton wheezed. "Joshua is with the DFA. He can—"

"He won't," I snapped. "Nobody in the Department of Fringe Affairs gives a damn about curing it. They'd rather burn down the Wilds than see if anything in there can help."

Peyton had grabbed my arm. Her grip was stronger than it'd been in weeks, her eyes more lucid and shock-white against her fever-flushed skin. "I need to tell you... I should have before... Don't go, Val. They'll find out you're there. They'll find *you*. The Wilds lost you once. It won't lose you again."

I must have heard this story a dozen times. How Peyton and her ex-husband had given birth to Joshua, but how she'd always wanted a little girl. How, the day she'd found me, blood-covered and alone at the edge of the Wilds, it seemed like I was the answer to her prayers. But those prayers weren't enough to ease her fear of losing me.

"I'll be back soon," I'd whispered, pulling away.

I broke off another sprig of herb bloom and stored it in my backpack. I picked up the beast's tracks. Fresh, with the deep indentations of five claws, its entire foot as big as my head. I swallowed the fear creeping up my throat. I was closing in. This wasn't the time to second-guess.

My legs burned as I hiked up the next hill. I smelled fresh water, heard the slight trickling of a stream, or maybe runoff from a nearby lake. The perfect resting spot for a wandering beast to quench its thirst after a full day carving a path of destruction.

Staying crouched, I carefully parted the undergrowth until I made it to the edge of a pebbled shore. I barely stopped my gasp.

Trees nearly as thick as skyscrapers—trunks scarred by fire and age—grew half-submerged in pools of crystalline water so clear I could see the roofs of the sunken houses twenty feet down. A drowned city, now a habitat for fish and water beasts. I could just make out murky shapes flitting out of the build-ings' long-shattered windows and broken doors.

Islands of green moss and ferns dotted the surface beneath a canopy so broad that only thin rays of light made it through. All was still.

All except for the boy.

He was crouched on the nearest island of green, completely dry as though he'd managed to jump the ten feet across the water. His back was to me, but it looked like he was examining something. He brought it to his nose and sniffed.

My first thought was that he had to be the pilgrim who'd left the glint bush leaf. No one else would be out this far, and he was dressed strangely enough for it: a mottled green tunic with a hood as deep as the one on my rain jacket. His entire form, even crouched, was hard around the edges, crackling with strength. A circlet of ivy and nightshade was woven within his dirty-blond hair, clasping itself closed at the back of his head. The entire outfit was ridiculous, but I had seen worse among the sick and desperate who braved the Wilds.

I started to rise from where I hid, to call out that if he didn't head back soon—if we both didn't—we'd be dead.

As though sensing my movement, he stood and turned.

Tall. He was tall. And he didn't try to blend in as any prey or human would, but instead stood out like a predator daring anything to attack. His eyes were gold-red. His mouth was sharp and thin like a sliver of broken glass, and it cocked into a smirk.

"Come out, come out, wherever you are," he said, voice lush with threat.

Everything about him made me want to scream danger. He might have been the most beautiful boy I'd ever seen, but in the Wilds, the worst things for you looked the best.

That was most true for him: a wildling.

I stayed crouched, barely breathing, as he turned his focus from one island and tree to the next.

It was impossible. Nobody had seen a wildling this close to Seattle in two years, since the last envoy failed. For a while, I even doubted they existed. Surely they were figments of fairy tales told to entertain primetime viewers or conjured by veteran hunters to scare off the newbies.

But there were stories; human cities pulled deep into the Wilds' depths, and the survivors made slaves to inhuman masters. Wildling kingdoms, each with their own rulers, all viciously fighting for territory and claiming parts of the human world inch by inch. All of it sounded like fabrications of a fevered imagination.

And yet here he stood.

"I know someone's there."

My skin chilled. The wildling was looking down at a collection of butterflies at the water's edge, their vibrant wings flashing in the sunlight. His eyes rose and scanned his surroundings again. "Don't worry, I'll find you."

I slowly started to back up. Paused. Now that I'd tempered my panic, a couple things became startlingly clear:

If half the stories of wildlings were true, I wouldn't make it five feet before he discovered me.

Then there were his eyes. Violently gold and red. Every beast with eyes like that had a heart gem. Who was to say he wouldn't, too? One powerful enough to buy Peyton and me out of our crappy apartment. Enough to get her the treatment she needed with more left over for the necessities.

My body moved on its own, and I silently nocked an arrow and drew my bow before I finished the thought. I rested the arrow's vanes against my cheek. The tip kept shaking when I aligned it with his chest.

He deserves it. He wouldn't hesitate to kill me, not for a second.

I'd taken life before. Dozens of beasts of the Wild had died at my hand. This boy—this beast—wouldn't be any different.

I evened my breathing. The wildling turned, giving me an easier shot. My surroundings shrank to the single point that was the tip of the arrow. All I had to do was loose it.

Loose it.

Loose it.

I thought of all I had to gain. Peyton. Our life. Freedom from this danger.

My fingers stayed frozen in their curled position.

I couldn't do it.

I jumped, aim jerking, as the wildling laughed. "You'll only get one shot. Make it count."

I realized he was talking to me a moment before the ferns wrapped around my legs and pulled.

The arrow loosed, flying wide over his shoulder and embedding into the tree's trunk. The wildling's eyes zeroed on me. "There you are."

I ripped myself free of the mud, nearly losing my boots in the process. The ferns he must have magicked tried to hold me in place. Panicked, I whipped out my knife and cut myself free.

I nearly fell face first as I fled, not daring to look back. I didn't need to. I could hear the near-silent rush of air as something leapt across the water and landed on the shore.

He was after me.

I knew I couldn't outrun him. My only hope was to make it to where the bus picked me up, but that was at least a couple of miles.

More magicked plants reached for me from the undergrowth. I sliced them all away in a frenzy and kept running. Close behind, the boy who was not a boy laughed. "Good. Make this fun."

I wouldn't make it a couple miles.

I reached a rise and slid down a slick embankment, ending up at the bottom in a crouch, partially concealed by bushes. My harsh breath screamed in my ears, only just drowning out my thudding heart. I struggled to clench my knife with my sweat-slicked hand. I didn't hear the wildling pursuing me anymore, but that didn't mean much. He was part of the Wilds, as much as the trees and beasts. If he wanted me, I couldn't escape.

I had to fight.

I scooped a handful of damp dirt and forced my breathing to slow. Years of practice had me parsing out the surrounding sounds and smells, categorizing them into those that were benign and those that could cause me harm.

There you are.

I spun and threw the dirt. The wildling knocked it aside with a flick of his hand, sneering.

"That was alarmingly sad. No, *don't try to fight me.*"

I'd raised my knife when his voice hit me. It was thick and heady, dripping syrup into my veins and ensnaring every thought I had of resisting him.

"That's it," he said as my limbs slackened, knife lowering. "There's nothing to be afraid of. Certainly not from me."

He drew closer, confident his magic had me completely under his control. "Perhaps they were wrong. Perhaps you are not so special after all. I had hoped that you would be different. That's mine now."

He held out his hand for my knife and, despite my resistance, I started to give it to him, helpless under the wildlings' most feared ability.

Influence. Compulsion. Magic. Whatever you called it didn't make it any better. The horror stories the news played reminded us always. Scenes of people found frozen in place and succumbed to the elements, despite being mere feet from shelter. Some who had completely lost their minds and murdered their families or killed themselves. Others who had simply gotten too close to the trees and were drawn inside against their will, never to be heard from again.

My knife was nearly in the boy's hand. I willed myself to focus. I willed his magic to release me.

A second before his fingers curled around my knife, I whipped it upward, using every bit of my natural fighting instinct. It was a joke compared to the ex-military and government-sponsored hunters, but it was enough to throw the wildling off guard. He snarled as the blade nearly caught his cheek.

I swiped again, driving him back. He was fast. Too fast. I couldn't hit him, but stopping for even a moment meant giving him a chance to counter—

"You will *stop*."

His compulsion hit me again, and my body briefly stuttered to a halt, magic settling over my bones like a leaded suit.

"You *are* something," he mused, recovering. This close he smelled like earth after the rain, like a charred tree following a lightning strike. "I've never encountered a human with the ability to resist compulsion as strong as mine before. But you still couldn't stop me."

My cheek tingled as he traced a finger around the edge of my face.

"I can make it quick," he whispered. "Turn you into a tree in the span of a heartbeat. Or keep you immobilized until the wolves come and tear off pieces of you bit by bit. What do you think? Do you agree that's a suitable punishment for trespassers like you? Now, now, don't do that."

My entire body had begun to tremble. But not from fear, as he likely thought. His compulsion was no stranger to me now, and I knew how to fight it.

The moment I broke his magic's hold on me, I plunged my knife straight into his chest, burying it to the hilt.

"How about a third option?" I said. "You die."

He didn't scream. He barely let out a gasp as his body hit the ground. The Wilds went silent, and for one terrible moment, I feared retribution. I'd just killed one of their masters.

I wiped at my cheeks. My face still tingled with the feel of his fingertips on my skin. Extremely human fingertips. Everything about him looked entirely too human. Even now he appeared as though he were merely sleeping, eyes closed, a smirk on his lips.

Maybe I should have felt horrified at what I'd done, but there was only relief. He'd have done so much worse; he'd basically said so. This was nothing less than he deserved.

I had no time to linger. Not as late as it was, while standing over the body of a wildling, and very much still in danger.

I knelt and, with a hard tug, removed my knife from his chest. Only a thin smear of blood coated the blade. Red as bittersweet berries. Seeing it turned my stomach. I'd expected sap.

Small white flowers had started blooming across his chest, as though trying to cover up the unsightly wound.

I followed the line of flowers to where his heart gem should be, just beneath a few layers of now-dead flesh. Less than a minute. That was all it'd take for me to carve it out, and my problems would be solved. At least for a time.

I rested my knife over his chest, letting the tip sink past his damp shirt and into his skin. Just a little more pressure. I could do this.

A strange rhythm radiated through my hands. A heartbeat, steady and strong.

Not mine, I realized too late. His.

"You should have gone for my heart first," the wildling said.

Then all I saw was darkness.

TWO

Strong arms cradled me when I came to. For a long moment, I existed in the state between waking and dreaming before realizing that I was being carried. My cheek rested against a chest.

I wasn't dead. Some other hunters must have found me. I tilted my head up and could just make out the bottom of a sharp jaw. "Thank—"

I plummeted into water a fraction above freezing. The cold punched the air from my lungs and seized my muscles. I gasped on instinct but only managed to swallow a mouthful of water. When I tried to swim to the surface, I discovered my hands were tightly bound behind my back.

Not good. So not good.

I flailed and breached the surface, gulping a single breath before my head was pushed under again. Any thought that this was accidental vanished. This guy was trying to kill me!

I flailed again but this time my hair was yanked above the water where I got a brief, blurry look at the wildling I'd stuck my knife into.

"Y-you should b-be dead," I said.

"You wouldn't be the first who's disappointed," he answered. "Your smell offends me."

He dunked me again. Something coarse scraped my face—moss or lichen—as he scrubbed at it, and chunks of dried berry juice and blood were carried away by the current. I struggled, but between his strength, my bound hands, and the frigid cold, it looked like I was going to die.

Then the wildling scooped his arms beneath my knees and back and hauled me, dripping, out of the water.

"Y-you b-b-bastard. P-put me d-down before I—"

"As you wish."

I was dropped unceremoniously against a large tree trunk. Vines circled from behind and pinned me to the bark.

"So you don't try anything stupid. You've already done plenty of that for today."

I managed to flip my wet curtain of hair out of my face and blink until my vision mostly cleared. My head still throbbed from where he'd hit me.

Then I became *very* awake when I felt his hands moving beneath my shirt, near my collarbone and above my heart.

"Are you... *Are you feeling me up?*"

I lashed out with my still-free legs, but he easily leaned to the side and caught them, pinning them between his arm and ribs. His smile was malicious.

"Don't flatter yourself. You know very well I'm checking for the heart gem you humans so love to use."

I tried to bite him, but all I could do was wait until he discovered what I'd been hiding for years.

He pulled his hand back and frowned. "You don't have a heart gem. You resisted my magic by yourself."

"Maybe you're just weak," I spat.

He tilted his head, eyes glittering dangerously. "I am many things, but weak isn't one of them. Only the strongest wildlings can use compulsion on humans. And only the Lords can do so as I can. You are none of those things, and yet...you resisted."

I expected hatred in his face. Maybe disgust. The sort of reaction any human would have had if they found out what I could do without the aid of a heart gem. In these tense times, abnormalities were practically the enemy.

Instead, the wildling smirked. He went to my discarded backpack and started rifling through it. I didn't bother asking him to stop. Human courtesies didn't apply to monsters like him.

My mouth went dry as he pulled out the small pouch of heart gems I'd collected this trip. *Now* he looked disgusted. He dangled the bag at me, the gems inside clacking together.

"Much less than I anticipated, but this is just one of the many times you've taken, isn't it? You have no respect, just like the rest."

A grating laugh escaped my lips. "Says the guy—the *thing* —who tied a defenseless girl to a tree just to steal from her. Preach your twisted integrity to someone else."

"Please. You're far from defenseless." He rubbed at the spot on his chest. Exactly where my knife had gone in, I noted with some satisfaction. It looked healed. Unfortunately.

"I hope that hurt," I said.

"More than you know. But I've endured worse."

He dumped my heart gems into his hand and, before I could protest, cast all but one into the river.

"I needed those!" I struggled against the vines, but they only held tighter. "You have no right—"

"I have *every* right," he hissed. I blinked and he was crouched before me, crackling with rage. His mouth was thin as a razor, eyes equally as sharp. The plants around him began to frenzy, vines flailing, new shoots spewing forth with rampant growth. "My kind rules the Wilds—"

"That took over *our* world—"

"—therefore, everything in it belongs to us. You are just another thieving little fox."

"Then why not kill me?" I leaned as far forward as the vines allowed. "Kill me like vermin and leave my body as a warning. At least then it'd save me from talking to you."

It wasn't the damp chill settling into my bones that made me shiver as the words left my lips. What was I doing? I shouldn't be baiting him, planting ideas in his head when I was sure he had far worse ones of his own.

I flinched as he raised his hand, but he only pressed the remaining heart gem over my heart.

Nothing happened. I felt no surge of power rush through me, not even a tiny one. There was no glow that every full heart gem made when placed near a human's heart.

"Interesting," he said. "It wasn't a fluke. Your magic comes from within. You're just like a wildling."

"I'm nothing like you."

He removed the heart gem and pressed it above his own heart where it remained as cold and dead as it had over mine. "No, you're not. But you're not like them, either. And that's precisely why I was looking for you."

He flicked my last heart gem into the river. Then he stood and gazed down at me, the heat in his expression searing my damp skin. "Now that I've confirmed what I needed, what should I call you?"

I glared in answer.

"You will call me Rune." He bowed, bending at the waist, one hand splayed over his heart. "If you won't give me your name, I'll give you one. Perhaps grub. Or would leech be more appropriate..."

There was no use reasoning with him, or appealing to any sort of sympathy that didn't exist. The most I could do was stall, or maybe get some information I could use to plot my escape. He wasn't the first bully I'd faced. Though he was certainly the most dangerous.

As Rune turned to examine something by my pack, I quickly gauged my surroundings. While I'd been knocked out, night had swooped in, and the cold temps with it. I'd long missed the bus back. Peyton would be frantic with worry. Some of the other hunters, the ones who saw me as their biggest competition or simply a pest, would be overjoyed.

"What are you doing here?" I said. "If you hate us so much, why are you so close to the edge of the Wilds?"

"Isn't it obvious? I was waiting for you."

My shock jolted some feeling back into the parts of my arms that had started going numb. "Because of my magic? How did you—"

"Someone who is loyal to me knew of a human who consistently defied the dangers of the Wilds. The trees and birds and deep, dark things told her of you, who, against everything we knew, had a unique, impossible magic. And so I wondered, what trickery did they possess that allowed them to accomplish this? And what else could they do?"

I shook my head. "I don't know what you think I am, but I'm nothing special. Just an abnormality."

"So you don't agree that your survival in our Wilds is unusual?"

He drew closer as my stomach twisted uncomfortably. "You pretend that you don't hear the rhythmic breath of life around you or see patterns in the green where others don't?"

"That's not... None of that's true. I've just been out here a long time. I've learned things." The excuse sounded hollow, even to me.

Rune stared at me for so long I had to resist squirming under the intensity of his gaze.

"So what now?" I asked. "Are you going to kill me? Spirit me away in the night?"

"Perhaps. That depends on how you answer what I'm about to offer."

The distant snap of a sapling made him jerk in surprise. It was my turn to smirk.

"Is someone afraid of the big, bad Wilds?"

Rune's lip curled. "Nothing would dare attack me here."

We were in a small depression of earth carved by years of overflow from the river. The exposed roots of the enormous trees wove natural walls on either side that kept us hidden while simultaneously offering a number of ways to escape. It was the sort of place I'd pick if I didn't want to be found.

"Of course. Nothing would dare," I said.

Rune ignored me. He placed his hand against the nearest root and whispered words in a language I couldn't hope to understand. The roots reached up with alarming ferocity, intertwining to close the gaps above our heads. Bioluminescent mushrooms sprouted along them. The bleached yellow and green light glowed strongly enough to cut harsh lines in Rune's already harsh face, the bladed edges of his jaw and pools of darkness that were his closed eyes.

Rune dropped his hand and the sensation of his strange words fled my body, leaving me shivering worse than before. I'd been so terrified I'd lost touch with how desperately I needed warmth.

"Is something wrong with you?" Rune said.

I kept my lips clamped together, but my teeth chattered against my will. "N-no."

"You're a terrible liar."

"Pity. According to y-you that's another wonderful human q-quality."

Rune knelt before me, holding what looked like a shriveled chili pepper, or maybe the half-rotted root of a plant. "Eat."

"I'm not eating anything you give me."

He grabbed my chin. I tried to bite him again, but he expected that and forced whatever he held down my throat. An overpowering peppery flavor filled my mouth and made me cough. A flush of heat rushed through my entire body until it was as though I sat beside a furnace. I almost expected my clothes to start steaming and smoke to pour out of my ears. I waited for the poisonous side effects, but only the pleasantly warm feelings remained.

"Why?" I managed after I finished coughing.

"You can't freeze to death before you hear what I have to offer."

"I don't want to hear anything you have to offer."

"You didn't want the pepper root, but you had it anyway." The mushrooms' glow lit up his obnoxious grin. "Humans always want something from the Wilds. Why else would you be here, if not to take?"

"Like the Wilds haven't done the same to us."

"I'm not here to argue subjective morality. You resisted my magic; therefore, you're someone I can use. You've survived numerous times in the Wilds, which means you have some semblance of skill, no matter how rudimentary."

I waited for him to stop insulting me and get to his point.

"My offer is this: I want you to help me take the high throne of the wildlings," Rune said.

I coughed again. Partly from the lingering taste of pepper root, but mostly from the insanity of what he'd just said. "Maybe you left some lichen in my ears. Help you take *what*?"

"Even someone like you has heard of how the wildlings rule."

Of course I had, as much as I'd heard trickled whispers from those few who escaped the Wilds or the rare hunters who went deep within and saw impossible things. Once-human cities claimed by jeweled frost and moss and glittering with lush plants, all led by savage wildling rulers. Wild kingdoms filled with glimmering rot and delights and dangers too great for any human, made to ensnare and entrap the weak or desperate. I knew rationally the few liaisons from the human world had to be meeting with *someone* with authority. But still.

"This is modern day," I said. "Nobody needs kings."

"Yes, which is why your human government has worked so flawlessly," Rune said. "We have Lords and a single high ruler because there's one thing wildlings respect above all else: power. And I plan to have the most."

He towered over me as he stood, looking into the blackness just beyond the luminescent glow of our little sanctuary. "The throne of the high king has sat vacant for years. In that time, the Lords of these Wilds, in the places you once called Portland and Vancouver and Victoria, haven't made a move to claim it, and the ones on the western edge of the peninsula are too weak to try. All of them have been busy squabbling with each other and dealing with minor affairs. As long as the throne remained empty and none attempted to claim it, they had no reason to go to all-out war. Mostly, no one took it because they had no *right*."

He squeezed his fist, no doubt imagining it being the throat of someone he hated. "I have that right. I will take it, and I will make them all heel."

"And then what?" I said. "Unite your stolen kingdoms to destroy the humans?"

He smiled. "Your bloodlust is commendable, but you have

a simple idea of what it is to rule. As long as the humans remain where they belong and keep their hunters away, we won't have a problem."

He knelt again, and his focus told me my part in his insane plan was coming.

"Dead wildlings have been appearing lately, killed by powerful magic. Unlikely the work of a human, so don't get your hopes up," he said as I failed to hide my surprise. "My guess is that one of the Lords has become discontent with their status. The kingdom responsible hasn't claimed it yet, but it has thrown them all into disarray. They are tense and alert, yes, but they are more suspicious of one another than ever before. It is in this chaos that I will take my throne.

"That's where you will help. For as bad as you think I am, the Lords are worse. With their strength they can compel anyone who opposes them, wildling and human alike. They can whisper dark thoughts into your mind and drive you insane or make you turn on your allies. With an errant command, a victim would happily swallow broken pieces of a blade or eat the flesh of a loved one, aware the entire time of what they were doing, but unable to stop it. There are few ways to guard against such magic.

"But you resisted my compulsion, as strong as it is. With your...unusual skill, you will help me, and I will reward you in kind. I am cruel, but I am also fair. Become my killer and my blade. They will be focused on stopping me and never suspect you waiting to put a knife in their backs. And because of that you will be my...what's the phrase humans use? The ace up my sleeve?"

"You have to be kidding," I said. "The moment they see I'm human, they'll kill me on sight."

"I can disguise you."

What little I knew of wildlings and their magic made me

suspect a little trickery wasn't going to fool some powerful Lords. "And if that doesn't work?"

"As part of my deal, I'll ensure that nobody will kill you."

"Please. Don't make promises that are impossible to keep."

"I don't."

I looked for any tell that he was lying. The twitch of a muscle in the severe lines of his face. The barest shudder of his gold-red eyes unable to hold mine. He truly believed that he could keep me safe from all the horrible things he'd described.

"Lucky me," I drawled. "I won't die. I'll only get dismembered or frozen or turned into some horrendous, barely alive thing. And what do I get out of all this?"

He flicked his hand, and rubies, emeralds, sparkling glass, and gold appeared in it. "I'm not as good at conjuring such things as others, but I could give you enough to satisfy any taste."

"Keep trying. Those are unnatural. There's a shine about them that's wrong. People will take heart gems, and they'll take a few other things from here, but some they don't bother with. Some are cursed."

"Very well." It physically hurt to watch the jewels melt back into the dirt. Rune raised a finger and tapped his heart. "Then how about this? All the magic you could ever need."

"I get to cut out your heart? Good deal. Except for one small problem: I can't use any wildlings' heart gems, even if you did actually give them to me."

I was pleased to see an annoyed muscle feather in his jaw. "You could sell them, likely for more money than you'd ever need. Help me, and I will let you carve out all the heart gems of the Lords. Help me, and you can carve out the hearts of any who stand against me. No use letting them go to waste."

His eyes glittered. "And you, little fox, with the money you could get anything you ever wanted. The highest loft atop a glittering tower of wealth. Perhaps food to fatten your belly, men to fill your bed. Or women, it doesn't matter to me." He curled his nose. "Perhaps new clothes and a bath."

"Screw you." If he'd been a little closer, I'd have tried to kick him again. He knew nothing of what I really wanted, but I was more tempted by the offer than I cared to admit.

"Don't lie to yourself." He leaned in, and his breath tickled the side of my neck, voice thick like honey. "You may be something different, but you're not too good for human wants. But there's more: I also offer you something intangible that can't be easily bought."

"And that is?" I hated how my voice came out breathlessly light.

"The power I know you crave, enough to hurt those who hurt you. That's something I understand."

Goosebumps spread across my skin. Our bodies were nearly touching.

"And there is another reason you'll accept," Rune said. "If you help me, you'll find answers to questions you didn't even know to ask."

"I don't have questions."

Lies. All of it lies. Rune smiled like he knew it, too.

"And yet here you are, back again. You can't stay away, can you? The Wilds tug you like a thorn buried in your heart. You might have escaped them once. Twice. A dozen times. But you never leave, not really. A part of you is here. The Wilds never give anything back unless they have a reason. Something happened to you here. You just don't want to remember."

A dark sky covering a shaking earth. Bright light and screaming and then...nothing. Nothing until Peyton took my hand and led me away. "I'm not talking about it."

"Good. I don't particularly care to know."

Rune leaned back, smirking like he'd already given me

exactly what I wanted. "Consider wisely, little fox. You *want* me as High King of the Wildlings."

I knew almost nothing about the politics between humans and the Wilds, only that neither side had made any obvious attacks against the other in years. The last human attempt had been the Reclamation where we burned huge swaths of the forest to try to make the land livable again. Instead, all we'd done was seriously piss off the Wilds, and it'd taken everything back with a vengeance. Hundreds died. Entire cities were overtaken in hours. We never tried again, and the Wilds since hadn't spread. Mostly.

But despite our stalemate, we were teetering on a knife's edge. I could feel a restless energy every time I entered the Wilds. Like cresting a waterfall and waiting for the inevitable drop. There was a jittery nervousness in the city, too. The news hadn't said much, but attacks along the edge were growing more common. There was a tint of fear anywhere outside of the padded comfort of Seattle. People were looking for something, anything, to keep them safe.

"So as high king you'd stop the Wilds from taking any more of my world," I clarified.

"I make no such promises," Rune said. "All I want is the throne."

That wasn't a yes, but it wasn't a no. "And why do you want it so bad? If you're the rightful ruler, why haven't you taken it already?"

His entire body went taut. "Because it's my right. Because it's *owed* to me. Others, however, don't agree."

There was more to it than that, but I didn't care about the details. I shouldn't have cared at all.

"I've laid out my offer," Rune said. "What is your choice?"

Some "choice" it was. "I need a little time to think it over."

His smile was indulgent, maybe even a little playful, like he knew I was stalling. "You will decide now. Or I will leave you tied here for whatever beasts are nearby. Maybe they'll be kind enough to bite your head off first. Or they'll go for the entrails and pick away at them piece by piece—"

"Okay, okay." I tried to look downcast, as though he'd bullied me into agreeing with what he wanted. "I...guess I'll do it."

"There, that wasn't so hard. This way we'll both get what we want."

He placed his fingers on the vines pinning me to the tree. "Some advice: let any traitorous thoughts you have die. Run and I will find you. Go back on your word and I'll think of creative ways to make your end as unpleasant as possible."

This guy didn't give an inch. What did I expect from such a merciless creature? "I understand."

The vines drew back, and I was free.

"Now my hands?" I said, showing him the bindings.

"I don't think so. You'll stay like that tonight. You can have your full freedom when we meet with the others tomorrow."

"Can't you make an exception? I promise I won't...oh..."

I tried to stand and immediately flopped back down. I shook my head as though to clear it. "Ow, ow. That hurts so bad."

"What is it?" Rune snapped.

Beneath the curtain of hair obscuring my eyes, I watched his feet as he drew closer. I let out another pathetic groan. "That pepper root you gave me. I think it's messing with my stomach."

"Liar. It's entirely harmless. If you think for a second I'm going to tolerate antics like this—"

The ropes around my wrists—weakened by the sharp rock I'd used to saw at them for the last few minutes—ripped as I tore them apart. I slammed my palms against Rune's chest. An electric buzz ran between us. I'd learned long ago to hide my magic. A secret I had buried deep.

Now I released what little I'd collected after years of repression. A furious force, unrestricted and vengeful, pummeled through Rune.

He went flying back. His head glanced off a far tree with a dull *crack* and he slid, unmoving, to the ground.

I stood, shaking from both the cold seeping into me again and exhaustion. After years of keeping my magic cooped up, it'd become like an atrophied muscle that needed working out. But it *had* worked. Barely.

You never left, not really. A part of you is here now.

I scowled at Rune's unconscious body. He knew *nothing* about me. Clearly, or else he would have foreseen that I'd never accept his terrible deal.

I scooped up my backpack and knife. The blade *snnked* as I pulled it free of the sheath. I stood over Rune.

A mottled black spot near his right temple marked the future site of a wicked bruise. The tips of his coarse hair sparkled with blood.

I squeezed the knife handle. I should kill him for good this time, straight through the heart gem. He wouldn't think twice about doing the same to me if I wasn't useful to him.

A long, low growl shook the trees and trembled the ground. Something immense prowled through the moonlight close by. A slow smile spread across my face.

On second thought, I didn't need to do anything. I'd let the very Wilds he thought he commanded finish him off. Oh, the irony.

With that pleasant thought, I managed to find a couple remaining heart gems the river had washed ashore and hurried to escape into the dark.

CHAPTER

THREE

I couldn't slow down. No matter how much my side felt as though it was tearing open. How scalding my blood and throat burned, as though I was exhaling hot coals with every breath.

I crashed gracelessly through the trees, chasing the barest peach pink of the rising sun. Every time I stopped, I imagined Rune's shadow following me. It always flickered away when I spun to look, but I swore I could see his gold-red eyes glittering in the dark.

When I blinked, those eyes changed to the glassy sheen of a doe before she bounded away. I whirled to find more eyes peering from a hole in the ground. A badger. Only a badger. Normal creatures with normal eyes. I was nearly to the edge of the trees.

The same thought kept pace with my legs: *You'll regret not killing him. You'll regret it, you'll regret it...*

By the time I could see the trees break, my burning blood had turned to a jittering that wracked my entire body. Pain stabbed my eyes. Colors were too vibrant, like they'd been cranked to the farthest ends of the spectrum, splitting into shades I didn't think possible for any human to see. The murmur of voices, the growl of the approaching bus climbing the steep hill, the clatter of metal from weapons, all of it chipped away at my eardrums, an excruciating, keening pitch.

I threw down my backpack and tore it open. They had to be here. That jerk couldn't have taken them or I was—

I let out a small, desperate cry of relief as my fingers closed around the bottle tucked in its own separate pocket. My hands shook as I unscrewed the lid and poured a single tablet out, catapulting it into my mouth and crunching down.

Near-instant relief flooded me like a gentle rain. My limbs sagged, and I had to lean against a tree to avoid collapsing.

"Hypersensitivity," Peyton had called it. "Probably tied to that magic of yours."

We hadn't talked about it since I was nine and the episodes had gotten too much to bear. One day, soon after I'd used my magic for the first time, I'd awoken to find the world too much. Sounds blocks away made my eyes water. Dim light gave me vomit-inducing headaches. Even the gentle brush of air across my skin grated like sandpaper. My body had become a prison I didn't think I'd ever escape from.

Peyton had gone out early one morning, leaving me in a padded cell of pillows pressed tightly against my eyes and ears, the windows of our tiny apartment drawn, a damp rag against the back of my neck, knees tucked to my chest.

It'd been dark and late when she'd returned. She'd smiled tiredly and pushed a small bottle into my hand.

"From the doctor. It'll help the hypersensitivity and, I think, hide your magic. Take it every day, no exceptions. Take it and stay hidden."

My heartbeat was slowing, and my panicked breathing along with it. Satisfied I was okay, I stepped to the edge of the trees right as the bus rolled up. The medicine had slightly dilated my pupils, so I had to squint at the bus's headlights as the doors flung open and the heart gem hunters from the camp at the base of the hill stepped off.

I waited until the last one exited, ensured no one was looking my way, and then kept my head down as I crossed to the bus.

"Payment, then seat," the bored driver said. He looked over as I fished out a soggy, crinkled five-dollar bill from the bottom of my pocket and slid it beneath the glass. "You weren't here last night," he noted. "Thought you'd be coming, but you never showed."

I was surprised he remembered me at all. I forced a shrug. "You must have missed me."

"Doubt it. I don't miss anyone."

I shoved the five farther under the glass and took a seat in the back. My leg jittered as I waited for anyone else going down to get on board. I didn't recognize most of them, which wasn't surprising. Turnover rates for freelance heart gem hunters tended to be high.

At last, the driver shut the door and turned us around to start the descent down the winding road. A couple miles later the trees thinned, and I felt knots unwinding in my shoulders. The gaze of the Wilds seemed to turn away from me and rest mercifully elsewhere.

The road curled around Hood canal and nipped the coast of Case Inlet before the edge of Port Orchard came into view, the largest city this end of the peninsula, and my way back home. I looked at my hands. Thanks to my medicine, the warm blush of magic had left, and they were just shaking and cold.

I had never questioned what I could do, and neither had Peyton. I'd heard that before the Wilds, magic was an impossibility. And soon after, there was talk that those who lived near the Wilds had *changed*. It wasn't anything anyone would notice, at least not at first. Some people were simply peculiar. Or downright odd. They'd be overheard talking to beasts, or found alone, naked, staring at the moon, even on the coldest nights. In the right light, their eyes appeared to glow.

I shoved my hands under my legs. To investigate my own oddities was to invite dangerous questions and even more dangerous scrutiny. I was human. I knew that much. That much was safe, and that was all I cared about.

The bus driver pulled into the terminal at Port Orchard, and I used the doors near the back to avoid more curious looks. The part of Port Orchard the heart gem hunters had taken over was a Sharpie-d line of cracked asphalt with barred shops on either side, and small tent cities capping either end. The ground warmed as the sun rose. The moist air coated my skin and reeked of bagged trash and traces of sewage.

The heart gem hunters' camp was little more than stained mud-brown tents and the occasional RV outfitted with grill guards and weapon racks. Clusters of hunters—preppers, ex-military, self-proclaimed bounty hunters—sat around fires glowing dimly through the morning mist, checking and double-checking the gear that'd keep them alive. Some were just here for the day, shuttled up from Seattle. Others stayed the season, until it got too cold or they lost too many from their outfit to keep going.

I skirted around the one put-together office along the street—where the government-sponsored hunters of the Department of Fringe Affairs congregated—and made a straight shot for the one place I knew would buy the few heart gems I'd salvaged.

The stench of an unwashed body hit me a moment before someone grabbed my arm and whipped me around.

"Hunter!"

The man's beard was a nest made by a blind bird, unkempt

with strands sticking out in every direction. He had on a simple green habit, like something a monk would wear, and looked underfed, though his grip didn't feel like it.

"Let me go," I said firmly.

He made a grab for my other hand, where I held my heart gems. "Heresy! An affront to everything the Wilds have offered us. You pillage and steal what doesn't belong to you!"

A few of the government-sponsored hunters nodded in my direction. I tried to rip my arm out of the man's grasp, and when that didn't work, I used my free arm to push against his neck. "Let. Me. Go."

The man's pupils shrank as though he'd stared directly into the sun. He threw his head back, seemingly unaware he still held onto me. "The great Mother Tree grows from the deep, her trunk wide and strong, her roots thick and hungry, her branches enveloping all her children. Do you hear her below? Do you hear her growing, waiting to join us?"

"Your ears work? Let her go," someone roared, and I was torn from the man as Rylan intervened. He glared daggers at my attacker. "Keep it up and I'll really give you something to pray about."

"An abomination...an affront..." The man continued muttering. He tried to reach for me again, but Rylan's large frame blocked him. Between his turban that made him look a few inches taller than his already immense height, and his scowl, *I* wouldn't want to mess with him.

Apparently, the man thought the same. "When the time comes and the key turns the lock, you will see. All will be dazzled by their brilliance."

Rylan took a heavy step toward him, and the man scampered off down the street.

"Trouble, trouble everywhere you go, Val," Rylan said, shaking his head. The rings on his fingers, each inlaid with a small heart gem he could activate for unruly customers, glittered as he scratched his beard. "Is it too much to ask that you not attract it for one day?"

"If I knew the secret to that, trust me, I'd be doing it," I said.

Rylan laughed. Then he stopped when he noticed the government-sponsored hunters still giving us an uncomfortable amount of attention. "Let's get inside."

I followed him through the front door of his shop and heard the snick of the deadbolt behind me, ensuring no one else would bother us. Rylan wasn't much older than I was and used to be a hunter before a leg injury forced him into early retirement or, if he'd kept pushing it, an early grave. But he was still young and daring. Which meant he was bold—or stupid—enough to buy from me.

"You wouldn't believe the annoyance those religious nutjobs have already caused." Rylan squeezed himself behind the counter and leaned on the glass covering the heart gems he already had in stock, sleeves rolled to his elbows and showing off his scars. "Wasn't enough that they hung around, but they've only gotten worse this past month."

"Why doesn't the government stop them?"

Rylan laughed, and even I felt a slight flush crawl up my neck at the stupid question. "You know as well as I do they do what they can. But the farther you get away from the big cities and closer to the Wilds, the more the laws become..."

"Flexible?" I said wryly.

"Open to interpretation," he answered with an indulgent smile, which quickly shriveled up. "The exact same kind of interpretation I do for you each time you come in here. What do you got?"

Feeling embarrassed, I laid out the few heart gems I had. Rylan held a small magnifying glass up to his eye and got to doing what he did best. He turned them over, weighted them for size, and checked the exterior for any cracks that could cause the magic from within to explode upon use. I tried to distract myself by examining the jewelry he inlaid the gems into. Necklaces and brooches, some rings like the ones he wore. Items that could be discreetly fastened near the heart, or placed there swiftly when the need arose.

"Hate to say it, but I can't take these," Rylan said, placing the last one down. "I always process them, but the cut's terrible and the amount of magic is pitiful, even for gems of this size. What happened to your usual quality stuff?"

Rune's taunting smirk flashed through my head. My gut tightened. "I had some complications." I pushed the gems back to him. "I need the money, Rylan."

Rylan snorted. "Not to crap on your complications, but these aren't worth buying. The DFA is closing its grip on sellers like me, and I'm sticking my neck out every time I get product from a non-licensed hunter like you. When I buy, it needs to be worth it. Sorry, Val."

I pounded the counter a little harder than necessary, making the gems jump. "Don't give me the sales pitch, Rylan. Our rent went up again. Food prices are insane, not to mention the cost of getting out here, and Peyton needs medicine. Much longer and we—"

My throat closed up, and I swallowed hard. I hated how much it sounded like I was whining. Soliciting pity went against every fiber of my being. "Rylan."

"Sorry, Val, really."

"I *need* this."

"If I had my way, I would."

"I'll get you bigger gems," I said, weariness already eating at my bones at the thought of heading back home with absolutely nothing to show for it. "What do you say you give me a fair price for these, for being such a consistent seller?"

Rylan dropped his head with a sigh. I could see his mind running through the risks versus the rewards. I bit my tongue, waiting. If he needed bigger gems, then he needed me. At least I hoped.

At last he looked up, frowning. "I'm too stinking soft—"

Someone pounded on the door.

"Go away," Rylan barked. "I'm on a mid-morning break."

The door exploded inward, spraying glass across the floor. I ducked on instinct. Shouts rang out as men and women dressed in dark uniforms with blood-red patches on their chests swarmed inside.

I tried to grab my gems, but Rylan swept them off the counter. In seconds, the shop was almost entirely filled with uniformed bodies. I lunged desperately for cover.

"Don't move!"

One of the officers threw me bodily against the counter and wrenched my arms behind me.

"I haven't done anything wrong!" I snarled, struggling.

"The Department of Fringe Affairs," Rylan said pleasantly. "You should have mentioned you wanted a private meeting. My insurance already hates me, so repairing that door—"

The rest of what he said was muffled as he was wrestled to the ground.

"We have the owner, sir," one of them said. There was the metallic clink of Rylan's rings hitting the floor. "Heart gems removed."

The agent holding my arms pressed me more heavily against the counter. "What about this one?"

"Probably one of his suppliers. Cuff her and we'll take her in, too."

I thrashed harder. No way was I letting myself get dragged in where I'd be scrutinized with no escape.

"Someone hit her!" The agent holding me snarled.

"Leave her," a familiar voice said. The remaining agents scouring the shop jerked to attention. "The report talked about smuggling illicitly cut heart gems. You're not a hunter, are you, girl?"

I kept my face down, trying not to laugh at Joshua calling me *girl*, as though he hadn't been my stepbrother from the day Peyton brought me home. "Just trying to buy some camping supplies, sir. Heard he had a good selection of crampons."

"Crampons? What is that, woman's hygiene stuff?" one of the men said, scowling.

"Sir, she's lying," the agent holding me said.

"I said let her go," Joshua said.

"Sir..."

"Are you disobeying me? Don't worry, I'll question her personally."

Reluctantly, the agent relinquished his grip, and my bruised stomach got some relief. A vice-like grip closed around my upper arm and pulled me to the back of the shop. A door clicked.

"Joshua."

"Shut up," he hissed. He dragged me through Rylan's disarrayed office and out the rear of the shop. Once we were in the clear, I pulled myself free.

"What the actual hell, Val?" Joshua snarled. "We get a tip off about this guy buying illicit heart gems and *you're* the one doing the selling?"

"I'm sure it's not just me," I said. "And you knew I was hunting. What'd you think I was doing, padding my rock collection?"

At Joshua's growl of disapproval, I jabbed a finger at him,

"If I wasn't doing this, Peyton might already be dead, so you're welcome."

"Don't." His scowl darkened. His blond hair was slicked back, muscles angrily straining beneath his black DFA uniform, as though holding himself back from slapping me. I saw very little of Peyton's face in his, and I'd seen very little of *his* face in the five years since he'd had a blowout argument with Peyton about him joining the DFA and he'd stormed out. "Don't you dare turn this against me. I have a legitimate career doing legitimate good."

"And you're legitimately letting Peyton down." My finger pressed against his chest. "Do you know how bad she's doing, Joshua? How someone in the late stages of rot looks? Of course you don't, because you never visit."

"I send more than enough money every mont—"

"Which does nothing! Get out of your department bubble. That's barely enough to buy food. It's definitely not enough for medicine. It hasn't been for a long time."

I was being childish and petty, but it felt good to unleash all my pent-up frustration at one of the few people in my life who could make a real change but wouldn't.

Joshua's furious gaze remained fixed on me. "You have no idea how unselfish I've been, especially with all that's happening. They've got me running around at all hours, cracking down on illicit heart gem suppliers. If I haven't paid enough attention to you and Peyton, I'm sorry. I'll get in touch with her when I have the chance and see if there's more I can do."

I shrugged his hand off. Even if he meant well, his help would come too little too late. "The DFA is always cracking down on illicit heart gems. Just give Rylan a slap on the wrist like you do with everyone else and let him get back to business."

"Not this time, Val. This place is shutting down for good."

Cold dread curled in my stomach. Rylan was the only seller willing to buy from me. Without him, I really would only be collecting heart gems to pad my rock collection. "He's just one crooked buyer out of the hundreds, and he's not even close to the worst."

"Doesn't matter. He's getting brought in. Any and all we find are getting brought in."

He couldn't be for real. Corporations and the government bought and sold heart gems, and there had always been the little guy, trying to do what they could to get by. And if they were engaging in a little underhanded business on the side, then so be it. That was the price in the free market. And it was the only way people like me could possibly make it.

"Don't do this, Joshua."

He sighed, though it didn't sound that regretful. "Sorry, Val."

This wasn't the Joshua who'd helped an overwhelmed Peyton take care of a mute, bewildered child when she'd brought me back from the Wilds. Who'd let me snuggle against him during storms. Who'd taught me how to use a knife, a pistol, even a sword during summer break when the other kids were studying for college exams or posting pictures of their vacations.

"I don't have any other options," I said.

"And neither do I. If I had my way..." He blew out a long breath. "You've put me in a real situation here, you know that?"

I jutted out my chin. "Guess you'll have to take me in, too, then."

I held out my wrists for him to cuff me. A flash of anger bolted across Joshua's face, and for a moment he looked like he actually wanted to do it, before shoving my hands down.

"I have some pull, so I can let you off with a warning. I'll make something up to the others."

I laughed, though it came out mocking. "Don't strain yourself just for us. And stop pretending you're choked up about this. I heard they gave you your own task force in, what? Six months? Next thing, you'll be shooting for a higher position. It's just about power, and it doesn't matter what you have to do to get it."

He shoved off the wall and opened the back door. "Leave, Val, before they ask me why I'm taking so long."

I should have been grateful. Despite everything, it seemed Joshua was actually doing his best. Or what he believed to be his best.

"Val?"

Joshua's expression was hardened. Nothing remained of the kind, understanding stepbrother I once knew.

"No more going into the Wilds. We're cracking down on unregistered hunters, too, and there are rewards for turning them in. I'm sure more than a few hunters would love to line their pockets by putting you in jail. If you're caught again, I really will be taking you in, and you probably won't be getting out."

I DIDN'T REGISTER the ferry ride over to Bainbridge Island. I got on, drowned in my thoughts, and when I surfaced again, I was watching the bow of the ferry line up with the island's terminal.

I pushed off the railing and fully zipped up my rain jacket as the wind ripped at the hems. My movements were all in a daze. It was just now fully hitting me that I had...nothing. No heart gems to sell, and no one to sell them to. Getting a job was laughably difficult anywhere close to where I lived, and wouldn't pay enough, anyway. Peyton was probably sick with worry, and I dreaded the talk we'd need to have when I got home.

I jumped as the ferry horn blared, a last warning before it disembarked the other way.

I hurried down to the deck and scrambled onto a waiting bus at the terminal. As I sank wearily into the seat, I could make out the glittering lights of Seattle through the window. So close and so taunting. Just another ferry ride away. I could take it anytime I liked, but I could never stay.

I pulled my hoodie farther up to cover my face as a group of rowdy guys got on, music blasting from their phone speakers. They passed a bottle around and spilled some on the already sticky floor. One of them looked my way. I tried to emanate as much don't-mess-with-me energy as possible and breathed a sigh of relief when he turned back to his friends.

I stayed tense for two more stops before hurrying off at mine. I kept my hands deep in my jacket pocket, but still in reach of my knife. Flags hanging outside storefronts rustled in the wind carrying the smell of impending rain. I shuffled past other people heading home from work, heads tucked deep in the collars of their coats, muttering apologies to the few I bumped as I tried not to trip on the cracked asphalt. I turned onto the street leading home and left the noise and others behind.

Whispers behind me. They crawled into my veins and curled up inside, quickening my heart.

I didn't slow, but subtly tilted my head so I could glance behind me without tipping off my pursuer.

All that was there were shadows and a vacant street. The neon sign of a pawn shop still open bled red and blue light on grimy concrete.

The boys hadn't gotten off after me. I'd triple-checked. That didn't mean I was safe. I was out of the Wilds, but the human world held monsters of a different kind.

I shook my head until the sensation of the whispers fled. Just my imagination. Sleep-deprivation, semi-hypothermia, running into Rune... I was practically delirious.

I hurried the rest of the way to our apartment complex and didn't remove my hands until I needed to grab my keys.

More whispers at my back.

Abandoning all subtlety, I whirled around. Still nobody there, but I couldn't deny the painful pressure in my ears, the squeezing feeling on my limbs.

It took me three tries to fit the right key in the lock. I turned it and the entire hallway turned too, spiraling like a terrible carnival ride. Instead of curiosities and delights, roots burst from the walls and tightly wound over one another as they devoured concrete and metal. Flowers bled from the cracks, their scent so thick I choked. They clambered toward me as the buzz of insects and howl of beasts grew louder, louder...

I shoved the door open. Everything stopped. The hallway was just a hallway.

I rushed inside and only breathed when I put the door firmly between me and the outside world.

"I need sleep," I said. "Sweet, sweet sleep."

I ensured the deadbolt was secure but didn't call out that I was home. Waking Peyton to worry about me could wait until she'd had a few more minutes rest.

The apartment smelled of stale air freshener that had long lost its potency. From the fridge, I pulled out the milk that was starting to turn and grabbed a well-bruised banana. I ate that over the sink and drank straight from the carton, staring into the black abyss that was the garbage disposal. The silence rested on my shoulders, heavier with each passing second until it felt like my spine would snap. In the vast, quiet emptiness of this moment, I could see what my life was. More importantly, what it would become. No heart gems. No help. No hope.

I leaned over the sink and clapped a hand over my mouth to stop a sob that rose to my throat.

Don't you dare vomit. And don't cry. I had to be stronger than that. Crying didn't do anything except make my face wet.

When I was sure I wouldn't waste my dinner, I poured the last of the milk in the drain and went to check on Peyton. I'd made enough noise that she was likely awake.

I slowed in the hallway, remembering the hallway outside the apartment that'd twisted, flushed with impossible greenery. In the dim light I swore those flowers were back, this time with shadow-edge petals. The smell of mist-dampened pine thickened the air.

None of this was real. But my heart sped up anyway.

"Peyton?" My voice cracked the silence. "I'm back. Sorry to make you worry. Some things came up. We...should talk when you're feeling up to it."

I pushed open the door to Peyton's bedroom.

The scent of the Wilds poured out. I knew he was there—that he had somehow followed me, that my mistake of letting him live had already caught up to me—even before I saw him.

"I agree, we should talk," Rune said.

He sat beside Peyton at the edge of her bed as though they'd been having an important conversation about me. Peyton's sunken face was blotched with crying. Her shriveled hands clenched the sheets, speckled with droplets of blood.

"Val," she gasped. "Run!"

"Please don't, *Val.*" Rune held a glass knife closer to her throat, his other hand on the back of her neck. "You still have a choice to make. And I'm not leaving until you do."

"Take what you want," Peyton pleaded. "We don't have much, but it's yours. Just don't hurt her."

"But she's what I want." Rune turned the glass knife so that the flat edge rested against the blood vessels of Peyton's throat. Each one bulged against sickly thin skin. "She and I had a deal, you see, and I plan for her to honor it."

"What is he talking about, Val?" Peyton said.

"She doesn't know, *Val?*" Rune said, eyes brightening. "Does she have any idea how you bring food to the table? Who you've spoken to? Perhaps that stepbrother of yours would be interested to learn. I know his type. The kind that would burn the entire Wilds down just to get what or who he wanted, consequences be damned."

There was no point wondering how he'd followed me, how he'd been watching. My every nerve hummed with fury. "Let her go. She's not part of this."

"You made her part of this the second you attacked me and ran," Rune said. "That was some fair magic. Untrained, but effective, and quite the surprise."

"I hope it hurt," I snarled.

"Unimaginably, yes. But as I said, I've endured worse."

"Let her go and I'll come with you."

Rune's smile was predatory. "You will. Because if you don't return with me to the Wilds, I'll cut her throat. A shallow cut at first. Here, and maybe here."

Peyton sucked in a breath as he traced the point of the knife from her chin to the top of her collarbone. "We'll both watch as she bleeds out. Then, when she's near death, I'll cut out her heart like you do to those beasts. Or perhaps I'll force you to do it. Even resistant to my magic, I'm sure I could get you to start. When that's done, I'll kill you and leave your corpse as a warning. Do we understand each other?"

I shook with rage, helpless to do anything to save Peyton. But Rune stripping me of all other choices had made his offer of power even more tempting.

It wasn't enough to get the heart gems and money that would come from helping him. Money was finite. But power, if you had enough of it, never lost value. I wanted to do more than survive; I wanted that power, so much that nothing—not even Rune—could ever hurt me or those I loved again.

"I promise I'll come with you," I said, defeated. "No tricks."

Rune cocked a lazy eyebrow. "And?"

"And I won't run."

"Or try to kill me. Not until the completion of our little deal. Not that I'll give you the chance again. Not that you could. And if you try, I have a hundred different ways I could end your life that wouldn't even use magic. And when I'm done with you, I'll come back for her."

"I already said we have a deal!"

Rune held my gaze, the vividness of his gold-red eyes searching me for any sign of a lie. "Excellent."

Smooth as air, the glass knife vanished into a sheath up his sleeve, and Peyton slumped, panting, back onto the bed.

"I don't understand, Val," she babbled. "Why is a wildling here? What does he want with you?"

"Shh..." I swept past Rune and pulled her back onto the pillows, even as she tried to fight me. Her blood-splattered, sweat-soaked hands tried to grab my wrists but kept slipping off. "Peyton, listen to me. I have to go do something, then I'll be back. I swear I'll be back."

"What do you have...to...do..."

The exertion of everything was taking its toll, and Peyton's eyes fluttered.

"Please, Val," she whispered. "Don't do this. He won't keep his promise, no matter what he told you. I can talk to Father Dumas and get help. There are things we can do. I feared this, dreamed about it, you know. I...I..."

Her eyes bulged. She gripped me tightly with the last of her waning strength. "The Wilds," she hissed, "they want you back, and this time they won't let you go."

They already have me, I thought. *Maybe they always did.*

"Rest." I kissed her fever-hot forehead. "Just rest and don't worry about me."

Rune's impatient form loomed in the doorway. "You've wasted enough time."

My hands clenched on the covers. He couldn't even grant me the dignity to say goodbye to a loved one for what might be the last time?

I forced myself to let go of Peyton and charged into the hall after him. "Rune!"

He turned, eyes glimmering in the dark. He was still tall enough to look down at me, but outside the Wilds I could almost pretend he wasn't as dangerous as he actually was. "Yes, *Val?*"

The way he said my name with such seductive venom caught me off guard. Deadly and alluring. Like a beautiful viper. "I have one more condition."

"You had your chance for bargaining before you accepted our deal. Before you betrayed me. You have no more conditions."

"She's *dying*," I said, plunging on. "Wild rot is eating her alive. She can't be alone without care."

I poked a finger at his chest. "And if she dies because I'm not here, your stupid Lords will be secondary worries behind me."

For a moment there was a flicker of something—not compassion, but its cousin, understanding—across his face. "How long?"

"What?"

"How long has she been afflicted?"

"How— Does it matter? A year, year and a half, I think?"

"And she hasn't succumbed yet." He looked over my head into Peyton's room. The silence weighed heavily with his deliberation. "I'll have her taken care of. That will be part of our deal, but nothing more. Don't test my generosity."

Generosity my butt. "How do you plan on that?"

"I have my ways. In that you can trust me. As long as you keep your end of the deal, you won't have to worry."

I could trust him as little as I trusted a beast not to bite. Still, what choice did I have?

I stuck out my hand. "Shake on it?"

His grin was as sharp as his glass knife. He engulfed my hand in his. It was surprisingly warm, rough with calluses and long-healed scars. "*Now* we have a deal."

THE CITY THRUMMED with electric life. We stayed well away from the crowded streets and bars where people gathered after work. I wondered if the few people we passed noticed something amiss about Rune. Here among the fluorescent light and concrete and metal, he stood out like he'd been drawn in the foreground with hard, sharp lines. How would others react if they knew that one of the creatures that kept us on edge, the boogeymen in every child's bedtime story, walked among them?

I glanced over at him as we waited to cross the street. For all the stories I'd heard, there was little I knew as absolute fact. Few people outside of the higher ups in the government had ever seen a wildling, and of those who had, most lived near the Wilds or were dead. If anyone ever managed to kill one, then that was kept under wraps as well.

Back before I'd dropped out of school, some other girls and I used to spend a pathetic amount of time speculating what it'd be like to meet one of the mysterious creatures. Would they be like trolls of the stories, smelling of rancid meat and afflicted with a deadly aversion to sunlight? Or would they appear even more inhuman? Maybe they'd be like the beasts, nothing we could possibly reason with.

With his tussled hair—interwoven with the circlet of nightshade and ivy—and his hands uncomfortably stuffed in his pockets, Rune just looked like a boy. A sharp, dangerous boy, but a boy. Not a monster.

"You're staring."

I jerked my gaze forward as the light changed for us to cross. "No, I wasn't."

"Perhaps you find my beauty alluring. Like a poisonous lotus flower."

"I *wasn't* looking."

He appeared smugly satisfied with himself, which only made me angrier.

"Is it true you eat humans to gain their life force?" I asked.

Rune stopped in the dead center of the crosswalk to stare at me, earning him a couple protesting honks from those trying to turn. "By the blood, what are you talking about?"

That answered my question. "Forget it. Keep standing there if you want to get hit. You'd be doing me a favor."

It took him a few more seconds to follow me to the other side of the street. "What venomous stories have you been fed? Plants, beasts, water, air. The Wilds sustain us. We take only what we are given. Not like some—"

"Yeah, yeah, a leech, or a grub, or whatever it was you called me. You made it clear how terrible humans are only half a dozen times. Now are you going to keep leading me on a scavenger hunt or actually tell me where we're going?"

"The Wilds. Obviously."

I made a show of looking around at the loud, dirty street corner where we stood. "Obviously."

Rune pointed. "There. A spot of greenery in this Wilds-forsaken place. Hurry up. I tire of being in your disgusting home."

He looked it, too. Out of the close confines of the apartment it seemed the largeness of our world had begun to take its toll. His skin had grown sallow and lost some of its luster. His eyes twitched to every passerby as though to gauge how much of a threat they were. For a moment, I entertained the idea of attacking him while he was clearly at a disadvantage. I'd kept my backpack and knife, and if I managed—

"I wouldn't."

"Wouldn't what?" I said innocently.

Rune smiled. "You know exactly what. My magic may be

weakened here, but don't forget about that companion of yours. Something happens to me, bad things happen to her."

I shoved past him. The tiny park he'd led us to was hemmed by hedges taller than me, with the few trees the city allowed overshadowing the empty playground equipment. "What are we supposed to do here?"

"Try to keep your pointless questions to yourself." Rune moved past the playground equipment and walked straight up to the hedge wall. He let out a long exhale, eyes closed. Then they flew open and were vividly glowing.

The hedge shivered. Each branch parted as though he'd stuck two enormous hands inside and peeled them back. Flowers sprouted in an arch among the top, and within seconds, a gaping hole had opened up.

I glanced back to make sure nobody else had seen us. When I turned back around, Rune was motioning at me. "Hurry up."

I had no idea what he wanted me to do until I looked into the hedge. The hole he'd created didn't pass straight through to the other side but transitioned into a spiraling path. The same path I'd seen in my hallway earlier. I'd be like Alice falling into Wonderland. Or whatever the far more dangerous version of that was.

"We haven't got all day, little fox," Rune said.

I hesitated for just a moment longer then stepped through. The tunnel closed in behind me, and I panicked. I wasn't a fan of tight spaces, and this felt like the worst way to die.

"Keep moving forward. It makes it easier," Rune urged. "It's not far."

I couldn't bring my foot up. Couldn't do anything as my breath grew steadily heavier.

Rune growled in annoyance. "If we don't move out of here quickly—"

Vines lashed around my arms, roots around my legs, and I

was yanked forward. I felt a sort of *pop* that might have announced that whatever magic Rune was using to transport us was working.

At last the vines and roots let go, and I fell to my knees in soft dirt, desperately trying to suck in air.

"Don't be sick," Rune warned. "I don't have time—"

A wave of nausea overtook me. I crawled over to a bush and purged what little I'd eaten over the past twenty-four hours. With it came the renewed taste of the pepper root and a woody flavor that might have been my medicine.

When I'd finished gagging up everything, I wiped my mouth and stood. "Tell me we aren't going to do that often."

"We'll do it as many times as necessary. But only if—"

He went still. The night-cloaked Wilds teemed with life as they always did, but within the lulls of silence he'd obviously sensed something I hadn't.

"...walking the path doesn't call attention to us," Rune finished in a whisper. "Follow me. And keep quiet."

I made a rude gesture at his back but fell into step behind him. Rune wasn't my friend, but he was certainly the devil I knew. I kept my senses alert for what he must have heard, but something about the magic jump—or walking the path, as Rune called it—must have rattled me worse than I thought. My nose felt as though flowers had been stuffed straight into it, and every breath clogged my head with spore-scent. The shriek of a night jar and low growl of a beast overlapped each other until it was impossible to tell them apart.

I let my hands brush over the wet ferns and linger on moss-covered branches. The sensations helped center me, if only for a few stolen moments. Hopefully, I'd stay that way before we ran into anything serious.

Rune stopped and swore. "I believe we're being tracked. I knew this would happen. Get your knife out."

Deal or not, I was already sick of him directing my every move, but I felt better once the hilt was snugly clasped in my palm. I crouched until the tips of the fronds tickled my nose, stilling my entire body down to slow, even breaths. I kept having to squeeze my eyes shut to clear the popping lights. My senses felt dialed to eleven, every inch of me on edge. Something was very, very wrong.

A spike of awareness pinged the back of my brain. I swiveled on the balls of my feet. "There!"

Rune pounced, a static image that was there one moment, gone the next. He stopped, looking into the thick brush where I'd pointed.

"What's the problem?" I hissed.

Still staying low, I swished over to him. The smell of fresh rot hit me first, like roadkill baking in the sun. "What in the—"

"A wildling," Rune said.

The wildling had been dead for less than a day, judging by how little it'd been overgrown or chewed at. Its heart gem had been entirely punctured by a shaft of lapis-blue rock, semi-transparent like quartz.

"One of yours?" I said.

"They belonged to one of the Lords. Who will almost certainly be made aware of an unwelcome presence very soon, if they aren't already. We're moving."

Rune took off without waiting.

I covered my nose with my sleeve and—against my better judgment—knelt to look closer. With my nose so strangely sensitive, it was almost impossible to see through my watering eyes. The shaft of the rock through the heart had clearly been the killing blow, but it wasn't the only one. Clusters of crystal jutted from the wildling's joints, through its gaping eye sockets, forcing themselves out its screaming mouth.

I'd seen death, but this...this was brutal.

"Val!" Rune's voice was tinged with anger and...worry?

I slowly stood and caught up. He glared, looking between me and where the dead wildling was.

"Taking notes for future reference? In these parts, we keep moving. No slowing. Not until we get to safer territory."

"Did another wildling kill that one? I've never seen anything like it before."

Rune's mouth thinned, as though some great secret was being forced from him.

"Our magic is varied, and very few of us, the ones who are still alive, choose to reveal the full extent of our power unless we have to. That wildling strayed too far into someone else's territory and paid for it."

That didn't answer my question. "They strayed too far... just like we are."

"Yes. Hence..." He put a finger to his lips and walked on. I thought I knew how to move quietly, but Rune practically cloaked himself in silence. If every wildling moved like he did, then special magic or not, I was in trouble.

Though my head was hurting again—the light too bright and the sounds too keening—I needed answers.

"Do you actually have a plan for taking this wildling throne?" I whispered.

Rune closed his eyes for a bit longer than a blink. Probably praying for patience to whatever gods he worshipped. "If I answer, will you be quiet?"

"To quote you, 'no guarantees.'"

What might have been mistaken as a smile appeared at the corner of his mouth. "My plan is this: I remove everyone who would oppose my ascent. The Lords of their different realms have each claimed their territories of these Wilds and control those who have pledged loyalty. Some Lords have formed alliances and others remain independent. This lack of unity is why none have claimed the seat of high king, legitimate or not. At least, it's one of the reasons. We remove the main Lords, and no one will question my rule when I take the throne."

I ducked beneath a branch and let it snap back into place.

"So that's it? You kill all these other wildling Lords, and no one's going to question your rule?"

Rune stopped walking long enough to give me a cruel, lazy smile. "Yes. Because anyone who does will be dead. A plan doesn't need to be complicated to work."

Cold, but ruthlessly efficient. If there ever was the chance of maneuvering himself politically into the throne, it seemed Rune had no interest in it. "And how do you plan on kicking off this master plan? Other than blackmailing me, of course."

"You ask...*a lot* of questions."

"You're asking a lot from me. The very least you can do is let me in on exactly how I'll be involved."

"We start with this: In due time, I will have a very special person for us—for you—to help me remove. Once they're gone, the rest should fall into place."

And before I could ask anything else, he picked up the pace. I swallowed hard. He meant for me to kill someone. Of course he did. He'd told me as much during our first meeting. I'd had no trouble killing things in the past, but those had been beasts. These were wildlings. They weren't human, but I wasn't sure how I'd react trying to kill again.

Rune kept up a relentless pace through the moonlit forest, leaving me panting and with a damp chill that never left my bones. The towering spruce and cedar of the Hoh Rainforest, cloaked in moss, wove their branches high above. Ferns burdened by clinging mist ran their fingers across my legs as we sloshed through shallow streams and muddy morass.

I was annoyed to see that no matter how filthy I got, none

of it touched Rune. Every inch, from the sharp lines of his face to his shockingly bare feet, was pristine as always.

"Can you hurry it up?" he said when my pace continued to slow, my stabbing headache now joined by even more shakes and a churning in my gut.

"I'm trying the best I can," I snapped. Something was wrong with me. A wildling sickness, perhaps, or we'd landed in the toxic hold of something and I hadn't noticed.

"I'd like to be at the hollow before—"

He suddenly lunged, dragging me into cover before I could take another step.

"What a—"

His hand clamped over my mouth a moment before I felt it. The air became charged and raw, licking trails of energy down my skin that made my hair stand on end. The same magic reached inside me and scraped me clean of every thought, save *run*.

I breathed through my nose as both of us waited for whatever it was to pass. When it finally did, it left behind a presence like a heavy rain soaking the trees. Enough of a powerful afterglow that I shivered.

I ripped Rune's hand off my mouth. "Things like *that* live here?"

"Obviously." He still watched the trees, an edginess to him. In his face was something like reverence. Something like fear. If he was a monster, then we'd just brushed up against a god.

It was good to know there were things that scared him, like they did me. It made him and others like him a bit more... mortal.

"We're moving faster. Don't fall behind," Rune said.

I stood and my legs immediately gave out, dropping me back into the mud. The sick feeling in my gut and headache double-teamed me, along with the shakes. To my horror, I slumped against Rune's legs. A small note of disgust escaped his mouth.

"Get ahold of yourself."

I tried. I didn't want to be touching him any more than he clearly didn't want to be touching me, but the overwhelming sensation of the Wilds I'd tried pushing through had caught up.

"Medicine," I gasped.

I managed to throw myself off him and dropped my backpack. My fingers fumbled with the zippers, but I knew in moments I'd be all right. I was just exhausted, and vomiting must have purged my stomach of more medicine than I realized.

"We don't have time for this," Rune said.

My fingers wrapped around the bottle. Rune eyed it as I pulled it out. "You don't need that."

"What do you know?"

I tried to open the lid, but my hands shook so badly they kept slipping off. "You're probably born without any sicknesses or diseases. Not a single disfigurement or insecurity. You're disgustingly perfect in every way, I bet."

I finally managed to pry the cap off right as Rune grabbed both my wrists and slammed me against a tree. I tried to fight back, to use the special magic he said I had, but whatever abilities I might have used weren't working against his brute physical strength.

"You don't need that," he repeated. He smelled like bleeding pine and smoke, his face so close we could almost kiss.

"It suppresses my magic," I said. "Everything here is too much—"

"That's simply your magic responding to the Wilds. You're

untrained and weak and letting it run wild. Control it," he said. "Take everything big and make it small."

"I. Can't," I said through gritted teeth. I tried to force him off, but I might as well have tried to move a statue.

"Because you have no discipline. You may have slithered around death before, but with me you won't survive long if you let the Wilds win. Every new magic you encounter, every new threat, you'll let it eat you alive without a fight. Control yourself!"

"I can't!"

I kneed him, just missing his sensitive parts. He grunted, but the distraction was enough to wrench my arms free. Pills exploded everywhere as the unlocked cap went flying. With a cry, body shaking, I fell to my knees, trying to find one that hadn't been covered by mud.

Strong hands ripped me up, even as I flailed mindlessly. Rune's iron-like fingers pried the now-empty bottle from my hand. He brought it to his nose and sniffed. Exhausted, I watched with some morbid fascination as his eyebrows went up and then slashed down with such intensity I was sure he was going to murder me on the spot.

"Where did you get this?"

I jerked free from his grasp again and sunk to the ground. Spots of light and color popped in my eyes. "I need that. *Please.*" It felt demeaning to beg. To feel so weak. "Give me one, just one."

"Tell me where you got this!"

"A friend back home; they get it for me," I lied. "They never said, some doctor... Please..."

Rune tossed the bottle aside and squished the closest pills into the soggy ground. I nearly cried.

"You've become addicted," he said. "If you keep taking it, then the withdrawals will be even worse. It's good you're stopping now because you're not getting any more. Perhaps not ever."

I wouldn't allow that. I couldn't live like this for the rest of what would be my very short life.

I started to claw my way toward him, my other hand reaching for my knife. I wouldn't let him do this to me. I'd end his life before he could—

I didn't make it to his feet before darkness took me.

CHAPTER
FIVE

"You're very special to me, do you know that, Val?"

The first time Peyton said those words, we were in Seattle, back when Peyton had a car and a good job and a great place to live and Joshua didn't hate me. Back before everything fell apart.

"Never let anyone make you feel otherwise," she said. "You're so very special."

Out the window, snippets of the world flashed past the pylons of the underpass. I glimpsed other cars. The glistening chop of Elliot Bay. Tents of the homeless. All of them bright snapshots like the flash of a camera.

"I love you." Peyton looked back at me. "I love you so much."

It was hard to feel that way at the moment. Peyton had moved us down south to find a job. To get out of the cluster of the city and find cheaper living in a place called Centralia. She'd found work almost immediately, and almost immediately Father Rathers, a friend of Father Dumas, had come by to check on us. I hadn't realized Peyton was that close to the worshipers of the Mother Tree. Or maybe that was how the worshippers welcomed everyone.

I hadn't liked Father Rathers. He'd smelled like cough drops, wore too many heart gems jangling on a gold chain around his neck, and had a laugh that sounded like a chipmunk being strangled. He always asked me questions I didn't understand and offered more than once to watch over me when Peyton was at work. She always refused. And I snuck away to spend the day closer to the Wilds when she was gone, anyways.

I couldn't say why I always ended up there. I would leave the house and start walking, and when I looked up, there would be the trees, thick and inviting.

I met Brandon not long after we arrived. He was nine instead of eight, like me, but I liked him in a way I didn't totally understand at the time. Though he was scared of it, he would meet me by the Wilds and play hide and seek and walk with me to collect smooth, colorful stones and berries. Sometimes, we'd both sit in the grass, the blades tickling our legs, and talk. I didn't talk much then, but he easily filled the silence, and I appreciated that more than I could ever tell him.

One day he gave me a flower he'd picked from his parent's garden, grown small enough that nobody was afraid the Wilds would claim it.

I'd taken the flower in awe. I'd never gotten a gift from anyone other than Peyton, and it made my heart soar. Then my fingers had buzzed, and the flower turned into an entirely solid, lapis-blue crystal.

Before I could try—and fail—to explain, Brandon had screamed and run off. Peyton had found me crying behind the house. She'd found the flower crushed to pieces in my tiny hand.

We left the next day. My headaches and hypersensitivity had started soon after.

"Do you love me, Val?"

I snapped back to the car. The bright flashes between the pylons grew faster and faster until they were like a projector, showing me images I couldn't remember, or things I'd wanted to forget.

I'd been broken and then formed, piece by piece, until I felt like something real. Weighted. Substantial. There was an exhaled breath, and my wants and needs were given existence. In my memories—or were they dreams?—I felt the pangs of hunger for the first time, the chill of cold, the pain of an open wound.

"Val?" Peyton's voice sounded brittle. "Do you...love me, too?"

She stared into the rearview mirror, as though my answer really, truly mattered to her. As though *I* really, truly mattered to her. I'd only recently started saying more than a few words at a time, and this, it seemed, was one of the first things she wanted to hear. I tried to form the clunky sounds with my tongue.

"I...l-love you, too," I said.

Peyton relaxed, beaming. "I know you do, love. I'll keep you safe, always. I'll protect you, no matter what."

"What in the green hell is that *thing* you're carrying?" a girl said. "In case you missed the smell, that's a human, Rune. Dump it and let it rot. It'd do the same to us."

My body moved as whoever was carrying me shifted their arms. "Take her," Rune said. "She and I have an unfinished deal."

"A deal?" There was a bitter laugh. "That's not like you. We're not desperate enough to align ourselves with *them*."

"I said take her. Make sure she doesn't die. She still has use to me."

I was barely aware of being turned upright on my feet and shuffled forward. Every time I slowed, a painfully tight grasp yanked me forward again.

"Can you hear me?" the girl hissed, low enough I wasn't sure if she was really talking or I was imagining it. "You're already dead here, no matter what he promised you. You should die and save us all the trouble. Maybe, if I'm nice, I'll help you."

Physical sensation returned to my body in fits and starts, and it was *not* happy. A wave of agonizing pain ripped at my guts, my limbs, my head, and I fell back into darkness.

REALITY WAS a puzzle I didn't have all the pieces to. At times I awoke covered in sweat, clenched so tightly into a ball I was surprised my bones didn't snap. Even the cool mist of the forest didn't help the heat radiating off me like a furnace.

Other times, when I slipped back into the waking world, it was almost bearable. I lay beneath a curtain of moss, slick bark sliding across my shoulder blades as I tossed and turned in a bed-like chute of tree roots.

Maybe it was merely a hallucination, but once I swore Rune stood over me, a scowl on his face. He was covered in mud and unhealed, bleeding scrapes.

"Where were you?" the girl said. "Wait. You actually *got* one of those? For *her*? Why?"

"She needs it."

"She doesn't deserve it."

"I'd do the same for any of you."

"But she's not one of—"

"Marian."

There was a disgruntled silence. Rune knelt, offering me something resembling a walnut that'd been charred in a fire.

"Eat it," he said.

My stomach churned at the thought of eating anything. My lips and tongue felt swollen as I managed to say, "No."

"I woke the entire nest as I stole it. You will eat it. It will make you feel better."

"I said no."

"Let her refuse," the girl said. "Let her die."

"Go help the others," Rune said. "Come back in an hour."

The girl huffed and walked off. Rune scowled at me. "You're unbelievably difficult."

Before I could answer, he pinched my jaw open and crammed the walnut inside. I chewed. I had no choice. Chunks of it scraped my throat as they went down.

I slept easily after that.

The final time I awoke I couldn't breathe. I waited for the feeling to dissipate, but it only grew worse. Darkness threatened the edge of my vision.

A ragged gasp escaped my throat as I sat up. A girl squatted on the tree root overlooking my bed, lazily curling her fingers back and forth. Her skin was colored as dark as burned bark, scars along her arms. Spider-web-like silk threaded her clothes, shimmering like a sun-dappled stream.

A trail of something not unlike smoke wound its way from her hands around my throat and forced itself into my mouth.

I sprang at her. My speed and sudden strength must have surprised her as much as it surprised me because she nearly fell from her perch. Her eyes widened as my hand clamped around her neck and squeezed with a strength I didn't know I had.

"Looks like Rune's little fox has teeth," she managed. "Pity you survived."

"Keep choking me, I dare you."

It looked like she would, and it'd be a battle to see which one of us passed out first. Then she held up her hand, and the last of the pressure on my throat vanished.

"It's no fun when you can fight back. Welcome to the land of the living. Your reprieve here won't be long."

"I've heard that before, and I'm still kicking."

"But you haven't been with us. With *me.*"

The trunk of the tree I'd slammed her against groaned as my fingers continued tightening around her throat. The girl's eyes flared.

"Are you going to do it?" she hissed.

I could. I felt good. Really good. Stronger than I had in a while, like the Wilds were an outlet I'd been plugged directly into. "Not unless you make me."

"Pity won't win you points here," the girl said. "Just what did Rune do to you?"

I recalled flickers of pain from the withdrawals of my medicine. Recalled Rune's face over me, feeding me something that cleared the last of the medicine's effects and left nothing to stop my magic from returning in full force. "It wasn't what he did. It's what he stopped me from doing."

"Stop playing around, Marian," someone said.

A guy about my age glared at us from outside the nook of the hollowed tree I'd been sleeping in. "If you're done babysitting then we could use your help."

Marian slapped my hand away like she could have at any moment. "Clean yourself up and try to look somewhat presentable. Now that you haven't died, our king-to-be would like to see you."

"Rune's still here?"

"Of course he is. This is King's Hollow. If anyone has the right to be here, it's him. Now do what I say."

Seemed many of the wildlings were as charming as Rune.

"I'll wait outside." Marian parted a curtain of moss and left me alone.

I sagged back onto the root-made bed, spent. Just that brief bit of exertion, no matter how strong it was initially, had left me feeling drained. I guess I wasn't as recovered as I thought.

I was somewhat surprised to find my knife and backpack both untouched beside me. No medicine, though, and my tongue tingled at the memory.

I took what I needed from the backpack and strapped the knife where I could easily reach it on my belt. I splashed moss water on my face from where it'd pooled in a small basin and caught a look at myself in the fractured water. My face was ragged and drawn, cheeks pinched and hair in knotted snarls. But I was alive and planned on keeping it that way.

I tied my hair out of my face and stepped out of the sleeping nook.

"Finally," Marian said. "You take too long. I have other things I could be doing."

I followed her through a cluster of young trees until the space between them widened and led us into a clearing. I gasped. Marian looked back, glaring. "What's your problem?"

"This is..."

"King's Hollow, yeah. Hurry up."

I could just make out the peak of Mt. Olympus looming over the trees that cradled King's Hollow. To my right was the still surface of a languid blue lake, islands of green on top. The brick and rusted-metal remains of a ranger's station sat on its shore, its last remnants consumed by greenery. Decorative arches of woven branches and flowers entranced underground passages, sky lighted with glass awnings the color of smoke.

We walked toward the centerpiece of the hollow: an enormous, uprooted tree, its base nearly as big as a skyscraper's. The inside was entirely carved out, like the mouth of a gaping beast. It was so thickly covered with flowers and fungi it was difficult to make out the throne set in the dead center.

"That's the throne of the high king," I guessed.

"My, aren't you observant?" Marian said.

"Where are the other Lords? I thought Rune had to fight to get here."

Marian laughed. "Getting here was the easy part. None of the Lords would trade their cushy kingdoms for this unless they were ruling. Most don't even remember it exists. It's the last place they'll look for us."

"Then that means Rune's won; he's the high king!"

"Really? Does that throne look useable to you?"

As we drew beneath it, I saw she was right. It was made entirely of gnarled wood and encrusted with jewels and gold and, strangely, ice. It'd be impossible for anyone to sit on it.

Marian started up a wooden path leading to the throne. I paused and then turned slowly around as the sensation of stares scuttled down my spine like a spider.

At least ten other wildlings watched me from different parts of the Hollow. They were young. Or maybe they were old and that was how all wildlings looked. Their skin was the color of dirt, sap, pale mushroom, or tender green branches. Some were covered in wisps of feathers, scabs of scales, and small sprouts, complimented by jewels and other finery, whether conjured or scavenged, I didn't know. The mossy green and bark brown of their clothes made the gold-red of their eyes pop even more.

They were wayward princes and queens, and beautiful, every one.

"Now you understand where you are and who you're among," Marian whispered. "The few of us here who have seen humans don't remember the experience fondly. If it weren't for Rune, they'd likely make flowers rip from your fingernails and hang your corpse from the highest branch where it'd be a feast for eagles and finally of some use. You're in our home now, and that means we're your masters."

"I've been in your home for years. You haven't bothered me before. And I have no master except myself."

And Rune. *For now.*

Marian's face pinched into a frown. "Whatever Rune thinks you can do or deliver for him, he'll be proven wrong. And when you're done being useless, I'll happily peel your skin off and feed it to you."

Marian was already becoming reliable with her threats. If anything, her attitude was comforting. I'd met people like her, those who were so upfront about how much they hated me that I could almost relax around them. "I'll remember, so I know exactly who to stab first when the time comes."

That got a wicked grin out of her, and despite myself, I couldn't help smiling either.

"Don't worry, she's mostly bite," someone said.

It was the boy who'd yelled at Marian earlier. He was stocky, with what might have been the nubs of horns just poking out from his nest of brown hair. A bow was strapped over his back. His thick, calloused fingers, bent like he was constantly crushing a rock, told me he knew how to use it.

He threw his arm around Marian, who immediately squirmed away. "Touch me again and die, Xander."

"See?" Xander said. "She says that to everyone. It's her own sadistic sign of affection so it means she already likes you."

He playfully tried to pull Marian toward him again, and she jabbed a knifed hand into his side. "What did I just say?"

He grinned at me. I waited for him to grow disgusted once he got a clear look at what I was, but he seemed more curious than anything. "Thought you weren't going to make it for a little while there. You're stronger than you look." He cocked his head, curious. "I can see why Rune brought you here."

"*I* can't," Marian said.

"We know. You've made that abundantly clear. But Rune brought her, and to you Rune can do no wrong." He grinned wickedly. "Not when you have such a *fond* affecti—"

Marian tried to sink a fist into his stomach, but Xander darted out of range, laughing. Someone touched my arm and I jumped. A wildling with eyes as large as emeralds, hair the color of ash, snapped her hand back.

"Uh, excuse you," I said.

The girl's cheeks turned blood-blossom red. "Sorry! It's just... I wasn't sure when I'd get another chance, you see."

"Chance to..."

"View one up close. The few humans we've ever encountered, they don't last long here. Can I..." She timidly held out her hand again. I cocked an eyebrow but offered an arm for her to touch.

The moment she did, light spread from her fingertips. It spiraled through my arms and body, lighting up the veins until it reached my heart where it dimmed.

"Whoa, whoa," I said, pulling away again. "What did you do to me?"

"It's true, you don't have a heart gem," the girl said. She placed a finger over her chest where I could see the faint glow of her heart. "This is amazing! You're amazing!"

I stared at her. "I'm just a human. We're all like that."

"Really?" she clapped her hands. "How incredible! I didn't

know. None of us did, not really. We've never spoken to a living human."

"And we should have kept it that way."

Marian had returned, Xander with a mischievous grin right behind her. She jerked her head toward the hollow. "Enough wasted time. Leave us alone, Xander."

"Triss and I will go test the perimeter," Xander said. He gave me a playful salute. "Don't piss Rune off too much. He's in a mood, and you know how those get."

I didn't, not really. I wasn't sure I wanted to find out.

Marian and I continued up the narrow path to the opening of the fallen tree. Behind the throne, some pieces of the inside remained, creating woody walls cordoning off small rooms.

We found Rune in one of them.

"Knock, knock," Marian said. "I brought her like you asked. She didn't choke on her own spittle. Unfortunately."

Rune leaned over a wooden table with what looked like a topographic map of the Wilds spread out before him. He moved his fingers across, not looking up. "Good. Go help Triss and Xander. I'll have something for you when you get back."

Marian didn't move. Rune looked up, the start of a scowl on his face as though he couldn't believe she hadn't jumped immediately to do as he'd asked. "I believe I gave you a task."

"I'm not leaving you alone with her. Not while she's armed."

Rune gave a barking laugh. "That nub of a weapon won't do anything. And she won't try to harm me."

"That depends on how much you insult me," I said.

"See?" Marian said.

Rune glowered at me. "Don't bait her. Go, Marian."

Clenched fists at her side, Marian stalked out, leaving faint icy footprints on the floor.

"You have a special skill for angering people, did you know that?" Rune said.

"I'm multi-talented, what can I say?"

He smirked, teeth slightly sharp and slightly crooked. There was a pause, a held breath. His smirk fell, replaced by a scowl that looked almost...disappointed?

"So I was not mistaken the first time. You don't remember me, do you? Typical human selfishness."

"Remember you where?" I asked, confused. "I remember you assaulting me, taking my heart gems, bullying me into this. I remember that *very* well."

"Before," he said, though it came out as a murmur. "When you, I, both of us, were children."

I squinted at him. "What the hell are you talking about?"

"Never mind."

He turned back to the map, and that was that.

The rest of what I assumed was his room was surprisingly... domestic. A single, simple bed fit in the corner, covered with silk-like sheets. Crystal lighting emanating from heart-gem-like stones painted the walls in warm streaks of orange and deep shadow.

Strangest of all was the shelf beside the table—full of human books and trinkets, rusted cell phones, faded cigarette boxes, and a chipped coffee mug from Forks, WA.

"Didn't think you were the sentimental type," I said. I came over to look at the map. "What're you—"

Rune flipped the closest side away so I couldn't see. "No."

I nearly laughed at the childish move. "No?"

"I give you tasks; you fulfill them. That's all you need to know."

"Let's get something clear: I am not your servant, I am not your slave, I am someone with whom you made a deal. If you want what I can give, then how I carry that out will also be up to me, or at the very least have my input. Right now, I want to see exactly how you plan to go about doing this. It isn't like I'll be sharing it with other wildlings."

Rune's expression was a carefully calculated mask, but I almost fooled myself into thinking I could see him slowly agreeing with me.

"Very well." Rune unfolded the map. There were charcoal circles around different areas where Portland, Victoria, and Vancouver used to be and where the husks of those cities still remained, likely overgrown and crawling with beasts.

"Those are the wildling kingdoms," I said. "Where the Lords are."

"The ones we need to eliminate, yes," Rune said.

There were more circles, some near the coast. One in the north, along the Salish Sea, was simply labeled Undersea. I knew more inhuman beings had appeared as the Wilds spread, but it was still surprising to see such stark confirmation. "And those?"

"Future problems. Now that you're not dying, we can finally get started," Rune said.

"You gave me some kind of new medicine when I was sleeping. I remember that."

"Don't mistake it for any sort of kindness. I need you."

I wouldn't dare mistake anything he did as kindness. "What happened to me?"

Rune pulled his glass knife and stabbed the corner of the map in place. "I should be asking you that, since your answer may be just what I need."

He moved to his shelf and held up one of the items. Under the crystal light, the red medicine bottle looked even more like spilled blood. My tongue tingled with the memory of when I last took it. My throat went dry.

"Do you know what this is?" Rune said.

"My medicine, obviously. To suppress my magic."

"No. Do you know what *it* is? Do you know what it's made of?"

"Of course not. Pe— My friend always got it for me. I never cared what it was, only that it helped me."

"And where did your friend get it?"

"Can you just ask what you want to ask, Rune?"

Rune squeezed the bottle until the plastic creaked. "The pills you were taking contained powdered shavings from the bark of a heart tree."

He waited, as though expecting me to have the slightest idea of what that was. The Wilds had many different types of flora and fauna not native to the human world. Frost bloom and dragon's heart, cupid's arrow and death thrall. Engorged blossoms with scents that could lull to sleep, or invigorate, or tempt into a ceaseless rage that had you lose all your senses until you woke up days later naked, lost, and half dead from starvation and thirst.

"That name would have stuck out to me. What is it?" I said.

"A superstition, and my way forward," Rune said through clenched teeth, as though annoyed by the very thought. "How much do you know of wildling myths?"

Just as much as I knew about the wildlings and how they ruled, which meant frighteningly little. "We have believers in the Mother Tree and other primeval forces that are found in the Wilds."

"Those are but a couple. There are many others. There are the gods: Rhasahlyn the Gentle, Mishari of the Beasts, Nieriati the Bloom Tender. There is also the Mother Tree, believed to have given life to all wildlings. Some myths are used to mislead and control through fanaticism and fear. The Mother Tree and its ability to conjure life to the Wilds is a story for the suscep-tible and stupid, but its present-day effects are very real.

"What are believed to be the offshoots of the Mother Tree, the heart trees, weave the crown for the future high king during their coronation, and *only* for the future high king. I need the heart tree to take my throne. *That* will seal my rule, and even if others dispute it—and they will—I will have legitimacy above all others."

"Then use the heart tree," I said. "Go make it weave your crown."

"I would. If I could find it. There is only one heart tree in this part of the Wilds. The other wildling Lords have kept its location hidden." He tossed the bottle to me, and I snatched it out of the air. "But your *friend* knew where it was."

"No, they didn't," I said, trying to keep my voice steady. "They got it from some doctor. They probably have hunters that go out and collect it."

"You expect me to believe that?"

"Yes, because it's the *truth*."

He stepped closer. I brought up my knife and pressed the tip to the hollow of his throat, stopping him. "Trying to scare me won't change my answer. I don't know how they got it. And I'm sure my friend doesn't either."

The tip of the knife depressed his skin as he drew closer. "I could find out. I could make Peyton talk."

My breath caught. Of course he'd sniffed out my lie. "Try it. Waste your time getting the same answer I'm giving you."

He searched my face. Looked into my eyes as though he could dive in and see any deception.

At last he stepped away, and I let myself relax, but only a little.

"If I'm unable to find out where the heart tree is from other wildlings, then I'll seek out humans who might know."

"But you don't need it." I pointed with my knife. "The

throne is *right there*. Just chip it out and take it if that's all you want."

Rune brightened. "Why didn't I think of that?" He made a grand gesture toward the door. "Would you do me the honors?"

Knowing he was up to something, and not particularly caring what, I headed back out to the throne. Up close, I realized that the part I thought was ice was actually aquamarine crystal, pale as the purest heart of a glacier.

"It's terribly uncomfortable to sit on." Rune leaned against the wall of the hollow. "Maybe you could remedy that."

I angled my knife between the slim cracks of crystal. When Rune made no move to stop me, I raised it up and brought it down.

A startling, electric crackle. I was lifted from my feet and thrown into the wall. It hurt to breathe. I could hear a strange sound, and it took me a moment to realize it was Rune laughing.

"I haven't been that entertained in a while. Thank you, Val."

He knelt beside me, laughter replaced by his normal hungry expression. "It's not enough to simply take the throne, otherwise those other Lord leeches would stay here. It needs power, a crown. In olden times, the wildling leaders would come together to lend their power to create such a crown and free the throne. Without them, I need what the heart tree provides to get my own, on my own."

I wheezed as I rolled over, trying to get air. Rune stood. "If you're lying about what you know of the heart tree, I'll find out."

"I'm not...lying...you insufferable...jerk."

"Good. Now get up, we have—"

"Rune!"

I staggered to my feet as Xander swung in from the nearby tree, panting as though he'd fled from something. "Pitus just got back. She said Jezaline and Mordecai, they..." He grimaced. "You'll have to see for yourself."

Rune gave a jerky nod. "Show me."

MY STOMACH HEAVED, but I managed to keep its contents down as I stepped out of the path Rune had summoned. Rune, Marian, Xander, the girl named Triss, and a few other wildlings I didn't know were crouching, nearly invisible, in the greenery nearby.

"It's Erza," a tiny wisp of a girl said in Rune's ear, her voice trembling.

She must have been Pitus, one of Rune's spies. "I was coming back here and thought I'd pass through and check on her, and I found... I found ..."

"*That*," Marian said grimly.

I looked where they were. Wherever this Erza and her wildlings once lived hadn't been a human city. There were no skeletons of metal and stone for the foliage to transform. Instead, magic had reshaped the earth to form cathedral-like structures and simple living spaces, all decorated with glittering stones, gold, and droplets of frozen water.

Wildling bodies littered the ground. Moss had already begun overgrowing some of them.

"Raquel." Rune curled a finger at a boy with buck teeth and a fang hanging from one ear. "Tell me if any of the attackers remain. Keep it discreet."

The fang bounced as Raquel vigorously nodded. "Got it. I'll make my own."

He cleared out a space of ground. He muttered beneath

his breath, fingers pinching the earth together as though molding with Play-Doh. In moments, two marmot-like creatures, slender and black-furred, sat dutifully in front of him. Raquel spoke another word and their eyes burned blood red with life.

"Your sight is mine. Your smell is mine," Raquel murmured. "Go, and I will see as you do."

The creatures scurried off toward the city.

I gaped. Raquel grinned at me, clearly happy to find someone in awe of his magic. "You like pets? I could make you one. I'm really good with rats. But if you want something real, I know a few wolves that probably won't eat you."

"This is not the time, Raquel," Triss said. Her large, rounded eyes turned on me. "But I heard humans *do* keep pets. Little tigers and small wolves. Is that true—"

"Triss," Marian snapped.

Raquel turned his glowing eyes toward the city as his furry shapes deftly scurried in and out of the houses, wove between low-hanging vines, and dipped into shallow tunnels. I scooted closer to Xander. "You know who did this?"

"Jezaline and Mordecai," Rune answered for him.

"Two of the Lords," Triss said to my questioning gaze.

"Why would they kill one of their own?" I said.

"Erza isn't. She didn't pledge allegiance to them. So it looks like they might have...dealt with her."

They would do this to their own people? Humans did the same, but for some strange reason I thought, for all the wildlings' faults, they'd be better than that.

"It was only a matter of time," Pitus said softly. "Rune, if they come to King's Hollow..."

"I'm well aware," Rune said sharply.

Raquel stood as the two ferret-like creatures scurried back. He scooped his hand over their backs. The glow in their eyes faded, and they melted back to dirt. "The Lords are gone. I found Ezra."

"Where?" Rune asked.

He ordered a couple of the wildlings to stay behind just in case this was still a trap, and he, Raquel, Triss, and I snuck to the center of the city where Raquel led. He stopped, face paling.

They'd strung Ezra up by roots pierced through her fore-arms and calves. Her chest squirmed, and it wasn't until I looked closer—and nearly lost my stomach again—that I real-ized it was covered in small black worms chewing on her flesh. She stirred as we approached.

"Rune..." Erza's chest gurgled with blood, lips dribbling red. "We meet...again, though this time it's not as favorable a circumstance...for me." She sucked in a wheezing breath. "You asked me to join you...once. I'm...regretting saying no right about now. Oh well... What's done is...done."

"Don't try to speak, you'll only bleed out faster," Rune said. "Triss is a good healer, she'll—"

"No, please..." Erza said. "It is...too late. You and I both know it."

"Triss can fix you," Rune insisted. "No matter how broken your bones or torn your flesh. Let her—"

"Even if she healed me, I'd be less than. Look at me, Rune."

Erza managed to pull her head up, giving him a broken grin. "Do I look...whole to you anymore? They came and I could do *nothing*. Not when they killed my friends, not when they slaughtered my lover. You understand some of what that's like, so tell me...if you wouldn't feel the same. I know you could move on after that, but I'm...not so strong as you."

Rune might as well have been a statue, staring at Erza as she gave another hacking cough. "There must be something I can do," he said.

"There is. Do me that one last favor. I beg you, please."

"Rune?" Triss whimpered. She twisted a small pouch that smelled of mint and glasswort, tinged with a cloying sweet scent of eclipse flower to ease pain. "She doesn't have much time."

She took a step toward Erza, but Rune put up a hand. "What did Jezaline and Mordecai want, Erza?"

Erza managed to grin. "You, I'm sure. But though they suspect who they're dealing with, they don't know it with certainty yet. You are a wraith, a spirit who should be dead if it weren't for folly and dumb luck."

"And strength," Rune added. "Always strength."

Erza weakly nodded in agreement. "Don't let them get you. Make the bastards pay."

Rune drew his glass knife. I forced myself to watch as he stepped up to Erza and, in a swift, practiced stroke, drove it into her heart. There was a sharp flash that brightened her skin and then dimmed. She shuddered once and went still.

Rune stepped back and, with a disgusted snarl, flicked off some of the worms that had latched onto his hand. "Take her down. Bury her with the rest," he ordered Raquel before stalking away. Raquel started summoning more dirt creatures with enormous digging claws while a couple more gnawed at the roots holding Erza up.

I jumped as Triss put a hand on my arm. "It's a lot, I'm sure. You okay?"

I should be. I knew some of the terrible struggle I was getting involved in, but somehow it still ended up being worse than I thought. "He could have saved her. He has powerful magic. He could have done more!"

My voice had risen enough that the other wildlings were shooting me concerned looks. I bit my tongue. "I thought she and Rune were friends."

"They were…" Triss paused, as though the word *friend* and Rune didn't go in the same sentence. "They respected each other dearly. That's why he honored her choice. She'd been broken in more ways than one. She thought it better to go this way, so he allowed it."

I brushed off Triss's arm, trying to be gentle for her sake. "It wasn't *her* choice as much as Rune's."

Triss gave me a sad smile, as though I was a child who hadn't yet understood what all the adults were talking about. "I know it's hard, but it was best. She'll return to the earth and become one with the Wilds again. If you want to talk about it later, let me know."

I swallowed hard and thanked her and then went to find Rune who was staring at another dead wildling. Beautiful, multi-colored mushrooms had started growing from their back. "How often does this happen?"

He looked up, clearly irked at being distracted. "Does what happen?"

"You're not stupid, so don't act it. This." I gestured to the carnage. "Have the wildlings always slaughtered each other like…like…"

"Beasts?" Rune's eyes flashed. "Does that bother you? Isn't that what you and other humans think of us?"

I wasn't sure what to think of them anymore. I once believed that the wildlings' savageness and cruelty extended only to those outside their borders. Now they seemed doubly cruel to their own kind.

"Can you stop this?" I asked. "If you become king, will you stop things like this from happening again? Will you talk things out? And not just with wildlings. With everyone."

"You don't know what you're asking."

"Yes, I do."

"No." Rune held my gaze, unflinching. "I can't talk it out!

Do you think it's possible to do so with beings who are capable of such cruelty? Who butcher and hang each other like trophies—"

He bit back his words, furious expression receding to something more calculated.

"But eventually," I said in a quiet voice. "You could try eventually."

"If that is ever possible, I will try. That's all I can promise. You will help me realize that possibility. Marian!"

The other girl was at his side in an instant. Rune jerked his head at me. "The task I gave you earlier. Val's going with you."

"What?" the other girl looked outraged by this. As outraged as I was.

"I'm not—" I started.

"I'm not dealing with some pathetic, weak human," Marian seethed. "I haven't done anything to be punished like this, Rune!"

Rune either didn't hear us or didn't care. "Val will do the honors; you stay out of the way. This particular wildling's magic is strong enough to stop even you. Think of this as Val's practice run. Do what I ask and come back. Or don't come back at all."

Before I could continue to protest, I felt an uncomfortable prickling running down my spine. I turned. I swore I saw the glassy sheen of eyes in the trees.

"Someone's watching us."

"Pitus!" Rune barked.

The wisp of a girl vanished without stirring a leaf. The other wildlings had frozen in place. Rune swore. "It's time to move quickly."

For once, I agreed with him.

CHAPTER
SIX

Marian opened a path back to King's Hollow, barely allowing me time to step through before it started closing. I barely had time again to grab my backpack, refill my water bottle at one of the waterfall's offshoots, and rush after her, wondering why I was. I didn't need her. Didn't *want* to be around her, as much as I was sure she didn't want to be around me.

"If Marian gets on your nerves, just hit her," Xander had said. "She responds well to violence." Then he'd laughed.

I had no idea how to feel about that.

It took less than a minute before the Wilds swallowed King's Hollow, replacing my surroundings with towering trees. My shoulders relaxed. My heartbeat slowed as I deeply breathed in the earthen scent. If only for a moment, I could forget the last couple days and pretend Rune and I had never met. I was simply out on another hunt. I could go as far as I wanted, or turn back at any—

I realized Marian wasn't in front of me anymore, a moment before she materialized beside me. She looked frustrated that I hadn't squealed in surprise.

"A few rules," Marian said.

"This ought to be good."

"First, you listen to me. Always. Second, we cannot be seen. We cannot be discovered. If the other wildling Lords find out Rune is here—that he's alive at all—before he's ready, it'll be a disaster. They'll crush us before we can make any move against them. What they did to Erza was the least of what they're capable of."

"Anything else?" I said.

Marian thrust her hand out, and I had to duck as a ball of ice barely missed my face. I pulled my knife, but Marian's crooning voice, thick with magic, said, *"Stay where you are."*

I froze as though rigor mortis had gripped me.

"Please, try to fight it," Marian cooed, hand gently waving as she layered on more magic. "You're not as special as Rune thinks."

She reached for my knife as both my anger and the heat within me built to a boiling point. Her magic hold broke. I stabbed upward and managed a tiny, stinging cut across the back of her hand before she leapt away.

I pointed my knife at her. "Try that again and see what happens."

Marian pressed her fingers against her hand, and they came away bloody. She scowled at them, as though not believing she could be hurt. Then she laughed and kept walk-ing. "I will. You can bet on that. That was good, but I'm nowhere near as strong as the Lords. I wonder how long you can resist them? Would you like to try again, for practice?" She waggled her fingers back at me.

I held my knife up in answer.

"Hmph. Guess not. You're too scared. I understand. It wasn't like you *meant* to break my hold on you."

"Does it matter? The result was the same."

"It matters because I say it does. And because Rune wants you to learn control. You're untrained, and those who blunder about not knowing what they're doing…"

Frost consumed a nearby bush, and she shattered it with a single blow. She held out her hand. "Give me your knife."

I laughed. Marian scowled. "That wasn't a joke. You're going to kill this wildling using magic, not a weapon."

I turned the blade toward her, taunting. "Blades kill just as well as magic. Would you like to see?"

"Those pathetic, helpless beasts you hunted don't count. If you want to be strong enough to truly hurt a wildling, you will give me the knife—"

I felt her magic reaching out and snatched my hand back. Marian gaped before re-arranging her expression into nonchalance and walking off. I warily sheathed my knife and followed.

We hit a shallow river. I pulled off my shoes and socks, rolled up the bottoms of my pants, and waded into the frigid water, doing my best to avoid the ankle-breaking rocks. Marian jumped across in a single leap. I refused to look at her smug face as I finished crossing and put everything back on.

"Who is Rune sending us to kill anyway?"

"Someone named Twicca," she said. "He's a minor wildling Lord who's gotten a little too close to discovering us than Rune would like."

I nearly tripped as I put my shoes back on. "So he just kills him? Wouldn't that make it more obvious we're out here?"

"The wildling Lords fight all the time. Some die. Nobody cares. And yes, we kill them. If you don't like how we do things, then you never should have come here."

I didn't like it, but I understood it, especially after seeing what those hunting Rune were capable of.

"Don't even bother, he's not interested."

I looked over to find Marian sneering at me. "What?"

"I see that stupid, moon-eyed look you have. You're thinking of Rune. Like *that*. Well keep dreaming. He'd never be interested in someone like you."

I'd been accused of many things, but being romantic was never one of them. Other than the childish feelings I'd had for Brandon when we were kids, I'd had little to no experience with romance. I'd dated a boy in middle school when we were both laughably innocent, one who left scribbled notes in my locker and slipped candy into my hands when we walked home. After that had been other hunters who'd vanished one way or another, either within the Wilds or after a turbulent couple of weeks.

The last relationship I'd had, as though to prove I could feel *something*, was a fling with a heart-gem dealer even further entrenched in shady business than I was. It'd ended when he was arrested, and I'd narrowly escaped joining him in jail. Lately, I'd begun wondering if I was capable of loving anyone else, or if I was doomed to be cold-hearted.

Marian's scowl had only deepened the longer I didn't answer her accusation. I forced myself to laugh. "Trust me, I'm not interested... But you are, aren't you?"

Her cheeks darkened, something that looked disturbingly human.

"Does he know. Better yet, does he care?" I pressed.

"Keep your mouth shut."

"Do you try to kill him like you do me? Is that how you flirt—"

"I said..." The temperature plummeted, and my next breath came out as crackles of frost. "Keep your mouth shut."

I smiled as I mimed zipping it closed, and after a moment our surroundings warmed back up to their usual chilly wetness.

"Rune only has one love and that's the throne," Marian said. "That's all he's wanted for as long as I've known him."

"So all those wildlings back at the Hollow, he doesn't love them, is that right?" I said. "I'm sure they hang around because of Rune's sparkling personality."

"They stick around because they have loyalty and honor. Something you know very little about."

"Don't tell me what I know. You don't know anything about me."

"And I plan to keep it that way."

Marian forcefully slapped away some branches near her face. "Rune saved them and cared for them when no one else would. They respect him. Some fear him, the smart ones anyway. That's better than love. Stronger than it, too."

It sounded like she was lying to herself. But what did I care? If they hated each other, then that was just more chance they'd rip each other apart and save me the hassle of doing all this.

We hiked. Long enough for dew to completely soak the calves of my pants and my stomach to start ripping itself apart with hunger. I was regretting not taking the time to scrounge up food.

"There."

Marian was pointing up at a tree. A golden-red-eyed squirrel chattered down at us, trying to scare us from its territory. "Eat that. Your stomach's so loud they'll hear us coming miles out."

I showed her my empty hands. "No bow." And I didn't want to eat it, anyway. I'd cut out enough heart gems and seen enough animals of the Wilds turn to rot that I'd stopped eating any beast from here long ago.

"Kill it with magic," Marian said. "Obviously."

"I can't."

"You will, or we go no farther." She smiled.

I glared at her and then the squirrel. The pangs of hunger fed the magic whispering to me. Without the medicine blocking it, I sensed the current of power in my blood, something I hadn't felt since I was a child. But I couldn't use it. Doing so would make me more like *them*, and less like *me*.

With one hand, Marian leveraged herself up the slick trunk of a nearby tree and broke off a blood fruit—the skin spotted yellow—and bit in. The crimson juice of its namesake dripped down her chin, and my stomach growled louder. She dangled it over my head, juice dribbling at my feet. "Eat up."

"I'm done with this," I said. "If you don't have anything better to do than torment me, then don't bother."

Marian leapt down and grabbed my arm, squeezing hard enough for my bones to protest. "I'm telling you to—"

Then my magic *did* work. I struck out faster and harder than ever before, breaking her grip and sending speckles of blood flying from where my nails broke her skin. Marian looked stunned.

"How dare you!"

She lunged at me. We went tumbling to the ground, ferns and thorns tearing at our clothes. Marian's fist caught my jaw, and I returned with a blow to her ribs that made my knuckles sting. I kicked out, desperate to hit her again, to hurt *something* in a way I hadn't the power to before.

My kick missed. Marian's didn't. It robbed the air from my lungs and threw me back, but I had enough sense to drag her with me. The ground vanished under my feet.

I twisted on instinct. My hand caught the sharpened point of something, and I bit down a scream as the flesh of my palm was torn away. I managed to wedge my other fingers in a small crack, and my fall came to a jarring halt.

"No, no, no."

Marian dangled in the open air beside me, barely hanging on as I was. We'd fallen into an enormous chasm hidden by the underbrush. The sharp point my hand had caught was the top of a blue crystal. There were dozens of them—no, hundreds— extending down the chasm walls until the endless bottom swallowed them up.

"I'm not dying like this," Marian snarled. "Not after everything, because of some...*stupid*..."

"Relax," I said. "Your swinging is making things worse."

Marian didn't stop swinging but managed to throw her other hand up and grab a small shelf of rock. Arms trembling, she grabbed another and another. In seconds, she'd reached the top, stood, and dusted herself off, legs shaking.

"A little help?" I said.

Marian looked down at me. She knelt and reached. I tried to grab her hand, but she knocked it aside and took my knife. "Help yourself. Maybe use your magic. Or let go. I don't care."

A thousand different insults, curses, and terrible, terrible things I wanted to do to her flashed through my mind, but none of them were going to help me. I tried to find another ledge to grab, but they were all woefully out of reach.

"Magic," she drawled. She twirled my knife over me, taunting. "Figure it out or prepare for a *looong* fall. I wonder if I'll even hear your body hit the bottom."

I tried, truly. But after years of suppressing it, nothing happened. I didn't even know *what* I was supposed to do. Marian sighed loudly.

"Don't think about it," she said. "It's magic, and it's wild, like everything here. The Wilds don't overthink. They *do*, they act, they survive. Bringing thinking into that ruins it."

My grip was slipping from the sweat coating my palms. All I could imagine was plummeting before being impaled on a crystal. *Oh no*, Marian would say, and she'd be overjoyed at my demise. Rune would move on, and Peyton would never know what happened to me. I had to hold on. Had to find a way out of this—

My hands gave out.

Like wings unfurling, my magic surged. The crystal I'd gripped melted like wax to fall with me, before hardening again. My shoulder popped as I came to a sudden, jerking halt.

I dangled for a moment, legs kicking over open air, until I found purchase. Another crystal softened until I could just reach up and grab it.

Trying my best not to think about what I was doing, how my magic was simply *working*, I climbed, again and again, over reforming crystals until I pulled myself over the edge and flopped onto my back, exhausted.

Marian's face appeared over me, twirling my knife in her hands. "Get up. I'm not waiting around for you to nap."

I weakly snatched at my knife, but Marian pulled it away.

"Magic doesn't come naturally to you, but if you're going to be of any use to Rune—which I doubt—then you have to *make* it come naturally. It has to be your first defense, your first attack."

She jabbed a finger at my head. "Don't. Think. You humans are already good at being brainless, so it should be easy."

I managed to stand, shoulders aching. "Do you have any other insults besides that I'm human, or is that as far as your creativity goes?"

Marian grumbled something. I looked back at the chasm. The earth had split too far for me—a human, as I was constantly reminded—to jump across. Now that I wasn't dangling for my life, I could see that the crystals I'd pierced my hand on had a faint glow. Like heart gems.

"I've only seen these once."

Marian snorted. "Then you haven't gone very far into the Wilds. They're pretty common around here."

"For how long?"

"Does it matter? As long as I've been alive. They started showing up years ago, right after the Cataclysm. Every wildling knows that."

I wracked my brain for what I knew of the Wilds' history. It was said that not long after the Wilds appeared the Cataclysm happened, when the wildlings, monsters, and gods of the Wilds caused massive amounts of destruction as they settled into their new home and formed their hierarchies of power. The fighting and destruction were so bad it spilled into the human world. Thousands died, humans and wildlings alike, and it wasn't until the Forming that things were made safe. For some.

"Every so often another chasm will appear," Marian went on. She tucked my knife into the hem of her pants. "We've wasted enough time."

I looked at my palm. The skin had broken where I'd pierced it on the crystal, and there was the start of a dark, blood-crusted bruise.

"I *said* we have to go," Marian called. "You make me wait any longer and I'll start testing how sharp this knife is. On you."

I forced myself up.

Eventually, the perpetual green became dotted with remnants of the old world. We crossed roads that were so cracked they were basically rubble. Summer cabins overgrown with green and filled with nests of small beasts. There wasn't a single human and clearly hadn't been for some time. The farther we traveled, the more it was like a time capsule, showing signs of where the Wilds started and how much of our world it'd devoured since appearing.

It was as we passed a long-rusted gas station and grave-yard of cars that I knew we were getting close.

"You ever killed anything before?" Marian said. We slowed as the outlines of what remained of a town the Wilds had claimed came into view. "Besides beasts?"

I knew I was capable of it, in self- defense. I tried to convince myself that this was all I was doing. A little dirty work to defend myself against much bigger threats. "Let's just find this guy."

Marian shook her head, mumbling, "We're going to get ourselves killed."

We approached the town cautiously, dampening our shoes in rivulets and crossing the spongy dirt beneath a small over-pass. I'd never seen any place the Wilds had taken over after the fact, but I wasn't prepared for the sheer beauty of what they'd created.

Within the concrete, glass, and metal structures humans had left behind, wildlings had built their own magic-crafted palaces and dwellings fit for the royalty they thought they were. Domed rooftops speckled with glittering gemstones magicked from the earth, colored with bioluminescence. Wooden walls that had regrown to attach to the enormous trees alongside them. The scent took my breath away, so rich with sweetness I temporarily forgot myself among the smells, the colors, the raw taste of magic on the air.

Everything here had been enchanted to ensnare and entice and entrance. More than once I had to stop and remind myself why I was here and what I was doing. Once, I sensed move-ment and pushed Marian into cover as a wildling appeared. He wasn't looking around, but I had no doubt he was on guard.

Marian gave me a disgruntled look. "Twicca will likely be in the center of town," she whispered.

We continued creeping, running across a few more

wildlings; though like those in King's Hollow, they didn't appear to be guarding anything so much as living. It was strange. Almost...domestic.

"There."

Marian pointed at the community center. Like the others, magic and the Wilds had reformed it into a green cathedral of sorts, with metal and glass flowers sprouting along the outside. "We'll climb to the top to get in."

It took me more than a few tries—Marian muttering impatiently—to find enough handholds to climb until we were on the roof. Marian froze an air vent and popped it off, and the pair of us dropped inside. It was barely big enough for us to fit side by side. Sunlight streaming through numerous holes in the ceiling lit our way as we slowly crawled toward what I guessed was the lobby. I heard the problem before I saw it: voices, multiple.

An enormous table had been placed in the center with chairs on all sides. At one end of the table stood a wildling who looked as though he was giving a presentation. Though by how sweaty and nervous he was, it didn't appear to be going well.

Marian jerked back with a barely muffled curse. "Not good —don't look! They'll see us!"

But I shrugged her off and tried to get a better look at the other three wildlings that were his audience.

"*This* is why you summoned us, Twicca?" the woman at the other end of the table said. Her dark skin was awash with sun, hair coifed in elaborate curls. She stared at the man who'd been speaking, while a small, furred beast tried to squeeze from her grasp. She magicked it in place and sank her long nails into its flesh. Blood seeped onto its fur. I could almost imagine its high-pitched screams as she refused to let it die. "Falsehoods and fleeting sightings?"

The man, who must be Twicca, gulped. "My spy swears

that's who he saw. And the boy didn't escape that many years ago, so the timeline matches. There's a possibility—"

"There is no possibility. We came here because we believed your report to be about a *real* threat."

"Now, Jezaline," the wildling beside her said. He was compact in his chair, mustached and dressed almost laughably like a jester. I almost expected to see shoes with little bells on the toes as he pulled them up and brushed them against his puffy sleeves. "To him this *is* a threat. He doesn't have the luxury of loyalty or power like we of the great kingdoms."

"Nor will he ever."

Jezaline waved a hand, and figures peeled out of the walls. Where their faces should have been were whorls like bark, arms and legs woven of branches. One put a softly glowing knife to Twicca's throat, who had begun to cry.

"P-please, I swear it! The trees speak. He who should be dead walks. There are whispers, groans from the earth, something that could hurt even you."

"*What*?" Jezaline said. "I've heard enough. Kill—"

"Patience, patience, my dear Jezaline," the other wildling admonished.

"Mordecai, you and this whimpering toadstool have worn mine out."

Mordecai smiled as though the threat and fury in Jezaline's face amused him. "My young friend, Cobb, what do you think of our sweaty Twicca's ramblings? Has your master, the Lord of Portland, had any such trouble about what he speaks?"

The third member of the audience finally moved. There was something strangely Rune-like about his face, but he was stockier and soft around the edges, skin like the flesh of a hard-boiled egg.

He looked between Mordecai and the trembling Twicca with the knife at his throat, who was pleading with his eyes for

Cobb to agree with him. "Apologies, I'm just Lord Aleki's attendant."

Jezaline's nail sank deeper into the small creature in front of her. "Mordecai asked you a question. You will answer."

"I really can't—"

"Answer!"

Cobb stared down at the table. "We...have not heard such rumors or dire premonitions, no."

Twicca whimpered as Jezaline looked at him. There was a small *snap* as her nail completely severed the creature's neck. "So you've wasted our time. Kill him."

Before the guards could do it, other wildlings dropped from the ceiling and burst through the doors on all sides. In seconds, Jezaline, Mordecai, and Cobb were surrounded.

"Another audience!" Mordecai gave a tinkling laugh. "Jezaline, I could, but would you rather greet these interlopers?"

Jezaline barked an order. The first of the newcomers were cut down almost immediately as more of her guards molded around them. A couple of the newcomers hacked away at one of the guards, fighting with desperate ferocity. A third's magic soared just over Jezaline's head, who snarled. "Enough of this! Mordecai!"

"If we must," Mordecai sighed.

The two Lords entered the fight, and the other wildlings never stood a chance. Thorns and vines spewed from the ground, skewering and cleaving anyone they touched. Jezaline shot silver needles from her sleeves that punctured flesh and bone. Mordecai, like the maniac court jester he appeared, giggled as he easily bounded around blade and arrow alike, cutting limbs and glamouring others to freeze so that he could easily snap their necks.

I could do nothing but stare, trembling, until at last only a single girl and Twicca remained in the center of a closing circle of Jezaline's guards. Jezaline flicked her fingers to remove some of the blood dripping down her nails as Mordecai giggled.

"The resemblance is uncanny," he said. "Yours, Twicca?"

"Spare her, please," Twicca begged. His legs collapsed. "Kill me if you must, but spare my child. She's not part of this."

The girl drew her chin up, and I was awed by her defiance, even when facing death. "Don't beg for me, Father. These beasts are worse than any the Wilds could offer, and I'd be glad to die fighting them."

"And indeed you will, my dear," Mordecai said.

Jezaline was looking at the girl. "Your pathetic begging hasn't fallen on unkind ears, Twicca. *We* will do her no harm."

Twicca gratefully sagged in his captor's hands, clearly missing the insinuation in Jezaline's voice. "Thank you, oh thank you. She has made a mistake; we both have. Show us your mercy and it will be repaid tenfold."

Jezaline's lips curled in disgust. She conjured a large silver thorn, bladed like a knife, and tossed it at the girl's feet. "As I said, no harm will come from us. Do it, girl. We show you this small mercy. Refuse, and I promise you it will be infinitely worse for you."

Both Twicca and the girl stilled. Then, as terrible recognition dawned on Twicca's face, the girl grabbed the thorn and placed the trembling tip against the base of her throat. "Better to die by my choice than be killed by cowards. I will not be the last."

Jezaline raised her hand in warning. I forced myself to look as the girl plunged the thorn into her throat. Her eyes bulged. Her body swayed and then pitched forward.

Twicca gaped at the growing pool of blood beneath her, snot and tears running down his cheeks. "My child... Oh, my girl..."

"I forgive you your slights, Twicca. This was far more entertaining than I hoped," Jezaline said. "Now you can die."

Twicca had no time to scream before one of the guards sliced his throat while the other plunged a hand into his chest and ripped out his glowing heart gem. Red sprayed the table, and the husk that was his body fell away. The guard tossed the still-glowing gem to the ground, where it cracked and went dark.

"Go and find anyone else loyal to him," Jezaline said with a lazy wave of her hand. "Finish them in whatever way you see fit. Neither I, nor Mordecai, need weaklings as subjects."

With barely a brush of air, her guards absorbed back into their surroundings.

I pulled back from the edge, fighting down a tide of nausea. Marian was shaking.

"I guess they did our job for us," she whispered. A soft, hiccupping sob escaped her lips. "Oh gods, I think I'm going to... No...no..."

It was a struggle to keep my own fear from taking over. "I'm guessing those are the other Lords."

"Yes. Mordecai's from Victoria. Jezaline from Vancouver." Marian grabbed the sleeve of my shirt. "We have to go, now."

For once I agreed with her. Getting involved with more wildling vendettas than necessary seemed like a quick way to end up like Twicca.

Quietly as I could, I scooted my body backward until it was easier to turn around and crawl inch by inch back the way we'd come. My leg bumped the side of the metal, and I sucked in a sharp breath.

"Keep quiet!" Marian hissed. "Almost there—"

She let out a little gasp. I felt their presence before I saw them. The arms of Jezaline's guards peeled through the flimsy walls of the air vent. Their whorled faces swirled to look right at us as their root-woven arms started to wrap my ankle.

"Crawl!" I shoved Marian. "Hurry!"

I tasted the charred scent of magic on my tongue. My leg was jerked back.

"We've got other visitors!" Mordecai crowed somewhere below us.

I tried to face the guards, to use my own magic before they could slit my throat like a pig.

"Val!"

I looked at Marian, right as her spell hit me full in the face.

I screamed. It felt like she'd sprayed burning acid on my eyes, and no matter how hard I rubbed, the searing sting wouldn't abate.

Marian shouted obscenities. Hands wrapped my limbs and dragged me backward, until I felt the cold of being removed from the air vent and dropped to the ground. A large weight pressed a knee against my back, pinning my arms. I heard a struggle and another thump as Marian was brought down beside me.

"W-who are they?" a timid Cobb asked. "Are they from here?"

"Come to avenge their dear departed master, no doubt," Jezaline's cold, clipped voice said. "Let them join him."

I tried to blink the streaming tears from my eyes as a thorned blade rested against my throat. My pulse jumped.

"No, no, not yet," Mordecai said. "Look at them. These ones are strange, can't you tell? Where's your sense of curiosity, Jezaline?"

Through the slits that were my swollen eyes, I saw boots stop before me. My chin was grabbed and raised.

"This one appears to have a problem looking at us. What's wrong with her eyes?"

"She's blinded by your radiance," Marian said, voice dripping with sarcasm. There was a snap of fingers, followed by another snap, this one of a bone breaking. Marian screamed into the ground.

"Keep mouthing off and I'll break the others, one by one," Jezaline said. "Followed by your jaw. Then every other bone in your body. Which kingdom are you from? Why were you watching us?"

"Such a crude method, simply asking," Mordecai said. He dropped my chin. I blinked until I could start to make out the lines of the floor and feet through the stinging tears. Mordecai smiled down at me.

"There we are. That wasn't so hard. However, you might want to close your eyes for this next part. It tends to hurt a lot, I'm told."

I tried to squirm out of his reach, but one of Jezaline's guards smashed my cheek to the ground, and Mordecai easily pressed his cool fingers to either side of my temples. He spoke a word. For the second time in as many minutes, searing pain was all I knew as my skull felt as though it'd been ripped open for all to see. An ethereal hand entered and began trying to force its way into my thoughts.

No you don't.

Through the splitting pain, I willed my mind to tighten, closing my thoughts off behind an iron lock. The rummaging magic turned to ransacking as it fought against my resistance but eventually receded. I panted into the floor, totally spent.

Mordecai sighed. "Your magic is strong. I could break it, but I don't need to resort to that just yet, right, Jezaline? That's why we keep them alive, for a time. It draws out the experience."

"Yes, yes, you've made that clear. Stop playing and get what we need to know," Jezaline said.

Mordecai approached Marian, and she started to thrash. "Don't you dare touch me, you—"

The guards broke another one of her fingers. Marian screamed right before Mordecai put his hands to her head. Her eyes glazed over, mouth going slack.

After a moment, a delighted grin slid over Mordecai's face. "Really? *Really?*"

"Out with it," Jezaline said. "Before I get impatient."

Mordecai patted Marian's cheek as he drew back. "Our deceased friend Twicca wasn't entirely wrong. It seems our dearest Rune has come back to life." He smiled down at me, and a chill ran up my spine. "Why don't we all go pay him a little visit?"

I never thought I'd fear for Rune. But seeing him alone in front of Mordecai, Jezaline, Cobb, and a dozen enemy guards surrounding King's Hollow, I could admit I was terrified.

Yes, Rune was horrible. Wicked, even. But I *knew* him. Knew what he wanted, at least. I had a higher chance of surviving with him than with any of the vipers who stood across from him.

"The prodigal son returns," Mordecai said gleefully. He sat on the bough of a moss-covered branch, swinging his legs. "Rune, Rune, Rune. We thought you were dead!"

Even outnumbered, Rune managed a villainous smirk. "If Lord Aleki had his way, I would be." He jerked his head at Cobb. "How is my uncle, cousin? Regrettably alive, I hope?"

Cousin? Rune had family? But then, the slight resemblance Cobb had to Rune now made sense.

Cobb had paled. "Lord Aleki would never—"

"Send his own nephew to Mog Moren?" Rune said, smile dangerous. "As naïve as ever, Cobb. You clearly don't know him as well as I do."

"So *that's* where you vanished to all those years ago," Jezaline said. "There were rumors... Even as we all looked so terribly hard for you."

"Lying witch," Xander muttered beside me. He, Marian, Triss, and I stood just behind Rune, a foil to the guards behind the other Lords.

The rest of those loyal to Rune watched tensely from the trees and the water or peeked out from root-arched passageways. Marian cradled her broken fingers in one hand. Triss had rushed to her and slathered a salve on them moments after Jezaline's guards had dragged us back to the hollow. I'd gotten drips of honeydew water to help the stinging in my eyes. I'd caught a glimpse of myself in a puddle. My eyelids were puffy, but my irises were red and gold, just like a wildling's. Marian had illusioned mine to match theirs. She'd saved me from Mordecai or Jezaline killing me on sight.

I wasn't sure how to feel about that. Grateful, I suppose.

Rune spread his arms out. "Unfortunately, we're not quite ready to entertain guests. You want to enlighten me as to what you're doing in King's Hollow?"

"We should ask you the same thing," Mordecai said. "The lost heir, gone for years, at last returns during a period of growing unrest. We've enjoyed relative peace between our different kingdoms. You wouldn't be thinking of upsetting that, would you?" His eyes flickered to the throne. "Though I suppose we have our answer."

"I've only returned to take what's rightfully mine," Rune said. "If any honor remained among the Lords—"

"There is no honor for the bastard son of Rowan, I'm afraid." Mordecai didn't sound the least bit sad. "You have no claim."

Bastard? I mouthed to the others. Xander shrugged. Marian

remained stone-faced, glaring at each guard as though sizing up how many she could take.

"As his son, I still have the only legitimate claim," Rune said.

"You have *nothing*." Jezaline's sharp voice rang through the Hollow. "You should be dead, your corpse feeding the worms. You come back and think we're suddenly going to give power to you?"

Rune's smile was petulant. "Yes. I expect it."

Jezaline was a blur. Her nails raked across Rune's face, and blood sprayed the leaves. Marian and Xander reached for their weapons, but Triss put an arm up to block them.

"Don't! It won't help!"

"We owe you nothing," Jezaline seethed, standing over Rune. "You will not lord over us. You will not take the throne."

Rune touched his cheek and stared at the blood on his fingertips. He straightened up. "Tradition says otherwise."

"Tradition." Jezaline spat. "That died with Rowan, as you should have. No wildling will ever follow you. You can get as many crowns and take as many thrones as you want. You may even try to kill us, as I can tell you so desperately wish to do. But you will still be playing at king. A leader that no wildling will ever respect."

Rune stared at her, the ribbons of Jezaline's claw marks cutting a brutally beautiful image across his face. "They don't need to respect; they need to obey. And they will, once my biggest obstacles are out of the way. All those who stood by and let the house of Rowan fall, who allowed Aleki to do what he did, will pay."

"No, they won't."

Jezaline raised a hand and more of her guards unwound from the treetops and rose from the pebbled mud around the water's edge. One buried a fist into a girl's stomach. Someone screamed, and fighting broke out among those in the root-arched passageways as they were dragged out. More guards approached Triss and me, and I softened my knees, waiting for the first blow.

"Stop!" Rune's voice rang above the struggle.

A crossbow twanged, and one of Rune's followers cried out as an arrow sprouted from his shoulder.

"Call them off, Jezaline," Rune snarled. "You will deal with me and leave them."

I held my stance, Xander beside me with his bow drawn, arrow pointed dead center of the whorl of the nearest guard's face.

"Try it," Xander said pleasantly. "I'll at least take down three of you before I go."

"Only three?" Marian said. "At least get to five before you fertilize the ground."

Triss clutched her bag of healing remedies, a pathetically small knife in her hand.

"P-Please! Do as he asks!" Cobb grabbed at Jezaline's arm, causing her to jerk away in disgust. "I'm sure it's just a misunderstanding. I'm sure Aleki wouldn't really want his nephew dead!"

Nobody moved. Nobody uttered a sound, except for the boy softly whimpering, an arrow in his shoulder.

"Don't be a fool, Cobb," Jezaline hissed. "One doesn't *mistakenly* send their nephew to Mog Moren. I'm sure this is exactly what he wanted. Even if he hadn't, Rowan is dead now and no longer has any say in our affairs. Stop your blathering nonsense."

"But he does have a point," Mordecai said.

Jezaline's eyes narrowed. "I grow tired of these games. Explain."

Mordecai bowed to Rune. "Though I don't believe you have

claim to the high throne, some royal blood, thin though it may be, still runs through your veins. There is far too little of that in the Wilds these days. I knew your father, boy. I wouldn't want to sully his memory by killing his only son, no matter how illegitimate."

"Of course you wouldn't," Rune said pleasantly. "Just by killing him."

"Now, now, you know that wasn't me! The Sundering took so many from us, and the history of who did what has become incredibly...muddled."

"Sure it has. But you never inconvenienced yourself by coming to help him, even when he called for it."

Mordecai gave a falsely pained grimace. "I'll admit his demise was...opportunistic for me and others to seize a little piece of power in all the confusion. But please, the past is past! Now we cripple ourselves with infighting, and the more we do, the more we weaken against the humans. We forget our true enemy."

"Spare me, Mordecai," Jezaline said. "Let's kill the little pest and be done with it."

More scuffles broke out. Jezaline's guards closed in around Rune, and he sized them up. I might have been able to make it there in time to stop one, but I'd get a thorn or blade between the ribs likely before that.

"Banish him!" Cobb shouted. "Spare him and banish them all."

Everyone stopped.

"Do you have moss between your ears?" Jezaline said. "He would just come back."

"He wouldn't," Cobb insisted. "Not now that he knows the other Lords are aware he's alive and won't accept him. His element of surprise is gone. You could kill him at any time. You have all the power. He won't risk it."

"Or I could kill him *now*—"

"And once word reaches the other wildlings that you killed their high king—even a bastard one? There may still be more than you realize who follow the old ways."

Jezaline blinked, clearly caught off guard. "They wouldn't dare rise against us."

"T-they haven't yet because they've had no reason to," Cobb said. "But once they learn of his death, at your hands..."

Jezaline was quiet, thinking.

"Though he's a simpering weakling, Cobb speaks truth," Mordecai said. "Hope is a powerful driver and even stronger cage, my dear Jezaline. If word is to get out about our dear Rune—and word *will* get out, no doubt about that—it's best our subjects have hope that someday he may return and the old ways with him. But in the meantime, they will continue to be subservient to the stability we provide, content in knowing that the bloodshed his attempted ascendence might bring is temporarily avoided."

Rune stiffened as Mordecai placed a hand on his shoulder and squeezed. "That's your best course, Rune. We'll spare you and your followers, in honor of our dearly departed Rowan. Go south, to the Wilds the humans call Flagstaff and Phoenix. If they don't kill you right away, then build your little empire there. Fight the humans and leave our kingdoms alone."

"Two days," Jezaline growled. "I'll give you two days, and then we'll start hunting."

A muscle feathered Rune's jaw. I waited, every nerve tensed. His choice would either save us or damn us. At last, "We'll go."

"No, Rune," Marian said. "You have *every* right—"

"We'll go," Rune said, glaring at her. "Give us three days."

"One," Jezaline said with a smile. "Don't bargain anymore, or I'll slaughter you all where you stand."

Rune nodded again. With a flick of her hand, Jezaline's guards melted back into the surroundings. "It was good seeing you, Rune. But if I see you again, I'll put your head on the end of a stick."

THE MINUTE the other Lords and guards left, I went to find Rune in his room within the hollowed tree. I heard raised voices as I approached.

"You can't run." That was Marian, insistent. "Those Lord bastards think they know everything, but after all you've been through—"

"*We've* been through," Xander said. "Everyone here has sacrificed and plans to sacrifice much more for this, for you."

I peered inside. Marian and Xander stood shoulder to shoulder, watching as Rune strode around the room, stuffing some things into a bag, waving his hand over others, and letting the earth swallow them. His silence was unnerving.

"Rune? We can't run," Marian repeated.

"If you hadn't been caught, we wouldn't have to," Rune said, and Marian's head snapped back as though a wasp had stung her.

"That's not fair, Rune," Xander said. "They were Lords—"

"I didn't ask for your opinion."

Rune straightened, and both Marian and Xander went rigid. "Despite its cowardly appearance, we aren't limping away like a wounded beast, we're speeding things up. They didn't take the chance to kill me. They'll regret that."

When he turned, I could see lines of rage etched in his face. My heart sped up. "Get the others moving. Break them into smaller groups so they can't be easily found. You two are with me, along with Triss."

"And the human?" Marian said.

Rune looked right at me, as though he'd known I was there the entire time. "She hasn't fulfilled our end of the deal. She stays with us."

We'd see about that.

"But—" Marian said. I stepped into the doorway. Marian glared at me.

"Go deal with the preparations," Rune said to them. "The Lords will probably start hunting us sooner than they said. I won't allow anyone to be caught off guard."

"Sure." Xander tried to gently lead Marian away, but she shrugged him off and roughly shouldered past me.

Xander sighed. "Thanks for standing with us back there," he said to me.

As if I had a choice. "Sure," I said. Then, because I felt bad about that, "You're welcome."

Xander sighed again and followed Marian.

"You're getting to be quite the voyeur," Rune said. He turned back to deciding which things to take, and which in turn to discard. One of the books was the next to vanish. "So, you've met my competition. What did you think?"

"You lied to me."

"I lie to a lot of people about a lot of things. You'll have to be more specific."

"You're not the true heir."

Rune tensed, and for a second, just one, I questioned my sanity for provoking him. Then I remembered what he'd done —what he'd do—and felt better about it. "It's one thing if the other Lords won't back you. If all I had to do was take down a few wildlings and your precious throne would be clear. But even if you take the throne, what if others don't think you're legitimate? I'm not fighting a civil war!"

"And what did you think would happen even if I had the

strongest claim?" Rune said softly. "That after years they'd all step aside and grovel at my feet? We're beasts, Val. Like you humans, we're rage skinned in flesh, and most will take no master, even a true one. It doesn't matter what they do after I take the crown. I never planned on ruling with benevolence. Not with them."

"Then you'll do it without—"

"Rune?"

Rune's cousin Cobb stood in the doorway, wringing his hands. His eyes flicked around as though Jezaline's guards would peel from the walls and slit his throat. Which, to be fair, they might.

"You're safe here, dear cousin," Rune drawled. "Mostly. You can speak freely."

Cobb nodded, gulping. "It's just...what Jezaline and Mordecai said is true. Neither one will back your claim. Aleki won't either."

"Really? How strange, I was under the impression they threatened my life and banished me because they liked me."

"W-what I meant to say..."

"I don't need Aleki's favor. And I don't need theirs, so if you've come to remind me of that, you're wasting your breath."

"Of course, I-I know," Cobb said quickly. "But you do need the heart tree."

"The one we don't know the location to," I said pointedly. Cobb glanced at me.

"Who is she?"

"She can be trusted," Rune said, surprising me. "Did you come here to recap everything or give me something useful?"

"I know where the heart tree is."

Rune kept a perfect poker face. Not an eyebrow twitched, not a muscle feathered. "Is that so?"

"I overheard Jezaline and Mordecai talking about it on the

way here. They say things around me as if I'm deaf or mute. It's in the low marshland, what used to be part of your father's kingdom."

"I remember," Rune said.

"Yes, well, some smaller wildling Lords had the territory there, but after your father died and you...after nobody could find you, the other Lords killed them and installed their own people so they can visit whenever they want."

"Am I missing something?" I asked. "I thought this heart tree only works for someone who has blood claim to the crown."

"Does she really have—" Cobb started.

"Yes," Rune said. "Answer her."

"Technically, yes, it only works for blood heirs," Cobb said. "Though a wildling *can* rule as high king without a crown if they have enough support and power. Jezaline and Mordecai visit the heart tree for the magic. It's strong there and replenishes their own." Cobb shuddered. "The things they can do, Rune..."

"Power without vision is useless," Rune said. "Thank you, Cobb."

"Y-yes, of course. It's the least I could do for—I'm so sorry, Rune," he whimpered. "I had no idea what Aleki did to you. One day you were there, and the next I woke up and you were simply gone. Aleki said you committed a crime, that you deserved to be in Mog Moren. If I had known the truth...if I had been stronger... I'm so sorry."

"Not sorry enough to find me and discover the truth for yourself," Rune said. "But I understand. You were young and innocent and powerless. We both were. Two of those things have changed for you, but you're still as spineless as ever."

Cobb hung his head.

"Consider this a small penance," Rune said. "When I take the throne, you'll be rewarded."

"Oh, thank you, thank you—"

"Get out."

Cobb scrambled to do so, nearly tripping on his own feet in his haste.

"I'm not going with you," I said.

"You don't have a choice. We have a—"

"The *deal* was when you had a legitimate claim. This is..." I shook my head. "I'm not a miracle worker, Rune. I can't be what you want."

"You can be exactly what I need."

"No. I'm leaving. Don't try to stop me."

"Why would I do that when it'd be so much easier to let the DFA and other humans do so?"

I looked back at him, suspicious. "Nice try. They won't know I've worked with you."

"They won't have to." He gestured to me. "They'll take one look at you and you'll never be free again."

It took me a moment to understand what he was saying. I rushed out to the throne, kneeling next to the stillest puddle of water I could find. My eyes were still the gold-red of a wildling. More than that, something was off about my image, as though I had a glowing filter all around my body.

"Unglamour me, Rune," I said as he came up behind me. "Undo all of this now."

"It won't help, and most of it's not my doing. You've been off the heart-tree medicine long enough that your magic has made itself known. You can see it, can't you? Most humans can't, but it won't matter. They won't know why, but they'll know you're different. They'll ask questions and won't like the answer. And when the DFA finds out, they'll kill you on sight. I wouldn't even need one of mine to kill Peyton. The DFA will do that, too."

I stood, trembling.

"How strange, isn't it? You've spent your whole life hidden, and now you're a bonfire shining in the night—"

I whirled around and punched him in his unguarded stomach. He wheezed, air exploding from his lungs. He clearly didn't think I'd dare attack him, but he'd known this would happen the moment he'd taken my medicine from me. He'd *let* this happen.

I punched again, but this time Rune was ready for it. The wood beneath his feet bent and flexed to his command, letting him evade. I tried to use my own magic—to call it to me as the second nature Marian thought it should be—but nothing answered. All I could focus on was wanting to tear Rune apart with my bare hands.

"Think of the great service you'll be doing for humanity. Do you really believe," Rune wheezed, grimacing, "that Jezaline and Mordecai are gathering power just to sit idly around? They want more, always more. They want what they don't have yet. And as Lords of the Wilds, what do you suppose that might be?"

"Shut up!"

I tried to hit him again. Rune danced just out of reach. "You know the answer."

Rylan's words came back to me. How the rich and the government in Seattle were asking for more powerful heart gems. What other need would they have for strength like that? What else, except to prepare for the threat of war?

"They won't stop at slaughtering us." Rune kept his feet light as we circled each other. "First will be the outskirts of Seattle and then the city itself. And that's just one city. You think *I* hate humans? My dislike is nothing compared to the bottomless well of their loathing. Your kind won't stop them. Nobody can stop them. Except for me. And I can only do that as high king."

I didn't want to hear his reasoning or his trickery cloaked in truth. I let out a growl as I struck again. This time Rune didn't just dodge. With one hand, he grabbed my wrists and slammed me to the wall. The other he moved closer to my face, almost caressing my cheek. I could feel the heat of his magic emanating from his palm. Enough to burn my skin.

"I can always count on you to keep me on my toes, little fox," Rune said. He was smiling, perhaps the first real one I'd ever seen from him. "But you won't wriggle out of this. I'll make you a new deal."

"Stick your deals right up your—"

I gasped as he pressed my wrists harder against the wood. My cheek was growing unbearably hot.

"I'm getting my crown from that heart tree. And when I do, you'll get some of its bark. Enough to make you new medicine. Enough for you to blend back in among your humans. And you'll keep getting it. *After* I get my throne."

"And how do I know you won't go back on *this* deal? Or keep adding to it until I'm trapped with you forever?"

"Trapped forever, yes, how terrible. There are no more tricks. We both get what we want."

He lied so easily I was almost impressed. He *said* there was no more to trap me, but by helping him I was trapping myself.

"Your answer?" Rune said.

Heat like magma flowed from my core and spread through my arms, fueled by my anger. Rune hissed and let me go. He looked down at his blistered palm and then up to my glowing eyes. I hated how there was no fear in his expression, only triumph.

"Now you get it. The only way you—we—survive this is to fight to end them before they end us."

Every cell in me wanted to attack him again. To hurt him as much as he'd already hurt me. But he had a point. And though he'd lied, I had to admit in some ways he'd assured my survival, too.

I drew in a deep breath, magic returning to wherever it lay dormant. I could feel the barest crackle of it beneath my skin, reminding me that I could use it.

I wouldn't. I couldn't. Not if it meant becoming more like them.

"We have to move fast if we want to stay ahead of the Lords," I said.

Rune's smile was all menace. "You've already pissed them off enough, something you're very good at. First, we take the heart tree. Then we pay my uncle a visit and their downfall begins."

EIGHT

The rest of the wildlings scattered within hours, while Rune, Marian, Xander, Triss, and I disappeared into the Wilds, leaving King's Hollow behind.

"We'll be back," I overhead Triss reassuring Rune. He was particularly unbearable the first day. He snapped at every noise we made and forced us to double-back at least a dozen times to avoid being followed. After he'd gotten onto me about my growling stomach, *I'd* snapped at him. That'd earned me a murderous look from Marian, but he'd deserved it.

We moved south, following tributaries feeding into what I thought was Lake Quinault. We were so deep into the Wilds I couldn't be certain of anything, since humans hadn't been here for years. We stuck to mist-filled valleys and woke one chilly morning to birdsong that sounded disturbingly off.

"They're after us already," Rune whispered, eyes scanning the trees. "Jezaline has no intention of letting us leave their territories alive."

With Xander and his bow scouting a safe path, my head on

a perpetual swivel for so much as an unnatural-looking leaf, we picked up the pace until we left the false birdsong and immediate danger behind. It was impossible to say for how long.

I helped the others hunt on the days it felt safe to do so. I never ate what we killed, remembering the rotting carcasses the beasts turned into, but that never happened to the wildlings. Not even when Marian would rip out their tiny heart gems and toss them at me.

"For your collection."

Triss always looked imploringly at her but never spoke up. Rune didn't notice, too pre-occupied with where we were going next. Instead of fighting back, I would forage the underbrush for mushrooms and berries bursting with sweetness that Xander had pointed out as edible. There was honey, too, in a beehive I smoked out using a dried branch, old cloth, and my matches. I cherished the surprised look on Rune's face when I returned to camp smokey, covered in bee stings, but chewing on a honeycomb.

"None for you," I said, taking a seat by the fire.

The morning of the fifth day, Xander came back from scouting with a spring in his ghostly quiet step.

"We've crossed the border out of their territory," he announced.

"That means we should be good, right?" I said.

"We're never *good*," Marian snapped. "But if Jezaline and Mordecai still aren't around, then we've lost them. Since Aleki's wildlings aren't here, that means he doesn't know we're coming."

"The heart tree is close, less than two days," Rune said. "I want to be in Portland within the week."

"Rune, that's still over a hundred miles away," Triss said wearily.

"Unless you summon a path for us to travel," Marian said, and I could already feel nausea churning my gut.

"I would, if I wanted to announce to Aleki that I was here," Rune said. To Triss, "And I don't care how far it is. You knew there would be difficulties when you joined me. If it's too much for you, you're free to leave."

She shrank back. "That's not—I didn't mean—"

"We should rest," I said. I'd noticed the weariness hanging off all of us, Triss especially. She was the gentlest wildling I'd met, and the brutal pace we'd kept had been hardest on her. Even now, she sagged against a tree while we packed up camp. "We should take the chance while we're safe here."

"Rest?" Rune said, as though the word was foreign to him.

"Relax, chill out, recover so we're not zombies when we go to the heart tree."

"What are zombies?" Xander said.

"Every moment we waste is one we're not moving forward," Rune said to me.

"And any good leader would know when pushing too much does more harm than good," I shot back.

Triss sucked in a sharp breath. Xander stilled.

Rune stared at me, but I refused to lower my gaze. Marian came over and whispered something in his ear. His eyes flickered to Triss.

"We'll... Rest," he said at last. "For today."

Then he took off into the trees, leaving us alone.

"Thanks for saying something, Marian—" I started.

The other girl was already gone, too.

I shook off the stiff exhaustion that was my constant morning companion and spread out to find a better place to lie down for a few more hours. We'd been walking along the upper crust of a valley, where boulders and slabs of rock had scoured the trees nearly bare. One of the overhangs looked perfect to keep me out of the worst of the morning's chill. I laid my sleeping bag down and started stuffing what little dry clothing I had to make a pillow.

"I brought you some things that might help."

My heart didn't jump as badly as it usually did when the wildlings appeared out of nowhere, but still it lurched uncomfortably.

Triss held out a small handful of multi-colored flowers, herbs, swollen roots, and things I couldn't identify. She nodded to the cuts and stings I'd collected over the last few days. "I thought I could heal those up. My magic isn't as strong as Marian's, but I have some useful skills."

"Thanks, but you should be resting, not tending to me," I said.

She tugged my sleeve for me to kneel beside her. She spread out what she'd brought with careful, practiced movements. "I want to do this. It makes me feel useful. Sometimes it's hard to feel that way around the others."

"You are useful," I insisted.

She gave me a grateful smile. "In my own way, I suppose. I've never had a strong stomach for violence, and no matter how many fights we get into, I can't seem to enjoy it."

She indicated for me to hold out the arm with the worst of my injuries. She took one of the red leaves, rubbed it between her fingers until it caught fire, and then held it under a root until green goop bubbled up from the center. She let it cool a moment in her palm before wiping it over the cuts. The cooling sensation tamed the angry sting. I watched, astounded, as the small cuts stitched themselves together before my eyes.

"But I'm good at this," Triss said. "Perhaps better than any of them. Over the years I've read so much and explored so much I'm practically a walking compendium."

I let her work in silence as she burned more of the root and then sprinkled some powder over my eyes to ease the still-lingering pain of Marian's alteration. Xander had told me it would fade eventually, but that changing my appearance so fast—especially to someone who'd had little exposure to direct magic—had made the experience more painful than it had to be.

"All done," Triss said happily when she'd slathered the last of the roots' goop onto me. She gathered up her remaining supplies and stood, the movement whisper soft.

"How do you do that?" I asked. Learning about the various plants of the Wilds, and the ones that could heal, was useful. But if I could walk softly enough to never need healing? That was even more so. "Move that quietly, I mean?"

She paused, thinking. "It comes naturally to me. But I suppose if I were to describe it..."

She held up a finger, wanting me to listen. I did, until all I heard was the Wilds, the subtle chirps, trills, drips, and faint whispers of animals passing by.

"There's a rhythm of life here," Triss said. "Find space within that rhythm and move there. Your sound will simply become one with everything else around it."

I stood, brushing the leaves off my pants. "That sounds much easier said than done."

"Which is why even some wildlings have trouble with it. But you don't need stealth, Val. You're strong enough that you *want* them to know you're coming. To know and be afraid."

I had no idea how she'd gotten that idea. I was terrified. All the time, it seemed.

"If you really want to know, ask Pitus when we're back with the others," Triss said. "She's far better at it than I am. I swear she has the ability to turn to smoke."

I thanked her, and she left me to marvel at my newly healed cuts and scrapes. Marian had returned and now picked her way through the trees below, trying to find her own spot to rest.

"Thanks for speaking up back there," Xander said. He crouched on the overhang of my spot, bow clenched in his hands. He scanned our surroundings before deciding we were safe and jumping down. "I thought Triss was going to drop."

"Someone had to say something," I muttered. "Rune would have driven us into the ground."

"I know he can be...intense."

That was one word for it. I nodded at the bow. "You actually know how to use that?"

He pretended to be offended. "Your doubt wounds me."

"Not as much as you might wound one of us if you don't know how to shoot."

He smirked. "Touché. Willing to learn something else from a wildling?"

Despite my tiredness, I was, and he took me to the edge of the rock-scoured hillside, where the line of trees began. He pointed to one of them, drew an arrow, nocked, drew, fired again, and again, until the same foot-wide circle of its trunk resembled an arboreal porcupine.

"That answer your question?" he said smugly.

I rolled my eyes. "Do all wildlings have big egos? Let me try."

He gave an indulgent smile as he handed it over. "If you can."

I evaluated the bow as Xander went to remove the arrows. He pressed his hand over the chunks of missing bark. A moment later, it reverted back to a smooth, unmarked trunk. He handed me an arrow. "Good luck."

He wasn't kidding. The bow was clearly made for his strength and more. I managed to draw it all the way back once, but my arms shook so much that my shot went laughably wide.

"It's imbued with magic," Xander said, failing to hide a smile behind his hand. "You have to connect with it, direct your will to let it help guide you."

"Of course you do," I grumbled. "And quit laughing."

Xander put on a stoically somber face, though his eyes danced with mirth. "Apologies. Your ineptitude is no laughing matter."

It took a lot to silence all the thoughts whining at how stupid this was and really *feel* the warm sensation of magic imbued in the wood, let it guide my movements.

The next time I drew back was easy. I managed three arrows close to where Xander put his. He whistled.

"That's...not bad, actually. You picked up on that quick. Thought for sure you'd be one of those humans who only used guns."

I handed the bow back, shoulders and back aching. "Not unless I wanted to miss every shot and let the entire Wilds know where I was."

"Smarter than most," Xander said.

I drew my knife and used the tip to dig the arrows out of the trunk and returned them to Xander's quiver. He healed the tree and nodded at my knife.

"That isn't going to do much, not for what we need. I'll trade you."

He pulled a blade resembling a slim machete, the tip of it set at a slight angle.

"There was a steel factory where you humans used to call Olympia. Before some of the Lords shut it down, they made a few of these. Enchanted with anti-rust, and ever-sharp magic. Overall better for blocking and stabbing from close range. Much easier to get inside an opponent's defenses."

I took it almost reverently. "You'd give this up?"

"As nice as it is, I'm more of a long-range kind of guy. If I'm close enough to use a blade, I'm out of luck." He met my gaze, all traces of humor gone. "And Rune's trusting you to watch his back. You need something with a little more bite."

I unsheathed the sword and swung it around, hoping I didn't look too inept. I'd had some experience learning sword-play from Joshua, but it was more questionable than my knife skills. Still, the weight and feeling of power the blade gave me felt good. I could definitely see myself getting used to this.

"And you just want my knife in exchange?" I said, suspicious. "I'm tapped out of making deals for the time being. Maybe ever, after this."

"Just the knife. Promise."

I hesitated before handing my knife to him. "Treat it well. I may want it back."

"No, you won't." He nodded to my blade. "What's its name?"

I scoffed. "It's a sword, Xander. I'm not that sentimental."

"You humans," he said, but not unkindly. "It's not senti-mentality, it's practicality. Unlike guns, blades kill intimately, using your life to take another, watching closely as they die. A sword is an extension of yourself. And since you have a name, it should, too."

I'd never thought of myself capable of such small destruc-tions, but in the short time I'd been with Rune and his wildlings, I realized he'd changed that.

"Okay. Then I'll call it, uh...Stabby."

Xander frowned. I shrugged. "No good? Then what would you suggest? What did you name it?"

"Doesn't matter." He put out his hands. "Can I look?"

I held out the sword, but he grabbed my entire arm instead, moving it as though striking and then stabbing. He adjusted my elbow and wrist so that light glinted off the sharpened edge. Even in his awkward position, every movement flowed from one to the next.

"You seem to know what you're doing," I said.

"My parents were metal forgers," he said offhandedly, still focused on the blade. I held in my scoff. Out of all the things I expected wildlings to have, a job wasn't one of them.

"They seem to have taught you a lot."

"They did, yes. They were the best in our realm. There are beasts that even we wildlings find dangerous, and many sought my parents out for means to kill such beasts. They worked for smaller Lords, normal wildlings, armies, and the common folk. It didn't matter the lineage; all were equal under the blade."

I hadn't missed him talking of them in past tense. "What happened to them?"

Xander held my arm in the position of a perfect finishing strike, as though driving the sword cleanly through a heart gem. "They made a weapon for a Lord who used it to murder a rival of another house. The murdered Lord's son blamed my parents and had them publicly executed. I was to join Rune and the others in Mog Moren but escaped and lived with some outcasts called the Mysts until Rune found us."

Xander let go of my arm, and I swung the sword around a few times before letting it hang at my side. "I'm sorry."

"It's the past. No sense mourning about it, and there are those with Rune with much more tragic beginnings. All of us have been hurt in one way or another."

"Still—"

"Name the sword."

I was about to say that it was *his* job to do, since he'd just taken the time to look it over, but I was surprised to find a name readily pop into my head. What was more apt than something that slid between ribs and into hearts, that was small in the grand scheme of things, but could still burrow deep and fester?

"It's named Sliver."

"Fitting." Xander nodded. "Slight, but capable of great damage if placed in the right spot. You're connected now, to bring death or, if it's your time, accept it."

It took me a minute to position the scabbard so I could easily draw the blade. When I looked up, Rune had returned. He seemed to be scanning the lower valley, triple-checking we were alone as he meticulously did every time we stopped, even though the rest of us had assured him multiple times we were safe here.

"What kind of weapon does Rune use?"

"Rune?" Xander looked. "He has a glass knife, but he doesn't need it. He's one of the strongest fighters I've ever seen, which makes sense for an heir to the high throne. Was quite the shock when he first showed me what he could do."

"Why's that?"

"Not every wildling has the ability to manipulate the Wilds, or compulsion half as powerful. His heart gem is strong enough to handle all of that and be a true terror, even without the knowledge of a blade. I assume he had some formal weapons training from his House, but he's never used it. At least not that I know."

I rubbed the pad of my thumb over Sliver's hilt, watching as Rune knelt and placed a palm to the ground. After a breath, he stood and moved on, satisfied.

"Doesn't he ever quit, even for a second?" I said, exasperated. "We're supposed to be relaxing!"

Xander laughed. "Rune? Absolutely not. Hasn't since the day I met him. The fact that he actually listened to your suggestion to stop is a minor miracle. He almost never takes advice like that. And, of course, never from a human. No offense."

I took none. After so many other slights, what was one more, especially one that was true? "You said he was part of a House?"

"You know of them?"

"Only a couple."

They'd been a product of the Forming, following the Cataclysm, when the wildlings at last stopped their internal fighting and united. They killed most of the major beasts and minor gods destroying the Wilds and established their first high king. Peace had reigned for a long time after that, and even fighting with humans had lessened. But all good things ended eventually.

I counted off on my fingers. "I've heard of the House of the Glittering and... House of Worms, I think? That can't be a real one."

"It was," Xander said, leaning against the tree. "Jezaline's House. House of Sovereigns is another. House of Knives. House of Small Cuts."

"You can't be serious."

Xander grinned. "Jealous of our gawdy conventions, are we? House of the Fallen Star was Rune's. But don't tell him I told you that. Every member from that House is gone."

I looked for Rune again, but he'd walked off.

"I've heard Mog Moren mentioned a few times," I said. "What is that?"

Xander grimaced like I'd poked an open wound. "I don't think..."

"*Xander.*"

I hadn't heard Marian approach. She glared at me, bristling, before turning on him. "It's time to get food. Hurry up. I want an actual nice meal tonight."

"As the lady demands." Xander sighed. "See you," he said to me.

"And *you*," Marian sneered, "keep your questions to yourself and nose out of our business. Or I'll cut it off."

I placed a hand on Sliver. "Sure you will."

Marian's eyes flared wider when she saw it. Then, seething, she stomped off.

<hr>

We might be safe for the time being, but that didn't mean I slept any better.

I rolled over, turning from the pitch black of the small overhang I bunkered in, and got a face full of milk-white moonlight. Gentle coos and song—interrupted every so often with an animal scream—tried to lull me back to sleep. It was no use. Years of being an alert sleeper had me totally awake now.

I wasn't the only one. As I stepped out of the overhang, gold-red eyes peered down from above.

I wrapped my sleeping bag around my shoulders and walked to where Rune sat. He didn't speak, didn't ask what I was doing up. I should have still been furious for what he'd done to me, but keeping the resentment going was exhausting and impractical. I wouldn't forget, but I would move on. For now.

"I've been wondering, did you trap them?" I gestured to where Marian, Xander, and Triss slept. "Like you did me?"

Rune chuckled, deep and rumbling. "You always think so highly of me."

"You haven't given me a reason not to." Not entirely the truth, but he didn't need to know that.

"They are here because they choose to be. And if they decide to leave, they're allowed to do so."

"And you wouldn't have a problem with that?"

"If they are with me, then they are mine and I will protect them. If they are not, then they're my enemy and not my concern. You put too much weight on things like honor and loyalty. We are together because we provide each other something. Nothing more."

"Like the two of us," I replied sardonically. "Together under mutual agreement."

He looked at me long enough that my face started to heat through the nightly chill. "Exactly. We wouldn't be together for any other reason."

I needed to hear that. In case I was starting to see him as anything else than the infuriating, sometimes cruel, means to an end that he was.

"You asked before whether I recognized you, when we were children," I said. "Why would I?"

"You, the only survivor amongst a town the Wilds devoured," Rune said, almost a mirror of what Peyton always told me. "Plucked from the remains by a magnanimous individual who called you her own."

I turned to him, mouth falling open. "I never told you that. How did you..."

A flash of memory struck me upside the head. Peyton scooping up child me. Peyton turning us both back to the Wilds' trees to curse at them.

There had been the flash of something in those trees. A boy's face? I had never been certain of what I'd seen. The memories were so mucked up and murky. But now...

"You?" I breathed. "You were there? I thought I made that up."

"Val," Rune said mockingly, "I'm hurt! I'm guessing you'll also say you don't remember me finding you, alone and covered in blood, wandering in the forest, a most delectable snack to any passing beast. Or how I led you back to the humans and to safety."

"But...*why?*"

He looked genuinely surprised by my question. "Would you rather I hadn't?"

I gave him a cynical smile. "Altruism isn't exactly a shining quality you possess."

He paused for so long I thought he might have fallen asleep. "Marian told me of the chasm you two found," he said, entirely avoiding the question. "You've seen those before."

I thought back to the blue crystals and the deep gorge in the earth leading into darkness. "Yeah, I have. When you and I found that dead wildling. And again..." The memory hurt like a firework going off in my skull, but it was there. "And I think something like it was there the day Peyton found me in the Wilds. She said there were a bunch of earthquakes around that time."

"Is that so?" Rune seemed to be thinking. "There have been similar earthquakes for years following the Cataclysm, and more often than not a few chasms appear."

He looked across the tops of the trees. The moonlight was starting to blend into the orange yellow of the horizon. "The crystals always vanished after a few weeks, but they've been lingering longer this time."

I traced a crack in the rock between my legs. "What *were* you doing out there, the day you found me? Really?"

Rune held my gaze for a long time before I begrudgingly looked away.

"I was trying to escape what I was," he said, voice soft. "And stumbled across you. I wonder, only now, what *you* were doing out there."

"I don't know."

And I couldn't remember, even if I wanted to. Everything I

wanted was in front of me, and with Rune. Despite my intense dislike—and I realized with a shock that was what it was: intense dislike, not venomous hatred—Rune had what I wanted. He had power, always, even when he was at a disadvantage. Yes, he was callous and cruel and savage, but he was nothing other than what he'd promised to be. I wanted some of that power and security, if only a taste.

"It is a terrible thing," Rune said. "The rot," he clarified when I looked over at him. "What's currently consuming your guardian. It's something no one should have to experience."

My mouth hung open. I quickly closed it. That was as close to sympathy as I was probably going to get from him.

"Thanks," I managed. "And I'm sorry, for what happened to you. Nobody—"

Rune unfolded his long legs and abruptly stood. His expression was a closed door the orange and yellow melted across. My heart spiked as I heard not-quite-right bird calls in the distance, growing closer.

"Time for us to move. We need to reach the heart tree before they reach us."

CHAPTER

NINE

I smelled the marsh before I saw it. It was a rotting dumpster in the sun. Shoveled muck-water and soggy greenery. The mosquitoes and biting flies that had been tolerable up to this point became a menace. None of the others seemed bothered by it. I caught Marian smirking at me as I smacked away the bloodsuckers.

"Having trouble?" she asked sweetly.

I glared at her, trying to figure out how she was completely unaffected by any of the pests. "Let me guess. Magic?"

She continued smiling before hurrying to catch up to Rune.

Triss sidled up to me. "It's not magic. Here." She held up a small, corked bottle. "I mixed some this morning. Dab this on your wrists and throat—"

I snatched the bottle from her with a muttered thanks. Rune, Marian, and Xander had stopped at the edge of the marsh's soggy ground. Marian was seething to Rune about something while he in turn looked as unconcerned by her outbursts as always.

"—makes no sense!"

139

"You've never been around it, so of course it doesn't to you." He jerked his head at me. "Hurry up. The heart tree is only a little farther."

He pointed through the marshland—interspersed with tufts of tall, dead grass—to where I could just make out a golden glow, like a halo rising through the low-hanging mist. "You will be joining me, Val."

"And the others?" I said, guessing where Marian's fury stemmed from.

"We'll be going, too," Marian said fiercely.

"*You* will be dispersing and keeping watch," Rune said. "The tree may not be left unguarded, and you can't approach with me."

"And why is that?" Xander said. Like Marian, he looked put out, but more curious than furious.

Rune exhaled a sharp breath. "As I explained to you numerous times, the heart tree is composed of incredibly old magic, stronger than any other in the Wilds. I'm a true heir, no matter how diluted my blood, so it won't be a problem for me. You three are not, and getting as close as we require will only make you sick or incapacitated or overwhelmed. You won't be any help then. I'm telling you to disperse and keep an eye out. We'll meet with you after I've gotten the crown."

"Rune, please—" Marian said.

He took off across the firmer marsh ground, avoiding the worst of the sucking mud puddles. "Val, with me."

"Be careful," Triss said softly.

Marian grabbed my arm.

"I already know," I said. "Hurt him and you'll hurt me."

"In ways you cannot even begin to imagine," she agreed.

She let me go, and in seconds I lost the three of them amongst the trees. It took me a moment of picking out the most solid path forward before I joined Rune. "What makes you think I won't betray you?"

Rune threw me a hard smile, like we were both in on a joke. "I *know* you might betray me. It won't sting as much if I accept that possibility."

What a lonely existence to have indeed.

The snarl of marsh trees draped with stringy moss, shallow, putrid puddles, and absolutely too much mud ended at a broad clearing. Rune crouched at the edges, staring hungrily ahead. "There."

The heart tree looked like a grown-up version of the near-mystical glint bush, its sprawling branches decked in leaves of gold and silver. The trunk was a brown richer and warmer than anything I'd ever seen. Within the wood was a small depression scooped smooth. Exactly the sort of space one might sit in if they were expecting to get crowned.

Something bothered me, though. I'd obviously never seen a heart tree, had no clue something like that even existed until a week ago, but the way the other wildlings put such weight and reverence on it made me think it'd be...more substantial. I'd seen glamour and experienced enticement beyond anything the human senses were supposed to endure. That which was too perfect was often the most dangerous. This tree was that. A lamp drawing us in just to zap us.

"Rune, stop. I think this is a trap."

Rune slowed. The hunger in his eyes was now tempered slightly by reason. He took in our surroundings.

"I don't see anything."

"But something's wrong, I can feel it."

"You...*feel* it?"

"I'm telling you there's—"

"If it is a trap, no one's here to spring it. If it is a trap, they'll regret standing in my way."

I gawked at him. This casually heedless Rune wasn't making any sense. Maybe he was right, and the magic of the heart tree was stronger and more compelling than I thought, even if I didn't feel a whisper of it.

Rune's long strides ate up the earth, making barely a sound or ripple through the marsh. Cursing, I scrambled to follow him.

"You will protect me while I get the crown," he said. "When I have that, use your sword to carve off shavings from the bark, as much as you need."

"And *after* you get the crown?" I asked, still fervently looking around as we left the higher grass and started across an unnervingly soggy open field. "The Lords want you dead. Doesn't matter if you have a shiny crown on your head. It'll just give them something to aim for."

"*After*, they won't be able to stop me."

He slapped at his neck and glared at the palm of his hand. Something bit my neck and then my forearm. Though I'd applied the ointment, the bugs were back with a sharp vengeance. Rune slipped in the mud, and I caught him. He barely said a thanks before he was walking again, and I could have screamed with frustration. My entire body itched at how exposed we were.

I stumbled after him, and my foot sank deep in the murk, muscles burning as I heaved it free. The thick stench of rotted water was making my head fuzzy. This close, the tree looked even more wrong, though it was difficult to say why.

"Finally," Rune muttered. He stared up at the glittering branches. "You don't know how long I've dreamed of this, Val. How many nights I spent planning exactly what I would do."

I turned to watch for an ambush while he reminisced. This was great, really, so great. But we were way too exposed and an unnatural mist was creeping in on us. "Just hurry it up."

"I've waited years. I won't rush this." He ran his fingers along the trunk, gaze distant. "I despise hope, but I will admit that this hope kept me alive. Every time I watched someone die, every night I lay awake in that hell, talking with the others about how we would change the Wilds into the way we wanted it, I never truly thought... I never *dreamed* I would actually..."

He let out a barking, half-crazed laugh that made me jump. "I should have died a hundred times over, but instead, dozens have died in my place, or under my hand. All for this."

Maybe it was my steadily aching head, but his voice had taken on a thickened, strange pitch. He turned to me. The strange mist had devoured our surroundings, leaving only us in the center, lit beneath the gold-silver glow of the heart tree's branches. Rune's eyes were the same color they'd always been, but covered in a thin sheen, like oil.

"And you are here, by my side," Rune said. His words were slurry, but my own thoughts were so cloudy it was too much effort to care. The mist...right? There had to be something in this mist.

So? A new thought lazily rose up. *Doesn't matter. This is nice, isn't it?*

Rune took his hand off the tree and stepped over to me. Not away in disgust or disdain. Toward me, willingly. Even without touching, I was hyperaware of the warmth radiating off his body. He might have acted cold—and he was that at times— but right then the heat between us was anything but.

"Val..." His hand reached out and brushed a strand of hair from my face. His touch was electric, thrumming through my every vein. I shuddered, happy, but not sure why. "You asked about after. *After*, when I become king, I'll need a queen."

My breath stopped. "You can't mean..."

"I could take a wildling wife, but you there's something

about you that draws me. Maybe it is because you are not afraid of me."

"I am." I didn't mean to say that. My tongue had taken over, and my muggy thoughts clouded any desire I had to rein it in. "I'm terrified of you."

"Perhaps a little. But you are stronger than that. It is them who should be afraid. I was loved, once. Then hated, then feared, then pitied."

He continued brushing the hair from my cheek, one careful strand at a time, his oil-sheen eyes roving hungrily across my face. "I prefer being feared over pitied, but with you, pity's something I cannot have, nor do I want. I find your resilience... intoxicating."

"It would never work. The other wildlings would never accept me."

"They would hate it," he agreed. "But they've rarely liked the things I've done."

This—all of this—was wrong, but the warning bells in my head were muffled by the surrounding mist and my own desires. Rune was...was...

Infuriating, callous, and...

He wrapped an arm around me and pulled me to him. His hand cupped the back of my neck, and though parts of me fought against this insanity, the other parts of me didn't mind when he lowered his lips to mine and kissed me. Tenderly, gently, achingly sweet, all opposites of what he was.

I had kissed boys before. When I was sober, when I was drunk. Ones I liked and ones I didn't, either because I felt like I needed to or because I wanted to feel needed.

Rune was different—and not because he was a wildling, but because *I* was different. I relished this more than I ever had before, and he responded in kind. Kissing him was like going so deep into the Wilds there was no possibility of coming out, of flirting with death and enjoying every moment of it. So, in a way, I should like it. And I did, I really did.

For someone who frowned so much, Rune's mouth was surprisingly soft and cocked in a smirk as I fumbled to readjust my lips. I blushed at my own inexperience at simple kissing but didn't stop. His touch was shockingly gentle as his hands ran up my arms, as a finger traced the calluses of my hands and the small, seemingly constant cuts I had there.

"Don't move them," he murmured as I tried to pull my hand away.

"They're hideous," I said. Why was I saying this? I'd never had a problem with how I'd looked, but somehow, under his almost-reverent gaze, every imperfection and fear had been laid nakedly bare.

"They're you," he replied. "And they're anything but."

I shouldn't want this, and even Rune seemed to be fighting against kissing me, though admittedly not very hard. He hungrily deepened the kiss as my hands wove through his hair, catching in the ivy of his circlet. Unsure of where else to move my hands, I frantically ran my fingers down the lines of his neck to his throat. Had I really put a knife to it before? Why had I done that, when kissing it seemed a so much more appealing option?

Rune grunted as I pulled my lips off his and brought them slowly, tenderly, to the angles just beneath his jaw—

No! My inner voice exploded, as though having broken through whatever silenced my sanity. *This is so, so wrong.*

It's fine, the lazy voice said. *Let it happen, give in...*

But I was aware now, and there was no going back.

I shoved Rune away. He splashed backwards and nearly stumbled, still grinning stupidly. "Too much? I understand. I have a certain appeal..."

"You don't want this," I said even as the cloudy thoughts

that I *did* want this tried to swarm me again. "You don't even *like* me."

"That's not true." His voice was a purring whisper. "I find you exhilarating."

I shuddered beneath his words, but they were empty. There was no passion in kissing me. He would do it simply for the thrill, not unlike sticking his head in a wolf's mouth.

He reached out for me once more. Whatever temporary insanity had gripped us both, I had to break free of it.

I shoved him away again, drew my sword, and plunged the tip into my thigh hard enough that blood quickly spread in a dark-crimson spot.

I gasped. Any murky thoughts were secondary to the pain, and they fled, along with the mist.

We were surrounded.

I used to think the most dangerous things in the Wilds—other than wildlings—were bears, wolves, other hunters, and the occasional beasts I heard but never saw, the ones that spread rot and screamed from the deep, dark places.

These creatures oozing from the marsh mud had too many eyes, set within slick, moisture-covered bodies glistening with mucus. Their mouths were horror-filled rows of teeth, circular like a leech, and within them ran a single tentacle, with a needle-tipped point, stuck directly into Rune's and my neck.

I sluggishly sliced away my tentacle and stabbed the nearest creature in the mouth, grateful for the reach of my new weapon as the tip sank deep into its fleshy skin. It screamed as it died. Its friends closed in.

"Snap out of it, Rune!" I yelled. "We have to get your stupid crown before—"

I looked at the heart tree and realized we weren't getting Rune's crown. We never had any chance of getting his crown. Because where the heart tree had stood was a long-dead trunk, rotting from the inside. It had been an illusion, and suddenly my reluctance made sense. We'd been led here like idiots—like cattle to a feeding frenzy.

"Rune!" The nearest creature surged toward me. I cut it down and severed the tentacle dug into Rune's neck. He fell back, the grin slipping off his face. His legs appeared to lose all strength and he crumbled to a crouch.

"No…please stop." He covered his head with his arms, protecting himself from something that wasn't there. "Don't make me do it, please!"

I didn't see anything hit him, but slashes suddenly carved shallow grooves in his arms and legs, which wept blood into the mud. I gaped. What *were* these things that could hurt you without touching?

I yanked my arm back as one of the creatures tried to sink its teeth into my hand. I stabbed my fingers into its flesh and dragged it to the ground before driving my sword into its screaming face. Rune still hadn't moved.

"Listen to me, Rune, follow my voice," I said. "Whatever you're seeing isn't real. You have to fight it. You have to come back to me."

More of the beasts were dragging themselves up from the mud, and I was struck with a startling thought: why did I care whether they got him or not? We were outnumbered five to one. I had a clear shot at a river and the Wilds beyond. I could cross that and make my escape, leaving Rune here to buy me time.

I glanced back at Rune. He'd pulled his face up, looking around with an expression that was so, so lost.

"Val?"

That one word made my choice.

I stabbed another beast and hauled Rune to his feet,

bracing myself beneath his shoulder. I kept forgetting how big he was, and my feet sank into the mud.

"Fight it, Rune," I said through gritted teeth. I swiped at another beast as it snapped its circular jaws at my leg. They were getting closer. "Fight it and come back to fight here."

Rune blinked until the film over his eyes had mostly cleared. "Val...?"

"Yep, still me, your favorite human to hate on. Plan on helping her get out of this?"

"My thoughts... I remembered things that... It's been so long, I..." Rune blinked again. His face contorted in rage. His free hand crackled with heat. "They *made* me re-live that. I swore I never would again, and I meant it."

He pressed his hand into one of the still-bleeding cuts on his leg, hissing in pain. I smelled burning skin as his head snapped back, eyes hardening. He pulled away from me and straightened.

"Stay down."

I dropped to the ground as the earth shuddered. The creatures squealed in a panic, looking for where the threat was, until roots and vines burst from the ground and sank deeply into them, ripping their mouths apart, exploding from where their eyes had been. Those that escaped the first attack desperately tried to squirm away, until Rune flicked his hand. The air rippled, and they were torn in half. I could only stare in horror and awe at the destruction.

His heart gem is strong enough to handle all of that and be a true terror, Xander had said. He hadn't lied.

When the last of the beasts' flesh was dispersed across the marsh, Rune turned on the false heart tree and destroyed that, too. Branches snapped like toothpicks. The trunk fractured in a dozen places as destruction spewed from within. The devastation was so great I thought for sure he'd collapse, but Rune didn't so much as stagger, hatred etching every line in his face, as the tree was dismantled inch by inch and crushed to dust.

"Rune," I yelled. "That's enough!"

He didn't stop. The vines and roots and plants were nothing but a coiled serpents' nest where the stump had been. I stomped over and yanked his arm down. "It's dead! We have to go. Now!"

Rune looked at me then to the dead tree and the new wave of creatures crawling free from the marsh, tentacles waving with menace.

"You're hurt. I'm hurt. There's nothing more we can do here," I said. I looked at the tattered remains of what he'd been desiring for years and said something I never thought I would to him, "I'm sorry."

"Don't be sorry for me. Ever." Rune raised his hand at the nearest creature. A single root rose up before withering. Rune slumped against me. A bit of clear liquid oozed from his cuts along with more blood. "I appear to have overdone it. And the cursed things poisoned me. How unfortunate."

Not waiting for him to go berserk again, I wedged my shoulder beneath his, and we limped toward the river. Not fast enough. The beasts were gaining on us.

"You really are soft hearted," Rune said. "You didn't let me die when you had the chance."

"Some of us actually have a heart," I grumbled.

"Yes," he said softly. "Thankfully you do."

"For the record, I thought about it."

"Good. Then you possess some sense."

I meant to wade across the river and lose the beasts in the trees. I didn't realize how close the beasts had gotten to us, until one shot out a poisoned spike.

Rune reached out and caught it inches from my neck. The

movement threw me off balance, and we went tumbling into the frigid current.

I was pulled under the fast-moving current almost immediately, the cold like liquid nitrogen on my skin. Rune was torn from my hands. I fought until I broke the surface and gasped for air, swallowing a mouthful of water in the process. My hip slammed against a rock. A branch tore at my jeans, sending a fiery slice of pain up my leg, right before the river's grip pulled me down again.

The next time I managed to claw my way to the surface, I could just make out Rune swimming toward me, cutting through the water with hands like knives. One strong arm pulled me close.

"You aren't dying on me," he said. "I owe you a small debt, and I plan to repay it."

My soaked clothes shrank against my skin like an icy straitjacket. My kicks grew feebler. A solid gray shape rose out of the whitewater ahead.

"Watch—"

Rune tilted our bodies so that he bounced off the boulder. My vision stuttered. On we floated, thrashed about by the river. My jaw was locked together so tightly my teeth didn't even chatter. My core temperature was like a small candle, slowly dimming out.

Rune said something, and I managed to peel my eyelids open. "What?"

"Swim. There's a shore we can reach."

He was right. The river's current had diminished to something almost swimmable. This would be our easiest chance to escape.

Like unused machinery, my limbs moved slowly, joints creaking, as I pathetically started paddling that direction.

"Faster!" Rune said. A long pause, in which a terrifyingly recognizable sound rose in volume. "Swim faster."

"I'm g-going as fast as I—"

My words were grabbed, chopped up, thrown back at me by the unmistakable sound of crashing water. White rapids frothed and, beyond them, open air.

Rune snarled and tried to propel us away from the edge of the waterfall, but it was too late. We were both pushed over, and I was weightless, nothing but another water droplet plummeting toward the pool below.

I crashed into the surface and nearly blacked out. At first all I saw was swirling debris and the flicker of fabric. Then Rune reached out a hand and a vine unfurled from above, close enough for him to grab it and have it pull us toward the rocky shore.

With numbed fingers, I held tightly to him as we were dragged onto mud and pebbles. I still didn't let go of Rune. He wasn't much warmer than I was, but he was something my hypothermic body could latch onto.

"We have to move," Rune said after a moment.

"J-j-just a little l-longer," I chattered. I tried to rub my hands, tried to will the cold to go away. I needed to build a fire. Needed to strip out of these wet clothes. I even tried reaching for my magic, something, anything to get some warmth. "C-can't move."

"You have to. We have to—" He giggled. Actually giggled.

I managed to tilt my head. "W-what is wrong with you?"

Rune turned over and spat. Water and something thicker, maybe poison, dribbled out of the corner of his mouth. He giggled again. "Better. I'll be better soon. I think the river cleaned me out."

I managed to force myself up and look toward the top of the waterfall. The one good thing about nearly dying was that it wasn't likely those creatures would follow us. But we couldn't take any chances.

I shoved my arm under Rune and started to haul him up. "D-don't make me carry y-y-you."

Rune ran a hand over his face, laughing again, but his expression was dead serious. "Find...shelter... Oh, my head..."

"A lot more than t-t-that is gonna hurt in a bit, trust m-me. One step at a time."

He was big, far bigger than I realized, covered in cords of tense muscle. *One step, two steps, three steps.*

"...you." Rune's lips had moved, but I barely heard what he'd said.

"What?"

"Thank...you. Thank you f-for not leaving me there to die."

I shifted my shoulder farther under him and started walking again. I'd barely made it to the count of four when I looked up.

Wolves surrounded us. They used to live on the Olympic Peninsula long ago but had been driven away before the Wilds had appeared. The Wilds brought them back, but they weren't the same.

The alpha, nearly as tall as I was, stepped in front of the pack, lips pulled back against snarling, stained teeth. Her body was mottled fur and bare flesh consumed with clusters of greenery. Her legs were sowed with roots and wrapped with creepers, as though she'd grown straight from the ground itself.

"Don't thank me just yet," I whispered. "Looks like we're both about to die."

CHAPTER

TEN

Rune pushed off me and stepped forward. He stumbled a little, but by the time he made it into the center of the pack, he stood rigid, head cocked haughtily, eyes locked on the alpha. I prayed he wasn't about to do something that would get us both mauled.

"These are my Wilds," he said.

The alpha snarled, and I went for my sword. I hoped, as numb as I was, I could still swing it fast enough to wound a couple of them before they tore me apart.

Rune didn't flinch. His eyes glowed brighter, and the pack shifted nervously. One yipped, a nervous, keening sound, its gaze moving between its alpha and Rune.

"You will obey me," Rune said. "Submit."

Another wolf yipped nervously, and the alpha nipped at it. Rune stepped forward and I did too, thinking, crazily, that if the alpha wolf tried to rip him apart, maybe I could prevent it. The wolf's growl deepened. Rune didn't blink.

"I said, submit—"

The wolf snapped her jaws around Rune's arm so fast I barely had time to bring the tip of my sword up to its eye.

"Stop, Val!" Rune barked.

"And let it finish you off?" I shot back.

"I said stop."

The bite hadn't taken off Rune's arm. In fact, it seemed the alpha had held back, her fangs piercing his skin but sinking no farther. She pulled at him, perhaps threatening him with what she could do with a single, lazy toss of her head. Rune didn't pull away.

"You will yield," he repeated. "I am the Wilds, and you are of it. I have faced creatures of the depths and my own kind, who are worse than any beast, and lived. I will face you and survive. If you wish to remain alive, you will *yield to me.*"

I didn't drop my sword. This was crazy. This couldn't possibly work.

Yet, slowly, ever-so-slowly, the alpha released her jaw and lowered her head. She nuzzled the bite marks with her nose and lapped off the worst of the blood.

"We need shelter," Rune said. "Somewhere to dry off."

The alpha shuddered, still trying to resist his command.

"Now," Rune said.

The alpha dipped her head lower then took off into the trees. One of the smaller wolves jerked its head, as though gesturing for us to follow as the rest of them went after her.

The moment the pack was gone, Rune staggered. I managed to catch him before he collapsed. Despite us almost freezing, his skin was fever hot.

I grabbed an over-large frond and sloppily wrapped it around his still-bleeding wounds to cover the worst of the bite. "You either have a death wish or you're better with animals than I thought."

"I can't control them, not like Raquel," Rune said, gasping

as I tightened the frond. "If they'd chosen to tear us apart, I wouldn't have been able to stop them."

I finished tying off the frond with a sharp tug, and he hissed. "Maybe next time don't bet our lives on a bluff."

"Noted. You'll be happy to hear that I'm in an immense amount of pain."

"Shockingly, I'm not happy about that," I said. Then, against my better judgment, "Good job."

A malicious smile pulled at the corners of his mouth. "I do have my uses."

He pulled himself to standing but didn't move away from my side. Throat stinging as I sucked in a sharp breath, we moved stiffly toward where the wolves had gone. Despite our glacially slow pace, we didn't have to go far. Soon we found the alpha and pack circling a small cabin that'd been mostly untouched by the Wilds, half-wild as it already was. The logs that made up the walls had regrown anew and fused themselves with the surrounding trees. The roof was an entire biosphere unto itself, thick with a riotous euphony of blushing yellows, reds, and purples. Unless someone was looking for us, they would pass it by.

"Thank you," I said to the alpha. I started to nod in thanks, but Rune jerked me back, hard enough to hurt my neck.

"Bring us food," he commanded the alpha. "You will also let us know if there are enemies nearby."

The alpha chuffed in annoyance but dipped her head low before slipping into the trees, her pack close behind.

"Never show weakness or submission," Rune said. "Not to them. Not to anyone."

"There's nothing wrong with showing gratitude."

He looked hard at me. "If we'd done that, we probably wouldn't still be here."

I was too tired to argue. My muscles were stiffening. I   wo

—needed warmth, or else we'd soon go hypothermic. I'd seen enough missing tips of fingers, toes, and dead patches of skin on other hunters who didn't take precautions to know we were in danger. I glanced at Rune's bleeding arm.

"Hurry and get inside." I wearily helped Rune up the cabin's stairs and pushed open the door to the sparse interior. No bed, only some lichen and leaves somebody might have used to rest on, once upon a time. I left him there and even with stiff fingers somehow managed to crawl atop the roof. Among the plants, I found the red-leafed fern Triss used to start a kindling fire and dug up the root she'd used on my cuts. I brought down as much as I could carry. By the time I was back inside, my body had begun to shiver violently.

"Lie down," Rune commanded.

"I n-need to heal you," I said. "Get your clothes off."

He raised an eyebrow. "I didn't realize you had such affection for me. This is hardly the time, don't you think?"

If I had any heat left, I was sure it'd be rushing to my face. "Get out of your wet clothes, now. And if you make one more remark like that, I'll warm up by chopping you to pieces."

Rune's smile was devious, but that was a secondary concern. I was growing too sleepy too fast, my body shutting down. I practically threw the things I'd gathered at Rune's feet, and I tried to sit before I collapsed. My shivering had stopped. Another bad sign. No matter how much I rubbed my hands, they didn't get any warmer.

I didn't think as I stripped off my coat, my shirt, wanting only to grasp some glimmer of warmth. And then I was lying on the bed of leaves and lichen, strangely comfortable, and I couldn't remember anything else.

I awoke with Rune's arms around me.

My steady breathing hitched as my muddled mind tried to make sense of our positions. I couldn't remember falling asleep, or whether I'd willingly chosen to curl up beside him. When had we gotten tangled up? The last hour—or was it a day?—was so hazy.

I ignored my first instinct to throw him off and allowed myself to relax against his chest, breathing deeply as I reoriented myself. Strangely, this close he smelled of more than earth. Of flowers, and...absinthe? Or something sharp and bitter like it. Maybe like a clouded sky right before the rain.

There was gooey green salve slathered over the cuts along Rune's arm where the wolf had bitten. So he knew how to apply it. I was oddly happy about that.

I didn't enjoy being close to him, of course. It was just because he was warm, and we were both very much still trying to keep from freezing. That was it.

I curled closer, and as I did, I realized I was wearing practically nothing. Survival often dictated throwing modesty out, but necessity aside, I was at the end of what I was comfortable with.

I moved his arm off.

Rune grunted, shifted, but didn't wake. The faint light through the cracked slats of wood and busted windows highlighted the chiseled lines of his chest, carved shadows along his face. In sleep, he appeared shockingly serene. Vulnerable, even. Our makeshift bed was warmer than I remembered. After I'd fallen asleep, Rune must have used his remaining magic to grow us blankets of moss. It wasn't much, but it was something.

The cold kissed my bare skin as I slipped my still-wet pants, shirt, and jacket over my underwear. The part of my back that had been pressed up against Rune was the only part of me still warm.

A soft yip drew me to the cabin's porch. The alpha stood there, surrounded by her pack. A dead deer lay at her feet.

I glanced back at Rune, still very much asleep. I could handle this.

"Thank you," I said. I stepped off the porch to take it. "I appreciate—"

The pack surrounded me before I could blink. The alpha stalked closer, jaw slightly open, growling as though *I* were the prey.

"Stop," I commanded. "I'm not your enemy."

She didn't stop.

I held up a hand, trying to make my way back to the relative safety of the porch. "I won't hurt you."

Of course you won't, the alpha seemed to say. *I'll eat you before you do.*

I tried to calm my thudding heart and stood as tall as I could, pretending the alpha couldn't take my head off in one swift snap. "I said *stop*. I'm stronger than you."

"You don't believe it, so they won't believe you."

A shirtless Rune leaned against the porch railing.

"Why are you looking at me?" he asked. "I'm not the one eyeing you as my next meal."

"We're on the same side!" I protested as I turned back to the alpha. She had faltered when Rune appeared but resumed her approach. I could smell her rotted breath, see her stained teeth as she bared her fangs. "I'm not a threat!"

"Which is the problem," Rune said. "Here, strength is everything. You don't believe you're powerful, so they won't believe you."

I *was* powerful. I couldn't bend the Wilds to my will, or walk as softly as Triss, or summon beasts to do my bidding. My magic was survival, adapting to any situation. I could survive this. I *would* survive this.

The alpha snarled, opening its jaws wide. In a burst of desperate insanity, I reached into her mouth and grabbed her tongue.

The alpha froze. The pack whimpered. Rune gave a barking laugh.

The tongue was difficult to hang onto, but I wrapped it around my wrist and pulled tighter.

"I am not your enemy," I repeated. "Thank you for the food. Now leave us in peace. If not..." I pulled her tongue harder.

The alpha's gaze bored into me. We both knew she could take my arm off at any moment. But finally, she gave the shallowest of nods, and I released her tongue. She smacked her lips as though to clear away the taste of my skin. Then she cast a final look back before she and her pack vanished into the trees.

It took my legs a moment to stop shaking enough to walk. I grabbed the deer and started hauling it to the porch.

"Interesting tactic," Rune said, on the verge of bursting into more laughter. "I believe humans had an adage about sticking things in a wolf's mouth, but you clearly took a different moral from that."

"You going to keep making smart remarks or help me with this?"

He brushed past me to the side of the porch and whistled sharply twice. A gurgling croak rang through the trees, and a moment later a raven soared down and landed on the railing.

"Berries," Rune said. "And some pepper root."

"Please," I added.

Rune frowned at me and then back to the raven. "Now."

The raven cocked its head. Rune sighed and repeated his request, more slowly this time, after which it finally flew off.

"Raquel could sing them a sonnet and they'd understand," Rune said, disgruntled.

He grabbed the deer's antlers with his un-injured arm and easily dragged it the rest of the way inside. I was grateful when he pulled on his shirt so I didn't have to keep myself from staring.

"Take out your sword, start skinning," Rune said.

"You aren't going to help?" My teeth were chattering again. I grabbed some of the red leaves I'd collected earlier, but everything was too wet to catch. "Can you at least magic a fire? Something to warm us up?"

"I can only do so much, little fox. Every magic has its limitations, and you have found mine. Don't think about the cold. Focus on working and you will find it doesn't bother you as much."

I doubted that, but with my hands shaking, I drew my sword and started cutting pieces of meat.

"Talk," I said. "Distract me."

Rune cocked his head in what I imagined was mock surprise. "How strange. You wish for me to open my mouth instead of keeping it shut?"

"I'm too cold to think. You always seem to have something to say, whether I want you to or not."

He collected the bits of meat I carved and ran his hands over them. The meat turned dark red and then black as the blood drained out of it and soaked into the cabin floor. A moment later, sprigs of greenery poked their heads up, small, bulbous fruit growing on the ends of their branches.

"More meat," Rune said. "Life doesn't come from nothing. There must be an exchange, and right now I am too drained to offer my strength. Tell me, have you heard of our creation myth."

I handed him more pieces, wracking my brain for what I

knew of wildling myths. "I've probably heard them once or twice. You already know that some humans believe in the Mother Tree."

"Many wildlings believe in the Mother Tree as well, the core root which all the Wilds, wildlings, and beasts sprang from."

"Like Yggdrasil, from Norse mythology. I think we still have believers of that in the human world, too."

He frowned at me. "Are you telling this, or am I?"

I dipped my head in a pretend bow. "By all means."

The fruit from the plants he'd grown seemed nearly ripe enough to eat, and despite seeing what had grown them, my mouth watered.

"At the base of the Mother Tree is a being of destruction, Grislehaut, who continually gnaws away at its trunk," Rune said. "When we were first created, the Mother Tree's leaves became the clouds and the sky. The sap dripping from where Grislehaut chewed became the oceans and the forest, and its flecks of bark the people. But though the tree formed everything, it was the great heart gem at the center that gave everything life and purpose. Shards of that heart gem exist in every living being within the Wilds."

Rune put a hand to his heart. "It is reviled to take something so precious from another wildling."

I carefully maneuvered my blade to avoid slicing off my finger. "Yet you're still giving them to me."

"Luckily, I'm not a believer in such myths, except that which serve my needs. You will get what you're owed. In that, you have my word."

For what the word of a wildling, especially one like Rune, was worth. But I believed him. In spite of knowing I shouldn't, I believed him.

I continued to carve until my fingers became too numb to

move, while Rune summoned more food. I managed to pick the nearest dew-kissed fruit and bite into it. Its sweet juices ran down my chin and made the collar of my jacket sticky, but at the moment it was the tastiest thing I'd ever eaten. I tried to eat another, but the temperature had fallen again, and I hadn't recovered enough to endure it.

"Lie down," Rune said. He'd taken up a side of the moss bed, leaving space for me.

I didn't argue, cold as I was. But I kept my clothes on. The embarrassment of enjoying his warmth, his closeness, was still fresh in my mind.

I lay down on the other side, closest to the edge. I expected Rune to keep his distance. Surely, he'd only gotten close to me in sleep. He would never do it voluntarily.

"Don't be so prudish, little fox."

Rune wrapped an arm around me and pulled me close. A sigh of warm relief escaped my lips.

"If this is a problem, tell me," Rune said.

"No...it's fine," I muttered into his forearm. I traced the lines of slowly healing teeth marks with my eyes. "And I'm not prudish."

"Oh? Are you thinking this is more than it is?" Rune's breath was an annoying tickle against my ear. "Does the thought of that make you nervous?"

The moment of Rune's kiss in the marsh flashed through my mind. How his eyes had been full of desire, but his mouth twisted in disgust, even as he hungrily brought it against mine. Without the drug ensnaring my thoughts, I could see that moment for what it was: there was no longing, only dislike. He could never want me. And I would never want him, no matter what he said or did.

"We have a...mutually beneficial relationship; that's all this is." And as if to prove I believed these words, I confidently sank closer to him. "Don't *you* make it more than it is."

"I'm in no danger of losing myself. But you..."

The planes of his cheeks rested at the top of my head, smoothing the tangled snarls of my hair. "Have you ever been in love, little fox? Ever had a longing need to be with someone that superseded everything else, to the point where every breath, every moment, was filled with only them?"

That was a shockingly personal question. Our situation was making us both too comfortable with things we shouldn't have been.

"Don't ask if you don't really care about the answer," I said evasively.

"But I do care."

"You first," I said, turning it back on him. Because learning that Rune—that this *wildling*—wasn't capable of love would help build up the walls that were supposed to be between us. "It sounds like you have."

"Mmm..." he mumbled into my hair. "Perhaps. I'm not sure I would know it for what it was. I have hated a lot of people, and I know that emotion well."

I was drifting off, his voice lulling me to sleep.

"But maybe..." Rune said softly. "The feelings love and hatred evoke are not so different."

I didn't know how long we stayed like that, or if I even truly slept. The next thing I remembered was a sharp *caw*.

I blinked awake as the raven landed in the broken window. It hopped inside and deposited some pepper root and a few berries. Its black eyes glittered as though it'd caught us doing some terrible, illicit thing.

"The raven's back," I said to Rune, pushing out of his arms again.

"Good," Rune grunted. He stood. His hair was more tangled

than a briar bush. His eyes flickered to me and then to the raven. "And...thank you."

The raven cawed again. Then it screeched a cry of alarm and flapped out the window. I was in a crouch, stiff, cold muscles protesting even before I heard bootsteps crunching outside. Wood creaked as someone stepped up the porch and pushed the door open.

I followed the boots up to military pants, to the shrewd eyes—human eyes—of a man standing over us. A hunter. With a sword pointed at my throat.

"A pair of wildlings," he said. "I think you need to come with us."

ELEVEN

I was so tired and numb, and we were so outnumbered, that even if the hunters were driving a knife through my heart, I wouldn't be able to fight.

But instead of that, we were walked away from the cabin, until I could barely feel my feet and I was hoisted onto someone piggyback. The same thing might have happened to Rune, though I couldn't see him.

I faded in and out of cold-induced sleep. If I was going to die, at least I'd die well rested. The few snippets of the surroundings I registered didn't make sense: houses clustered along a small street. More humans, their curious faces peering at me. Even children, though there was something unsettlingly different about them. I was too tired to think what. Too tired to even move.

I was brought inside, wrapped in so many blankets I was practically immobilized, and then I truly slept.

Everything was stiff when I awoke. My skin still felt damp and cold, but was growing steadily warmer, as though I was a vampire regaining her humanity.

I was in a bedroom, simple and clean. A light rain pattered the window. I was alone.

I sat up. My sword was propped in a chair across from my bed, and I grabbed it and strapped it on, while fighting down panic. Rune wasn't here, and if my garbled memory was correct, we were somehow in a town of humans. A hunter camp, most likely. And though I was still alive, I remembered that the man thought we were wildlings. I was sure they wouldn't take kindly to Rune. *Especially* to Rune. I might already be too late.

I threw open the door and nearly ran into a man on the other side. He was dark-skinned and muscled, likely ex-military, holding a steaming cup of what smelled achingly like coffee.

"Watch it, hot drink," he said. "Thought I heard you up and about."

He noticed the sword and pushed the drink into my hands where I cradled it, letting its warmth seep into my aching fingers. "Going already? It's safe to stay a little longer, if you can manage it."

"Ru—the guy who was with me. Where is he?"

"Hard to say. He's around, I assume. The moment he could move, he vanished into the Wilds. Probably waiting for you. Although…"

He peered closely at my eyes. "Human. Thought so. Whatever they did started to wear off right when we picked you up."

I stepped into a bathroom and checked my face. Much too pale, but he was right, my eyes were back to their usual human green.

The man leaned in the doorway, watching me. "It's okay, we won't kill him, if that's what you're worried about. I'm Garrett."

I pulled away from the mirror, suspicious. "I have a hard time believing that."

Garrett chuckled. "If we killed the wildlings... Heck, if we so much as appeared threatening to them, we would have been wiped out a long time ago. We're sort of in between kingdoms here. No reason for them to bother us."

I tried wrapping my head around that. Wildlings didn't *need* a reason to bother humans. And no humans survived very long in the Wilds. That reality plagued the back of my mind every time I entered. Same story for the cities the Wilds devoured. Swallowed up overnight. No survivors.

"You have a lot of questions," Garrett said. He gestured for me to follow. "Let's go see if we can coax your friend back out."

He's not my friend.

I held the words back. Rune wasn't exactly my enemy, and I didn't want them trying to kill him—if they even could—and someone getting hurt.

The house I'd slept in was one of a dozen in a neighborhood, all overshadowed by the trees. I could tell there used to be many more homes here, but either by design or other more violent means, the homes that remained were contained to a few blocks. They were simple but obviously well cared for. Where the Wilds intruded on them had clearly been worked around: walkways rerouted around roots; thickened, waxy leaves overlapped to cover torn holes in the roofs; gurgling springs made the centerpiece of the street.

"This is Castle Rock," Garrett said. A couple was staring at us, and he waved, likely to show them things were all right. Kids ran past, laughing as they swished through the Wilds' underbrush. None of the parents looked concerned. One of the little boys stopped and stared at me, and I gasped. His eyes were vibrant blue and glowing.

"Yes," Garrett said, clearly knowing what I'd noticed.

"They glow almost like the eyes of a wildling. Are they...?"

"They are not children of wildlings and humans, no. Even if wildlings lived around here, I doubt any of them would ever choose to sire a child with a human. Frankly, I think they find us disgusting."

There's something about you that draws me. Rune's poison-thickened voice filled my head. He'd been delusional. Nothing more. We both had been. "Then how are the children like that?"

"We don't know." Garrett stopped at the end of the street. The base of an enormous tree stopped Castle Rock from going any farther. Garret and I watched a few of the smaller animals who called the trunk home scamper above us. "No children like that have been born back in the human world, at least not last we heard. The ones here don't have magic, not like the wildlings. They don't have heart gems, either, but they have a connection to the Wilds. It accepts them, and they aren't afraid of it."

Some of the children had wandered closer. They stood in an eerily silent group. One of the smaller ones whispered to a tree and then giggled.

"I'm guessing you don't leave here because of them," I said. "I don't know how the human world would react."

"Not well, I imagine. We're safe here. *We're* changed. Even if we went back, that would only cause problems for them." He looked at me. "Judging by who we found you with, I'm guessing you understand a little of what I'm talking about."

If he was curious about why I was working with a wildling, then he would stay curious. "I'll get Rune."

"We've got medicine here if he needs it. And we'd love to invite him for dinner, if he's up to that."

I had no clue what Rune would be up to, but I nodded. The children watched me as I slipped into the trees.

It didn't take me long to find Rune, lounged in the bough of a tree, tossing ripened berries into his mouth and spitting out the seeds. He really had no manners.

"You survived," he said.

"Same to you," I replied. There wasn't a trace of the wolf bites on his arm or any lingering effects from the poison. I cursed his speedy wildling healing. "I'm surprised you waited around. Have the others—"

Marian, Xander, and Triss came around the side of the trunk. Triss surprised me by giving me a big hug, and I surprised myself by hugging her back. Xander jerked his chin at my sword, grinning.

"Rune told us a little about what happened. Good trade?"

"The best. How'd you guys find us?"

"After scouring the marsh for the rotted remains of your body, just to be sure, Marian followed the blood trail. She may have the personality of needled thrush, but she's a good tracker."

I braced myself as Marian stalked up to me. "You were supposed to keep him safe," she seethed.

"He's still breathing and has all his limbs. I think I did my job."

"You were tricked!"

"We were both tricked!" Not to mention it had been Rune's stubbornness that had put us in more danger.

"It was an illusion, Marian, and a powerful one," Rune called down, clearly unconcerned that she looked on the verge of running me through. "For added nastiness, they also baited the surrounding marsh with Gelvenans."

Xander grimaced. "Those things are disgusting. Some of the smaller Lords of the coasts like using the toxins as a hallucinogenic. They can make you see anything you want."

Rune's look to me was all suggestion, a single eyebrow

cocked. "Val and I both experienced the potency of their poison firsthand. Fortunately, she had the cunning to overcome it. I was right to bring her with me."

Marian let out a hiss of annoyance.

"But what was a random tree doing with an illusion on it?" Triss asked.

"It was simple, really," Rune said arrogantly. "Jezaline and Mordecai used poor, stupid Cobb to draw me there. They had him "overhear" exactly what I wanted to know, guessing he would immediately pass it on to me to ease his guilty conscience."

"They *knew* exactly what you wanted, and they nearly got you," I said. "If you had just listened to me, we wouldn't have been in trouble!"

Rune popped the last fruit in his mouth and slid to the ground, lithe as a cat. "I was in total control."

A hollow laugh bubbled up from my throat. "You were *not.* You couldn't focus on anything else but that stupid tree."

"I was in total control," Rune repeated in a tone that dared me to challenge it.

I threw up my hands. I was so sick of him, sick of his arrogance and single-minded focus that was going to get us all killed. "If I wasn't there, you'd be dead. You were anything but."

"I," he said, voice low, "am always in control. They took that control from me once, and I will never give it up again. So, I suppose it's a good thing I chose you to ensure I didn't lose it."

"Does it get heavy carrying that massive ego?"

Rune's smile was full of daggers, eyes like hardened smoke crystal. "It will be heavier when I have my crown."

He broke away from me, and I let out a pent-up breath.

"I hope you have all your things," Rune said. "We're almost to Portland and Aleki's kingdom."

"The people of Castle Rock want us to stay for dinner," I said.

"Absolutely not," Marian said.

"How strange. They're not afraid of us?" Triss said.

"We could use the break, if only for a little bit," Xander said to Rune.

"We've already wasted enough time," Rune said.

My back was already aching at the thought of sleeping on the ground. "If you plan on taking Aleki's kingdom, then consider this an opportunity to build ties with your future subjects."

"I said no—"

Rune's eyes flickered over my shoulder.

"How did they sneak up on us?" Marian said.

The children from Castle Rock peered around the trees and rocks, eyes glowing blue. Rune cocked his head, as though hearing unspoken words on the air.

"Maybe we can stay one night," he amended.

I watched as the kids tried to teach Triss how to kick a soccer ball. For as swift and coordinated as the wildlings were, it was like watching someone with crutches walk across ice.

Triss missed a kick by a mile, and the children squealed with laughter. I caught Rune smirking and even Marian let out a snort. Xander and Garrett were deep in discussion about weapons at the other end of the veranda that had been converted to our meeting place. Between us were the few citizens of Castle Rock brave enough to join wildlings for a meal.

They'd brought foraged mushrooms and beasts with their heart gems still intact. For drinks, they offered flasks of watered-down wine distilled from fermented fruit and mixed with honey. Rune had taken one look at all they'd offered and immediately magicked more fruit, sugar-coated flower petals, and small trees swollen with nuts that sprang up from the ground around the table and grew to their full size as though in time-lapse.

Everybody had been wary to touch anything he'd conjured at first, but once we were all a few drinks in and inhibitions lessened and the humans had tried his offerings. I felt a gentle, pleasant buzz from the honeyed wine, even if it made my tongue dangerously loose and my muddled thoughts feel as though they were under the Gelvenans' poison again. Rune, too, had partaken in a little more than he should, judging by the tint on his cheeks. I was surprised the wildlings had so quickly dropped their guard. I also knew their vulnerability was an illusion.

"They make my skin crawl," Marian said.

She was staring at the children as they ran past. Triss came over, sweating slightly and panting. She glared at Marian and swiped a fattened peach.

"Keep your words to yourself. They are children, and they aren't trying to kill us. We don't meet many like that."

"They aren't right," Marian said louder, and a few people nervously glanced over. Marian took a long drink. "They should be dead, all of them. Either skewered by Aleki or eaten by the beasts. This magic is tainted."

"You're what's not right," Triss said fiercely. She swiped another fruit. "These are not the ones who made us who we are or have hurt our kind. Remember that."

She rejoined the children, and Marian's lazy grin turned on me. "You not going to stick up for them? You're always so eager to give your opinion where it's not wanted."

"Silence, Marian," Rune said.

"I was just—"

"You're being insufferable right now."

Marian drowned her next words with a big sip. I watched her take her time to swish it around in her mouth before swallowing.

"You..." She seemed to think over her next words surprisingly carefully, considering how much she'd had to drink. "You listen to her too much. It's as though what we say bears no weight."

"Don't be like this."

"Like *what*?"

"Obstinate. Obtuse."

"Are you commanding me not to be?"

She had trouble meeting Rune's laser-like gaze.

"There are decisions that require neither your involvement nor your input," Rune said. "This, obviously, is not one of those times. I respect what you have to say, of course."

"But you respect what the human has to say, too."

"Val has proven herself," Xander said from down the table. "We've gone over this. It doesn't hurt to hear her thoughts on matters we might not have much experience with."

Marian sunk sullenly back into her chair. It was clear they'd had this conversation before. Rune might be a prince, but he was still a prince in exile. Where to draw the line between following him due to his command or loyalty likely got a little hazy at times.

Rune crooked his finger to one of the little girls who had strayed outside the game. She looked back at her friends for reassurance and then shyly walked over. He held out a candied blossom.

"Wait," he said when she reached for it. He made a show of waving his fingers over it, and the blossom bloomed a second and a third time, until the smell of sugar exploded in the air and he held an entire candied bouquet in his hand.

"Share," he said as he gave it to her.

Delighted, the girl ran back to her friends, and they stopped playing and descended on it like a school of piranhas. Triss came over, still panting, and took a seat. "They don't need any more energy, if you were wondering."

"I didn't sense anything unusual with them," Rune said to Marian. "They are children. Their magic is that of the Wilds."

Marian scowled. She stabbed some berries with a fork and devoured them.

"Bribery will get you everywhere with them." Garrett chuckled as he slid down the table to us. "Not sure about their parents. They're the ones who'll have to deal with the consequences."

Rune raised his glass, and a little liquid spilled over the side. "Thank you for the hospitality, whether it be from kindness or fear."

"Or both," Xander said.

"Or both," Rune agreed. He took a large swig, and when he put the cup down, I swore his face was more flushed. How much had he drunk already?

"It's not you we have to fear," Garrett said. "It's the few wildlings who give us trouble."

"Around here?" Triss looked a little concerned. "Do they come by often?"

Garrett waved a placating hand. "You're safe for now. They roam outside here, but rarely come close. A couple have come into the city before, though. A few have bothered some of the older girls."

Garrett's hand tightened on his plate. "Those we shot at or chased off. It's always a dangerous thing. Most of them are here of their own volition, but every once in a while, someone from Lord Aleki's domain shows up."

Rune's expression didn't change at the mention of his uncle's name. "Courtesy call, I imagine."

"Something like that. He doesn't bother us, but he does like to check up."

"Because of the children." Xander voiced the exact conclusion I'd come to. "He's curious about the children."

"Either that or he's afraid, and I'm not sure which one's better," Garret said. "But so far he hasn't harmed us, and I don't see a reason why he would."

"He doesn't need a reason," Rune said with a slurry smile filled with too little inhibition. "One day he could wake up and decide he's bored, or needs some sport, or simply doesn't want whatever threat you humans could possibly cause so close to Portland and simply..."

Rune sliced a hand, and the top of a nearby fruit-laden sprig fell away, cut neatly in half. Garrett had gone still. The eyes of the other humans were wide with fear.

"But I will see to it that he doesn't bother you," Rune said.

Garret swallowed as he drew his eyes off the plant and back to Rune. "I didn't know you were going to speak to—"

"Are there any other surviving human cities?" I asked. "Any you know of near Seattle?" Rune had clearly drunk too much to think straight. I didn't believe Garrett and the others were in league with Lord Aleki, but I also didn't think blathering about what we were trying to do was a good idea either.

Garrett fixed me with a long look, as though seeing straight to the heart of what I wanted to ask. "Over the years we've had people sneak out where other cities have historically been. We've never found anyone alive."

Marian wore a sneer. "There are no surviving human cities outside Seattle. The Lords who were in power before Jezaline and Mordecai would have never allowed it." She cocked her head, voice simpering. "Who were you hoping had survived? Who did you think would be there for you?"

I took another drink instead of rising to her bait, but it didn't lighten the sting.

"Your parents," Rune said.

My gaze snapped to him, and his sloppy grin only grew. "Poor, lonely Val. It doesn't matter if they are alive, you know."

"Rune, that's enough," Xander said softly. "No need to be cruel."

"It's not cruel to speak the truth."

Anger sliced through the alcohol-induced headiness, enough to raise me from my seat. "Shut your stupid mouth."

"They never tried to find you, did they?" Rune said. "Never tried to take you back. I think that if they're dead, it's a mercy. It takes so much to survive in the Wilds as a human. Even more with a child weighing you down."

My hand tightened around my drink. Garret chuckled awkwardly. "I think we should all let the past stay in the past."

"You should be grateful," Rune said. "You're better off without them, and they, you." He raised his cup in a mock toast. "Neither one can use the other as a crutch."

It wasn't the wine but my anger that caused me to refill my drink. It was Rune's smirk—*knowing* that he'd cut me deeply— that caused me to walk over to him.

"Come back for more?" he said in a low voice, words slightly slurred. "Just like the swamp and the cabin?"

He was right, I'd been an idiot to think that he'd changed. The last couple days were already fading like a bad bruise, slightly unpleasant and not eager to be relived. This was who he was. I'd forgotten that. I should be grateful he was reminding me.

"Rejoice that your parents are dead," Rune said. "At least that way they don't have to see what you've become—"

I poured the entire cup over his head. The pavilion went dead silent. Marian was on her feet, reaching for her weapon before Xander managed to hold her back.

"Take that back," I said to Rune.

He kept his head tilted down as the wine trickled over his face, across the flush of his cheeks. Then he stood and towered over me.

"No." His breath was honey sweet. "You and I both know it's true."

"Just because you didn't have parents who loved you doesn't mean I never did."

There it was, a flash of hurt deep, deep down that showed I'd scored a hit.

"Marian, no," Triss warned as Marian freed herself from Xander and started coming around the table, probably to rip me into shreds with her bare hands. "Both of you, stop!" Triss yelled at Rune and me, grabbing Marian's arm.

"That's not how you get the ladies to like you, Rune," Garrett said, putting his hands up pleadingly. "Why don't we all—"

Rune's grin was petulant. "I have many who enjoy my company, whether I speak the truth to them or not."

I laughed, strained and too high-pitched. "The only way you can get a woman to stick around is to tie her up and threaten her life."

"It was either subdue you or take another knife to the chest."

Emboldened, I pulled Rune's cup out of his hands and drained it, not taking my eyes off him as I did so. "Trust me, I'd *rather* take a knife to my chest than talk to you longer than I have to."

I shoved the cup back into him and stormed away. The daylight had grown sparse, but I didn't care as I slipped into the Wilds, ignoring the others calling me back. I needed space, and I'd find it out here. Garrett wouldn't risk anyone coming after me. Triss and Xander wouldn't let Marian out of their sight for fear she'd murder me. And Rune...

I stopped to take deep breaths until a little of the light-headedness disappeared and some clarity replaced it.

No, Rune wouldn't bother coming after me.

The twilight sparkled with fireflies as I kept walking, heedless of where I was going, uncaring of the consequences. My thoughts were a tangled web. The Lords, my magic, the poison-induced kiss, and how—as much as it tore me up to admit—I hadn't entirely hated it.

Stupid, stupid, stupid. Rune had been nothing but uncaring and callous since the day I'd met him. He'd thrown others who trusted him into danger with no regard for their safety. He'd put aside all other needs but his own. He'd risked the ire of Jezaline and Mordecai to protect those who followed him, and showed a softer side I'd never seen around the kids in Castle Rock—

I punched a tree, earning me a bruised hand and startling a flock of grouse. If only I'd brought my sword so I could stab something.

I turned in a circle, trying to discern any familiar landmarks. The pain had superseded my anger and cleared some of the fuzziness from my head. How long had I been gone? Ten minutes? An hour? I needed to go back.

Not entirely sure which direction, I picked what I thought was the right way and started walking. My foot caught something.

Brain still wine thickened, I barely managed to recover

before faceplanting. I spun to find out what had tripped me and froze.

The body was human, of that I was sure. But like the wildling Rune and I had come across, crystals sprouted from his mouth and eyes, covering his skin like a rocky rash.

I carefully approached, as though worried he'd spring to life and grab me. I couldn't tell how long he'd been dead, but his outfit looked familiar to me. A worshipper of the Mother Tree, one of the religious groups that had been swarming Port Orchard. What was he doing out here?

With the night now deep, an unnerving glow caught the corner of my eye. I turned, dread mounting.

"Oh, no."

There were a dozen bodies, all dead the same way. Supplies were with them, too. Pickaxes and climbing ropes. Carabiners and headlamps.

Something was terribly wrong here. And yet I found myself stepping over the bodies anyway and quickly discovered what the equipment was for.

Another crevasse, wider than any I'd seen. I knelt at its edge, feeling the brief loss of gravity as I leaned over. More crystals lined the inside like teeth. A cool wind, dirt-scented and tinged with something not unlike flowers, wafted up.

The crystal nearest me glowed, enticing. Despite my better judgment, I reached out and put my hand on it.

My body seized. Something deep inside me jarred loose, as though freed from the shackles of lost memory. I smelled stale sweat and tasted the tinge of smack powder on my tongue—a stimulant favored by some hunters, cocaine-like without the addictive qualities. I heard the clink of something, too: Pickaxes.

Then the screaming began.

My vision shook. Wide-eyed zealots ran as the earth tore

itself apart. Vines snapped; trees groaned. Bile rose in my throat, and it was as though a claw hooked my midsection and tore me back in time to the day Peyton found me. Fear clogged my throat. I turned, knowing what I'd find: the pulpy, barely recognizable bodies of my parents.

Nothing was there.

This wasn't right. They were supposed to be here. In every memory I'd had of that day, no matter how fractured, they were always here.

I took another step back. Hands sprang from the dark and grabbed me. Despite the weakness of my child body, I turned feral, thrashing, biting, clawing to free myself, but the hands didn't relent. The trees parted as I was dragged deeper, until I saw a blue light and the gaping maw of an opening in the earth.

"No!" I screamed until my throat was raw. "Don't take me there! Don't—"

I rocketed back into my present body, ripping myself from the crystal before collapsing to the ground. A rock dug into my low back. Cold, damp sweat coated my forehead, and no matter how many breaths I took I couldn't seem to fill my lungs. Every inch of me felt charged, as though I'd stuck my finger in a socket.

Someone else was here. I could sense them in the darkness.

I rolled over, biting back a groan. I could make out a shape and gold-red eyes peering from the underbrush.

"Stop lurking, Rune, it's creepy," I said. I squeezed my eyes to clear the drink-induced fuzziness from my head. "Have to admit, I'm surprised you're here. Let me guess: You've come to apologize?"

Rune said nothing.

"You're right, that's too optimistic." I rubbed my face. "See these dead guys? They were searching for something. Sounds crazy, but I think it might have to do with me. No, that *does* sound crazy. I don't know. Ugh...my head's killing me."

The figure stepped into the moonlight, and my blood chilled.

"I'm sure Lord Aleki would be interested to hear what else you might have seen," the wildling who was not Rune said.

Before my sluggish reflexes could respond, his hand was around my throat, choking the fight out of me.

"Don't die yet," the wildling said. "There'll be time for that later."

The Wilds around us swirled as a path appeared and I was dragged through.

TWELVE

The wildling's iron grip didn't relent as we hurtled through the blurry green. I couldn't hit anything vital, no matter how much I thrashed.

"Keep struggling and I'll break your neck," the wildling growled. His grip tightened, and I swore my windpipe cracked. "What did I just say?"

Through my fuzzy vision, I could see the end of the path, where no doubt I'd be surrounded by other wildlings and any chance of escape would be gone.

I kicked out hard, my heel connecting with the inside of his knee. There was a loud pop. He screamed.

He clubbed me on the side of the head, but his leg crumpled. I ripped free from his grasp and tumbled out of the path.

I stood on wobbly feet, gasping. I must have succeeded in disrupting where he wanted to take me, because we weren't anywhere special; beneath the overhang of what might have once been a skybridge, now collapsed, shavings of rusted metal scattered at my feet.

"I'll kill you," the wildling gritted out. He stood, leaning heavily on his still-functioning leg, and drew a knife. "I'll gut you and feed your insides to the crows."

"I thought you needed what I knew," I said.

"Not anymore. No amount of information a human knows is worth this pain. Now *stand still.*"

His compulsion immobilized me for all of a second before I broke free and rushed him. He snarled in surprise but still managed to dodge my punch. I was forced to duck a crackling spell that soared over my head. With no weapon, I had to keep him close and hope he had lackluster fighting skills and weak magic.

I cross-blocked his swipe. His magic-laden fist just missed me. The aftereffect briefly seized me in place, and I had to let myself fall back in order to keep him from stabbing me.

"What is the bastard heir doing traveling with a human?" the wildling spat as we broke apart. "Give me something to share, other than your corpse."

"He enjoys my company," I said. "We have stimulating philosophical discussions."

He growled and tried to immobilize me again, but it worked even less the second time, and I got the jump on him, pinning his knife arm down with my knee, hands on his face.

He screamed as my thumbs found his eye sockets. His arms flailed, and I felt like I was being ripped in two as a spell hit me in the gut. Magic, white hot and furious, broke free.

Blue light burst from my fingertips, burning where it touched. The wildling's screams pitched. He thrashed even more, slicing my thigh with the edge of his knife, but it didn't stop the flesh from peeling from his face.

Horrified, I leapt off. His skin continued to split, channels of blue tearing him apart piece by piece until his screams gurgled to silence.

I stared at the smoke rising from his body. The smell of

charred flesh and magic made me want to vomit, but I choked it down. What I'd done—*whatever* I'd done—he'd deserved it. I had no time to question how. I could already hear loud voices.

I cast a final look at the body before ducking through the shattered windows of an old sports store.

I'd heard stories of how, even before the Wilds took over, Portland was already one with the earth. The environment here didn't devour so much as integrate. The sharp, metal lines of buildings flowed into a swirling chaos of greens. I shrank back as the canopy rustled. Something watched the street. The roads were overhung with branches, on which perched gold-red-eyed birds obscured by leaves, watching for any sign of movement.

To be safe, I stuck to moving within the buildings whenever I could. I slipped between long-rusted shelves of a grocery store, careful not to disturb the small nests within. The street signs were covered. Though I couldn't read them, I seemed to be near downtown. I hoped I was making my way north out of the city.

My only chance at living through this was making it out undetected. Rune and the others, likely still insufferably drunk, hadn't seen me taken. Even if they knew where I was, Rune wouldn't risk putting himself and his entire plan in jeopardy by alerting Aleki just to rescue me. I was very much alone.

I found a small hole in the wall and, avoiding the scattered glass, crawled through to the next building. Shouting voices rang out one street over. The wildlings must have discovered my handiwork and were combing the area to find me.

I emerged in what looked like a boutique-type store on the corner, with what had once been two enormous glass windows at the front. I could see the dark edge of the Wilds across the street. Potential safety. If I could reach it.

I double-checked both ends of the street and the overhanging canopy before taking a deep breath and sprinting. My shoes slapping the pavement sounded like gunshots.

I tightened my gasping breath. Too loud. I was too loud. My heart thumped so hard I was sure any nearby wildling would hear it.

Even still, I was almost to the safe embrace of the Wilds.

A loud shriek. Wing flaps battered the back of my neck a moment before a feathered body slammed into me. Talons like needles sank into my shoulder and wrenched me up. I was airborne an entire second before my shirt and skin tore and I plummeted back onto concrete. I swallowed a scream as my shoulder throbbed. *"Son of a..."*

The beast let out another earsplitting screech as it circled. It might have once been an eagle, or it might have been something of the Wilds' own making. Its wings were leaves instead of feathers, its body that of a bird but with a needle-sharp mouth perfect for tearing apart whatever it caught in its enormous talons.

My magic stirred, and almost on instinct I raised my uninjured arm.

Let it be part of you. Don't deny what you already are.

A small shard of blue erupted from my hand and just missed the bird as it veered, shrieking. I staggered, exhausted. I grabbed a dead branch to use as a weapon, cursing that I'd left Sliver in Castle Rock. I shouldn't have taken it off, not even for a second.

"Found her!" someone yelled.

I blinked as wildlings surrounded me, a half dozen in all. More than even my freak magic could handle.

One of them, a man with hair the color of autumn leaves and roots curling like horns on his head, smiled lazily at the branch in my hand. "Cute. Drop it and come with us. Lord

Aleki wishes to speak to you. But after he's done, I promise we'll make your death quick."

I raised my stick. "Yeah, cause *that's* going to make me give up."

"Take her alive," the wildling said. "Break her if you have to."

The first one tried immobilizing me, only to find out how much that didn't work when he got too close and I broke a few of his ribs with a baseball swing.

"You see what she did?" another hissed. "No effect! That's not—"

"Doesn't matter!" their leader snarled. "I want her—"

One of the overhanging branches shot down and skewered him in the chest. He lurched, gasping, right before flowers ripped from the wound and reduced him to a gory bouquet.

"It's strange, Val," Rune said. "I recall recruiting you to fight for me, yet I find myself doing an awful lot of fighting for *you*."

He stepped through the path that had carried him here and let it close behind him. His glare at those surrounding us was all menace. "If you leave Lord Aleki now, you live," he said loudly. "If you choose to stay loyal, you die. I know firsthand that Aleki couldn't care less whether you draw breath or fertilize the earth, so choose wisely."

Maybe they were loyal to Aleki, or maybe they didn't like being told what to do by the bastard heir to the throne. Regardless, they hesitated before attacking.

Shoulder screaming in pain, I managed to punch one before spinning out of the headlock of another. Vines scrambled to hold me in place. I scurried out of their grasp and found myself close to Rune.

"Is that a stick?" he said, raising an eyebrow at my weapon of choice.

"I improvised. I can't believe you came," I said.

"Sometimes I surprise even myself," he said. "Don't make me regret it."

A wildling grabbed me, and my magic chose that moment to work again. My glowing fingers burned his grip until, screaming, he let go.

"That's new," Rune murmured.

"Behind you," I shouted, but it was too late. Four wildlings simultaneously attacked him. Rune's flowering vines cast one away, but the other three managed to wrestle him down and pin him to the ground, knife at his throat.

"Rune!"

Fingers sank into my wound. I screamed until I was brought down beside him.

"Bind their hands," a woman spat. One of Rune's spells had hardened half her arm into something like bark, and she held it stiffly at her side. "Take them to the grotto."

WE WERE DRAGGED through another bending tunnel of green and wound up surrounded by walls of rock. To my left, a mansion sat just in sight through the trees.

"Move," the woman said, shoving us.

We shuffled past weeping stone angels to the center of a grotto. The weeping angels at the front had been shoved over to make room for a single wooden throne. In the magic flames of hundreds of candles, I counted ten wildlings populating the pews of the audience chamber. Far too many to fight, as weak and weaponless as I was. Too many even for Rune.

"Get Lord Aleki," the woman snapped. "Tell him his nephew's come to visit." She shot Rune a cold smile. "The moment Lord Aleki heard that you'd escaped, he knew you'd come here. I never thought you'd be stupid enough to actually do it."

Rune returned with a cold smile of his own. "He has a lot to answer for. I figured, as family, I'd make him the first."

"Not anymore, it seems." The woman looked me up and down. "You blew your element of surprise to come save *this*?"

"I'll admit, it's not my brightest plan. I'm still waiting to see her return my kindness."

"Aleki was right; you are a disgrace. Now on your knees."

Something like hatred flickered across Rune's face. "I don't grovel before anyone. Especially not him."

"I wasn't asking."

My legs were kicked out from behind, and my knees smarted as they jarred on the stone floor. Rune fell beside me but kept his head high as the woman smirked at him.

"Much better. Where you belong."

She walked off, and I scooted close to Rune without alerting the guards.

"She's right. You blew it coming to get me."

Rune's gaze snapped to me. "Perhaps this is a human tendency, but I believe what you should be saying is thank you."

"Yes, *thank you* for making things worse and getting yourself captured. What do you plan to do now?"

"The same thing as before: kill my uncle."

I briefly closed my eyes, trying to quell the panic setting in. "That's not a plan. And even if you had one, there's no pulling it off now."

"Remember, I'm always in control." For a moment there was no smugness in his expression, only naked earnestness. "Do you trust me, Val?"

What a loaded question. One that should have been easy to

answer with a hard no. But for some reason I said, "I want to, but I can't."

Rune's grin was like a wolf baring its teeth. "Smart."

"I don't believe it."

An older wildling emerged from the walk between the grotto and the mansion and stepped into the light of the candles. There was nothing in his physical appearance that reminded me of Rune—soft, dumpy flesh, with coal-black hair and a mouth ornately stained with color—but the triumph in his tone said he was someone used to getting his way. "When they told me who they caught, I didn't believe it." He gave a high-pitched, delighted laugh. "To think, after all that scurrying around, you still wound up at my mercy."

"But of course," Rune said. "What kind of nephew would I be if I didn't visit, Uncle?" Rune jerked his head beside Lord Aleki. "And Vanesi."

The girl beside him could have been carved from ice, from her snow-pale skin to the tinges of blue on her fingertips. Her thinned lips stretched into a snake-like smile.

"Dearest little cousin Rune? How many years has it been? Seven?"

"Nine. But who's counting?"

Vanesi floated down the steps to us. She tenderly brushed a hand across Rune's jaw, and I saw him suppress a shudder. "How's your eye? That sasic berry juice really did a number, I remember."

"Healed, unfortunately for you."

"And the fingers? And all your smaller, more brittle bones?"

"Also healed. Everything you physically did to me has."

Vanesi clucked. "Such a shame. Maybe if Uncle's nice, he'll let us play one last time."

Her eyes, bottomless pits of black, swept to me. My skin

grew clammy. "What have we here? Oh, little Rune, so it's true. You're working with a *human*?"

"How far you've fallen," Aleki said. "A member of the once great House reduced to employing their kind."

"Fortunately, it's difficult to bring shame to a House that no longer exists," Rune said. "What's your excuse, Uncle?"

I tried not to pull away as Vanesi put her fingers against my cheek and then grabbed my hair and forced my head back. "My, look at her. Do you think we could keep this one, Uncle? There are a few new tricks I've been dying to try out. I think she'd do wonderfully."

"I don't see why not." Aleki settled his bulk on the throne and gazed at Rune with a sneer. "I'm in a good mood now."

Vanesi smiled and then hit me over and over until my ears rang and a trickle of blood stung my eyes. She laughed and threw me back down. I barely managed to catch myself with my bound hands to avoid smashing my face into the stone.

"I see you haven't changed, Vanesi," Rune said impassively. "So blunt and unsophisticated." He cocked his head toward the lone figure who'd slipped in behind Aleki's throne. "Cobb, is that you cowering back there? Your tip about the heart tree was missing a few important details."

"Rune, I, ah, I didn't—couldn't have known—" Cobb babbled.

Aleki raised a hand, glaring at him, and Cobb went silent. "Keep your mouth shut unless you wish for Vanesi to remove your lips. So you shared what you believed to be the location of the heart tree? That's something you failed to disclose to us, isn't it, Vanesi?"

"I'm sorry, you have to believe me," Cobb said, shrinking back. "I only thought—"

"She'll teach you what sorry means later, Cobb," Aleki said.

"Or maybe I'll send you back to Jezaline and Mordecai and let them decide what to do with you."

"No cousin Luella?" Rune said. "I would have liked to see at least one friendly face."

"You'll find none here." Aleki leaned forward, his girth shifting with him. "Let's hear it."

For once, Rune looked confused. "Let's hear what?"

"What you want, of course. You might have been the weak bastard of my brother, but you were never without your spineless tricks. Perhaps you thought my heart had softened after all these years and we could put old transgressions aside? Perhaps I could even give you the true location of the heart tree. So let's hear it. Or better yet, I want to hear you bargain for your life, though I assure you that won't get you very fa—What is it?"

Rune was shaking his head. "I'm not here to offer anything. I'm here to take. You're dying tonight, Uncle."

Vanesi laughed, and even Aleki grinned, his jowls quivering as he shook his head. "That's some gall, I'll admit. Maybe you're not as smart as I thought. Vanesi, would you kindly?"

Vanesi stepped up to Rune and placed her hands on the sides of his head.

"You obey him just like a beast, Vanesi," Rune said. "Are you allowed to sit at the table, too? Does he let you out of your cage every once in a while to run wild?"

Vanesi's fingers turned whiter as she pressed them against his skull. "He finds my abilities useful. And I enjoy using them. Time to open up your secrets."

Rune gasped as Vanesi leaned in. He began to shake, blood leaking from his nose.

"Give—them—to—me—*gah!*"

With a snarl, Vanesi threw him to the side and sank her foot into Rune's gut, over and over until she was a sweaty, panting mess.

Rune's teeth were stained with blood as he grinned. "Temper, temper, Cousin."

"As strong-willed as ever," Aleki said, amused.

"But *she* won't be," Vanesi said, coming over to me. She brushed a crazed strand of hair away. "Let's see how you fare."

I tried to scramble away, but my back hit a pew, and Vanesi's claw-like fingers easily found either side of my head.

"Don't mess up her face too much." Aleki's lips stretched into a lecherous grin. "She may be human, but I could still have use for her body. Do what you will to her mind. I don't care if she can speak or move, other than giving me a little fight."

"Gladly," Vanesi hissed, and then her magic invaded my head.

I couldn't even try to stop it. This wasn't Mordecai's magic rummaging through my brain. This pierced through any mental defense I might have had like a hurricane. It speared my thoughts and tried to pull them, thrashing, out of me, until all I felt was pain and all I heard was screaming.

I opened my eyes and realized the one screaming was me.

"Shut *up!*" Vanesi's foot connected with my gut, and my screaming turned to gasps. "You stupid, worthless worm!"

"You must be losing your touch, my dear," Aleki said. "All that effort just to fail to scry from a human?"

Vanesi straightened up and took a deep breath. "Maybe I need a little more practice. A few sessions should do it, and then she's yours."

"Yes, later." Aleki stood and motioned to one of his guards who handed him a sword. He idly nudged the point at Rune. "Pick them up."

The wildlings behind us started to lift us to our knees, but Rune jerked his head back. The man's nose broke, and before anyone could move, Rune was charging at Aleki. The other guards raised their crossbows and pulled weapons, but Aleki merely laughed.

"Rune, please. You know you can't do anything to me. See?"

Aleki waved his hand, and Rune seized in place, feet from him. "Did you really think you'd come into my domain, kill a few of my people, and kill me? You *wish* you had the power to do that, *wish* you had power like mine. But alas, all your strength isn't enough against true will."

Aleki rested the sword on Rune's shoulder, blade turned against his neck. I tried to stand but was roughly shoved down.

"You have no idea what you were up against taking on the Lords," Aleki said. "Hatred for what they stole from you made you stupid."

"For—they—" Rune strained to speak, neck muscles taut. Aleki moved closer.

"What was that?"

"For what *they* did? No, Uncle. In Mog Moren, I was beaten and violated and broken in ways that no human or wildling should ever have to suffer. That was because of *you*."

Aleki frowned. "Interesting, and yet all that didn't teach you. I admire that, stubborn to a fault. Your father was the same. I imagine that hubris was what got him killed."

Rune managed to tilt his neck, giving Aleki a wider target to strike. "I'm exactly where I wanted to be. Don't miss, Uncle. You won't get another chance."

Aleki raised the blade. "I don't intend to. Goodbye, last of the House of the Fallen Star."

I didn't understand what the meaty *thwack* was until an arrow pierced halfway through Aleki's hand. He cried out, the sword falling from his grip. The magic on Rune unfroze, and he swept the sword up while the rest of Aleki's guards looked around in panic. A second arrow passed cleanly through another's heart, and she went down.

"They've surrounded us, idiots!" Vanesi screeched.

The remaining wildlings scattered. I spied the flicker of shadows in the nearby trees before someone's knee clubbed my face. Blood sprayed. Stars spun.

I managed to roll beneath one of the pews, and as soon as no one was close, I crawled to a sword embedded in the ground and furiously rubbed my bonds against the blade until they cut. I yanked the blade free and tried to orient myself.

The audience chamber was in chaos. Aleki cowered in the alcove behind the throne alongside Cobb, all while the dark shapes continued to move around the outside, downing wildlings who didn't know where to look. I finally understood Rune's plan. He *wanted* to be caught, wanted all their attention on him, the big prize, while Marian, Xander, and Triss got into position.

I deflected a wildling's blade before slicing his arm and kicking him in the chest. More arrows sprouted from the backs of those trying to flee. Vanesi continued to scream. Her eyes found me across the carnage, and she pointed her razor-thin sword.

"*You.* You die here, human."

She came at me much faster than I was ready for, as dragged down by fatigue as I was and with blood stinging my eye. Her first swing broke my defenses, and pain radiated up my injured shoulder. I tried to adjust and she drew close, elbowing my cheek and spraying blood.

"You think you know of our world, but you are a mouse among lions, little girl," Vanesi snarled.

I rolled and she somehow cleaved one of the pews nearly in two. I tried to dart in, but the severed wood stretched out hands and would have grabbed me if I hadn't rolled again. "Did you enjoy the time you had feeling powerful? Because that ends right—now—*Stop.*"

Her compulsion staggered me, but I scooped up a rock and threw it haphazardly, forcing her to duck. Her shock bought me time, and I managed to slice her arm before losing her in the rest of the fighting. I ducked as another wildling swiped at my head. He raised his blade again, and the point of a knife appeared in his gut. When he collapsed, Marian stood in his place, glaring at me.

"Get to Rune!"

Rune had gone for Aleki, clearly intent on finishing him off, but Aleki's magic had found him first. Under his furious spell, Rune was slowly raising his sword, point pressed against his own stomach. His arms shook with the effort to resist.

I spun under another wildling before Xander shot them. Triss knocked another aside. "Val, for you!"

She threw me Sliver. I caught it, cast the other blade aside, and charged toward Aleki. A delighted smile had spread across his face as blood started seeping across Rune's shirt. I wouldn't reach him in time.

Still running, I scooped up one of the dropped crossbows and, with one arm, aimed and fired. The bolt sank into Aleki's shoulder and spun him around.

"Don't kill him!" Rune roared as I drew Sliver.

Aleki was scrambling back on his good arm, lips pulled in a menacing sneer. "Stupid girl, did you really think you could kill me? Here, I'll allow you to do the honors and *kill Rune.*"

His magic washed over me and faded. I enjoyed watching his face move from shock to panic as I stepped beside the throne and pressed the blade to his throat.

"I recommend you stay very still."

"Impossible," he wheezed. "My magic—"

"Is just like mine," Rune said. "And she resisted it, too. Don't kill him yet, Val. That honor belongs to me, and I want to make him watch, first."

"Watch what?" I said, but Rune was already facing the remaining few wildlings as Marian, Xander, and Triss cleaned them up. I hadn't realized how good of fighters they were, but the bodies of nearly a dozen wildlings littered the grotto's audience chamber.

"Whatever he's offering you, I'll give you more," Aleki fervently whispered. "Precious jewels, land, lovers, food, anything."

"How about heart gems from other wildlings?" I said, and Aleki fell into stunned silence.

"He can't promise you that."

I looked at the bodies, ignoring the uncomfortable churning in my stomach. "Looks like he delivered. Stay there, Cobb."

Rune's cousin froze midway through slipping from behind the throne. "I wasn't running, merely—"

Marian grabbed his collar and hauled him down to stand beside a sneering Vanesi.

"Well done, Cousin," she said. She looked at the carnage with undisguised appreciation. "All those years I took you for a soft weakling. How much more fun it would have been if you'd had this much fight bef—"

Rune stepped forward and drove his sword through her chest. Vanesi's eyes bulged. She tried to speak, but only gurgled blood came out before she collapsed.

"Check the mansion," Rune said to Xander. "Bring anyone there to me, alive."

Xander and Marian vanished. I stared into Vanesi's dead eyes, still grappling with the suddenness of her death. Had I expected that taking a seat of power would be a bloodless affair? I knew only a fraction of what Rune's supposed family had done to him, but still...

"Leave everyone else alone, Rune," Aleki said. I still held him by his collar, sword resting on his throat. "You've had your fill of blood. If you think this display will make the other Lords bend—"

"They will break, not bend," Rune said. "And groveling is beneath you, Aleki. If he does it again, hit him," Rune said to me.

He crouched before Aleki. "You took everything from me, Uncle. And so far, I must admit I've enjoyed doing the same in kind. Answer me this: in all the years I was gone, you could have gotten the high throne at any time. You could have promised me my freedom if I only compelled the heart tree to give you the crown or murdered the few I still cared about until you got what you wanted. Why didn't you?"

Aleki's mouth had gone slack. "You don't understand anything, do you?"

"Then enlighten me—"

A woman screamed. Xander and Marian had returned, Marian dragging a wildling woman, a little girl clutched in her arms. The other two wildlings looked like hired help, people to work the mansion.

"These were the only ones we could find," Marian said. She threw the woman before the throne as Rune folded himself into it. The woman saw Vanesi's body and clamped her hand over the little girl's eyes. She looked, shocked, up at him. "R-Rune?"

"Luella." Rune sounded almost surprised. "And a child. Who is this?"

The little girl pulled her mother's hand from her face and gazed around, seemingly unperturbed.

"Your name?" Rune repeated.

"Olette, she's Olette," Luella said. "Rune—"

"You killed Aunt Vanesi," Olette said softly. "Are you going to kill my grandpa?"

"Yes, I am," Rune said.

"Leave them, Rune," Aleki said. "Whatever your hatred of me, spare them from it."

"Don't worry, there's plenty of my hatred to go around. Marian, bring her here."

"Rune, I said—"

Marian pulled Olette from a crying Luella.

"Rune, this has gone far enough," I murmured. "She had nothing to do with this. Kill Aleki and call it done."

Rune ignored me and placed Olette on his knee.

"Don't do this, Rune. Don't be like them."

"I'm already like them," Rune said. His hand gently rested atop Olette's head. "He—they—made me that way."

"You're not. You're better than them."

"You think too highly of me."

Rune continued staring at Olette, but his gaze was far away. I wasn't sure I was even getting through to him.

"How old are you, Olette?"

She stared at Aleki and then her mother.

"Look at me, Olette," Rune said. "How old are you?"

"P-please!" Luella sobbed. "Please don't hurt her!"

"I'm eight," Olette said.

"Eight!" Rune said. "That's something. That's the age your grandfather had me taken away. To a place where I had to work and fight. A place where I was beaten and more. A place where he wanted me to die."

"Rune, stop," I said. My body was growing hot. "This isn't right."

"Your grandpa did that to me," Rune said. He looked at Aleki, fury carved on his face. "What do you think I should do,

Aleki? Let her live, as you did to me? Give her years to build up resentment and come back for revenge?"

I straightened up, dropping Aleki at my side. "I won't help you anymore if you do this. No matter what you threaten me with."

Rune raised his other hand, and magic crackled to life in it, reflecting off Olette's wide eyes. "*Now* I want to see you beg, Aleki. Beg like I had to so many times."

Aleki's throat bobbed up and down as he struggled with the words. At last, he bowed his head. "Please don't kill her. I'm...I'm begging you, don't kill her."

Rune brought the magic closer to Olette's cheek. "Not good enough."

I took a step forward. "This has gone far—"

One of the wildlings Marian and Xander brought from the house moved, snatching up a crossbow and shooting Triss in the chest. Time stopped for what felt like an eternity. I watched the pain register in Triss's face, watched her vibrant emerald eyes go dim.

She collapsed, shaft quivering through her heart.

Marian roared something unintelligible and, in a spray of blood, the man went down, throat savagely cut. Luella screamed. Rune started to rise.

That was when Aleki pulled the knife from a flap in his coat. He lunged at Rune.

I saw Rune turn in slow motion, saw him push Olette off his leg and bring up his arm. It wouldn't be in time to stop the blade from burying into his stomach.

I grabbed Aleki's arm, my other hand on his back, opposite his heart. My only thought was stopping him, no matter what.

A blue flash. My world snapped.

I could almost hear it, like a glowstick breaking. I could certainly feel it, a rush of magic so strong I went limp and crashed to the foot of the throne. Aleki's dead body fell next to me, pale flesh sagging. His eyes were dull, as though there'd never been any life in them at all.

The last I saw before the darkness closed in was Rune peering down at me from the throne, as though seeing exactly what I was for the first time.

THIRTEEN

Conversation darted in and out of my head like fireflies, blinking to life and then dying just as quickly.

"What she did, Rune...you saw."

That sounded like Marian. And she sounded scared.

"I know what she did. I was there."

Rune's voice was soft, as though he didn't want to wake me. Or he was scared, too.

"This changes things," Marian said.

"This changes nothing. We accomplished the first step, and they'll react exactly how I expect them to."

A severe sigh. "I know you have this...*deal*, but look at what happened! She can't remain alive. Not with that kind of power."

I sensed the presence of someone beside me, though my eyes refused to open. A feather-light touch brushed a strand of hair from my cheek. "She's not done being useful to me. Not yet," Rune murmured.

I fell back into the dark.

The next time I came to my senses, I found myself looking

at the moth-chewed curtains of a canopy bed, the rotted fabric eventually transitioning to trailing lines of ivy and flowers. The pillows I lay on felt stuffed with spider's silk.

I sat up and immediately regretted it. My head throbbed. My chest ached as badly as if someone had driven a knife through it. Getting to my feet was putting myself at risk of falling on my face, but I managed.

The rest of the room was as decadent as the bed: a marble vanity in the corner and an enormous clawfoot tub inlaid with jewels in the bathroom where I went to splash water on my face. One look out the window showed me I was in the mansion beside the grotto. While practical, it was also gaudy and oozed the arrogance of its former master. Of course Rune chose to hole up here.

I checked myself in the mirror, and a memory flashed across its surface. Rune peering down at me from his throne, bodies surrounding him. He'd been unnecessarily cruel, and I wanted answers.

I turned my face this way and that, looking for...

I wasn't sure. Something that would explain what had happened to me when I'd tried to stop Aleki. I felt fine. Well, lousy, but not like something catastrophic had happened. If anything, with my initial grogginess gone, I felt more energized than I had in a while.

Something else I needed answers to.

I walked out onto the upstairs landing. Xander stood at the foot of the stairs in the atrium, talking with one of Rune's wildlings I hadn't seen since King's Hollow.

"When did they arrive?" I called down.

The wildling he was speaking to looked at me warily; Xander said something and they left. Xander's expression was hard to decipher as I came downstairs.

"Most joined us the last two days, after Aleki died, after

you killed him. Some of his wildlings fled and some of them joined ours from King's Hollow."

Xander wrinkled his nose at the garish furniture and decorations. "Most have chosen to stay in Portland, and I don't blame them. You should see the private wing. Makes the rest of this look tasteful."

"I was out for two days?" I said, trying to ignore his offhand comment: *after you killed him.*

"You were." Xander's brow furrowed. "You feeling okay?"

"That woman, Luella, and Olette. Rune didn't…"

"A question for Rune. He wants to explain."

"Xander, just tell me—"

Xander jerked his head, and I reluctantly followed him through a dining room to the front door. "Go talk with him. After that we need to make a plan. We've learned of the location of the heart tree. The *actual* heart tree."

I was momentarily distracted. "How?"

Xander gave me a look that said I was again asking the wrong person. "I think Rune's in the grotto. Not to rush you, but we can't stay in this cushy place long. Now that Aleki's dead, Jezaline and Mordecai won't hold back. They'll want us all dead no matter how far we run."

"I don't think Rune has any intention of running."

Xander grinned. "Strangely, I don't think so, either. Listen, Val," he said as I stepped outside. "You should still talk to him, but what Rune did—"

"I don't need you to make excuses for him."

"Just…listen, really listen to him when you do. Don't judge him too harshly."

I wasn't ever going to promise that. I knew a little about what had happened to him and how terrible his past had been. But that was no excuse for him to act as he had.

What did you expect? You knew exactly what he was from the very start.

Yes, but somewhere along the way, I'd started hoping I was wrong.

I walked down the garden path to the grotto, bracing myself for what I'd find there. The entire battle and bloodbath seemed like a particularly bad nightmare in a long sequence of them.

I stopped above the grotto's audience chamber and for a second thought the nightmare hadn't ended.

The wildling bodies hadn't been removed. They couldn't be. Blue crystals, like enlarged blades of grass coated in frost, grew out of them. They skewered through limbs and torsos, sprouted from skin, anchoring the bodies to the floor and creating a spiked trap for anyone who wandered too close.

I took a deep breath to steady my heart.

I really needed to find Rune.

He wasn't anywhere in the grotto, so I wandered to the back of the mansion to what looked like a guest house built among the flourishing garden that bled into the Wilds' trees. I heard voices as I stepped inside.

"I thought you were going to die."

That was Marian, in the last room down the hall.

Rune gave a dark chuckle. "I owe too many people too much pain to go out yet."

"I know *you* were prepared for killing him or dying, but do you think that made it easier for any of us? For me? I couldn't stand seeing that... Couldn't stand you not knowing how I truly felt."

"Oh? Do tell me what it is you fe—"

He stopped speaking, and when I was able to see inside the room, I knew why.

Rune was seated in a plush chair, one that Marian straddled, fervently kissing him.

An unnecessary stab of...something pierced my chest. I scoffed it off. I had no reason to feel weird. Rune could kiss whomever he wanted, and Marian hadn't exactly kept her infatuation with him hidden.

Rune hissed as Marian grabbed at his shirt. "Marian—"

"You're—not—kissing—me back—"

"*Marian.*"

Rune pushed her off. Marian blinked at him, as though coming out of a trance.

"I had no idea wanton death made you desire me more," Rune said.

"They all had it coming. And you know I've always wanted you, don't pretend otherwise."

"I knew."

"And?" Marian demanded.

Rune rested his chin on the tips of his fingers, gazing at her. I could have sworn his eyes flickered to where I stood. "That's the last kiss you're getting from me."

"You've said that before."

Rune stood. "And this time I mean it. It does neither of us any good. Did Xander learn anything more about the heart tree?"

If Marian was disappointed at his rejection, she didn't show it. I rapped on the doorway. "Hope I'm not interrupting."

Marian shot me a scathing look before biting out, "He didn't learn anything you didn't already know. We might have temporarily escaped the Lords, but we're running out of time."

"We were always out of time," Rune said.

Marian shook her head with a loud sigh. "Yes, but this is worse, and you know it. Jezaline and Mordecai will be heavily guarding the heart tree now that Aleki's dead, and they'll assume you gleaned its location. We don't have the manpower to get through them. Your forces are scattered and low. If we fight them head-to-head, it'll be over fast, and we'll lose."

"Unless you get more manpower," I said.

Rune looked curiously at me. "And how do you propose we do that?"

I shrugged. It seemed obvious, from what little I'd learned of how the politics of the Wilds worked. "The same thing you're already doing. Get to the heart tree, get the crown. Jezaline and Mordecai were scared enough of retribution from wildlings not entirely loyal to them that they let you go. Who's to say those same wildlings won't be swayed to your side once you get the crown and become the true ruler?"

"Do you have flowers sprouting from your ears?" Marian seethed. "We *can't* break through to the heart tree; they'll be too strong. Worse, our element of surprise is gone."

"Then we need an alliance," I said. Rune leaned back against the table, watching me like he knew where I was going with this.

"I don't know how many times I have to beat this into your skull: None of the other wildlings will align with you before you have the crown," Marian said. "They won't risk it."

"Unless..." I said.

"I didn't go to any wildlings," Rune finished.

I'd assumed there'd be some outside of the other Lords' influence willing to hear Rune out, but it worried me how much Marian paled.

"You can't mean the Undersea."

"The Undersea has an army?" I asked.

"Yes, and a formidable one, should they stop infighting long enough to amass it," Rune said.

"Sounds familiar," I mumbled, earning a dirty look from Marian.

"Going to the ocean king for help is useless," she said. "He stays out of all wildling affairs."

"He stays out of petty squabbles," Rune said. "He'll listen to me."

"Jezaline and Mordecai probably already talked to him. You can't do it."

"I can't?" Rune repeated, voice lowering to a dangerous whisper. "Are you telling me I *can't?*"

"I'm saying you shouldn't," Marian amended quickly. "You know what he might ask for, and if he collects, if they take you, I—"

"You'd what?" Rune sneered. "You would *what?*"

"Forget it."

"Perhaps I didn't make it clear: you and I will never be. No matter how much you pine for me."

"Rune, stop," I said.

"I don't need you to defend my feelings," Marian snarled. She lifted her chin at Rune. "Even if it's one-sided, that's good enough for me."

"Ah, yes, unrequited love. Whatever works for you."

Marian's lip trembled. She gave a jerky nod and walked out.

I whirled on him. "You are beyond an ass, you know that?"

"More than you realize," he said.

"I bet if she confessed she truly loved you, you'd crush that too."

"She doesn't love *me*." Rune said, bristling. "She loves what I did for her. I'm the one who led her and others out of Mog Moren, who rallied allies and gave her the first safe place and people she's had in years, maybe ever. *That's* what she loves. But me?"

Rune chuckled darkly. "I think she's secretly disgusted with me, even if she doesn't realize it. I don't blame her. She doesn't want me. She doesn't *need* me. She needs someone to return the affection so she doesn't feel so alone and doesn't have to face what she is by herself."

Rune turned to the table, though there was nothing on it. "I hope you've healed up because we leave soon."

"And I'm not going unless we have a new understanding."

Rune flinched, hand brushing his side as he faced me. "There is no new understanding. We work off the same deal—"

"I'll kill for you, but only those who deserve it," I said. "What you almost did to that little girl—"

"And who gets to decide who deserves it? Me? You? Someone who hasn't an inkling of what almost any Lord or those in my family would do given half the chance? The depths of my depravity are nothing compared to them."

"We're not killing innocents!"

Rune shifted his feet and winced again. "I didn't kill innocents. Olette and Luella are fine. Well, they're alive."

I sagged with relief. "You didn't..."

"Kill them?" Rune cocked an eyebrow. "They were there to demean Aleki before he died. But when he lunged, and you killed him..."

Rune winced, hand going to his side again. I stepped closer and started raising his shirt.

"What are you—"

"Shut up and let me look."

"It seems women can't keep their hands off me today, no matter how much I try to stop them."

I glared at him. "You're not trying very hard now. Move your hand."

He did, and I pulled the shirt up. I tried to ignore the numerous scars crisscrossing his toned midsection and focused on the latest wound. Between the bottom of his ribs and top of his hip spread angry red skin and blackened veins.

"You'll be happy to know that magical wounds heal slower and are far more painful than knives. I'm in an incredible amount of discomfort," Rune said. He sucked in a sharp breath as my fingers brushed over the injury. "By all means, make it worse. I'm sure I deserve it."

"Aleki got you."

"No. This was my spell."

"This was...you did this on purpose?"

He grabbed my fingertips before I could touch the wound again. "I'm not a masochist."

I finally understood. He'd redirected his own spell into himself rather than hurting Olette or attacking Aleki and risk hitting me with the collateral.

I pulled my hand from his and dropped his shirt. "You do deserve this. I don't ever want to see you do that again. Promise me that you won't hurt any more innocents."

"I can't promise that."

"I know, but promise it anyway."

"Val..." I swore I could still smell the tint of honey on his breath. "I can't promise. But I'll try. Come with me."

He pulled away and stepped out the door. My body relaxed. He hadn't promised, but I would do my best to hold him accountable. And if he ever crossed that line...if he ever started becoming the same as the wildlings he was fighting against...

I looked at my hands. They'd been covered in blood during the fight. Would I have the strength to cover them again?

I followed Rune but stopped on our way to the mansion. Among the worn stone benches was a patch of freshly turned earth, blooming flowers ensnarled over top: drooping lilies, fire blossoms, ficus, bloodrose, and others from the Wilds with names I didn't yet know. Rune clearly hadn't buried his enemies in the grotto, so who...

"Triss. I saw her get shot, but I thought... I'd hoped..."

"Straight through the heart," Rune said. "She died instantly. She knew the risks of joining me." He rubbed his hands, and I noticed smears of dirt across his knuckles. "She knew what it meant to all of us. The wildling who killed her is dead, so she can sleep peacefully."

Rune stiffly continued walking. I broke off a bloom and laid it among the rest over Triss's grave and then followed him.

We went to the mansion's second floor and down the hall from where I'd woken up. Rune knocked twice and waited until a soft voice ushered us inside.

It was Luella and Olette's room. Olette watched us from the corner, unblinking. She'd apparently been playing before we'd arrived. Human toys were scattered over the floor of the enormous bedroom, though I didn't miss the wooden practice sword and shield in the corner.

Luella stood and gave Rune a short bow. "Did you need something, cousin?"

Rune gestured to me. "Val was concerned for your safety. I wanted to show her you two were alive."

"And well," I added. I checked around the room, as though I might find obvious signs of abuse or imprisonment. Bars on the windows. Trip alarms or guards. "You *are* okay?"

Rune scoffed as Luella's face softened. "We are well. And we're not prisoners. Rune...did what he needed to with Aleki." Luella cleared her voice as she took a seat again and watched Olette silently grab another toy and continue playing. "And he's been gracious enough to let us stay here. We have nowhere else to go."

"You have no other family?"

"None by blood. There are smaller, less organized groups of

wildlings scattered in other places of what you call America. None nearly as powerful as Aleki was. None that could protect us should a rival vying to hurt Rune want to get to us."

That made some sense. I also doubted any of the other Lords would take them in. And I couldn't imagine the gentle-looking Luella and a child roughing it in the Wilds alone.

I approached Olette and crouched. "Since he probably hasn't, I wanted to apologize to you, to both of you, for what Rune did."

"Rune already apologized," Luella said with a smile.

Rune smirked at me. "Surprised?"

"And you're not scared anymore, Olette?" I said, ignoring him.

The little girl continued methodically grabbing parts of a puzzle one piece at a time and trying to fit them together. I noticed they were all from different pictures.

"She doesn't talk much," Luella answered for her. "Vanesi—"

Luella glanced around the room, as though her sister's vengeful ghost lingered.

"She's gone, Cousin. I made sure of that," Rune said.

Luella's entire body relaxed, but only slightly. "Vanesi never liked it when Olette talked. She'd pierce her tongue with pins or beat her where Aleki couldn't see. Beat both of us. I don't think Aleki would have cared about her hurting me, but he had a soft spot for Olette. That is why Vanesi treated her "games" like they were our secret."

Luella shrugged a shoulder out of the top of her dress, until I could see the black bruises of jabbing fingers, reddened burn marks, and slender holes, not yet healed.

Luella pulled the dress back up. "Heated knives and needles were her favorites."

"Sasic berry acid in my eye and broken fingers were always

her choice with me," Rune said. "She'd heal the fingers and then break them again. My father never knew." Rune flexed his fingers. "They still ache from time to time."

"In a way, you saved both of us," Luella said.

"She really did that to you both?" I said in shock. "To her own family?"

"When I visited, yes," Rune said. "Wildling families are not what you're used to, Val. Blood does not bind here, power does. So you get enough power that nobody hurts you again."

"It's true, then, you really intend to take the high king's throne," Luella said.

"I do."

Luella watched Olette quietly moving the pieces around. "Good. You will make a good king."

Rune's grin was malicious. "No, I won't. But I'll be the only king they'll get. Time to go, Val. Luella." He bowed again and stepped out.

"I don't know how you caught up with Rune, but thank you for helping him," Luella said.

"Yes, thank you," Olette said, so softly I barely heard.

I nodded slowly. "You don't...mind that a human is helping him? Other wildlings aren't so understanding."

"After knowing me for a day, you've treated me with more kindness than my own flesh and blood did my entire life. It doesn't matter to me what you are."

"I see." I gave her a small bow like Rune, but one far more disjointed and awkward. "Let me know if you need anything."

In the hall, Rune leaned against the railing as if in repose. If he'd been stone, he'd have fit in perfectly among the statues.

"Thank you for sparing them," I said before I could think better of it. "I thought... I almost believed..."

"That I would have done it." Rune pushed off the railing, eating up the distance between us. "A thank you? You're growing sentimental, Val." He took a strand of my hair in his finger and twirled it. "Don't tell me you're growing fond of me."

I flashed back to Marian kissing Rune. Another flash and I was the one on top of him, the one kissing him.

I knocked his hand aside. "Not on your life."

"Good." Rune's expression turned serious. "I'm not good for you. I'm not good for anyone."

He started to walk down the stairs. Only then did I remember one of the reasons I'd come to see him in the first place.

"The crystals," I blurted out, and Rune cocked an eyebrow back at me. "Vanesi, Aleki, the others, they were all covered in those crystals. Is it spreading? Is there an opening around here they came from?"

"Of course not. That was your doing."

I jerked back. "I—That's impossible."

"I thought so too, at first. But they appeared right after you attacked Aleki, and..."

I didn't like the hesitation in his voice. "Attacked him and did *what?*"

"Tomorrow. I'll tell you tomorrow."

"I need to know now, Rune."

Rune held my gaze. I realized with some surprise that he wasn't stalling simply to be obstinate. He didn't *want* to tell me. Whatever had happened—whatever I'd done—had surprised him. Maybe even scared him.

"You attacked Aleki and stole his heart gem," Rune said.

I stared at him. "I would have remembered carving out his heart."

"You didn't carve it out."

There was uncertainty in his eyes, unguarded, before he mocked it again. "You killed him without a blade or any magic that I know of, drew the life from his heart gem until there was nothing left of him."

"How—How is that possible?"

"I don't know," Rune said, frustrated. "It seems you gained access to some new magic, but if that had been introduced since I was away, then I missed it."

His grin was crooked. "Don't worry. Your worst fear hasn't been realized: you're still not one of us."

Strangely, that wasn't reassuring. "Then what am I?"

Rune didn't answer. I wasn't sure I wanted him to.

CHAPTER

FOURTEEN

I stood over the dead bodies in the grotto.

They were, of course, exactly as I'd seen them the day before, frozen in the same death pose, all of them covered in the same blue crystal. I tried to remember exactly what had happened before I'd blacked out, but the only thing I got was a headache.

Something was wrong about this. *I* couldn't have done this. I knew my abilities, but they were limited, and I'd never seen any sign of being able to steal magic from anything, not to mention a heart gem. I'd never heard of *anyone* having that kind of power, especially not in the human world. If a way had been discovered to siphon magic, then it wouldn't have been kept a secret for long.

I drew Sliver and stepped over to the prostrate form of Aleki. The crystal prevented me from turning him over, but I could still see every clear detail of his body.

I placed my hand over his heart and closed my eyes. I tried to block out all distractions. Tried to call my magic to me.

It didn't work. Of course it didn't. What I'd done wasn't possible. Or I'd already taken his magic.

I found Vanesi, her face still frozen in shock as though she couldn't believe Rune would dare kill her. Even I still couldn't believe it, though from what she'd done to him and others, I could understand it.

I brought the tip of my sword down on the crystal above her heart and tried to chip some of it away. After two minutes of going at it, all I got was aching hands and the smallest fragment broken off.

Frustrated, I placed my hand over her heart anyway. My magic stirred.

I jerked back. It could have been my imagination, but the point above her heart was glowing. And when I concentrated...

My hand glowed where there'd been nothing before, cool blue magic curling around my fingertips. I gaped at it then placed my hand above her heart again and *pulled*.

It was weak, far weaker than taking Aleki's must have been, but I managed to take some magic from her and from the others, until my skin practically crackled with it.

I pulled back, horrified and secretly fascinated. No wonder I'd had trouble using magic. In some ways, I was like a battery. I couldn't use it easily if I wasn't charged up. And I could only do that by taking from another source.

I looked at the bodies then at my hands. I still couldn't believe that I'd created these crystals, but I could believe that there was something very wrong with me.

"IF YOU DON'T HURRY, I'll leave you out here."

I ignored Marian's empty threat. While I was past

expecting her to drive a knife in my gut any chance she got, she'd been extra prickly since I'd walked in on her and Rune.

Marian glared at me over the metal railing. "Did you hear me?"

"Unfortunately," I said.

"Then get up here. I found another."

I sighed and started crawling up the vine-devoured rubble into the latest apartment we'd found. While Aleki had made the mansion and grotto his own personal palace, the wildlings under him had created homes of their own in the city. Living spaces decked in pillaged human goods and given wildling touches. Root-made cages full of colorful songbirds I'd cut free, menageries of deadly plants that tried to spear or choke me before I shut the door on them. Entire roofs open to the canopy, with hammocks stacked ten high, made of thickened leaves and draped with woven silk.

Perhaps I was succumbing to Stockholm Syndrome, but I couldn't help thinking that, for all its danger, this wouldn't be an unappealing place to live. At least the air was clean.

"Food," Marian said when I joined her. She threw me hard cheeses and dried fruit, cured meats, and a still-corked bottle of wine. She jabbed a finger at it. "That's one of the few good things you humans make, so if you drop that, I swear to the green I'll gut you with the broken glass."

I threw all the food on the table. "Enough, Marian."

"Enough what?"

"Enough biting my head off. If this is about you and Rune—"

She stopped rummaging through the cupboard to glare at me. "This has nothing to do with that. I just don't like you. I made that clear."

More than once. Still, I'd experienced hurt well enough to

know I wasn't the real target of her ire. "I'm sorry about Triss. I didn't know her very long, but I liked her."

Marian slammed the cupboard shut hard enough to rattle my teeth. "Keep your sympathies," she growled. "They're only good for the weak and dead." I caught her wiping at her eyes as she turned her back on me to rifle through a smooth wooden chest. "Go next door and search there. I thought I smelled more meat."

I stowed everything in my backpack and tried to stay out of her way as we finished with the apartment and methodically searched the rest of the street. I spied a sign with POW and OOKS on the front peeking from the undergrowth. There were bookshelves inside, and I felt a pang of homesickness. Peyton used to love bringing back little treasures from the few times she ventured into the Wilds, my favorite being books. We could still buy them in the city, but scavenged ones were like lost treasures reclaimed.

I stepped through the front where a large pane of glass had once been. "Marian?"

I'd seen her go this way. I wouldn't have been surprised if she *had* ditched me.

"Marian...?"

I avoided sinking my foot into the numerous holes as I made my way upstairs. Husks of empty shelves, most pushed over, covered the space. A Rare Acquisitions room looked untouched, but not a single book was inside, or anywhere else.

Whoever lived here could have taken them before the Wilds overran it. But I'd been surprised to find an entire collection of human books back in Aleki's mansion, in a library I wouldn't have minded getting lost in. I'd had no idea wildlings cared about human literature, yet even monsters like Aleki appeared to have taste.

The weakened floor creaked as I threaded through the

shelves and came to where the books the wildlings hadn't wanted were thrown in a disorderly pile. Most had been there so long their yellowed pages had flaked away to papered dirt, years of rain mildewing the covers.

Marian stood next to the pile. She delicately peeled apart the wax-thin pages of a book on painting, looking startlingly serene.

"There you are."

She jerked in surprise. I felt her magic shoot through the floor toward me. I leapt aside but realized my mistake too late as my leg easily fell through the wood, followed by the rest of me. I landed hard, and my left arm immediately throbbed with stabbing pain.

With a cry, I yanked it away and rolled over. Needled thrush, an entire nest of it. Non-toxic, but I'd be picking the spines out of my skin for days, and the severe pain would last long beyond that.

I laid my head back with a groan as another flash of pain ran up my shoulder. Thankfully nothing felt broken.

"Serves you right for sneaking up on me."

I forced my eyes open. Marian peered down through the hole I'd made. "I hope it hurts."

"I called your name!" I snapped and then bit my tongue as even the slightest movement caused a fresh wave of agony. "I thought you wildlings had extra sensory hearing—gah!" I bit my tongue until I could risk opening my mouth without screaming. "I need help. Can you go get Triss—"

I realized my mistake the moment the words left my mouth. Marian scowled. Her face disappeared.

"I'm sorry, Marian," I called up. "I'm sorry we lost her, and I'm sorry you hate me. If I could change things, I promise I would."

No answer. I counted to three, taking deep breaths to

prepare myself, and then forced myself to my feet and began to search nearby for some of the plants Triss had healed me with. Multi-colored flowers and roots, and...what else? What had they been called? It was impossible to think straight through the pain.

Arm throbbing, head spinning, I sank back to the ground.

"You're so pathetic."

Chunks of wood barely missed my head as Marian dropped through the floor, landing inches from the needled thrush. She knelt to examine my arm.

"This stuff's super common. It doesn't hurt that bad."

"Great...for you," I panted. I'd have to sling my arm. Something to keep from moving it any more than I had to.

"Heal yourself."

I resisted kicking her into the needled thrush out of spite. "If I could do that, don't you think I would have?"

Marian grabbed my uninjured hand—making me hiss as I was jerked—and held it over the needled one. "The magic is there; you just don't trust it. Focus it. Become one with it, as we are one with the Wilds."

Sweat ran, stinging, into my eyes. "Your lessons suck, you know that?"

"Maybe. But if you want to fix this, then you'll shut up and listen."

I tried tapping into whatever feeling I'd had when Aleki had attacked Rune. Quieted all the pain, the outside noise, and settled firmly in my body.

I felt something, a tickle of power. I urged it toward my arm, but nothing happened.

"I can't." I flopped back.

Marian pursed her lips. "You can kill Aleki with some unknown magic but can't manage what every wildling child, even those with little magic, can do? Figures."

I lay there, urging myself to move through the pain when it began to lessen, like Novocain slowly being injected from my shoulder to my wrist.

I turned my head to find Marian running her hand over my arm. Slowly, ever so slowly, the needles were pushed out, and angry red, yet unmarked, skin took its place.

"Thank you," I murmured.

"I'm not doing it for you," she said savagely. "Rune needs you, as much as I hate it. I couldn't do anything against Aleki or Vanesi, but you did."

Whatever her reasons, I was glad for it. "You like painting."

Marian pulled her hand away, and the pain in my still-needled part of my forearm came back with a vengeance. "We are not talking about this."

"Sorry. Not talking about it."

Marian returned to my arm.

"You're good at that," I noted, since I couldn't seem to keep my mouth shut.

To my shock, Marian's face softened. "I healed much worse than this in Mog Moren. Bad breaks and knife wounds and beatings and...other things."

A faint smile flickered across her face, though I wasn't sure she noticed. "Rune's were always the worst. Most who were brought there avoided fights, but he actively sought them out. Seemed every night I was closing up one wound or another."

"You two were close."

"*Are* close," Marian growled. "All of us who follow him are. There."

She stood, and after a bit of stiffness, I did too. I flexed my arm. It still felt swollen, but the pain was nearly gone.

Marian hadn't bothered to check her handiwork but stepped over the needled thrush, back to the street. She clenched the window frame. "I'm not an idiot. I know Rune doesn't want me, not like that. I helped him through that dark time, but I'm also a reminder of the worst part of his life. Some days I think he can't stand being around me, and if I'm honest, I feel the same."

She sighed. "When things between you and him are done, I want you to leave, too. Leave and never come back. You'll remind him of what he lost, too. He doesn't need more darkness in his life. Not from you. Not from me."

She stepped out the window. I flexed my hand again, feeling the throbbing of my heart all the way to the tips of my fingers.

RUNE WAS WAITING for me when I returned to the mansion.

"I want to try something."

"Ominous," I said. "What?"

I'd dropped off what we'd gathered to those in the kitchen and joined Rune in the overgrown garden, where crested iron gateways split it into squares. Cobb was in one of them, wringing his hands and looking around as though he'd be run through by Rune or one of his wildlings at any second. I hadn't seen him since the night we'd—I'd—killed Aleki.

"I thought you left with the others," I said.

Cobb gave me a wan smile. "I might be a wildling, but I wouldn't survive very long out there. I guess you and I have that much in common."

"Speak for yourself."

Cobb coughed awkwardly. "I suppose I should. Thankfully, Rune graciously allowed me to stay."

"And now I'm graciously telling him to help you," Rune said. "Though he's unable to wield it, being around a Lord has given Cobb some insight into more advanced magics. I want him to help you figure out how you took Aleki's heart gem."

I stared at Rune. "And you trust him?"

Rune gave a wry grin, and even Cobb laughed.

"Absolutely not," Cobb said.

Rune nodded to the guest house he'd been staying in. "I'll be watching. And if he gives you any trouble, kill him. It'll save me the hassle of doing it myself."

"Oh, ha, ha," Cobb chuckled weakly as Rune walked off. "He's such a joker."

"He's really not," I said. "And after hearing what your father and sister did to him, I can see why."

"It wasn't *my* fault. If I'd have stopped Vanesi whenever she did those things, she'd do them to *me* and that wouldn't solve anything!"

"She was your sister, and he's your younger cousin. You should have done *something*. You should have told Aleki."

Cobb was shaking his head. "Aleki knew about it, at least what she did to Rune and Luella. How could he not? He allowed Vanesi her...enjoyment because it served Aleki's needs and kept her tame. Secretly, I think he urged her to target Rune."

I recoiled. "Why?"

"Because even though Rune's illegitimate, he still held claim to the throne. Rune's father Rowan was always the most favored in their House, so much so that their family exiled Aleki to 'trim the weak branches.' Aleki pretended not to care —and Rowan foolishly visited to try to keep the peace—but Aleki was overjoyed when Rowan was killed and the House fell. With it gone, even his little claim to the throne had a chance. It wasn't long after Rune came to live here that Aleki had him, ah, removed."

"Why not kill him?" I said. "Why send him to Mog Moren at all?"

Cobb eyed me, as though debating whether it was worth trying to explain. "Even with the House gone, as second born, Aleki's claim to the throne was weaker than Rowan's, and Aleki wasn't certain the heart tree would weave a crown for him. If that was the case, he wanted Rune there to claim it for him."

Cobb gave a chagrined smile. "Unluckily for Aleki, the other Lords caught wind of what he planned to do and... persuaded him that vying for the throne was unwise. It'd been too long after the Sundering and the death of the last high king. Any other claims to the throne had been murdered or imprisoned."

"That's sick, you know that?"

"Don't judge us too harshly, human. We have neither the luxury nor the desire to be kind to one another. There is no benefit, even toward family, if the family brings no value, protection, or power in return."

I let out a disgusted grunt. "Let's just get this lesson over with. And before I forget..."

I nudged Sliver's tip under Cobb's chin before he could blink.

"I may suck with magic, but I'm pretty good with a weapon. I haven't forgotten the reason we fell for the false heart tree was because of *your* information."

"That I overheard from Jezaline and Mordecai! How was I to know?"

"If this tree proves to be the same, I'm taking it out on you."

Cobb gulped. Point made, I put my sword to the side but within reach. Though I couldn't see him through the window, I swore I could feel Rune's burning gaze on me.

"All right, what do I do?"

"I'm…ah…not entirely sure."

I cocked my head. "Excuse me?"

"The power to take a wildling's magic from their heart gems…you understand we can't do that, right? Otherwise, we'd be killing whomever we wanted whenever."

"Some of you already do that."

"True. But your ability would certainly make it easier. You're a strange human."

I thought back to the children we'd seen in Castle Rock, how their eyes glowed blue. What strange abilities did they possess? Were there other humans who grew up in or near the Wilds who had the same? I was strange, but surely I wasn't the only one.

Cobb cleared his throat. "Let's start with the basics. Like any spell targeting a specific wildling, you first need to focus and find their aura."

My brow furrowed. "And that is…"

"Not as easy as it sounds. Try to feel it."

"I have no idea what I'm looking for, Cobb."

Cobb glanced at the guest house with a look of disgust. "Give me your hand. I don't like it either, but it's part of the demonstration," he explained when I hesitated.

I reluctantly let him clasp mine. He closed his eyes, and a moment later I saw it: a faint, hazy vapor outlining his body. Wisps of it trailed off him, like how I imagined an animal might discern a scent.

"Do you see it?" Cobb said.

"It's faint, but yeah. Maybe if I—"

When I reached out to touch him, Cobb squeezed my hand hard enough to hurt before he practically threw it back at me.

"Let's…not do that. I don't need you any closer to my heart gem than you are," Cobb said. "That color is the magic aura my heart gem produces. You'll need to home in on that. It's the same way we wildlings focus on another's magic when healing or trying to break through a magical defense. Why don't you try to find it again. Without touching me."

But after a half hour of digging deep and closing my eyes, breathing steadily and widening my stance, I didn't *feel* anything except like an idiot. Whatever brief burst of magic Aleki had given me was gone or out of reach again.

"I'm done," I said, exasperated.

"Are you sure?" Cobb asked, though he seemed relieved. "It almost looked like you had it there."

I flopped to the ground and glared at him. "Liar. I barely made any progress."

"Agreed. Now it's my turn."

My skin prickled. I hadn't heard Rune return, but now I was all too aware of his presence crowding my space.

"I have an idea," he said.

"Not now, Rune," I said. "I'm exhausted."

"And you'll be exhausted when you need your magic most, but you'll have to keep going or die. Get up. We're not done."

I managed to stare him down for a full five seconds before admitting he had a point. If I was going to intentionally use my magic, then I couldn't let this be my failing, especially not in front of him.

I reluctantly took Rune's offered hand and let him help pull me up.

"Leave," Rune said to Cobb, never taking his eyes off me.

Rune had always come off as a natural leader, and a natural jerk. His intensity, though—the unflinching way he stared at me, and only me—that wasn't something he'd been taught. That was him, through and through.

The kiss in the marsh had been poison, literally. The cabin had been about survival. Rune had been clear about that.

Still.

"Your heartbeat's sped up," Rune said. "You're scared."

The almost-soft way he said it snapped me back to the real world where I couldn't have him, where I didn't *want* him, and he felt the same. This Rune was a single-minded boy—and not a human one—who only had one desire. Nothing, not even any emotions he definitely didn't have for me, would stand in his way.

"I'm not scared."

"And now you're lying. It's easy to tell. You look away, just for a second. Like that," he said as I did. "Do I still frighten you?"

I unclasped our hands. "Of course not."

He gave me a not-quite-believing smirk. "Then it's the Wilds, and if they frighten you, there will be no point to trying this."

I'd let him think whatever he wanted. I forced myself to look right at him, unblinking. "I respect them. There's a difference."

Rune smirked. "Call it what you want, and I'll call it what it is. Wildlings draw their magic from the Wilds. It sustains us and aides us. It's why we can't stay in your sterile, dead human world for too long, and why so many of you pesky humans die in ours. You can fight against that magic or ignore it. But the magic is here, always. You must root yourself in it. Here..."

He touched my forehead.

"And here."

He touched above my heart.

I licked my suddenly dry lips. "It's not that easy."

"It is. You just don't want it to be."

"You have *no* idea what I want."

"Of course I do. Maybe even more than you."

I raised my hand, maybe to slap him, maybe to cup his cheek. "Of all the arrogant, self-important, th—"

He caught my hand and pressed my palm to his chest. He was incredibly warm and *alive.* I found his aura naturally, so vibrant that Cobb's appeared like a match beside an inferno.

"What are you doing?" My voice was higher than normal. I tried pulling my hand away, but Rune didn't let go. "Rune, stop—"

"Try again."

"You idiot. If I manage to pull this off, I'll kill you!"

"If you could, would you?" He sounded genuinely curious.

"I-I..."

"Try again," he urged. "Don't be scared."

Against my every instinct, with Rune's intense gaze still on me, I forced my eyes closed.

I didn't know what "rooted" felt like. But instead of resisting it, I used the warmth radiating into my hand to guide me, to bring down all the walls I hadn't realized I'd constructed and allow myself to truly feel whatever came my way. I focused on my feet, my legs, moving the awareness up through my body until the Wilds were a source and I was the conduit.

"Command it." Rune's voice reverberated through my bones. "Tell it what you want it to do."

Not kill you, idiot.

But why not? So what if I wanted him dead?

Him, the one who'd caused me and so many others pain.

Him, the one who showed me more kindness than some of my own kind.

The warmth in Rune's chest grew. My fingers felt like they were sinking into his skin. My own body responded, a static charge running through me.

Rune let out a gasp of pain.

"No!"

I tore my hand away and practically threw myself back. Rune was bent over, clutching at his heart. He grinned at me. "You started to do it. I knew you could."

"You...*idiot*," I seethed. "If you wanted to die, you should have let me finish you off weeks ago. I would have gladly done you the favor!"

Rune cocked his head, his smile still mocking. "You should see your face right now. One might get the impression that you truly cared about me."

A hundred thousand curses sprang to my lips. But before I could unleash any of them, there was a soft breeze and Pitus appeared out of thin air, dressed in mottled green clothes, with persimmons sprouting from her tangled strands of hair.

Rune straightened up. "Yes?"

Pitus crossed one hand over her chest and knelt. "My Lord Rune—"

"Prince, Pitus, not lord, not yet." He laid a gentle hand atop her head. "Exiled prince, if you're feeling especially specific."

Pitus mirrored his smile, bowing lower. "Prince, then. I was scouting the outskirts of Portland and intercepted something I think you will want to hear." Her eyes flickered to me. "Likely both of you."

"Is this message still contained, as my uncle so loved to do?"

"It is, My Lo—Prince."

Rune held out his hand and Pitus placed a small, burnished metal carving of a laughing bird into it, its eyes glittering with small jewels.

"An echo," Rune said to me as he turned it over in his fingers. "They're infused with short messages that only the intended listener can hear, either through magic or a password provided by the deliverer." He held it up to Pitus. "And the wildling you took this from?"

"Dead. I caught him as he was leaving. When it was clear I wouldn't be shaken, he tried to destroy the echo. I managed to remove it and let the Wilds end him."

"Excellent. You may go."

Pitus ducked her head. She gave me a soft smile before vanishing as quickly as she appeared. Rune turned the bird over in his fingers. "These are notoriously charmed. Some, if you attempt to break into them, will burn your lips and tongue off so that you cannot speak what was within. Others will clog your ears with rot so that you can never again hear secrets not meant for you."

Rune brought the bird up to his mouth and whispered something, fingertips glowing.

"Judging by your confidence, I'm hoping you know how to get it to speak?" I asked.

"Of course."

"Of course. How foolish of me to doubt."

His smirk was both infuriating and entirely expected. "Now you're getting it—"

"—*your support would be invaluable.*"

My jaw dropped as Joshua's voice came through the bird's open beak, as clear as if he'd been right beside me. Rune held the echo up between us, his gaze like a stabbing question straight into my heart.

"*I have yet to convince my contacts within the government that moving against the other Lords would be wise, but they'll come around. Every day, our sides extend this conflict when we should be cooperating. You understand, more than most. You share ambitions the others don't. I've considered your requests but need to see some reciprocation. More than you already have.*"

Rune placed a single finger on the bird's beak, and it paused, wings curling back in. "You know who is speaking."

It took me a moment to gather my swirling thoughts. I was too surprised to even consider lying to him. "It's my step-brother. But that's impossible."

"Clearly not so impossible," Rune said.

I wracked my brain, thinking back on the rare few times I'd spoken to Joshua since he joined the DFA.

"I didn't know he was a high enough rank that they were sending him into the Wilds, that's all," I said.

"Indeed." Rune stared at the laughing bird, contempt on his face. "And this clearly was something Aleki didn't want anyone to hear, or one of his underlings wouldn't have risked sneaking back in to steal it."

Rune tapped the bird's beak once more.

"My people are concerned about disturbing rumors we've heard of deeper in the Wilds. Things that even the Lords are having trouble dealing with. Confirm this isn't the case, and we'll move forward. As we've made clear, your support would be invaluable—"

I looked at Rune as he closed his fingers around the echo, silencing it. "Why'd you—"

Cobb stepped through the iron archway. He looked between the two of us. "Am I interrupting something?"

"What is it?" Rune said.

"Luella," Cobb said. He still looked suspicious, as if he had any right. "She said she wanted to speak to you. Both of you."

"Then we'll see her."

When Cobb left, giving a jerky bow as he did so, Rune stuffed the laughing bird in his pocket. I grabbed my sword, and together we went to Luella's room. She turned from the window as we came in.

"Olette," she said. The little girl ran over and clutched at the hem of her mother's dress. Luella knelt, smoothing down her daughter's hair. "I need to speak with them alone. Can you go play quietly somewhere?"

Olette looked at us as though we had the final say and then nodded and ran into the hall, giving me a shy look before vanishing.

"Nobody will harm her here," Rune said.

"Thank you." Luella swept over and closed the door. She was fidgeting, fingertips plucking at the hem of her dress.

"Is something wrong?" I asked.

"Not exactly. I..." Her eyes flickered to Rune. Though he'd promised she was safe, fear of her own family clearly ran deep. "It's..."

"Whatever it is, we'll listen."

Rune nodded.

"I didn't tell you before because I wasn't sure... Aleki never let me in on his important meetings. Vanesi always had more interest in the discussions, and Aleki sometimes needed her... talents during negotiations. But I did pick up some things." She sucked in a breath. "A little before you arrived, Jezaline and Mordecai came to visit."

Rune didn't seem surprised by this. "And what did they want? An alliance? To raise the bounty on my head?"

"I'm not sure. I couldn't hear everything. But they were afraid." Luella looked at me. "One of the reasons was the blue crystals. You might have noticed they've been spreading. More than the other Lords would admit."

My insides tightened. Rune might not have been all that concerned, but the fact the other Lords were nervous about them made *me* nervous.

"They didn't have any ideas what to do about them?" I said.

"None." Luella gave Rune a soft smile. "They weren't the Lords' top priority. I also heard them talking about something… I think the word was under. I couldn't make it all out, but I definitely heard that."

"Under?" I looked at Rune. "That mean anything to you? Like…beneath the ground, beneath the water… The Undersea." I finished at the same time Rune nodded.

"It's possible," Rune said. "The Undersea and the Wilds have never allied, at least not officially. Despite this, they may suspect that's where I'd go to try to broker an alliance."

"There is…one more thing," Luella said.

Rune cocked his head with a sardonic smile. "This has been quite the interesting meeting already. I'm sure your chest feels much lighter."

"Rune," I admonished. "What is it, Luella?"

Luella was looking anywhere but Rune. "I spoke too soon. There is nothing else I wish to share—"

"You can tell us," I said kindly. "It's okay."

"It's just…perhaps I was wrong…"

"Luella," Rune said more forcefully.

"Aleki wasn't the one who sent you to Mog Moren," Luella said in a rush.

Rune's face went slack with shock, before he straightened up. "Of course he was. It was his wildlings who took me in the night. They told me he did it. *He* told me he did it when I accused him of it."

"Despite what it may have seemed like, when I spoke to him soon after you vanished, he seemed just as confused about your disappearance as I was. He never wanted the throne of the high king, even though he had a weak claim to it." Luella spoke in a breathy rush. "He liked power, but he never played the political game. And getting you sent away wouldn't have helped him. Even with the crown, the other Lords wouldn't have accepted him. He didn't *mind* you ending up in Mog

Moren. It got you and the last memories of your father out of the way."

The room had darkened, and I realized thick green webbing was voraciously growing across the window. Rune's furious gaze didn't move from Luella. "Is that right?"

Luella cowered. "T-the other Lords suspected that he would try to take the throne anyway and barred him against it. If anyone else wanted the throne, it'd be another in his bloodline, one the other Lords didn't already suspect, if only they had the strength to take it."

"Vanesi," Rune spat her name like a curse.

Luella backed away from the nearly consumed window, looking between him and it. "Yes! It must have been Vanesi!"

The walls cracked as the green reached through. Roots spewed from the bedposts, snapping them like legs at the bottom of a long fall.

"Enough, Rune," I barked as the green leapt from the window and started devouring the floor toward us. "They're both dead; it's over now."

The green didn't stop. I tore my foot away from its grasping hold and grabbed either side of his face, forcing him to look at me.

"Don't you think Luella's been through enough? She doesn't need more pain from you."

I watched Rune as he seemed to return from that dark place the memory of his family dragged him to. He waved his hand, and the green stopped. A clear smear carved through the ivy covering the window, letting the light in again. Then he pulled himself from my grasp and walked out.

"I apologize," Luella said softly. "I should have realized what that news would mean to him."

"Don't blame yourself for his reaction," I said. "It was good to know. He's been through worse. He'll get over it."

"Perhaps. But wounds from family, by the nature of the ones delivering the blow, cut deeper. Rune has hated Aleki for so long, and such deep hatred cannot be easily redirected."

"Still, thank you for telling him. And me." I gave a short bow and moved to the door.

"Val." Luella wrung her hands. "There is something else you must know; something I trust you, as a human, with alone."

I slowly eased the door shut again. "I'm listening."

"There's a reason Aleki begged for Olette's life. A reason Rune was able to have so much sway over him, even if he didn't realize it. Aleki never cared for his own children, but Olette was different. Maybe he never saw her as a threat to his power, or his affection grew out of guilt."

I frowned. "Guilt?"

"Rune couldn't have known."

She looked close to tears. I narrowed my eyes, pieces slowly floating together into a picture I didn't want to see. "Luella, who *is* Olette's father?"

Luella kept swallowing, as though to get the taste of bile out of her throat. My mouth had gone dry, finding the words impossible to form. "Olette, is she Aleki's..."

"Yes." Luella sagged on the chaise lounge as though eight years of secrets were all that had been keeping her upright. "Aleki had many appetites, and not even I was safe from them. Vanesi would have never allowed him to sate them with her, but I am not as strong as my sister was."

My fist trembled. It was lucky I wasn't clutching Sliver, or I might have cut everything in this mansion to shreds. "I hope wherever he is, he's rotting slowly and painfully."

"I wish that as well. What happened to me is not a rare unkindness amongst those of the old Houses. I'm sure Rune could recall similar instances from his childhood. He was raised surrounded by such horrors. Rowan was nothing like Aleki, but that's not to say he was kind. Rune was always a serious boy, even from the beginning. And after the Sundering, he grew even more so."

I put the matter of Olette's parentage aside for a moment. "I've heard that term before. What is it?"

"When the Lords of the Wilds killed the high king and his lineage. I have no proof Rowan was in on the actual plot, but it seemed everyone had a part to play, no matter how small.

"The old House of Worms led it, Jezaline and her kin. They didn't want a single seat of power, and some of the other more powerful Lords agreed. Better to break it up and have a little than none at all. So one night they surrounded King's Hollow and slaughtered the king and his entire family. Rune was there, barely able to walk. Rowan brought him to watch what happened to rulers who didn't always remain strong and vigilant."

I could see it clearly: Rune, a little boy who had lost his innocence far too early, now desperate to grasp power if only to protect himself from falling victim to the same thing the high king faced.

"And after that, the other Houses turned on Rune's, didn't they?" I asked. "The House of Fallen Stars was destroyed and Rune's family along with it."

"His and many others. Nobody uses House names anymore except older wildlings or those looking to impress, but to do so is to bring up bitter feuds and old slights."

Luella smoothed the fabric of the chaise lounge with trembling fingers. "I love my Olette. Despite her origins, she is my sun and moon, and I would do anything for her, which is why..."

With great effort, Luella stood and briefly pressed her ear against the door. "With Aleki dead, technically Cobb and I have a small claim to the throne. But I don't care for it. Vanesi is dead, and Cobb is too weak for what would be required to take it."

I couldn't help grinning. "You and I can agree on that."

"But through me, Olette has a claim, too. I don't want her to be part of this world. I don't think he would, but I can't have Rune threatened by her. I want a new life for her, a safe life."

"And what does that have to do with me?"

"You have Rune's ear, probably more than anyone else, and perhaps more than you realize. You are not as entrenched in this world as his other followers. If you learn of a way to get Olette to safety, to free her from all this, could you please help me find it?"

I wasn't sure there would ever be safety, not where the wildlings and Wilds were involved. And I didn't want to believe that Rune would hurt Olette even if he believed her a threat. For all his faults, and recent actions to the contrary, I couldn't believe he would hurt or kill an innocent child and become the very thing he hated most in this world.

"I can't promise, but I'll try," I said.

"That's all I ask." Luella's shoulders sagged with relief. "Thank you."

I let her give me a grateful hug before I left. Rune was at the end of the hall, forearms resting on the railing, peering through the windows of the atrium into the Wilds. I tried to reconcile the severe image of the present with what Luella had told me, but only ended up feeling sadder.

"Are you upset about what Luella said?"

"What do you think?" he snapped.

"So Vanesi was the one who sent you away, and she's dead."

"*Vanesi* didn't do it," Rune seethed. "She was brutal, but she wasn't cunning or calculating. She would have simply killed me outright and been done with it. Besides, she had too much fun using me as her toy."

"Okay," I said, hating how that made sense. "So maybe it was someone else. Maybe they're dead already, because one of the other wildlings from the old Houses didn't want any competition."

I could tell the idea of him not being the one to end them irked him.

"I know you want to get back at whoever it was," I said, not believing I was consoling him about this. "But we have other things to worry about."

A slow, cruel smile etched its way up his face. "Wise advice. In time, I'll deal with this like I have everything else."

I didn't like the way he said that. Rune whirled and headed down the stairs. "Xander! Marian!"

They were there within moments, as though they'd been standing right outside.

"We move tomorrow," Rune said. "We're paying a visit to the King of the Undersea."

"Are you—" Marian checked her tongue. "Rune, their territory is near the Salish Sea. Mordecai's minions will be crawling all over, and the second you walk the path in, he'll know. Jezaline will know soon after that."

"Unless you feel like taking them both head on," Xander added. He flexed his fingers. "I'm a good shot, but I wouldn't advise that."

"Do you wish to weigh in?" Rune said to me. "Since the others have no problem giving their thoughts?"

"Only that I hope this is the only way," I said.

"It's the clearest path forward. We can't do anything about the Lords or the heart tree without more allies on our side."

He sounded convinced, and after thinking it over, I was too.

"Then we need a distraction for the distraction," I said. "Long enough for you to speak to the King of the Undersea."

Rune gave me a measured look. "And what do you propose?"

The fact that he was asking for *my* idea didn't shock me as much as actually having one. It was something that, if we didn't screw it up, might actually help us out, even after Rune got the crown.

"Easy," I said. "We just have to find someone waiting for an excuse to fight the Lords."

I nodded at his pocket. "I think I know just the person."

CHAPTER

FIFTEEN

I ducked as jaws snapped shut, barely avoiding getting my head bitten off. Through the night-washed trees, I could make out the lithe shapes of more beasts pursuing us, their masters' shouts not far behind.

"Nearly—there—" I heaved.

I slid beneath a low hanging bough, rocks and roots digging into my pants. Another beast lunged. I swiped with Sliver, glimpsing moonlight glinting off black fur—a body too bulky for a wolf, too lean for a bear, and a snarling mouth full of teeth—before my blade bit into its flesh. I jerked it free. Blood sprayed. The creature gave a final pitched whine and vanished, whimpering.

The wildlings' shouts grew louder.

"They have beasts?" I'd exclaimed the moment Rune and I emerged from the path just inside Mordecai's territory. Far enough in for over a half dozen of the Lord's wildlings to notice, yet far enough out for them to believe we'd mistakenly revealed our location.

Rune had flashed them an arrogant smile, and the chase had begun.

I could hear the scrape of claws on bark as something slithered through the trees, keeping pace. Dark shapes leapt overhead. I forced my exhausted legs to keep moving.

Ahead, I could make out the beach through a small break in the trees. We needed to reach that to start the next part of our plan.

A beast leapt from my left, and I barely managed to wedge my sword between its teeth before its sheer mass bowled me over. I released a hand to punch it in its beady eye then stabbed it in the tongue when it let go in surprise and pain.

I backed up, panting. My neck prickled.

I spun too late. A wildling with a second beast encircled me. The wildling pointed. "*Feast.*"

The beast leapt.

An enormous vine slammed the wildling against a tree hard enough to crack it, while an enormous thorn erupted from the ground and skewered the beast mid-leap. It yelped, before giving one last gasp and going still.

I swallowed hard and glared up at Rune, smirking at me from the tree above.

"You're welcome," he said.

"How are they supposed to follow us if you kill them all?"

Rune landed, quiet as a falling leaf, and cocked his head. The pursuing shouts were close. "Don't worry. There are more."

We stayed in place long enough for them to get a good look at us—to truly understand how big of a prize they were chasing—before taking off again. Rune moved so fast he never seemed to touch the ground, contrary to my still-recovering body, which was "sadly, humanly slow."

Rune's words, not mine.

"We need to go," I yelled.

He looked back. "We might lose them for real."

"They'll be able to track us. And I still need time for the next part. Make a path, now."

I had to dig my heels in as Rune stopped. He held out a hand, and the green in front of us curled into a tunnel.

"Remember, Val, if this is a plot to escape back to the human world, it won't end well for you," he said.

Though I was now used to wildling threats, Rune's cut strangely deep. "I told you already it's not. You just have to trust me."

He cocked his head with a smile that almost would have been cute were it not full of so much menace. "We're still working on that, aren't we?"

Of course we were. We probably always would be. Not that I cared whether he trusted me or not.

"Go." I swept past Rune and closed my eyes as we walked the path.

When I opened them, we were stepping out of a berm at the edge of a parking lot. A sign for Walmart glowed across a gleaming sea of cars. Glittering streetlights blotted my vision until my eyes adjusted. Despite the sensory overload, I was already grateful I'd picked here instead of downtown Seattle. Far less of a chance Rune would be discovered, but still close enough for Joshua to get here quickly.

"Change your eyes," I said to Rune. "And hurry. You stand out."

Rune grunted. He blinked once, and his eyes changed to a dazzling human blue. He softened some of the sharp edges of his form, too. He looked every bit a dangerous human, but still a human.

"I hope this works," he said.

"So do I," I said.

We hurried into the Walmart. Dry heat blasted across my skin. The ambient noise of so many people and beeping machines had me twitching. After what felt like months in the Wilds, I itched with edginess. I was sure I stood out. I was too dirty, too bloody, too wild looking. People would stare. People would know what I'd done, and who I was with, and once they did…

"What are you doing?" Rune asked as I stopped in an aisle of makeup and closed my eyes. All my thoughts collided in my head until I could barely think, barely breathe. I focused only on the sensation of my arm against the shelf. "Give me a minute."

"I doubt what we need is among the attempts you humans make to beautify yourselves."

"I *said*—Ugh, forget it."

I slowly forced a breath in, reminding myself that I was here, and for the time being, I was okay.

I pushed off the shelf.

Rune gazed at me, curious, and maybe a little concerned. "Out of all the things you've done, I didn't expect this to be the worst."

"You and me both," I said. "I just needed some air. Let's find the electronics."

But Rune stopped in front of a glass shelf. I started to panic as an attendant noticed us. Rune's illusion was flawless, but I couldn't help feeling they'd recognize him for what he was, regardless.

"What is it you have secured behind this glass?" Rune said.

The attendant looked between it and him. "You mean the baby food?"

"Food? For children?"

"For babies, yeah."

Rune's nose wrinkled. "Are babies really so dangerous that

you must protect it? Do they become so incensed with hunger they can't control themselves?"

I grabbed his arm and pulled him away from the gaping attendant. "Stop wasting time. The electronics are this way."

"How strange your world is," Rune said. "If staying here wasn't actively killing me, I might actually enjoy it."

I found the cheapest Pay as You Go phone, bought it with the few remaining, grime-speckled bills I still had stuffed in the pockets of my jeans, and within minutes was keying in Joshua's number as we loitered in the dark outside the back of the store. Since my time in the Wilds often destroyed my phones, I'd never been more grateful for memorizing the number of every important person I might ever need to call.

Joshua's voice was sleep-slurred when he answered. "Who is this?"

"Joshua? It's Val."

A pause. "*Val?*" There was rustling like he'd thrown himself out of bed. "You—where are you? Are you okay?"

Despite not being on the best of terms recently, I was genuinely touched he seemed so concerned.

I looked at Rune, watching the bits of green running along the edge of the water behind us. He gave me a look: *They're coming. Hurry it up.*

"I'm okay, for now," I said. "I can't talk; some wildlings are chasing me. We're in Lynwood, near Saltwater Park. I don't know how many there are, but I'll try to keep away from them as long as I can."

"In Lynn—Val, what the *hell* is going on? Wildlings have breached human territory? Have they—"

"Hurry." Feeling a massive twinge of guilt, I hung up and tossed the phone in the trash. My hands were shaking, but I dug my nails into my palm to make them stop.

"They've brought reinforcements," Rune said. I couldn't

feel magic the same way he could, but even I could tell we wouldn't be alone for long. "I hope this little plan of yours works."

"Let's try to stay alive long enough to find out," I said.

"How would you feel if you accidentally started a war?" Rune whispered.

We'd picked a quiet spot near the water, beside an old lighthouse the tourists loved. There was little greenery, which made Rune uncomfortable but me feel a bit better. The wildlings chasing us might be here in seconds, but they wouldn't get the drop on us.

"It's not that easy," I said. "Even if Jezaline and Mordecai were planning to invade, they don't have nearly enough strength to do so. And the human government wouldn't risk retaliating. Even when Joshua reports this, they'll call it an isolated incident, not an act of war. And they'll keep it hushed up to avoid panic."

At least until they had more powerful heart gems and more consistent ways to kill wildlings. "You of all people should know how this works."

There was his cocky grin. "Oh, I do. But I wondered if you did."

"You think I'd start a war between our people just to escape you?"

"Would you?"

Of course I wouldn't. I wouldn't put anyone in harm's way just to escape Rune.

Rune leaned against the wall. "It's fascinating, watching your conniving mind work. You pretend you're nothing like me, but I can see the truth. When there's something you want, and something stands in your way, there's nothing you won't do to get it."

"You're wrong."

"Hm... I don't think I am."

"I'm doing what's necessary. I don't *like* doing this or hurting anybody."

"Not even if they hurt you?"

"Of course I don't!"

"Of course you don't," Rune repeated, smirking.

He turned to me, voice pitching lower as his eyes drank me in. "There's a thrill to the fight you enjoy. You crave and covet power more than most. And now that you've had a little taste, and seen the results your violence can bring, you want even more. It's okay to admit it. There's nothing wrong with wanting to feel powerful in a world that makes you feel anything but."

All I did, all I'd ever done, from my best action to my worst, was so Peyton and I could get by. I didn't delight in it, not one bit.

I was almost better at lying to myself than I was to others. Almost.

"Rune," I said.

Pinpricks of gold-red eyes had appeared at the edge of the park. Even though we were hidden, the beasts the wildlings brought would have no trouble sniffing us out.

A sharp howl announced they'd been let loose, their snarling shapes charging toward us. I had to duck as an arrow zipped over my head, tip sparking off the concrete behind me. The green rioted where Rune pointed and there was a pained scream. Almost immediately, two more arrows shot past. I cut down one of the beasts, but more circled us.

"I'm starting to see the flaws in your plan," Rune said.

I was, too. We'd been surrounded far sooner than expected,

and our salvation hinged on not only Joshua believing me, but arriving before we were torn apart. He should have had enough time but until he got here, Rune and I were very much on our own.

Another beast lunged. I spun, arm jarring as I sank Sliver between its ribs and hit spine. As it died, its momentum ripped my sword away, and I scrambled to retrieve it as Rune conjured dirt from the ground and hardened it into fortifications. The next beast chewed away at it until Rune sank a muddy spike into its mouth.

"We're going back now," he said.

"Just a little longer, or else they'll definitely catch us over there," I said. "At least here they're weakened."

Rune ducked as a spell blew concrete chunks out of the lighthouse. "Here *I'm* weakened. If we don't do something—"

"Rune..." one of the wildlings taunted. I could see their murky shapes within the green on the other side of the park. "Not as clever as you thought, are you? Give up and make this easy. Let us bring you back to Lord Mordecai."

"In one piece, or many, your choice," another said. "But not the girl. Her filthy human blood spills here."

"Unless..." A third cackled. "Bring her along as a plaything for our beasts."

My grip tightened on Sliver. I'd slit my own throat before letting myself get captured by them. "New plan, maybe we—Rune!"

He stepped around his protection, putting himself in full view of the wildlings.

"There he is," one said, stepping out of his own cover. "Was it that easy to convince you to come with us?"

"I did want to make it easier," Rune said. "For me."

He was stationary one moment, gone the next, his glass knife slicing through the throat of the closest wildling. Another went down with a blade through his heart before the others reacted. Someone yelled a command. Rune turned to the next threat, but with all his skill, he'd only managed to get himself more surrounded.

Cursing, I charged out to help.

"There you are!"

The wildling must have used the others as a distraction to swing behind us. I tried to bring up my sword, knowing it wouldn't be enough to avoid the blade pointed straight at my gut.

A sharp crack split the night.

The wildling lurched sideways. His body clipped my legs, and when I stumbled to a stop, I found myself looking into his unseeing eyes. A large, bleeding hole punctured the center of his heart.

"Weapons free!" someone barked.

The night was suddenly full of earsplitting pops and muzzle flashes. I dragged Rune to cover as the wildlings who didn't react fast enough were torn down. A few managed to escape the first volley and tried to launch a counterattack, while others fell over themselves trying to escape.

"We're leaving!" one of them spat.

"They're coming from the right!"

"Back to the green! The green!"

Like a dark tide, more wildlings swarmed through the trees. Someone screamed. The chatter of gunfire was cut off. The humans had the element of surprise, but despite not being their turf, the wildlings had numbers.

Part of the greenery at the edge of the park tunneled. The first wildlings tried to step through to escape, only to explode in a screaming ball of orange and red. A Fringe Affairs soldier with a flamethrower continued spewing flames until the writing wildling went still. I felt like vomiting. I grabbed Rune's arm.

"Let's go."

Rune was frozen, staring at the charred husk of the wildling. The heat from the flames was growing more intense as a line of soldiers burned the wildlings back. I smelled gas.

"Rune! We can't stay here."

He turned to look at me. I saw something not unlike fear flash through his eyes. Fear of me and what I'd caused? Or fear of realizing just what humans were capable of?

"Yes," he said, "but we get far away before following the path."

I didn't know if I'd ever get the smell of charred wildling out of my nose. "Agreed."

The sounds of fighting continued as the two of us stuck to the outside of the park. I'd hated the wildlings all my life, felt oppressed by the DFA and their lack of caring, too. But I couldn't help feeling sick at what I'd done. I'd wanted a distraction and thought the two sides would be drawn to a bloodless stalemate as they always had in recent years.

This was so much worse.

You knew, a nasty little voice said. *You knew exactly what might happen. You just didn't care.*

I shook my head. That couldn't be right. That couldn't be *me.*

"There's a break in the fighting. There." Rune pointed. "Go. I'll follow."

I started to move, right as a soldier stumbled around the corner. He fired his sidearm twice before he went oddly rigid. I recognized the telltale sign of wildling compulsion holding him in place. He fought it, inching for his other weapon.

"That's enough," the wildling hissed. "I'd like you to *cut your own throat.*"

"Don't draw attention," Rune whispered. "We have to—Val!"

I swung around the corner, driving my sword at the wildling. He backed off, barely evading.

"*Enough,*" he said but the compulsion didn't slow my next swing, and Sliver bit deeply into his shoulder. He went down, eyes wide in shock, until I drove my sword through his stomach and he dropped, unmoving. Panting, I stared at my handiwork. Worth it. It'd been worth it. The guilt at killing him would be a small penance for what I'd already done.

"Val?"

Joshua's voice made my heart stop. Out of all the soldiers I could have saved, of course it had to be him.

"You're alive!"

He wrapped me in a tight hug before I could stop him. Physical affection had never been strong between us, so the move was even more shocking. "I thought—after I saw—But you're here, you're *safe.*"

"I'm sorry to do this to you," I said, squirming guiltily out of his embrace. He shouldn't be happy to see me. Shouldn't even want to *look* at me. "I didn't know who else to turn to."

"It doesn't matter; I'm glad you called. Everything's okay now. I've got more agents on the way. The wildlings are going to regret breaching our territory."

He took my arm and tried to drag me like a man possessed, like someone who'd found a precious heirloom they thought they'd lost. As gently as I could, I pried his hand away.

"I'm sorry, Joshua."

"It's not your fault," he said, driving the knife of guilt deeper. "Hurry, I need to keep you close. After what happened..." He scoffed. "I can't believe you survived! When I couldn't find you, I assumed the worst."

I stepped away as he reached for me again. "I can't go with

you yet. I have to do something first, something incredibly important. Give Peyton my love. Tell her I'll be back soon."

Joshua's brow crinkled. "Val, what are you talking about? Peyton is—"

His gaze drifted over my shoulder. I turned.

Rune had reappeared at the edge of the park. The illusion he'd used to conceal his true nature was gone, and his eyes glinted gold-red in the dark.

"Stand back, Val," Joshua said.

I grabbed his arm as he tried to raise his weapon. "Don't. Please. I'll explain later."

"Val, I'm telling you to step back. I can handle this."

"Joshua." I didn't release his arm, trying to convey what I wanted him to know without being forced to say it aloud.

Joshua slowly looked between Rune and me. "What is this?"

"We're leaving, Val," Rune said. "No more goodbyes."

Joshua yanked his arm from me and leveled the pistol at Rune. "Whatever magic you've used on her, undo it right now! I'll give you five seconds before I put a bullet through your heart."

Rune barely spared the gun a second glance. "There's no spell to unravel, nor glamour to reverse. Val—"

"Don't you dare talk to her!"

"Joshua, stop." I stepped in front of him and started backing toward Rune. "Pretend you never saw us. It'll be easier that way."

Joshua searched my face, maybe looking for some sign that I was doing this against my will. "No... Don't tell me. You're... You're working *with* them?"

He looked over at the ongoing fighting, pieces clicking into place. "You brought them. *You* caused this. I knew something wasn't right. Wildlings don't simply cross to the human world unless they have a reason. A big reason. Do you have any idea what you've done, any clue what this means? You're a traitor, Val."

"Look who's talking," I said.

"I've always been loyal—"

"I heard your message to Aleki. Were you trying to undermine the other Lords, or were you setting Aleki up to fail?"

Joshua's stance hardened. He stopped lowering his gun. "That wasn't for you to hear. There are bigger things happening than you understand—"

"Oh, spare me." Fury had temporarily taken the place of fear. Fury at myself? At him? "If I'm a traitor, then you're just as big of one. Let's go," I said to Rune.

The green behind Rune twisted as he called the path.

"You're the reason," Joshua yelled. "You're the reason Peyton's dead!"

I stopped, one foot on the path. "What did you say?"

"I went by to check on her—on both of you—a few days ago."

Joshua raised the gun again. His voice was choked, but the barrel never wavered from Rune. "You were gone, but so was she. No sign of her body, just blood all over the bed and walls. They tore her apart, Val. Did that monster promise she'd be okay? Because if you believed that, then you're a bigger idiot than I ever thought."

This wasn't making sense. Peyton was alive. I'd seen her *alive*. Rune had set his own wildlings to guard her. I'd trusted him to do that, at the very least.

I stumbled, and Rune caught my shoulder.

"Walk the path, now," he muttered.

"Get your hands off me."

"If you ever cared for Peyton, if you ever loved her as much as she loved you, come with me, Val," Joshua said. "Turn yourself in and help me make things right."

"Val—" Rune said.

I didn't see whatever Rune did that made Joshua react. There was a sharp crack, a grunt. Rune jerked, but his arms wrapped around me, too tight to resist, and I was pulled through the path, Joshua screaming my name until the greenery stitched itself closed behind us. We collapsed on the edge of a shoreline in a chilly salt mist spray, waves bashing ceaselessly against the beach.

CHAPTER

SIXTEEN

Rune stumbled away from me, holding his side. Blood leaked from between his fingers, but I didn't care. Not that Joshua had shot or that the bullet might have hit me if Rune hadn't stepped in front. It didn't matter that Rune protected me, because he'd failed to protect the one person I'd cared for most. My anger and sorrow were fuel, and I directed them at him.

The driftwood he leaned against grew a woody arm that held him in place. The rocks and sand coalesced into an extension of my will, wrapping around his throat like hands.

I hated how calmly he watched me. As though he'd entirely accepted death, and if I was the one who brought it, then so be it.

"I see you're putting that power you stole from Aleki to good use," he said. "I wonder how strong you'll be after stealing a few more heart gems."

"You were supposed to protect her!" I screamed, voice colliding with the crashing waves. "That was our deal!"

"I kept her safe as best I could. You had to know her safety wasn't guaranteed."

The sand around Rune's neck tightened, but he didn't so much as flinch. Why couldn't I scare him? Didn't he care about anything, even dying?

"That's no excuse," I snarled.

"It's not. It's a reality. I tried to protect her as best I could, but what did you think would happen when we went up against the most powerful Lords in these Wilds? Did you think they'd play fair? I wasn't strong enough to even keep one of my own safe."

Rune's voice had gone soft, though I couldn't tell if it was from emotion or his air being cut off. "Triss is dead. Others are dead too, and more will die before this is over. I don't keep anyone close, Val. Friends, family, lovers, they're all tools that can be used against you."

I couldn't stand to look at him. The shock was wearing off, and in its place was a gaping void that threatened to swallow me. The sorrow—the tenderness—in Rune's voice only added to the wrongness. He shouldn't be tender. He should be the monster I know so I could continue to blame him.

"I'm sorry, Val," Rune said.

"No, you're not." I pressed my palms against my eyes and the sand stirred at my feet, closed in on him. "You aren't... You could never..."

"We've all lost someone. You can let it destroy you, or you can let it feed you..."

His voice trailed off with the last of his air. I let him stay like that for a moment longer, as his lips began to tint blue and the slightest blush of purple leaked into his cheeks; let him wait to see if I'd be his salvation or undoing, before weariness replaced my anger and I released him. He rolled to the side, sucking in hacking breaths.

"It's my fault," I said. "I shouldn't have ever left her. I should have known one of them would figure out what I was."

"Regrets do nothing but chain you to the past," Rune said. He'd regained his composure, though I could see the bruised marks my magic had left around his neck. "My father said that right before he died. I think he knew what was coming. You have to let them go before you can be truly free."

I wiped at my eyes. I refused to show more weakness, give anyone else something to use against me. "You never let go of the past. Everything you've done has been to get revenge for it."

"And it has brought me nothing but misery. I only have hope that one day it will get better. That *I* will be better."

That was no excuse for letting Peyton die. The more I obsessed over that fact, the worse it got. I was pent up rage with nowhere to go. I was a howling maelstrom, barely contained.

"Did your father's death get easier?" I asked.

Rune thought about this. "No. But I got stronger. And that made all the difference. I—"

He hissed as he moved. I stared impassively as Rune examined his wound like someone would a painting: curious, a little awed.

"You're shot," I said numbly. "You turned me away when Joshua..."

I wouldn't think about that anymore. Not about Joshua, and not what Rune had done when Joshua had fired. I wouldn't give Rune the credit.

"This never would have happened in the Wilds." Rune grimaced and started picking at the edges of the wound. "The metal will poison me if left in too long. I need to dig it out."

I almost let him do just that. What did I care if he ripped his body apart trying to remove it? Or bled out like a hunted animal here on a beach? He would die just as Peyton apparently had. Weak. Bloody. Likely without much struggle.

"*You're better than that.*"

Peyton's voice rang loudly in my head.

"*You're better than* them. *Prove it.*"

"Stop that."

I knelt and shoved his hands away as he continued picking at the wound. This close, it was easy to find Rune's aura and the dark swirling place where the bullet was.

"Marian's been teaching you some of her tricks," Rune said. He groaned as I found the bullet and, inch by inch, pulled it out until the bloody metal fell into the sand, droplets of blood coagulating into pearls of crimson beside it.

Rune barely waited until I'd closed up the last of his skin before getting to his feet. "Thank you."

"Sure."

"The others will be here soon. We need to prepare to meet the King of the Undersea."

At the moment, there was nothing I wanted to do less. I wanted to leave all this. The Wilds, the Lords, the insanity. My life with Peyton was, *had* been, bad in its own ways, but it had made sense. I had a purpose, a sense of who I was.

I had no idea who I was anymore.

I stood and wiped the pebbles from my hand. I walked down the beach until I found a rock I could sit atop. To my left, across the dark, lapping waves, was the black mass of the Wilds Mordecai ruled. I wondered if Joshua was preparing to go there, to retaliate for the wildlings following us into human territory. Somewhere behind me would be the lights of Seattle. My home in the human world. Or where it used to be. I had nowhere to go.

I put my face in my arms and let the feelings wash over me as the tears broke free again.

I felt Rune approach, but he didn't try to comfort me. He

probably didn't know how. How could someone who was broken hope to repair the missing pieces of another?

He left me cold and alone atop the rock. I cried until I had nothing left. Until my sadness had frozen to ice chips of rage that scraped the hollowed-out husk inside me.

You can let it destroy you, or you can let it feed you.

Was this what Rune felt like each time someone who trusted him died? Was this why he shoved Marian away and always acted so cold and indifferent to the wildlings who followed him? If this was the result of caring too much, I would also do anything to never feel it again.

Eventually, Rune returned. He held out a small slice of candied fruit, shaped like a star and glistening with sugar.

"Why?" I asked when I took it.

"You need to keep up your strength. The King of the Undersea will be here soon, and I want you with me."

The fruit's sweetness exploded on my tongue, and the ravenous hollowness of a different kind opened in my stomach. I shook my head. "Our deal's off. You promised to protect her. Now you have nothing to keep me here."

Nothing but my life. We were both thinking it, but either we were past the point where I believed Rune would kill me, or I didn't care if he did.

"You could leave," he agreed. "Go back to Joshua and tell him nothing was your fault. He'll believe you, and it's true. I'm sure the reputation of a wildling isn't golden around the DFA."

He grinned. I didn't.

"You could try to put the pieces of your life back together. Try to push on as though the one you loved wasn't ripped away. Every day you could wake up and pretend there was nothing you could do. Lie to yourself to ease the pain. Or..."

"I could kill the ones who did this," I said. The thought simmered in me, fueled by anger.

"Help me create a Wilds in which that doesn't happen," Rune agreed. "Be my weapon, strong as an oak, honed as a razor."

"No."

"No?"

"I will kill them. But not for you, your throne, or your world. For me. For Peyton."

"Very well. Perhaps, in some ways, that's better." He held out a hand to shake. "Seal it in your human way."

I brushed his hand aside. There would be no deals other than our mutual vengeance. "I'm becoming as bad as you."

"Not yet. And is that such a terrible thing, to be more feared than loved?"

I didn't know.

Marian, Xander, and a few others from the Hollow waited down the shore. Out of reach of the ocean's surf, Raquel was laying a mostly flat slab of wood atop similarly sized rocks to make a table fit for a banquet.

Marian looked surprised to see me. "Rune told us what happened. You're not going to run back home? You're going to let them take more?"

"I'm staying to repay them in kind," I said. "I have nothing left for them to take."

"Not entirely true." But Marian looked satisfied with my answer. Maybe even glad. Xander gave me an encouraging smile, too; one shared by others. To think, all I needed to gain their acceptance was to lose everything dear to me.

"Have you asked for an audience yet?" Rune asked.

"Nearly," a boy named Grand said. He'd tied together what looked to be a collection of glistening holly branches and gnarls of incensed root. "Just needs the, uh, final ingredient. So they know it's not just anybody who wants to speak with him."

Rune stepped over and took a knife from Xander. He made

a shallow cut along his forearm and dribbled his blood across the offering.

While Rune handed the knife back, Grand muttered something over the offering, and part of it caught with the beautiful green-blue glow of everfire. He waded into the surf and, after determining the best location, let the bundle go. I watched the everfire glow drop until the depths swallowed it up.

"Now we wait," Rune said.

I paced the shoreline while the rest prepared and kept to the shadows of the Wilds' looming trees, as though Mordecai's forces across the water could see us.

After I tired of pacing, I helped Marian and Raquel drag more pieces of driftwood to enclose the table. I collected colorful starfish from the tidepools and handed them off so others could prop them on the table, nestled in decoratively woven bunches of sea grass.

"You want to talk about it?" Marian asked. I scooped up a couple urchins that one of Rune's more culinary talented followers had been making into something edible. "Whoever they took from you, I mean?"

"I really don't," I said.

"Good. I'm not great at talking about things like that."

"That's not true," Xander said. "You're great at talking. It's listening you have a problem with."

Marian swiped at him, and Xander scampered out of range, laughing. Grand looked disapprovingly at them while Raquel coaxed a line of crabs up the table to set up the final touches.

After all they'd lost, how could they still find joy? I felt like a barely-functioning, walking husk. I felt as though I'd never laugh again.

I saw Rune standing on a rock above the tide, hands clasped behind his back, watching the waves.

"How did you do it?" I asked the others. "Survived Mog Moren and everything else?"

"Not all of us did," Raquel said.

"One day at a time." Marian sat in a bed of dried bull kelp and set to sharpening her blade. "We had to believe there was something better if we just held on."

"Or we wanted to stay alive to piss off the ones who sent us there." Grand snickered. "*I* wasn't going to give them the satisfaction of dying."

"Rune became sort of a rallying point," Raquel said. "Survival at any cost."

"Why were you there?" I asked. "Why was anyone there?"

"Pick a reason," Marian said. "Family didn't want us or thought we were a threat to their power. Or we made somebody mad, sometimes without realizing it. In some of the Houses, you didn't even have to do anything wrong. Existing was offense enough. In Mog Moren, the guards like taking advantage of the female prisoners, so a lot of children were born there. Mog Moren was all they ever knew."

"Enough about the past," Xander said, more sharply than I'd ever heard him say anything. "The King of the Undersea will be here soon. That's what we should be focusing on."

"And what if he doesn't want to help Rune?" Raquel asked in a soft voice.

Marian drew the whetstone down the edge of her blade with a long, slow stroke. "Then we find another way. I thought this was a bad idea from the start. We didn't need any help to make it this far; we don't need it now."

"It's not just about taking the throne," Xander said. "It's about after. Even if Rune succeeds, he'll need the force of allies to get others to his side until he can amass his own."

"It won't be that easy," I said. The others looked at me. I

shrugged. I knew enough about human history, and had read enough stories about powerful rulers, to guess. "It won't."

Xander opened his mouth to answer as Rune strode over, face glistening with sea spray.

"He's arrived. Marian, Xander, Val, you will sit with me. He'll have his own guard and advisors, and I will have the same."

I grabbed Rune's arm as the others hurried to their places at the table. "I don't know anything about this kind of diplomacy. I shouldn't be with you."

"Don't worry. The Undersea has the same diplomacy style as the Wilds: claws and teeth."

He strode to the edge of the water as a dark shape rose from the churning sea and moved toward shore. I had to swallow a gasp as they came within the ring of everfire. The small entourage of the Undersea rode on the backs of orcas, with the fins of great whites flanking them.

"He's using orcas as horses?" I hissed.

Without turning his head, Rune raised a single eyebrow. "He *is* the King of the Undersea. What did you expect? Eagles?"

The orcas stopped in the shallows, and the figures stepped off and glided through the surf.

"Bendeti." Rune gave a shallow bow, and I mirrored him.

The King of the Undersea gave a small smile but didn't return the bow. His hair was damp and filmy like seaweed. I expected gills, but there were none along the long stretch of his neck, his skin the pale blue like that of a drowned man. He was adorned in rainbow shells, pearls, and jewels, all glistening like plucked stars. Tiny crabs scuttled beneath his sleeves and between the webs of his fingers.

"The one vying for the position of high king," King Bendeti said. "I smelled your blood before my messenger arrived. I had a feeling we'd be meeting sooner rather than later."

His cold eyes moved to me, and I was reminded of deep whirlpools, dark and drowning. "And a human pet. This *is* interesting. I have an inkling of what you desire, but I'll still hear you out."

If Rune was bothered by Bendeti's rudeness, he didn't show it. He swept an arm to the table. "Some light refreshments from our Wilds and your bountiful sea. As a soon-to-be high king in exile, I still provide well for my guests."

"By *providing*, you mean thieving from us?" said a small being with stalked eyes and armored like a crustacean. He sniffed haughtily. "How fitting that you would serve to our king what he already owns. The sort of backhanded trickery I'd expect—"

"Melik, please," the king chastised, and Melik fell into sulky silence. "Pardon my seneschal. He is overprotective."

"I am properly wary, My King," Melik said. "Especially when those of the *land*," he spit the word at Rune, "all seem to want a piece of what is rightfully yours."

"Others from the Wilds have approached you?" Xander said.

"Oh, yes," the king said. "For such interesting reasons and with varying propositions."

We took our places at the table. We hadn't removed our weapons, and at the king's words, my hand strayed to my sword. Marian wasn't subtle about shifting to grab hers, and the lobster-armored guards at Bendeti's back tensed, claws clasped around enormous spears.

Rune looked unconcerned. "I can promise that anything other Lords offered you is a lie."

"And anything you offer won't be?" Bendeti said.

"Do not forget that I am the rightful high king, a claim no other can make. The throne of the high king, if taken rightfully, provides more than status. My power will be amplified. Power that could be very beneficial to you."

"Or detrimental, I suppose, should we not agree to help you?" Melik sniffed. "Your threats are not so subtle as you think, baby king in exile."

Rune smiled and I got the impression that subtlety wasn't what he was going for.

"And how exactly—" King Bendeti started.

There was a muffled gunshot from across the water. About where Joshua and others from the DFA might have landed if they'd chased the wildlings back to their turf. Soft orange bloomed from the dark as a flamethrower went off.

"Oh, dear," King Bendeti said. "Seems some of your kind bit off more than they can chew."

To distract myself from worrying about Joshua, I picked up an enormous crab leg and snapped it in half, taking some delight in making Melik jump.

"Yes, they did," Marian said. "Something we know how to avoid."

"Is that right?" King Bendeti said.

"We know where the heart tree is," Rune said. "We only need the force to approach it."

King Bendeti continued looking at the soft flashes of light from the distant shore.

Rune leaned forward. "My request does require an answer—"

"You cannot have my army, nor a single one of my soldiers," King Bendeti said.

"But—" Xander started. Rune cut him off with a sharp look.

"Care to illuminate me as to why?"

"You're ambitious," King Bendeti said. "You may even be cunning. But you are not the ruler, not yet. There's a very real chance you'll die attaining that title. And if you do and it's revealed that I aided you so obviously?"

His seaweed-like hair swished as he shook his head. "That wouldn't look good to those Lords who remained. They may even turn on *me*. Though I doubt they would make any progress waging a war against the Undersea, they could make it very uncomfortable."

"I see," Rune said. "Then we can expect no help from you."

"I didn't say that."

"My King," Melik said, but King Bendeti held up a hand.

"I would greatly like you—the rightful ruler—on that throne," he said.

I watched King Bendeti closely. A lifetime of dealing with con artists, liars, and cheats had made me hypersensitive to what wasn't being said as much as what was. Bendeti didn't really care if Rune was on the throne or not. If I had to guess, he'd be happy if all the wildlings slaughtered each other and the Undersea slowly consumed the Wilds.

"So generous," Rune said. "Why the change of heart?"

"Because he'd rather you than one of the other Lords, one who's been ruling longer," I said. "You only want the throne, but have no plans after, and aren't as skilled at leading. I'm sure once you took the throne, King Bendeti would have some *suggestions* on how to rule."

"Impertinence!" Melik snarled, slamming a claw-like fist on the table and scattering a stack of oyster shells. "Blatant disrespect!"

"The pet speaks," Bendeti said, gazing coolly at me. "And here I thought you had it under control, Rune."

"If there's one thing I've learned about Val, it's that having her under control is rarely a possibility," Rune said.

I was briefly swallowed by the whirlpool in Bendeti's cold eyes. Perhaps he was wondering how I, a human, got involved in the political affairs of wildlings, why I cared at all. Or maybe he was wondering what it was I had over Rune to get him to allow me to join them at this table.

"You are a strange human," King Bendeti said. "Many of your kind rightly fear us, and yet here you are, willingly putting yourself in the middle of our affairs. You must be brave indeed. Or very, very stupid. Tell me, do you know what it is we of the Undersea do to those who are our enemies?"

"Likely nothing worse than the things I've seen the wildlings do," I said. "Or the things we *humans* do."

"Oh, yes. You humans and your love of violence." King Bendeti gave an indulgent smile. "Perhaps I spoke in haste. Could it be that you have joined us for the thrill of it?"

"Impertinence or not, my *pet* has a point, King Bendeti," Rune said. "Luckily for you, I don't particularly care what your plans for after my accession are, only that I get what is mine."

King Bendeti laughed. He stood, and Melik quickly scuttled to stand beside him. "Excellent. You are much more entertaining than the others. Then my offer of help still stands, and all I ask is a favor."

"And your favor is?" Rune said before I could interject that owing a favor, especially to King Bendeti, who had no love or loyalty to Rune or anyone else, seemed like a very bad idea.

"To be called upon at a later time. It is a good thing to have a future high king owe you something. I will call on you to deliver it when I choose," King Bendeti said. "For that and my help, you get access to your heart tree."

"I'm still waiting to hear of this wondrous help you're promising."

"As you're well aware, Lord Jezaline's and Mordecai's forces guard the heart tree. Nothing but a frontal assault will break through, and even that is likely to fail. They have watchful eyes everywhere. You'll be seen if you approach from anywhere in the Wilds."

"Thank you for reminding us," I said. "Anything else?"

"Anywhere in these Wilds, save one," King Bendeti said, looking irked that I would dare continue speaking. "A secret way."

"And how did you find this out?" Rune said.

"Secrets and information are the most powerful weapons a king can hold. Some free advice, baby king in exile."

"And where is this secret way?"

King Bendeti's smile was as cold as the depths. "Oh, you know it intimately well. It is in Mog Moren, the place of your imprisonment."

SEVENTEEN

"He's lying," Xander said. "That's obvious. He wants you to go back to Mog Moren, get yourself caught, and get out of his way. He's probably working with the other Lords."

"Except that if Rune does get caught, then he wouldn't be able to manipulate him once he has the throne," Marian said. "Val got him to admit as much."

She gave me a grudging nod. I continued running my finger along the rim of the sea-salted goblet while Rune leaned back in his chair, thinking.

King Bendeti and his entourage had slipped back into the waves, leaving Rune's offering untouched. He'd waved his wildlings over to eat what they wanted and had others clear the table. The fighting across the water had stopped, and worry for Joshua gnawed at my gut.

"He also wouldn't get his favor from you," I pointed out. "Which was a terrible idea to agree to, by the way."

"I wonder," Rune said softly, "when it was that I asked for all of your blunt input?"

Marian and Xander fell silent, but I rolled my eyes.

"You need it. You plan on actually trying what he said, right?" I asked. "King Bendeti even told you where to look."

And that bastard's smile had only widened when he'd said, "Through the serpent's mouth."

I didn't know exactly what that meant, but going off the haunted looks the others had worn, and their worry now, it wasn't good.

"It's suicide," Xander said. "The serpent is one of the guards of Mog Moren. We *might* be able to sneak by, but that's a big *might*."

Rune rested his chin on his steepled fingers. I let the silence drag on until it became clear he wasn't going to answer.

"I don't believe this," I said. "The answer is right there at your feet, but you won't take it."

"It's not so easy."

"It's exactly what you wanted. You want the tree; this is the way, Rune."

"Val..." Xander warned.

"I know it's in a terrible place, but you can't be scared—"

The chair toppled as Rune shot up, eyes flashing dangerously. "Don't talk about something you know nothing about!"

"What? Being scared?" I shot back. "I've been scared ever since you brought me to the Wilds. For Peyton. For my life. Of every Lord and wildling we've crossed. Of *you*."

Rune's face didn't soften, but I swore there was surprise in it. "You are stronger than you know. You have little to be scared of."

"And you do? You were thrown into Mog Moren as a weak child, and you still managed to escape. Surely, you're strong enough now."

"It's not..." Rune blew out a breath. "It's not a matter of strength. There are some things all the magic and power in the world can't overcome. I won't—" He sucked in a sharp breath.

"Mog Moren was created to break you down so you won't ever think of trying to escape. Even if you manage to get away, it never leaves you. I won't go back there."

He turned to Marian and Xander. "We'll rest here tonight and leave before dawn. We'll scout out just how formidable the Lords' forces are around the tree."

"I'll go," I said.

Xander's eyes widened. Rune's head snapped to me. "What?"

"I'll sneak into Mog Moren and find my way to the heart tree. Mog Moren's made to hold wildlings, not humans, and I can already resist some magic."

"No." Rune's voice was firm. "You have absolutely no idea what you're offering to do."

"If I can make it to the heart tree, maybe I can find a way to get you all there, too. At the very least, I can distract them—"

"*No.*"

"Rune—"

"You will not," Rune said. "If you do—"

It was my turn to explode at him, "You'll *what*? Kill Peyton? You missed your chance to do that, so what else could you possibly have over me?"

Rune jerked back as though I'd stabbed him again. Then his face morphed into a snarl. "As you once told me, if you were so eager to die, you should have let me kill you. I would have made it much less painful, and far quicker."

He stalked away.

<hr>

I COULDN'T SLEEP. I was too angry from losing Peyton. I was furious at Rune and what he refused to do.

Mostly, I was waiting for everyone else to go to sleep so I could leave.

Whe the night was thickest, I quietly got up. I slipped on Sliver, slung on my backpack, and stole to the beach to pillage what food remained from King Bendeti's visit.

I'd gotten a vague sense of where Mog Moren was based on one of the maps Rune, Marian, and Pitus had been going over earlier. It lay somewhere along the western shore of the peninsula. Probably four days of walking for me. If I made it that far. And even if I did, I had very little idea what to expect once I got there.

The wildlings slept deeper in the trees, high up in branches, or on hidden beds of moss. I kept a wide berth along the beach until I felt I was far enough away to risk ducking back inside. More than once I stopped, forced to resist the urge to go back and let Rune go through with his suicidal plan. What did I care? If he wanted to sacrifice those who followed him on the altar of his stubbornness, why should I stop him?

But I *did* care. That was the problem. After losing Peyton, it was as though a low fever of revenge had taken hold of my body, hot and constant. I didn't have the power to get back at the Lords. But Rune could. Or he could once he was high king. I'd help him reach that. For me.

"Out for a moonlight stroll?" someone said. "Without the moon?"

Marian and Xander blocked my path. Both looked as though they'd been waiting for me.

"I'm not running away," I said. "Not exactly."

"We know," Marian said.

"You're doing something even dumber," Xander said.

"We both know this is a better alternative than what Rune wants to do," I said. "I can't pretend to understand what you all went through there—"

"No, you can't," Marian snapped.

Xander put a hand on her shoulder. "Rune's only trying to do what he thinks is best."

"So, what now?" I asked. "You going to drag me back and tell him what I was up to?"

Xander looked at Marian. "Go get him."

"Get who?" I said as Marian slipped back into the trees.

"I hope you know what you're doing," was all Xander said.

After what felt like entirely too long, my nerves ratcheting higher every minute, Marian returned, Raquel the Beastmaster sleepily stumbling behind her.

"—don't understand why it has to be *now*. We're leaving early enough as it is."

Raquel stopped when he saw me and then looked at the others. "What is this?"

Quick as we could, we explained what was going on. Raquel's thin face drained of blood as we did, and by the time Xander and Marian said that I needed a way to get to Mog Moren, I could tell he was on the verge of exploding with reasons why he couldn't help.

"Rune will kill me if he finds out."

"No, he won't," I said. "He'll kill me. Do you have a way or not?"

"I *really* don't think—"

"Raquel." I gave him my best kindly smile, which, with how out of practice I was, likely came off more like a terrifying sneer. "I know you can do this, and I *promise* you won't get in trouble."

"And if you're dead, that's a promise you won't have to worry about keeping," Raquel muttered. He debated with himself for another few beats and then gave a shaky, defeated sigh. "I have one beast, but... he can only form at night or in the shadows, and he's not the easiest to control.

He'll take you there. I can't guarantee what he'll do after that."

"Will it work or not?" Marian snapped, glancing at where the other wildlings slept. "We don't have all night."

"Whatever the beast, I'll deal with it," I assured Raquel.

"If you say so," Raquel said. "Found him prowling around up north, when the moon was fully covered. He was eating the other beasts in the area, and the nearby wildlings were leaving sacrifices to try to keep him sated."

My stomach tightened. "You're really doing a good job of selling him."

"I'm just being up front about what you can expect. This is your choice. Don't get mad at *me* if it eats you."

I expected him to kneel and conjure this beast from the dirt, but instead he rolled up his sleeves and touched the inside of his upper arm, where a dark stain bled like a tattoo. The stain squirmed and then dripped off his skin like oil. The ground shivered where it landed.

Marian and Xander stepped back as the mud, brambles, ivy, everything on the forest floor began stitching themselves together, covering a solid, invisible shape like a ghillie suit. I could make out the sharp muscles of the beast's shoulders, the indentations of its enormous paws.

I could definitely see its teeth made of thorns and eyes shaped from two dull gemstones, glowing faintly when they turned on me.

"Erebus," Raquel said, though there was a tremor in his voice. The dark mass shifted toward him. "Carry her where she needs to go. *Don't* kill her."

Erebus, my new ride, let out a rattling, steaming breath.

"I mean it," Raquel said.

"I'm not so sure about this anymore," Xander said, and a small part of me agreed with him.

But *I'd* asked for this. Whether because I still wasn't thinking straight or had a death wish, I was going to follow through with it.

Shoulders back to make myself look as big as possible, I approached Erebus. "Take me to Mog Moren."

Those gemstone eyes held on my face. I forced myself to not break their stare. *I am stronger than you*, I thought. *I am stronger.*

You don't believe it, so they won't believe you.

Rune's words, once coming off as mocking, now rang true.

I willed strength into my stance, my voice. "You *will* take me."

Slowly, ever so slowly, Erebus bent the wet moss of his front legs and lowered his body enough that I could swing myself over his immense shoulders and settle in the crook of his back. Briars and sticks stabbed into my legs, but I forced myself to grab the slick bark of a tender sapling right behind Erebus's head.

"Good luck," Xander said. I nodded thanks, trying to ignore the look of fear in Raquel's face.

"I don't even know why you're bothering," Marian said. "You can't get the crown without Rune."

"Then I'll learn whether King Bendeti was telling the truth, and I'll find some way to get Rune to the tree safely," I said. "Don't let him get too mad at you for this."

I squeezed my sapling reins tighter. "Erebus, let's go—"

I was slammed back as Erebus took off. In seconds I was coated in frost and dew and had to clamp my teeth together to avoid biting my tongue off as trees and night blurred past. Erebus never touched the ground. He avoided every patch of moonlight, sticking only to shadows, bending around every trunk so fast it was difficult to force a single breath into my lungs.

How am I supposed to stop him? The thought squirmed into my head as the cold and frost burrowed through my skin and thin jacket and started to freeze my veins and turn my bones brittle. Though Raquel had given the beast specific instructions not to kill me, I wondered if that order applied to death from exposure to the elements.

Just as I was growing truly worried, Erebus skidded to a halt. My hands had frozen around the sapling, and I found myself flipped over Erebus' thorny snout. His hot breath coated my neck. He gave a warning snort, and I let go and scrambled away before he decided to go against Raquel's wishes. My hands crunched dead ferns.

We'd stopped at the edge of the trees, where the shadows ended. Beyond this, the greenery withered to a halt, turning to emaciated trunks, choked stalks, then nothing but dirt. In the distant night gloom, I could just make out an imposing line of circling green, but in the center was a dead wasteland with a deep pit.

I stood and rubbed my freezing hands. Erebus gave another low growl. We locked eyes, and despite my spine feeling as though it'd lost a couple vertebrae, I stood straighter.

"Thank you. I, uh, release you from my service, I guess."

Erebus growled again and then looked past me, to the wasteland. Tender green shoots raised along his back like hackles, as though to say, *you're going there* willingly?

"That's the plan."

I might have imagined it, but I swore he inclined his head ever so slightly. Then his solid form vanished into wisps of shadow, leaving behind only a pile of forest debris.

I walked warily toward the pit. There were a few dead trees to provide me cover. Not that I needed it. Even drawing closer to the edge of the pit, I didn't see any sign of prisoners or guards. Not good. No guards meant they didn't think anyone would ever make it out this far. Or that they didn't care whether you wanted to come in.

I peered over the edge of the pit and fought back a sense of vertigo. It had to be a quarter mile deep. In the center rose a cluster of pointed pillars, dotted with windows lit from within, giving the illusion of an illuminated spike pit.

There was no greenery, not even a husk of vine or leaf. The closest things were clumps of lulling yarrow sprouting from between the cracks in the rock wall. Their spores thickened the air, making me choke. I tied a cloth around my nose and mouth to try to keep the worst of it away. Still, I'd need to be quick. The spores didn't kill, but they were enough to make anyone, even wildlings, disoriented and weak.

Something large flapped over my head. I couldn't see it in the dark, but the dust around me swirled. I crouched, unmoving, as it landed on one of the dead trees, making the entire thing groan as it bent. Red eyes searched the dark.

Quiet as I could, I skirted the outside of the pit until I found a narrow path leading down. Again unguarded. I could practically feel the beckons of Mog Moren. *Come in*, it said. *You may come in at any time, but you'll never come out.*

"That entrance better be here," I muttered and started down.

Though I didn't see anybody, the closer I drew the more I heard the barking shouts of guards and screams of prisoners. Were it not for the spores, I could likely see the entirety of the pit from where I crouched.

At the bottom, the lulling yarrow spore was so thick it made my head spin, even with the cloth. The air stank of sweat and clung to the roof of my mouth. Now that I was down here, I could make out bars over the windows of the central pillars. The open space around them was filled with dirt-built structures where I assumed the guards lived.

Nearby, a group of prisoners was learning to fight in a fenced-in space. Every so often the brutish-looking guards, all wearing white masks caked in powder, grabbed two who were falling behind, gave them sharpened sticks, and forced them to face off against each other. As I snuck past, using the small dirt houses as cover, I heard cheering. One of the prisoners was stabbing the body of another. The guards pulled him off and grabbed two new fighters for the next round.

I swallowed hard, forcing myself to focus. Now I understood why Rune never wanted to come back. I couldn't imagine spending an hour here, not to mention years.

Down here, Mog Moren wasn't as big as it appeared from above. To one side was the gaping darkness of an enormous cave. That had to be my destination.

I started for it, just as a large rock broke from above me, nearly snapping my leg as it rolled past. I shrank back as the enormous shape that'd dislodged it crept silently along the wall. It was easily five times my size, its true form difficult to make out through that yarrow-made haze.

It stopped directly over me. The spores stirred as it sniffed.

Finally, it moved on. I stayed hidden for as long as I could bear, trying to block out the screams of the prisoners.

When I was sure it was safe, I broke for the cave.

Right as a pair of guards stepped out of a house.

"Who the—"

One of them grabbed me, yelling, "We got a runner! Over—"

I hit him, hard. With a curse, he let go long enough for me to free Sliver from its sheath and drive it into his gut. He went down, his shout turning to a final gasp. I spun to stab the other, only to receive an armored backhand. The cloth was knocked off my mouth, and the rush of spores made my world tilt.

I hit the ground and rolled on instinct, needing to get far enough away from him to reorient myself. I frantically felt for Sliver. I could feel the earth tremble as the guard stalked toward me.

"Stay down, girl. There's nowhere to go."

My fingers found Sliver's blade right as the guard grabbed my hair and pulled me up. "I *said*—"

I twisted, slamming Sliver's hilt into his temple, knocking his mask off. His eyes rolled back as he collapsed, but our scuffle hadn't gone unnoticed. More guards streamed out of the houses. Shouts rang out. I could break for the cave, but with that thing along the wall watching and the guards already alerted, my best bet was to hide out and wait for a better opportunity.

The central pillars were closest. Thin, worn stairs with no railing ringed the outside, wooden doors with bars on them inset into the stone. The bases of the pillars themselves created a maze-like network where I could lose the guards for a time, but—

A hand wrapped around my mouth and pulled me out of sight. I rammed my elbow back.

"Stay—*uff*—quiet!" Rune whispered.

"Rune!"

He released me, and I gaped at his furious face. "What are you doing here?"

"That's what I should be asking you. This..." He radiated so much menace that for a moment I was more scared of *him* than our predicament. "This is the stupidest thing you've done yet, and that's quite a list to top." He jerked his head back toward the path out of the pit. "We need to go before there's no other chance of escape."

"The guards are already onto me."

"Yes, thoughtful of you to cause a diversion. I barely had to kill anyone to get in here."

I hoped he was joking. He probably wasn't. "Why *are* you here?"

He gave me a long look. "I knew you'd try this. You, with your ridiculous ideas—"

"You mean the best chance we have—"

"—charging to your death—"

"—with you right alongside me, apparently."

"You were correct. I am much stronger than when I left," Rune said. "But that doesn't mean I want to linger."

His skin was speckled with sweat, breathing shallow. His eyes were slowly dilating. He was about to lose it, and if I had to keep an eye on him while avoiding capture, that could mean both of our deaths. Adrenaline or rage was likely the only reason he'd made it this far.

I stood. "We have to find a place to hide."

Rune took a rattling breath. I thought he was going to freeze up right then, but he picked himself up, and together we moved carefully through the dim maze of the column's base, keeping an ear out for guards.

I checked the next corner and snapped my head back. A group of guards were heading our way. No escape that direction.

"They're behind us, too," Rune muttered. "Close."

His back was pressed against the rough stone, and he started sinking to the floor. "I hope you came looking for a fight because we're about to get one."

There had to be another way. I wouldn't die in this hell, so close to finishing what needed to be done.

The soft patter of feet closed in on us. Someone grabbed my arm.

I spun, pressing Sliver's tip to the small depression of a

boy's neck. He was close to our age, early twenties at most, eyes hard, cheeks sunken, and skin the same sallow color of yarrow spore that caked everything in here.

We each held our breath, waiting for the other to make the first move. Would he scream to the guards, maybe to gain favor or get him out of the next round of punishments? Would Rune or I have to slit his throat right here?

Rune slowly pulled back my blade arm. "What do you want?"

If it was possible, the boy's face grew harder. "You've stirred them into a frenzy. If you don't want to die, follow me."

EIGHTEEN

"Forgive our lack of refreshments. We don't have food. Or anything to drink. Strangely, the guards neglected to provide either today. Perhaps they'll remember tomorrow."

The old woman gave a dry chuckle, almost as dry and cracked as the wrinkles on her face. Rusted circlets of metal held up the ringlets of her gray hair. Old blood and dirt caked her jagged fingernails, and she leaned heavily on a crooked cane etched with symbols I didn't recognize. "Mog Moren is not known for being especially hospitable. But you already knew that."

Rune didn't answer. The moment we'd entered, he'd crouched in the corner next to a horizontal slab of stone that served as one of the two tiny beds in the miniscule room. His fingers were splayed in front of him, head bent, eyes closed. I wasn't sure if he'd had a full-on panic attack, but he wasn't responding to anyone.

"Thanks for helping us," I said to the old woman.

"And no thanks to you for putting us in danger for it."

The door cased shut as the boy who'd led us up here

returned. He glared at me then peered out the bars, likely to double-check the guards weren't climbing the numerous levels to where their room was. "Lucky they didn't lock us in for the night. If they'd have seen me, it'd have been over for all of us."

"Cassius, peace," the old woman said. She rubbed her swollen knuckles. "I have witnessed many things in my time, but never have I seen a human in the company of Mog Moren's most famous former resident. Rarely have I seen a human at all who wasn't on the end of my spear."

She looked too old to be any sort of threat, but that meant nothing in the Wilds. I shifted Sliver on my hip, ready to draw it.

She gave a crackly laugh. "Tell me, girl, are you frightened of me?"

"Should I be?"

"If you've been in the presence of wildlings such as Rune and are still alive, then perhaps not. I've killed many humans who tried to destroy my Wilds, and many in turn killed my soldiers."

"You sound formidable," I said, erring on the side of flattery. The woman smiled, as though she knew exactly what I was up to.

"Was, child, *was* formidable."

"You're speaking to Narita Forcheck, human," Cassius said proudly. "Former General of the Killing Green, and you will show her respect."

Rune lifted his head slightly.

"Come now, Cassius," Narita said. To me, "There is no recognition or expectation in your eyes, and for that I'm grateful. The worst are those who come to me and have hope, for I have none of that to offer. I am not the general I once was. Obviously, since I'm wallowing here."

"But you *were* a general," I said.

"From Wilds farther south, yes, around what you knew as Yosemite. But as often is the case in our Wilds, power and respect breed mistrust. After a new Lord's bloody coup, I was banished from there and found myself in Mog Moren when I refused to pledge loyalty to the Lords of these Wilds. They're a spineless lot with no honor. I'd rather be in Mog Moren than serving them. Though I'd have spared my family the same fate."

"I would rather be here, too, than with them," Cassius said fiercely.

"No, you would not. I would have you free, even if it meant my death." Narita swiped her cane as one might sever a head. "Come away from the door, child, before you invite the trouble you're trying to avoid."

Cassius sighed as though they'd had this argument before. He took the only other chair, flashing Rune a dark look as he did. "What are you two doing here? You weren't captured." He nodded to my sword. "Not with that. Tried to start a riot? Wandered a little too close and thought you'd escape the vulture above?"

"We broke in," I said.

Cassius gawked. Even Narita cocked an eyebrow.

"Nobody willingly comes here," Cassius said.

"You obviously haven't met Val," Rune said.

"He speaks," I said. I waited for him to join the conversation, but after a minute it seemed he'd sunken back into sulking silence.

Without giving away our mission to find the heart tree, I told Narita and Cassius about the cave we needed to get to.

"Wish I'd known you were doing that before I risked my neck saving you," Cassius said. "You might as well go get caught now and let the guards finish you off."

"Cassius," Narita crooned. "Peace—"

"I will *not!*" Cassius said and then glanced at the door. His voice turned to a tense whisper, "They come all this way for some...secret path, not thinking what it would mean if *he* were caught."

Cassius jabbed a finger at Rune, and when there was no response, he bristled. "You have no idea what you are to people in here, do you, *Rune?*"

Rune's eyes remained closed, fingers pressed against his forehead, turning the skin pale.

"Maybe you could tell me," I said. "Who is he to the others here?"

"A survivor," Cassius said. "He escaped. And not just him, half a dozen wildlings with him, maybe more. They worship him in here. You want to talk about hope?" he said to Narita. "*He* is hope. Everyone who has even an inkling of getting out dreams of joining him. And now here he is, and he's pathetic."

He's stronger than he looks, I wanted to say. *He's one of the strongest people I know.*

"We have all suffered differently, Cassius," Narita murmured.

"Is that so?"

I stood, angling myself between Rune and Cassius as Cassius stalked to him. I didn't think he'd actually try anything, thin and sickly-looking as he was, but I wasn't going to risk it.

"My little sister was taken away a week after we were thrown in here," Cassius said. "The guards used her until they broke her, then they fed her to one of those beasts that guard this place. Did you hear that, Rune? How about this: my brother died in their forced fights. They're supposed to train them up to join the local Lords, but sometimes the guards get bored. He was stabbed so many times I could barely recognize his body."

He choked. "I'm starting training next week. I know some make it, but I won't. Is that enough suffering for you?"

"You're of my blood," Narita said. "You will endure."

Cassius wiped at his eyes. "I won't. You know I won't. But here I am, still fighting. I had hope because of you and what you did, and now you're here ..."

He collapsed in his chair, head between his legs. Narita rubbed his back before easing herself to her feet, joints cracking. She pounded the tip of the cane against the floor three times.

"Though I don't agree with my grandson's tact, I agree with his point. You, Rune, were given a chance many of us would have killed and died for. I knew of your father and his spirit, and to see yours so broken is not becoming of his memory. Do you remember me from when you were here last?"

Rune gave the barest of nods, and the corner of Narita's mouth twitched.

"I admit I kept a far distance from many I helped. My heart has hardened over the years, but still it's stricken with every loss. I would save myself some pain if only to save others from it. I helped you, in the little ways that those in here can. Would you throw that all in my face by coming back here and refusing to fight?

"If you want that throne as bad as the rumors say you do, then you have to get up and earn it. Don't let what happened to you here in the past ruin that. Don't let the shackles of fear hold you. There is more than enough holding us here as it is."

Rune still didn't move, and I figured it was my turn. I crouched beside Rune, looking for some indication he was listening.

"I can't imagine what you went through. But you're not that same boy anymore. You're stronger. You'd better be, because we still have to get out of here and get that crown, and

I need your help to do that. Are you going to screw me over before you can rub victory in my face?"

A flicker of a smile twitched at the corner of Rune's lips. "You are terrible at elegant speeches and encouragement, did you know that?"

"Much like you, I find brutality can sometimes be more effective than honeyed words."

"Indeed," he murmured. At last he opened his eyes. There was still fear in them, but his posture was rigid as he stood.

"I only wish my father had you as a general a long time ago," he said, giving Narita a small bow. "Perhaps things would have turned out different."

"What a pair of silver tongues you two are," Narita said, but she was clearly pleased.

"You are not going to die in the fights," Rune said to Cassius.

Cassius looked up, the splotches on his cheeks lending some pallor to his sickly paleness. "But—"

"You are not going to die. You are not going to give them that pleasure. Because you can only get revenge if you're alive."

Rune studied his hand. He rubbed the dirt between his fingers. "I will tell you what revenge means to me. When I was brought here, I met another boy named Kosta. It was he who got me through the first few weeks, the ones where they try to do everything to break you. You know what I'm talking about."

Cassius slowly nodded.

"Kosta was like a brother. He was the only one, at first, who believed we could make it out. We spent weeks planning, growing stronger, as much as we were able to on a diet of sour berry juice and silty water and rotten fruit. We tried to remind ourselves that the Wilds hadn't left us, that it was right out there, and we still had a connection to it. And when we actually *did* escape, I thought for sure that was the end of this hell.

But we were caught soon after that. We were brought back here. My cousin Vanesi heard about what I'd done and came to visit."

I had a sinking feeling in my stomach.

"She wanted to break my spirit, wanted to make sure I never tried to escape again, so she made me slit Kosta's throat."

Narita bowed her head, and Cassius mumbled, "Sorry."

"I'm not," Rune said. "It would have been better if she'd let him live. What she did, what the guards did after that, only helped fuel me. The second time I escaped was the last. I have since killed Vanesi and paid her back in kind. Like me, if you want any chance of revenge, you have to stay alive, no matter what."

Cassius clenched his fists. "I don't know—"

"You don't have to know. You just have to do. Stay alive. Build alliances but don't let the guards know. And when I'm high king, I'll bring this place to the ground, and you will get your chance at vengeance."

"A noble speech, so unlike your human friend," Narita said. She heaved herself up and hobbled to the door. "But now it's time to go. The guard will be calming down, and they will start patrolling again. You don't want to be here when they come by."

Rune nodded, jaw still tight. He was frightened, I could tell that much, but the worst of Mog Moren's terrible memories had been shrugged off.

"General of the Killer Green, if you survive this—*when* you survive this—find me. Your expertise would be greatly appreciated."

Narita cackled. "I suppose retirement isn't suiting me. And if *you* survive this, king-who-is-yet-to-be, I might take you up on that offer."

I thanked Narita and Cassius, and Rune and I slipped out and made our way carefully down the steps.

"I wish I could have met Kosta," I said. "I wish I could have helped *you* when you first escaped, just like you helped me."

"I think that debt has been repaid in our time working together."

I nudged him. "Is that what you call this? Working together?"

Rune smirked. "I have found many instances where it would be far more detrimental to work against you than with you."

We reached the final spot of cover. All that stood between us and the cave was fifty yards of open ground. We were about to break for it when a lone guard appeared out of the haze. He gaped at us, pointed, started to shout.

In a blur, Rune was on him, driving him into the ground. "Run," he snarled at me.

As though spilling from an upset ant hill, more guards joined the first, far more than we could hope to handle. Rock clattered from the wall on my right, threatening to trip me up. The creature was back. In seconds, it was keeping pace with me, and I poured on the speed for the final few yards, hoping it didn't pounce.

I practically slid into the cave, Rune right behind, and the beast and guards all stopped. They jeered as they stalked around the entrance but didn't step foot inside. They obviously thought we were going to die in here. What had King Bendeti led us to?

I kept Sliver drawn as we walked deeper into the cave. It was nearly as large as a football stadium, lulling yarrow sprouting from the cracked stone. We skirted around enormous fallen boulders, heading toward the back. A strange rattling sound shook the air.

"It's breathing," Rune whispered.

I rounded the next boulder, and my own breath stilled.

Peyton once showed me a Harry Potter movie, the second one, I think, with the basilisk. The giant snake curled along the wall might not be able to turn us to stone with its gaze, but it was enormous. More than my sword could cut through, with its armored bark for scales, a body that was a single line of rigid muscle, and a head that could snap me in two with a single bite. The venom leaking from the corners of its mouth hissed as it ate grooves in the rock.

I took a step back and ran into Rune. I must have made some noise—maybe the beast could feel my rapidly quickening heartbeat—because one of its eyes opened. It narrowed to a slit.

I practically collapsed into cover alongside Rune. I listened to the dry slithering of scales as it uncurled its long body, inch by inch. I imagined it peering at where we hid, as though we were children playing a very adult game.

I see you, snacks.

Rune shocked me by holding my shaking hand as the slithering drew closer. His face was drawn, ear cocked as the sound grew louder then moved past. Everything was quiet again.

He peered from our hiding spot. "Gone. Temporarily."

"What now?"

"You could be bait," Rune said. "Since you so love your high-risk endeavors. It likes things still moving. Habit, I think, more than instinct. The guards feed it some of the prisoners when they get bored of the forced fights."

I swallowed around the queasy feeling in my stomach. "Or we look for a way to the heart tree in another cave that *doesn't* have a giant snake."

"There is no other cave here. I knew this was the place King Bendeti spoke of the moment he said it."

"And there's no getting out and trying another way?"

"No. Not even I have enough power at the moment."

"You seem to be holding up just fine now."

"I," said Rune, "am terrified. I feel like a child again, waiting for my next beating. This place strips you of everything you are. It turns you from a wildling to nothing more than an animal to be used for others depraved sport or pleasure."

Rune glared at the cave entrance where the guards paced, no doubt imagining killing every single one. "But I won't let it control me, not any longer. We are getting to that heart tree. I am getting my throne. And when I am high king, I will bury this place and everyone responsible with it."

I touched his arm. He looked down at it, surprised. I was a little surprised myself. "Watch it. That sounded almost noble."

He gave me a wicked grin. "I'll have to watch that bad habit."

"Or maybe don't. And thank you. You know, for coming after me."

"Make no mistake, you and I will have a very intense discussion about this when we're done."

"You could just say you're welcome."

Rune's lips twisted as though he'd never uttered the words before. "Perhaps I will. You have a way of getting me to do things I don't want to. And I'm starting to think that not all of that is a bad thing."

"Rune—"

A shape rose behind him. For as massive as it was, I hadn't heard the snake return, hadn't seen it move. Not until it struck.

Rune twisted, but it was too late as one of the snake's fangs sank into his shoulder.

CHAPTER

NINETEEN

Rune snarled. He twisted again. There was the crack of magic, and the snake reared back, hissing. It slunk back into the maze of boulders then slithered up the walls, its scales somehow keeping its immense weight gripping the rock. I could hear it coiling in the deep shadows of the cave roof, seeking another opportunity to strike.

I tried to help Rune to his feet. "Can you stand?"

"Of course," he gritted out. He could, but already the snake's venom was turning the veins of his neck purple, moving toward his face. We had minutes, maybe, before he succumbed to it.

"Val—"

Rune dragged me behind him as the snake struck again. Its mouth collided against the thin barrier of earth Rune conjured, before drawing back to try again.

"Ideas would be great," Rune grunted.

The extent of my plan at the moment was to stab at something I couldn't reach. "You expect me to have one?"

"You have a knack for surviving things you shouldn't. I figured it was a safe bet."

Of course he thought that. But I realized he was right, I did have an idea. A terrible, desperate one.

"With me."

The ground trembled as the snake dropped to the floor and slithered after us. A boulder exploded as it pummeled through, showering us with chunks of rock.

"It's—" was all Rune managed before the snake lashed out again.

I pulled Rune to one side and we tumbled into a divot in the cave wall. My knees and legs scraped rock, and Rune cursed. The snake's head struck, but miracle upon miracles, it couldn't reach us.

"*This* was your plan?" Rune said. "I take back what I said. You've only escaped death by dumb luck."

He looked so terrible I didn't bother snapping back. I scrambled farther away from the opening as the snake struck again and again. Droplets of venom hissed as they sprayed the ground at my feet.

"Val..." Rune said.

"I know!"

"Do you have any idea—"

"I *know*. Don't let it kill me."

The snake drew back for the next strike.

I darted forward, swiping through the stalk of one of the lulling yarrow growing from the wall.

The spore-filled head of the yarrow was heavier than it looked, causing me to mis-time my retreat. I blocked just in time for the snake's fangs to knock me down. Stars bloomed in my vision.

I stumbled to my feet as the snake reared up.

"Not yet…" Rune said. He'd clearly caught on to my plan. "Hold… Now!"

The snake struck. Its head lodged in the opening of our hiding place. Venom burned my skin as I wedged Sliver between the tongue and roof of its mouth, holding it open long enough to throw the yarrow down its throat.

"Now, Rune!"

He was already grabbing a shard of earth and hurling it with inhuman force. It hit the yarrow head. The snake bit down, and I heard Sliver snap and felt a wave of hot, spore-filled breath wash over me.

The snake thrashed as it drew back. It smashed into a couple of the boulders and coiled over itself. I ducked as its tail smashed the wall. Eventually its movements slowed and the ground shook with its collapse.

"Dead?" I asked, swaying on my feet.

"Asleep," Rune said. "For now."

His words came out as a guttural choke. He'd collapsed against the wall. The purple venom running through his veins had turned black, and some leaked down his collarbone. He looked moments away from death.

"I need…" Rune managed. His hand twitched toward me. "You to…"

The spores had taken its toll on me, but I forced myself to stagger over and stand over him as he gasped for shallow breath. It seemed impossible, but I knew what he was trying to ask. "Say it. Say what you need."

"I…need…" His eyes were nearly black. "You know…what…it is…"

I collapsed to my knees. "I want to hear you ask for it."

I'd never seen such bitter disgust in Rune's face, though directed at me or himself I couldn't tell. There was something else there, too. Maybe…relief? Relief at surrendering even this small part of himself.

"Help," Rune whispered. "I need help."

"There, that wasn't so hard," I slurred. I nearly pitched forward onto him as I leaned over. Rune caught me, steadied me, hissed a little as the movement caused the wound to twinge.

"A little trust is all," I said.

"Like you…trust me?"

"Of course not. I don't trust you." *Liar.* And that was the problem. That had *been* the problem for some time.

"Val… I'd appreciate it if you hurried."

The strangest thing was that I didn't even consider using his predicament to my advantage. No wonder I was in the situation I was. I was too soft.

"Hold still."

It was a simple thing to find his aura.

"Easy," Rune hissed as I practically ripped his shirt to expose the wound. "With that much passion, a man might get the wrong idea."

I placed my hands around the angry puncture marks and willed the venom to leave his swollen veins and the skin to close up. It took a few tries, but at last it seemed I'd gotten the worst of it out.

Exhausted, I slumped against him, face resting in the warm crevice of his neck and shoulder. "Maybe a man would, but you're not a man."

"You're right." He might have actually sounded gentle, or perhaps I imagined his tender tone as I slipped into sleep. "I'm something worse. For your own good, never forget that."

It was dim when I returned to the waking world. My tongue smacked of yarrow spores and my muscles ached, though I was surprisingly comfortable. I might have slept for a few hours. I might have slept for a few days.

Rune's voice tickled my ear. "Did you have a nice nap?"

My legs were intertwined with his, my body in the crook of his side, face nuzzled beneath his chin.

"Rune," I said, trying to keep my voice even. "What are you doing?"

"Me? Simply trying to get the crown of the high king. But then you started grabbing me, and I found it exceedingly difficult to continue. You're very strong, even in your sleep, did you know that? I've encountered leeches less resilient to attachment than you are."

I closed my eyes for a moment. He had *not* just compared me to that again. "I was disoriented and not thinking."

"You're not either of those things anymore, and yet here we remain—Ow."

I pushed off him, hand brushing his still-tender wound in the process. My head swam before the world righted itself. We hadn't moved from where I'd healed him.

"You were supposed to leave," I said.

"This may come as a shock, but I've never been good at doing things I'm supposed to."

"Rune, why didn't you go for the tree?"

Rune stood. He offered me a hand up, but I didn't trust myself to take it. I couldn't make this situation any more awkward than I already had.

I got to my feet and saw the snake, still asleep, just outside our hiding place. The violent rush of what I'd done had me steadying myself against the wall.

"You idiot!" I hissed. "That thing could have woken up! You should have left me!" *Why didn't you leave me?*

"It'll be a while before it awakens," Rune said, unconcerned. "You recovered from that lulling yarrow much faster than I expected."

"Guess I'm lucky."

Rune threw me a half grin. "Yes, that's it. You were *lucky*."

"We need to move," I said, dismissing his insinuation.

Rune stepped to the open mouth of the serpent and ripped something free from the flesh. He handed me Sliver—what was left of it, anyway. The blade had snapped in the center, leaving me with a still-sharp, but much-less-effective bottom half.

"Xander will be disappointed at how you treat his gifts," Rune said. "He might not even care that it saved your life."

I shouldn't be broken up over the loss of a sword, but I felt sadness all the same as I sheathed what remained of it. Rune went to where the snake had been sleeping before we'd disturbed it. "Seems I'm indebted to King Bendeti after all."

There was a hole in the cave floor wide enough for a human to slip in. It was impossible to see the bottom. My stomach squirmed.

"You think there are more snakes down there?"

"There might be. But I can guarantee you there's a snake up here," Rune said.

Without preamble, he leapt into the hole, the dark swallowing him up.

I dreaded to hear the dull thud of his body hitting bottom, but a moment later, he called up, "By all means, take your time." He paused. "Strange. It's not difficult to see."

Pulse pounding, I turned and began crawling down, my feet touching ground not ten feet later. Rune was right, I could see, too. The tunnel was awash in a familiar blue-ish hue.

I rounded the corner and found Rune standing beside a

crystal twice his size. Dozens of them, equally sized, lined the tunnel.

"Look familiar?" he said.

"I don't get it. Where are they coming from?" I said. "Were they in Mog Moren last time you were here?"

"Not above. I obviously never ventured down here."

His face reflected off the smooth surface as he stepped closer. "Something's not right about them."

"You mean besides them showing up in the Wilds and no wildling having any clue what they are or where they came from?"

"None except for you. You're the only one to whom they've had any response."

I bristled. "We don't even know if it was me, or some coincidence."

If I didn't know Rune, I would have thought his smile playful. "You don't honestly believe that."

"I'm saying it's not *impossible*." I circled the crystal, instinctively crossing my arms. "But...what if I have something to do with them...? What does that mean?"

I dreaded Rune's answer as he stared at me for a long time. "It means that you are an enigma."

He continued down the tunnel. I lingered around the crystal. The others in the Wilds had felt strange, but this one felt... *good*. The energy emanating from it felt like a pleasant buzz on my skin.

"Val!" Rune said sharply.

I drew what remained of Sliver and rushed to catch up with him. "What is it—"

Trees, some rivaling the gargantuan size of those in the Wilds, filled the enormous cavern I'd stumbled into. All of them—every bough, leaf, and root—was made of blue crystal.

I turned in a circle, mouth hanging open. "How is this possible?"

"I don't know," Rune said, clearly irked at that. "We have to keep moving."

I lingered, brushing my hand against the nearest tree. I expected, upon closer examination, to find some flaw with them. Maybe, like the first heart tree, there was some glamour or illusion. Or maybe, like Rune's throne, the crystal was only a thin layer, a parasite of sorts that had preserved an entire grove that once existed down here.

But the entirety of the tree was solid crystal, so clear I could nearly see to the center of its trunk. It hummed with magic as I drew my hand away and followed Rune.

"Are these the same thing as heart gems?"

Rune looked back at me. "What are you talking about?"

"The heart gems always looked somewhat crystal-like to me. I was wondering if these were the same thing."

"Absolutely not. These are..." He looked at the nearest tree. I could almost fill in his unspoken words: *These are going to be a problem.*

Rune shook his head. "Let's hurry—"

He turned and stumbled to a stop. In the next tree was a person, a human or wildling I couldn't tell, half grown in the trunk. They were made entirely of crystal and were reaching out as though begging someone to pull them free. The howling scream forever chiseled on their face sent shivers down my arms.

"You didn't touch any of them, did you?" Rune said.

My hand tingled. "You're right; let's get out of here."

I tried not to let my fear fester as we wove our way through the rest of the grove. There was no proof that touching that tree had turned whoever that was to crystal. But it was only when we'd crossed the cavern and were back in a narrow tunnel that I allowed myself to breathe normally.

I nearly bumped into Rune as he slowed. "You can't tell the others about this. Not yet."

"How about, 'Val, could you please not tell the others about this?' Why sure, Rune, I can wait so we don't freak them out. Thanks for asking so nicely."

It was almost strange to see Rune smile. "Please. One problem at a time. Freaking them out could get them killed."

"Well, since you asked so nicely, I won't."

"Good. For now, we forget *that* exists."

I'd try, but the buzzing on my skin and the haunting, screaming face of the crystal person wouldn't leave my mind.

I wasn't sure how many miles we walked.

Rune kept up a relentless pace, only stopping to rest a couple times when I told him we might have to fight and that he would be too weak for it if he didn't slow. He'd grumbled but relented.

The tunnel eventually angled up. Rune stopped at the exit, where the blue light of the crystal and the thin red of dawn traded places.

"Prepare for anything," he said. "If they attack, kill as many as you can. The moment I have the crown, we leave."

"And if there are too many of them?" I asked.

"We'd better hope there aren't."

Not the least bit encouraged, I crept out of the tunnel with him, brushing aside the thick ferns and spider's webs that concealed our exit. No wonder it had been a secret. Someone would have to literally fall in to discover it.

"There," Rune breathed.

It was impossible to miss the heart tree. It grew in the center of an open clearing, giving off an ethereal light that set it apart from every other tree. The silver and gold leaf-covered ground at its base looked soft as silk and quiet as death, save for a faint, steady beat like a drum. It seemed the right kind of perfect, not an illusion.

I didn't see a single wildling. I didn't see any other wildlings. Not a flicker of gold-red eyes or the faint brush of a leaf.

"This is too easy," I whispered.

"Or it's as it should be," Rune said. "As long as King Bendeti didn't share this little path with anyone else—and he has no love for the other Lords, or even me—then we've given them the slip."

"We should still—"

But my words fell on deaf ears as Rune started toward the tree.

I grabbed his arm. "Did you forget what happened last time? We're not doing that again. Let me go first, make sure it's safe."

Rune considered this for all of three seconds and then pulled from my grasp. "What good would you be, my tricky little fox, if you couldn't come to my aid? If there is a trap, I will spring it, and you will save me from it."

I grabbed for him again, but he'd slipped away.

Cursing Rune and his stupidity, I circled the clearing until I found slender reeds hugging a creek bank where I could hide, distant but still watchful. Despite my trepidation, it seemed Rune was right.

The silver and gold branches shivered as Rune stepped beneath them. He pressed a hand firmly against the trunk, and the heartbeat sound sped up.

"It recognizes the rightful ruler," he said. He looked up at the trembling branches, his face consumed with a longing that made me hurt just looking at it. I hadn't truly understood, not until I'd been in Mog Moren, the hope this tree had brought him.

"Stay back," Rune said.

I crouched deeper in my hiding place as Rune dug his fingers into the bark, so deep that amber sap leaked onto his hand. He closed his eyes as the emanating hum grew louder, vibrating my bones.

"Blood of my father," Rune said, "child of the Wilds, true king over all other Lords, I am Rune, and I claim this crown and with it reclaim my throne."

The tree's branches began to twist on their own. Limbs rose as new sprigs of silver and gold leaves sprouted and melted together. More branches knit these melted parts into a crown. The delicate crest enfolded snarls of silver thorns, raven's feathers, and jeweled berries. When it was finished, it lowered toward Rune. Without opening his eyes, he reached up and removed the thin circlet of ivy and nightshade he'd worn since I'd met him.

"I will ruin those who stand against the throne," Rune said, "and destroy any who seek to threaten it. With my reign ends the Sundering. With my reign, the Forming will be made complete, any Reclamation stalled. Grislehaut's destruction will be halted, and Rhasahlyn's peace made true."

The branches placed the crown atop his head, and Rune shivered.

"The Wilds will rule forevermore," he murmured.

"How eloquently put."

My heart stuttered as Cobb stepped from the other side of the clearing. "Though I have one *slight* correction."

Like zombies, Jezaline's soldiers rose from the earth. Before

Rune could move, they held his arms, and one punched him in the gut. The crown slipped from his head, and Cobb caught it. It glittered as he turned it over in his hands.

"You finally played your part after all, Cousin. You might be the only one who could get the crown, but not the only one who can wear it. That honor belongs to me." Cobb placed it atop his head and sighed. "Where it should be."

"You were right," Mordecai said. "He was drawn to it like a vulture to a rotting carcass."

"A crude comparison, but apt," Jezaline said. I crouched lower, scarcely daring to breath. Where had they come from?

"Rune..." Jezaline clucked, lifting his chin. "I distinctly remember banishing you, under pain of death."

Rune sucked in a shuddering breath before answering. "I vaguely recall something like that."

"I'm sure you do. Luckily for us, you are more foolish than we thought, and our other heart tree didn't kill you."

"That almost ruined everything," Cobb grumbled.

"Cobb, how were *we* to know that behind your feeble facade lay a conniving mind?" Mordecai said. "We thought he would relay our trap to you, dear Rune, and that would be that. But Cobb had planted an irksome seed in our heads by convincing us to banish you."

"Loyalty," Cobb said, sneering. "Something in very short supply among many who believe in the old ways."

"You mean those who aren't a fan of having their rightful rulers murdered?" Rune said.

"But how to instill loyalty and unite them?" Cobb went on as though Rune hadn't spoken. He touched the crown. "The high king. A *true* high king, one who would be stronger than any before. You have no idea how long I've waited for this moment."

Rune stared at him. Then he began to laugh.

"You," he said. "Luella told me Aleki wasn't the one who sent me to Mog Moren, but I didn't believe it. Now I see, and I'll admit I am impressed. I probably did you a favor killing Aleki and Vanesi. Something you never had the guts to do yourself. With their deaths, that left only—"

"You," Cobb agreed. "The next in line, last heir to the House of the Fallen Star."

"I'll bet you tried so hard to forge the crown without me." The guards held Rune tighter as he moved toward Cobb. "Tell me, how many times did the tree reject you? Ten? Twenty? Did you beg? Offer it anything? How long did it take before realizing that you need me?"

Cobb jabbed Rune's neck, and he dropped to a knee, hissing as his neck smoked. "Not any longer, I don't."

"We other Lords believe that Cobb will make an excellent high king," Mordecai said. "He will unite the wildlings of each kingdom and bring peace."

"And he will leave us to run our own lands, as promised," Jezaline said, voice laden with threat.

"Of course, all as we promised," Cobb said.

"You could have just killed me," Rune said. "Or would the heart tree not accept you even then? Did you not wish to bloody your soft hands? You might have the crown, dear cousin, but you remain as unwanted and worthless as always."

Cobb's face purpled with rage. "I feel no need to explain anything to a soon-to-be corpse. Take him to King's Hollow. We'll kill him there in front of everyone."

"You'd better do it now," Rune said. "Otherwise, I promise I'll be the last thing you ever see."

"Unlikely," Mordecai chuckled.

Jezaline summoned a path. Rune caught my eye.

Hold on, I mouthed. I would escape, find my way back to Xander and Marian and the others, somehow. If we were quick, we might be able to save him.

"I think you're forgetting someone," Rune said. He jerked his head directly at me. "She'd like to join the fun."

TWENTY

Before I could move, the hands of Jezaline's guards reached from the murk and dragged me from my hiding place.

"You idiot!" I spat at Rune. "I would have saved you!"

"Would have, should have, could have," Rune said. "Consider this my ascension gift to you," he said to Cobb.

"Search for any others," Cobb said. The whorls of the surrounding guards turned to Jezaline, who sent them away with a wave of her hand.

"This is the human from before," Mordecai said, bouncing around me. "Incredible that you're still alive, though I'm afraid that ends now."

A knife appeared in his hand. I couldn't move so much as an inch as he brought it to my throat.

"You *could* kill her now," Rune drawled. Or... You could kill her along with me. You do so love your spectacle, and I think a double execution would start your reign off right, don't you?"

I tried to keep my breathing shallow as Mordecai's blade kissed my skin.

"And why would we care about pomp when killing a human?" he said.

"A normal one, I agree," Rune said. "But this one is...special to me."

"Even more reason for her to die." Mordecai's knife rested more heavily against my throat.

"Wait," Cobb said.

I couldn't understand it. Why would Rune reveal my magic? Why was he trying so hard to drag me down with him—

Then I saw Rune's wicked grin and realized that my magic wasn't what he meant by *special*.

"Human whore," Jezaline spat as Mordecai cackled in delight. "You're his...what? Concubine?"

"That's not—" I tried to protest.

"It never meant anything," Rune said loudly. "But I'll admit that I grew attached. I suppose it was inevitable. After all, war is not the only art form humans excel at."

"You perverted, lying bas—"

"Enough," Cobb said. "Take them both. We'll gut her before we do him. If anything, my new subjects will find the spectacle moderately entertaining."

We were dragged down the path to our execution.

KING'S HOLLOW WAS PACKED. In our absence, the other Lords had brought in their own wildlings, and not one of them looked friendly. Glass arrows were nocked; swords drawn and tossed from hand to hand, eager for blood. Some of the wildlings had conjured thickened walls of leaves to hide behind and scuttled along the uppermost branches to whisper to each other.

As we were brought to our knees below the throne, I

searched desperately for a glimpse of Xander, Pitus, Raquel, even Marian. Someone who would give me an inkling of hope that we'd make it out of this alive.

"Don't hurt your neck looking. None of them are here," Rune said. "I told them to stay away, no matter what happened to me. You'll be shocked to learn that it was surprisingly diffi-cult to get them to agree."

I scooted toward him. "I could kill you!"

"Better do it quick, then, because your window of opportu-nity will soon be gone."

He looked totally unconcerned that we were about to die, so different from the raw terror that tore at my gut. I worried at the bonds they'd secured our hands with. "I didn't think you hated me so much that you'd take me down with you."

Rune had the audacity to look appalled. "I don't hate you. I *need* you. You're the only way this could work."

"What could—"

"Quiet." A wildling kicked Rune in the side. When they looked away again, I leaned against a rock and subtly rubbed the ropes against it. They were giving, but too slowly. "This won't work, Rune," I hissed. "I can't help us."

Rune simply smirked. Cobb broke away from speaking with Mordecai and came over.

"I'm glad you're still finding humor in your situation, Cousin," he said. "Be sure to smile at the very end so it's forever frozen on your face."

Rune's smile grew. "Just for you."

Cobb's fingers twitched, no doubt wanting to strike him. "You always were too arrogant for your own good."

"Or perhaps I know my place and limitations." Rune nodded at the crown on Cobb's head. It was a little too big, sinking halfway down his brow. "You think that makes you high king? You knew from the very start you'd need me, and I'll bet even now you have doubts. Jezaline and Mordecai never give anything up, not unless they're getting something. Would you like to know what they're getting with you?"

Cobb's smile was brittle. "I have no doubt you'll tell me."

"They get the throne. Were I to take it, I would be a threat to them. But you?"

Rune's smile shifted to an expression that could almost be considered pitying, if I couldn't see his rage bubbling right beneath the surface. "You're a puppet. Easy to control and even easier to dispose of. They'll play their games for a time, enough to quell any dissent among their subjects, but eventually..."

Rune shrugged. "You'll be the one down here in my position."

Cobb glanced back at Mordecai and Jezaline. They were both looking our way, impatience etched on their faces.

"I'm no idiot. I know what they think of me. They believe me to be weak and bumbling. Someone who's easily manipulated."

"Then they understand you perfectly," I snapped.

Cobb smirked. "I can see how this creature ensnared you. Her tongue is just as sharp as yours. Maybe I'll have them cut it out before killing her."

He stood. "You underestimated me, Rune, just as they have. That will be their biggest mistake as it was yours. Die well, Cousin."

He turned to Jezaline and Mordecai as they approached. "My Lords! Ready for the main event?"

"I've waited long enough," Jezaline said.

She snapped her fingers, and we were marched up in front of the throne. I had nothing. No magic. No plan.

"Make sure to bring her close," Rune said, nodding to me. "Give her a good view of my death."

I'm always in control.

Rune believed it, but the words felt like a bad joke now. There was no *control* in getting me captured. No *control* in having us brought in front of the Lords, all of them together in one place—

Fast as a bolt of lightning, I understood what Rune was doing. The realization made me stagger.

"Keep walking." The wildling shoved me, but I barely felt it.

Rune had known the other Lords wouldn't be able to resist the spectacle of his death. It would be the one place and time they'd let down their guard, believing themselves victorious. He'd let himself get caught. He'd coaxed them into bringing us here. He'd even ensured I was taken with him and positioned me close enough to act when the time was right.

"You *idiot*!" I seethed, though Rune didn't hear. I couldn't use my magic reliably, even at the best of times, not to mention when we were about to die. Rune was relying on me to perform a miracle when it mattered most, and I knew—*knew*—I wouldn't be able to.

"Wildlings!"

Cobb had positioned himself before the throne. He wore a benevolent smile, arms out as though to embrace them all. "Today is the beginning of a new age. For years we have been without direction and without a high king. We've allowed the humans to maintain their poisonous hold on places that are not theirs. Is this acceptable?"

Dissenting boos and jeers answered. Cobb smiled wider.

"My reign will change that. As the high king, I will wage a righteous war on the humans. The Wilds will grow, and you will become more powerful than ever before. All will rightly fear us. But first we must remove one who stands in the way of this vision."

From the earth he drew an enormous thorn, grown at an angle, the sharpened tip near Rune's face. Desperate, I squeezed my eyes shut against the growing cheers and tried for my magic. The guard kicked my back. "Stop muttering."

"Yes, be sure to watch," Mordecai said hungrily. "See what all his promises and power have brought you."

Cobb had grabbed the back of Rune's neck and positioned him so that the tip of the thorn depressed his chin.

"The bastard exile must die," Cobb said. "And true blood, my blood, must take its place."

The guard pulled me up as I leaned forward. I'd nearly worked the ropes free. Rune's eyes flickered to me, expectant.

I can't! I wanted to scream. *I can't do what you've trusted me to, and now you're going to die. We're all going to die because of me.*

"And so ends the last of a line," Cobb said.

He pulled Rune's head back.

My ropes snapped.

I kicked back, foot driving into the knee of the wildling holding me. He screamed, clutching it. I yanked his sword free of its sheath and spun on the Lords and their guards.

"Let him go! Right now, or I'll...I'll..."

"*Drive that sword into your own gut,*" Jezaline purred, voice thick with compulsion. "*Slowly, one inch at a time so he can watch. Don't be shy.*" She bared her teeth in an animal grin. "*Do it.*"

I was halfway to pressing the point against my stomach when her hold over me slackened. I turned the sword back on them. Jezaline's smile faded.

"What trickery is this? What have you done?"

"*Crawl to me on your knees,*" Mordecai said, and when I didn't move, he gave a delighted clap. "Oho! Seems there's more to his pet than meets the eye."

"You gave her something," Jezaline says to Rune. "You made her this way!"

"He had nothing to do with it," I said. "And you will let him go."

"Be that as it may, my dear, surely you understand we can't do that," Mordecai said. "Your struggle is pointless."

I turned the sword from one to the next. My magic wouldn't listen. My arms started to shake as the truth of Mordecai's words sank in.

"Rune...if you have some way to save us, please, *please*, do it now."

"Put down the sword and your death will be quick," Cobb said. He still held Rune's throat against the thorn. "If not, I can guarantee you'll want to die a thousand times before we grant you the privilege."

I looked to Rune, seeking assurance, a clue, something that wasn't there.

"Don't let them kill you," I nearly sobbed. "Don't leave me here with them."

There was no trace of fear in Rune's face. "You can do it. Desperation makes monsters of us all, and they will all rightly fear you."

He jerked his head back, freeing himself. I let out a cry of relief.

Right before he stabbed the thorn through his neck.

TWENTY-ONE

Something in me snapped.

White-hot rage seized my muscles. Rage at the Lords for what they'd done. Rage at every terrible choice that had led me to this point.

And rage at Rune, for putting me here, knowing I was the only one who would, or could, save him.

A fist clocked me on the chin. My head spun, but I didn't feel the blow. It was as though my entire body had turned to iron, radiating nothing but anger.

"Kill her!" Jezaline barked. She'd backed away from me. She looked scared.

Good.

My instincts took over. I ducked an arrow and sliced a wildling open, each attack bringing me closer to the Lords cowering behind their forces. The blood and magic pumping through me drowned out almost everything else, but I could see Jezaline's lips move as she summoned more of her whorl-faced guards. They peeled from the ground, the trees, tried to wrap my feet and hold me in place.

I cut and hacked and sliced with a fervor. The ones that touched me withered away as though burned. I stabbed another wildling brave enough to come close. He screamed. Blood sprayed. I shoved him off my sword and kept stalking toward the Lords. No matter what they threw at me, I would stop it. It was inevitable that I would reach them and give them an end savage enough for the Wilds.

"I *said*—forget it, I'll do it myself," Jezaline snarled.

Stalks of silver needles rose like cobras to flank her. They spit at me, and I spun out of the way. A few needles punctured my arms and cut my side, but I was already numb.

"Jezi?" Mordecai gave a worried laugh. "You need to stop her. Now!"

Jezaline clapped her hands. The remaining guards twisted together, shooting upward until they were an under-growth giant, thorns for arms, feet made of root-wrapped stones.

"Crush her," Jezaline said.

The giant slammed an arm down. I dove, but my leg jerked, caught, and some of the thorns bit into my shoulder. Mordecai had turned the wood beneath my feet to liquid, and it slowly devoured my ankle, one inch at a time.

I snarled, willing it to free me, and the wood turned to blue crystal, shattering as I pulled my foot free. The giant reared up again. I couldn't hope to defeat that. I needed to get to the source.

"Don't let her—urk!"

Jezaline was pinned against the tree trunk as my hurled sword threaded the giant's rib cage and punctured her own. The giant's final attack withered as the magic holding it unwound and brought it crashing to the ground.

Mordecai tried to run behind the throne, but I was on him, clapping my glowing hand against his heart. His aura was easy to find. I was so lost in taking his magic that I nearly missed the light leaving his eyes.

I staggered as I pulled my hand off. Easy. I had killed one of the strongest beings of the Wilds as though they were nothing more than a hunted beast.

"*Heh, heh.*" Blood gurgled down Jezaline's collar as she laughed. "Rune really found himself a great—*heh*—tool."

It took a moment for the heady rush of taking Mordecai's magic to leave me, but when it did, I found I still wanted more. "I'm not a tool."

"We all are. You think he cares about you? You're a danger to him now. Once he gets what he wants, you'll be the next one he...he..."

I placed a hand on Jezaline's heart and took her life. Her jaw slackened. Her chin sank to her chest.

That left only one.

Cobb cowered behind the throne.

"You're...the same...those crystals," he blabbered. "How could you... How did you...?"

I twisted my hand, and blue crystal secured his legs. That done, I carefully removed Rune from the thorn and laid him on the ground.

"Yes—Yes, kill them!" Cobb screeched.

Once their Lords had fallen, a few of the wildling spectators had rushed to finish me off themselves. The closest one drew a knife, bloodlust on his face.

Two arrows appeared in his chest.

The others scattered as dark forms bled from the surrounding green. I saw the glint of blades, heard the twang of a bow as more arrows pierced flesh. Multiple flashes of white fur streaked below as the alpha wolf and her pack circled the hollow, coaxed by Raquel. They tore into any wildling trying to escape.

"Val? Rune?" Xander landed nearby. "Are you—" He whirled and loosed an arrow. "You two okay?"

"I've got him," I said, angling myself so Xander couldn't see the worst of Rune's injuries. "Keep them off me."

Xander nodded and leapt off to join the rest of the battle.

"You'd better not be dead," I muttered to Rune. "You better not have left me with this mess."

"Let him die," Cobb said. "Anything he offered you, protection, wealth, power, I could give you ten-fold. What is he to you?"

I stared at Rune's closed eyes. Through my fingers, I felt the faint, barely there beat of his heart. I *had* power. Unstable, and at times unusable and monstrous.

But I wanted him here, alive. There were still parts of me that hated him, yes... But more and more I couldn't deny that I liked him, too. Or at the very least respected how far he was willing to go for what and who he cared about.

"Time to wake up, Rune," I said.

I shoved magic into him. The large gouge in his neck closed. The wet blood dried. Some color returned to his paled cheeks.

"Get up," I said when he still didn't open his eyes. "I said get *up*."

Rune jolted awake. He blinked at the canopy and then cocked his ear toward the fighting before his gaze finally rested on me. His lips twisted in a crooked grin.

"Has anyone told you that you're glowing blue? The fact that we're both here and in one piece must mean that everything is going according to plan."

"You and I are going to have a very serious talk after this is over."

"Yes, yes of course." Rune noticed Cobb trembling behind me. "I see you got me a gift."

I helped him stand. It took him a few tries to stop leaning against me. I supposed that one might feel weak after returning from the brink of death. Again.

"I believe this belongs to me." Cobb flinched as Rune removed the crown from his brow and set it atop his own.

"I was only doing what was best for the Wilds," Cobb blubbered. "Be honest, you wouldn't enjoy ruling. All that responsibility and stress, and...and..."

"Val, do you mind giving my dear cousin and me a little privacy?"

Cobb's eyes bulged. "N-no, please don't leave, please don't —I beg you—"

Muscles stiff where Jezaline's thorns had found their mark, I left his pleading behind and went to check on how the rest of the fight was going. Many of the now-dead Lords' wildlings had managed to flee, the ones the wolves didn't catch. I wasn't terribly surprised to see a fair number of wildlings weren't fighting at all, but crouched in the trees and undergrowth, weaponless and waiting to see how this change of power played out. They hadn't leapt to the defense of their Lords or, it seemed, their supposed friends. So much for loyalty.

Marian rushed up to me, panting, shirt splattered with dirt and blood. "Rune, is he—"

"Fine," I said. "Better than ever now, I'm guessing."

She sagged with relief. "Good. And I'm...glad you're okay, too. You're glowing, you know that?"

"So I've been told."

Both of us turned as a small crush of wildlings rushed from the tangles of root-lined passages, breaking for the freedom of the surroundings Wilds.

"A little help?" Xander called.

I drew what remained of Sliver and leapt down to the forest floor. I'd never been in a battle this large. Every emotion seemed either amplified or subdued behind the shock of what I'd done. The lights were overly bright, the shouts and sound of swishing greenery as wildlings fled or fought or were killed was all stronger than ever before.

Finally, the last of the attackers were dispatched or allowed to flee, and King's Hollow fell quiet. I crouched, leaning on what remained of Sliver. "I think that's the last of the ones giving us trouble."

"Only leaves about two dozen more," Marian said darkly, looking at the wildlings who'd stuck around.

"Give them a chance," Xander said. "See what they're going to do."

"And let them stab us in the back? Don't be an idiot, Xander."

"Wildlings," Rune's voice boomed.

He stood before the throne, looking down at us. I wondered what had happened to Cobb, until I realized that the vaguely human shape at Rune's back, its skin skewered with thorns, flowers bursting from its skull, *was* Cobb. "Your false king is dead. Now I'll give you a choice: You can forgo the loyalty of your dead Lords and pledge your loyalty to me. You can help me forge a new age of wildlings under a single, rightful ruler and bring about a peace not had since the Forming."

He stepped aside, revealing the full extent of what he'd done to Cobb. "Or you can join him."

"You'd ask us to betray our allegiance?" one of the wildlings shouted. "What kind of choice is that?"

"Be glad you're getting one at all." Rune pointed to the wildling, as Marian and three others surrounded him. "Why don't we start with you? What is your answer?"

The wildling spat toward the throne. "Death to the high king and all who follow him."

"Come with me, Val," Xander muttered as the wildling had

a blade put against his throat. I brushed his hand off my shoulder and forced myself to watch as the blade was raised and brought down in a single, swift stroke.

"Does he have to do this?" I said as they let the body fall. "Isn't there another way?"

"I wish there was. I know Rune does, too."

Rune's face was hardened into a cruel mask as he oversaw the remaining wildlings making their choice. "He doesn't look it."

"He *can't* look it. If he shows any weakness, that'll encourage others to try to dethrone him."

Strength above all: the greatest trait the Wilds valued. How many times had Rune told me that?

Xander briefly shut his eyes as a scream rose through the Hollow then was swiftly cut off. "Are you okay? You're... glowing."

What a difficult question to answer. I felt...strong. And yet brittle. My body hummed with power, but it was wholly alien. I settled with, "I'm fine."

Xander opened his mouth, maybe to dispute me, but at another scream he closed it. "If you say so. Follow me."

We slipped away from the Hollow. In moments, the light thinned. The oppressive air and smell of blood faded away.

"I can't believe we did it," Xander said. "Rune talked about it for so long, but it never seemed possible, not really. Not until he found you."

"He could have done it without me," I said. "He almost did."

"Not even close. You were the trick." He glanced at my hands and then my heart, as though he could see the magic I'd stolen from Mordecai and Jezaline, as though afraid I'd do the same to him. "Still not sure how you did it."

"You and me both. If Rune hadn't..."

A sudden tightness squeezed my chest. I stopped, clutching at it.

"You okay?" Xander sounded concerned. "Val? Were you hit?" A sharp breath. "These thorns in your back. Give me a moment, this'll hurt—"

He gave three sharp tugs I barely felt. "There? Feel better?"

"Did we do the right thing?" I asked.

Xander threw away the thorns. He kept wiping his fingers on his pants as though he couldn't rid himself of my blood. "Rune is the true king."

"That's not what I asked."

"I can't give you an answer you can't give yourself. Rune will be a strong ruler. A good one. He cares for us, and he'll care for those who choose to follow him."

He will, I tried to convince myself. *He's a good person deep down. He cares for us. For me.*

He cares for us. He cares for me.

Maybe if I repeated that over and over, I'd believe it. I wanted to, so, so badly. I'd seen the good in him. I just had to hope it'd survive this.

"Too late, I guess," I said. "What's done is done."

"What's done is done," Xander repeated. "We're almost there."

Xander led me to a concealed opening beneath a waterfall, and after passing through a cave behind it, we emerged in another, much smaller, hollow. Trees hid it on all sides, and enormous lumps of moss-covered earth easily concealed discreet entrances to underground tunnels. A few of Rune's wildlings checked us out and then went back to their tasks.

"This is Wormwood," Xander said. "After they drove us out, the Lords never thought we'd dare get close enough again to pull off what we did."

"And why am I here?" I said. "We should be back with Rune."

In answer, Xander parted a curtain of moss and led me down a smooth-dirt tunnel into an earthen, root-roofed room. Compact beds of silk and satin hung just off the ground by vines.

And on one, the rot so bad it took me longer than it should have to recognize her...

"Peyton!" I gasped.

I shoved past Xander and slid to my knees at her bedside, unable to stop my tears. Disbelief at her aliveness collided with horror at her worsened condition. The rot had peeled back her skin and rashed along her arms and legs, oozing pus. Boils along her face looked ready to burst.

"Peyton... Peyton." I ran my hands along the little stretch of healthy skin that remained of her cheek. She stirred, but weakly. I couldn't imagine the amount of pain she was in.

"I don't understand," I said. "Joshua said... I thought they'd killed her. How did you manage..."

I trailed off. The answer was the same as it always was. "She was never attacked, was she?"

"Rune thought she could have been," Xander said. "In fact, the night he had her taken away, some of Mordecai's soldiers showed up as ours were leaving. They only barely avoided giving themselves away."

"He...staged her death," I said, mostly to myself.

Xander hesitated, before nodding. "He asked Pitus and Idwal, another spy, to make it seem like she'd been killed. He made a promise to you, and he intended to keep it."

I continued stroking Peyton's cheek, fury warring within me. A promise wasn't the only reason Rune had done what he did. He'd likely seen I was wavering in my resolve with each setback and as the Lords closed in. He needed to focus my hatred. What better way to do that than blame the very people he hated?

But like a cresting wave, my anger crashed down and drew back. Peyton was here, with me, as safe as she could be, save for the rot.

"Can you cure her?" I asked.

"She's too far along, or we would have," Xander said. He nodded to my arms, my skin still glowing. "But I imagine you have enough power now that you can."

I could. I would. "Bring me herb blooms, glasswort, and some eclipse flower. You have those around, don't you?"

"Of course," Xander said, catching on. "What about grubber's root? Triss used that a lot, though I'm not sure even it will be effective against rot that's so advanced ..."

"Yes, that too. Bring it all."

I gently stroked Peyton's arm, existing in the uncomfortable relief of finding her. I'd resolved to always have a hole in my chest where she used to be, but since she was back, she didn't fit quite right, as though bitterness had taken her place.

Xander returned a moment later and put everything on the table next to me. "Let me know if you need more."

"Thank you. Now leave."

He jerked a nod and was gone.

I recalled what Triss had done as best I could, letting the memory guide me. I used my magic to boil the grubber's root until the greenish substance leaked out. I mashed herb blooms and mixed the paste with glasswort, then smeared that over the worst of the rot before draping it with the petals from the eclipse flower. I sat back and waited for it to take effect, but after a few minutes, I knew Xander was right. She needed what only I could offer.

I placed a hand on Peyton's forehead and another on her arm. I forced myself to recall the moment the thorn had pierced Rune's throat. The desperation the act had awakened in me.

Magic flowed into her. Using the medicine, I fed the healthy parts of her body and ate away at the diseased. Like an archeologist, I removed the dead and rotting skin to uncover her, piece by piece.

The boils on her face receded. The scabs along her skin flaked off as new skin took its place. The eclipse petals, sucked dry of their essence, withered and fell away.

"V-Val?"

Peyton's eyes were open. They were milky white with disease. I knew by her shocked face that she could see me. "You're okay," I sobbed. "You're okay."

"I'm okay," she agreed. "Because you..." A weak gasp. "You're glowing, Val. Your magic, is it..."

"I have a lot to explain."

Peyton shrunk from my hold with a weary breath. "After all these years, I thought it'd go away. They said the medicine... Don't hate me, Val. I only wanted to protect you."

"Of course I don't hate you. Don't even say that."

Peyton stared at the rooted ceiling. "Don't use any more magic on me. You have to keep it. You have to stay strong."

"I will." I could make any promise now that I knew she was going to be okay. "You should get some rest."

"Yes. Yes, of course." Peyton's eyes fluttered. "I feel like I've been in one long nightmare. I don't know if I've woken up...".'

Her eyes closed. I held her hand until her breathing steadied. Peyton didn't let go of my hand as I stood.

"The wildling who took you from me, the prince, he's not here, is he? You managed to get away from him, didn't you?"

"Not exactly," I said. "He's High King of the Wilds now."

Peyton's eyes opened. "No... No...we have to leave him, do you understand? Before...before *they* took me, I saw... It was as

Father Dumas said. He knew this would happen, knew it from the very beginning."

I forced her back down as she tried to sit up. "You're not strong enough to move yet. Whatever you saw, it's okay now. We're safe."

"No, no, no... This is all my fault. It shouldn't be this way, *he* shouldn't have made it that far, and now that he has... We have to leave him, Val."

She was clearly still delirious. Either that or she'd been talking too much with Father Dumas and other worshippers of the Mother Tree. No doubt those vipers took every opportunity to fill her head with gunk and false prophecies whenever I was away. "I know. I'm going to talk to him one last time, then we'll go. I promise."

"Can't...be trusted... Can't..."

Peyton's hand dropped as she lapsed back into sleep. I waited to make sure she would stay that way before pushing through the curtain of moss to the surface to find Xander waiting on a stump.

"I need to talk with Rune," I said.

"He might be busy quelling any—"

"He'll see me." I took off toward the Hollow. After hesitating, Xander followed without argument.

The Hollow was eerily silent. I counted half a dozen of those who hadn't pledged their allegiance to the new high king, their bodies already overgrown with tender greenery. It wasn't as many as I'd thought there'd be. Either Rune's speech and claim of the throne was compelling enough, or wildling loyalty shifted to fit whoever was the most convenient master.

Marian intercepted me on my way to the throne. "Rune is busy right now."

"Did you know?" I asked. "Did you know he took Peyton? That she's still alive?"

The flash of genuine surprise in her face told me all I needed. "I'm sure he had his reasons."

"He always does. I'm ending our deal; you'll never have to see me again, just like you wanted."

She caught my arm. "Whatever I said... If I ever..." Her lips turned down in a sour frown. "Thanks. That's what I'm trying to say. Thanks for helping us—him—get this."

I couldn't help smiling at how difficult those simple words were for her. "Don't screw it up."

"We won't. We've spent years waiting for this day. The hard part is over."

She let go of my arm, and I continued up. The throne had come alive in my absence, melding Cobb's root-pierced body into the back. The crystals, jewels, and gold rearranged to coat the arms and high back where Rune's head would rest.

"Xander showed you," Rune said.

He sat in a crook of branches just out of sight of those below. His crown was askew, either on purpose or as though he hadn't grown into it yet. It looked fittingly insouciant on him.

I gestured to the throne. "You have a perfectly good chair right there. Isn't this what you wanted?"

A flicker of something—uncertainty?—moved across his face before he ripped his eyes away from mine and looked at the throne.

"I suppose it is. It's strange how something you've sought for so long can be exactly what you dreamed of and also nothing like it."

"You can't seriously be second-guessing now. Not after what you put me and everyone else through. Not after what you've done."

Rune's eyes were back on me. He languidly uncurled from his perch like a cat—

unfolding with grace and power—and closed the distance to me. I bristled, elated and tense as he cupped my cheek in one cool hand.

"Leave here, forever, Val," he said. "Take all the heart gems you want from my fallen enemies and never return to the Wilds again. Because if you do, the welcome you find may not be so welcome."

I knocked his hand aside and gave a mocking bow. "Gladly. Enjoy your reign, Your Majesty."

A hundred thousand things I wanted to say battled to free themselves from my lips. I stormed away instead.

That was it. No thanks. No acknowledgement of anything except that I'd done exactly as promised, as had he. That was all I *wanted*.

It didn't seem like enough.

"Val!"

Raquel raised a cup to me as I reached the Hollow's floor. Rune's wildlings—his *subjects*—had already begun regrowing the place into what it'd been before. Someone had summoned food and drink, and though I was sure the danger hadn't passed, they were already digging in.

"Come, grab a drink," Raquel called.

I gave a jerky wave, ignoring his confused reaction. I walked back to Wormwood to get Peyton, intent on getting her to safety before collecting my payment. My head was starting to hurt. All the problems I'd sworn to deal with until after I'd finished helping Rune were returning with a vengeance. Peyton was a victim in this, but me? Joshua might have been my stepbrother, but he couldn't ignore his duty to the DFA. Since Rune and I were done, I had no allies in the Wilds, and no friends in the human world.

Panic stabbed my chest, and it was a struggle to overcome it.

Damn Rune. Damn him so much.

Smoke was rising above the treetops, originating some-where farther down the coast. I watched it curl lazily upwards. Strange. Maybe Rune's ascension hadn't been as problem-free as I'd thought. But what did I care? I was done. My invitation to the Wilds had been revoked.

Right before I reached the waterfall, my skin buzzed. An energy in the air called to the magic in me. Curious, I followed the sensation until I parted a snarl of ferns and nearly stum-bled into the crevasse of glowing crystals.

"You've got to be kidding me." *More?* And so close to King's Hollow, too.

The crystals burned more brightly as I stepped closer. I could deny my connection to them all I wanted, but it was clear that we were connected. I just didn't know how.

Someone crashed through the trees. I whirled around.

"Peyton!"

I caught her as she pitched forward. Little remained of the rot, save for a few patches on her arms. Her face was slicked with sweat. "I told you to stay and rest. I was just on my way back."

Peyton's mouth gaped soundlessly. Her eyes darted from the crevasse to the smoke to the hole. Over the crash of the waterfall, I could just make out voices calling for her.

"What happened?" I said.

"No time," she gasped. "There's no more time. We have to... *You* have to... Now that you're strong enough... No more hiding. But I wish it didn't have to be this way." She pulled me close enough to smell the remnants of the eclipse flower wafting off her skin. "If you believe anything, believe that I didn't want it to happen this way, Val."

"What are you talking about—"

I gagged as Peyton hurled a cloud of spores into my face.

The familiar, cloying smell thickened my tongue and dulled my senses. Lulling yarrow. My body sagged, as useless as a puppet with severed strings.

"What'd...you...do...to me..."

I watched the next few moments as though they were happening to someone else.

Peyton dragging me to the edge of the crevasse. Peyton drawing a knife she must have grabbed from one of the wildlings. Peyton carving into the palm of my left hand. The lulling yarrow dulled much of my senses, but it didn't dull the pain.

"I'm sorry, I'm sorry, I'm sorry, love," Peyton repeated as she drove the knife deeper and my blood made a steady *splat, splat, splat* as it hit the ground. "I tried to keep you from the worst of it, but Father Dumas... He knew from the very beginning, somehow. He knew exactly what you were."

She threw down the knife and parted the skin of my palm. Tears streamed down her face. "I always knew, but I never loved you any less."

She tilted my palm toward me. If I could have screamed, I would have.

Where my white human bone should have been was glowing blue crystal.

"I have so much to tell you." Peyton used her shirt to wipe away the worst of the blood, leaving a semi-clean gash still awash in blue. "The legends of the Mother Tree, they're more than a history; they're our way forward. I swore it would never happen, that I'd help stop it before you needed to get involved, but then that stupid wildling boy interfered." Her voice shook with rage. "He got you involved. He messed this up, for everyone. He should have let the Wilds eat itself, but it's too late, there's no turning back now."

Peyton turned my limp palm over and touched my glowing bone to the point of the nearest crystal.

The magic I'd stolen from the Lords rushed out of me in such a rush I threatened to pass out for real. The crystals began to vibrate so violently they sounded like clacking bones. The ground shook. Voices screamed.

"It's begun." Peyton sagged to the ground. "They're coming."

CHAPTER

TWENTY-TWO

"You never had any parents." Peyton panted as she lugged my semi-paralyzed body through the trees. Tremors rocked the earth in sporadic waves. The screams were all around us. "Not as far as we know. When I found you, the people we thought were your parents..."

Peyton swallowed. "We think you killed them. You didn't mean to. You were so confused. Whoever they were, they were probably trying to take you back to wherever you came from. By the time we realized what you were, it was impossible to know for sure."

She was speaking, but the words might as well have been in a foreign language. None of this made any sense. The girl she was talking about wasn't *me*.

Peyton stopped to rest against a tree. She must not have used enough yarrow, because some feeling was coming back to my muscles. But what would I do, even if I could move? Everything I thought to be true had been shattered.

I had to find Rune and the others. Had to know if they were okay after whatever Peyton had made me do.

329

"Joshua's probably on his way." Peyton was looking in the direction of the growing smoke. "But you know how he is. He's been waiting for an opportunity to strike for a long time. My supposed death gave him that, though I suspect he's been working on a plan for much longer."

A tree crackled as it snapped in half, followed by half a dozen more. A group of wildlings streaked past in the direction of King's Hollow, shouting to one another and missing us entirely. Peyton waited until they were gone before hefting me again and continuing to walk.

"I'll answer all your questions soon, I promise. I don't have all the answers myself. Those Below are closer than we thought. They needed one more piece. They needed you."

My mouth tasted like yarrow paste. I smacked my tongue until I could manage, "What...am I?"

"You're my daughter," Peyton said firmly. "Never forget that."

"No... *What* am...*I*?"

Peyton's bottom lip trembled. She looked like she wanted to answer any question but that. "You are a glass god. Power clothed in flesh. You are the key to *them,* the key to everything."

Each word of her useless explanation was like a knife to my chest. Who was this person who'd kept such secrets from me? What had she done?

"You...lied to me."

"I had to. If anyone found out what you truly were, they'd have killed you. That's why Father Dumas got you the heart tree medicine. What you were had to stay hidden, even from yourself, until the time was right."

Peyton stopped, heaving for air. Despite her betrayal, it hurt to see her in so much pain.

"The Wilds have to die, Val, and Those Below can kill it. The Wilds knew." Her gaze darted around as though the very trees would awaken, enraged. "They devoured and devoured. It wasn't just keeping us out; it was keeping us from freeing them and freeing us. You don't have to be scared of the wildlings anymore, Val. *They* should be scared of what's coming."

But I wasn't afraid of what was coming. I was scared for Marian, Xander, and all the wildlings who didn't know what was happening.

I was scared for Rune. Truly, terribly scared.

"If we can reach Joshua, he can take us back to Seattle," Peyton said. "He'll cover for us, keep up the ruse. Nobody will ever have to know what really happened—"

The biggest tremor yet shook the ground. Peyton stumbled. I seized my chance and shoved her away. My legs and arms were still stiff and unwieldy, but I managed to lumber in the direction of King's Hollow as Peyton shouted at me to come back, that I was making a terrible mistake.

I stumbled into a shambling run, made treacherous as more crevasses, all spiked with crystal, ripped the earth apart. Smoke and soured magic coated my tongue. I followed the frantic shouts until I burst into King's Hollow.

A few of Rune's wildlings lay crushed beneath collapsed trees, their blood staining the lake crimson. Others were fighting. Marian had been right, some new converts weren't as loyal as I'd thought. I spied Xander and a few others dashing through the treetops. Xander's arm blurred. Arrows peppered a rogue wildling, and without a sound he collapsed into one of the multiple gaping chasms that had appeared since my absence.

"You!"

Marian spotted me. I hadn't expected a welcome reception, but the amount of venom in her expression made me step back. "Marian, wait, I'm here to—"

Her eyes widened. Too late, I realized she was looking at the palm of my hand and the blue glow within. "Marian, I can—"

I threw myself behind the cover of an enormous root as knives made of ice zipped overhead.

"You traitorous human!" Marian snarled. "You were against us this entire time!"

"I didn't do it," I yelled back. "Not exactly. I'm here to help!"

Marian laughed. More ice thudded against the root. I scrambled away from the frost gathering at my feet.

"I dare you to try explaining," Marian said. "Convince me you haven't wanted us all dead from the very beginning."

"I don't know what's happening, but we all need to leave right now." My cheek smarted as more ice cut dangerously close. "Marian, this part of the Wilds isn't safe!"

"None of it is safe, and none of it will be, not for us. Stop moving so I can—"

"Marian."

The attacks stopped. I warily stuck my head out.

Rune had appeared, glass knife in one hand, his other holding Marian's arm back. "Enough. Val couldn't have done this."

"Then why don't you ask her!" Marian jerked herself free. "Have her show you what's beneath her skin!"

Rune frowned. "What's she talking about?"

I slowly stepped out of cover. Out of everyone, I was sure Rune would listen. He had to. "I don't totally understand it either. I'll try to make some sense of everything, but right now—"

I was thrown to the ground as the earth shook with its most violent tremor yet. More trees snapped as they fell. Wildlings screamed.

I tried to stand and was pushed back to my hands and knees as a new chasm split between Rune and me, widening so fast I barely had time to push myself away before I fell in.

When I could finally stand, I approached its edge. I stared down into it, sure that I was imagining things.

The chasm didn't end in darkness, but instead revealed an entire other world below, as though, like my palm, the skin of the earth had been pulled back and revealed the underworkings beneath.

Trees, as big as those in the Wilds, reached toward me, almost close enough to kneel down and touch. Castles and spired buildings with purposes I couldn't begin to guess were interspersed between them. There were fields, too, stretching long into the horizon, glittering with grass like shards of fiberglass.

Though their color was correct, everything glowed with the same otherworldly blue light. Crystal, I was sure of it. The very kind I was made of. Its beauty was a cold thing. A glittering tomb that made me think of being buried alive, of slowly losing oxygen while yearning for even a second of real sunlight.

"Wildlings!" Rune said. Crown still askew, he leapt to a vantage point. "Prepare—"

A spear soared from below and struck the ribs of a wildling who'd gotten too close to the crevasse. Marian tried to catch her but missed, and the girl pitched forward and fell.

The beasts crawled up.

They were crystal creatures, mouths full of gnashing, glittering teeth. I barely had time to realize there were people riding them—their crystal skin speckled with human-like flesh —before the entire Hollow erupted in chaos.

Everything was happening too fast. I didn't know who this enemy was, but like any invading army, they'd want to quell resistance fast. They'd cut off the head of the snake. They'd go for Rune.

I dashed from cover, kicking off a trunk and throwing myself into Rune right as three shards of sharpened crystal stabbed where he'd stood.

We both hit the ground hard, me on top of him. He looked over my shoulder, to where the shards still quivered from impact.

"To think that could have been you," I said.

"You already have my gratitude. Up, get up."

I rolled off him, then he was grabbing my arm and pulling me beneath a tree whose roots parted for him before closing again.

"I don't know what's happening, but I will not stay here and let my own get slaughtered," Rune said. "I've gotten what I wanted. I'm not about to give it all up."

"I know, but we need to be smart about this."

A crystal beast gave a grating snarl as it stalked by. Rune parted the roots, knife ready. I tried to pull him back.

"You can't—"

He was gone. The roots started to close up after him. No doubt Rune thought to protect me by keeping me in a cage. I hacked away with Sliver and slipped free.

One of the beast riders waited for me.

I slid beneath his sword and swiped with my own, only managing to chip another piece off my already shortened blade as I connected with the back of the beast's legs. It chomped at my head, and I stumbled back, almost falling into the crevasse. The sounds of clinking metal on crystal swelled in volume. For all the wildlings' magic and ferocity, it seemed they couldn't do much against this new enemy. Regular weapons were useless. I had only one thing that might work.

I faked a swing, and when the beast went for where it

looked like I was going, I leapt atop its back. I slammed my hand against the rider's chest.

As I suspected, his crystal body—the kind that reminded me so much of heart gems—responded. Magic flowed into me. The glowing parts of the rider's skin dulled, and he slumped off, his beast collapsing after. I slid to the ground. They were tough, but not invincible.

"How peculiar. Why do you fight your own kind?"

Another rider watched me from the center of the fray. Her body was mottled crystal and skin, face carved into the sort of terrible beauty legends and nightmares were made of, crossed with thick veins of blue lapis. At her side hung a blade nearly as long as I was. She smiled, benevolent and malicious in equal measure.

I raised Sliver as I slowly approached her. "Who are you?"

"You already know the answer. You finally figured it out after all these years."

"She's one of yours!"

My heart stopped as Peyton stumbled through the battle and dropped to her knees beside the woman. "Don't hurt her, she's yours."

The woman sneered down. "Of course she is. She's the one we've been looking for." She raised her sword over Peyton's neck. "The same cannot be said for you."

Before she swung, I threw Sliver at her and threw myself in front of the blow, managing to catch the woman's sword between my hands. The blade still cut deep into my shoulder and lodged in something stronger than bone. I bit my tongue to keep from passing out.

"She means something to you?" the woman said.

"Leave," I gritted out. "Now."

The woman laughed. "I think not. Now that we're reunited, I won't lose you again." She shoved the blade deeper.

My vision flickered. "No! You're going back where you belong."

"But we belong *here*." She raised her hand, and a terrible fear filled me as the ground shook again. Then the throne—the one Rune had sacrificed almost everything to get—cracked down the middle, spewing shards of earth and wood.

I barely had time to cry out in horror before the entire Hollow seemed to tilt. I realized what was happening a moment too late.

"Run!"

Part of the ground collapsed, swallowed into the world below.

"Rune!" I screamed as he vanished out of sight. Something enormous slammed me from the side. The blade was torn from my shoulder, replaced with stabbing of a different kind all down my body. The woman's beast had trapped me in its jaws.

"I think it's time for *you* to return where you belong," the woman said.

I struggled weakly as the beast turned away from Peyton and leapt into the chasm.

The last thing I saw was the faint light of the sun through the rapidly shrinking sliver of earth, and Rune's face—his bloody, bruised but alive face—screaming my name until I couldn't see him anymore.

As Above, So Below

I didn't know how the light got down here. I didn't know how the air I breathed was so clean or how my surroundings were perfect, crystalline imitations of the Wilds and the human world, down to their texture and color. Though they weren't warm. Nothing down here was warm.

Mostly, I didn't know how I survived. It felt like only hours, but it might have been days since I'd been taken. Other than the guards outside the chamber, the only people I saw were some attendants. They were let in and quickly hurried to work, too scared to even make eye contact. Like the wildlings, they looked like me, but their patches of human skin couldn't hide the crystal beneath. One had growths of colored rock running along his arms and legs, while crystal ridges jutted from the girl's back.

I tried to talk to her while she tended my wound, but she never acknowledged me. With practiced care, she drew the point of a handheld crystal against the now-healed gash in my shoulder until any sign of injury was gone. When both were finished, they hurried out.

The door to the chamber opened again soon after. This time, it was the woman who'd taken me—Sotera. *Empress* Sotera. My skin had crawled when she'd told me the title.

"How are you feeling?" she asked. It was a silly question, partly because I knew she didn't care. Mostly because I felt drained. The moment the beast had dropped me, my arms and legs had been embedded between two crystal pillars that leeched what little magic I still had.

"I'll let you out in just a bit," Sotera said. "Until you can control your magic, we can't let you have any."

She trailed her finger along the pillars as she circled me. "There is a creation myth in the Wilds."

"I don't care."

"Of course you do. Their history is our history, and our history is yours, cherished one."

"I'm not your cherished anything."

Sotera smiled as though, like the rest of this, I'd come to enjoy the name in time.

"There is so much I want to tell you. Our history, our goals, and how they align with yours. We both seek to destroy the Wilds and the false king who resides in them."

I picked my head up. "So Rune's still alive."

Sotera's beautifully cruel face soured. "Do not allow yourself the luxury of hope. He is...for now. As is the one who called herself your guardian. She played her part, and her reward for that is to be spared our wrath."

I tried to summon some feeling of relief at learning Peyton was also okay, but I could only manage bone-deep numbness at her betrayal. All the times she said she loved me, I was nothing but a means to an end for her.

"As for you..."

Sotera pressed two fingers against the front of the columns. The crystals released me, and I fell to my knees. I was so, so weak, but I couldn't afford to be. I didn't care if I was one of them. I didn't care what Sotera wanted. Resolve had gripped me, along with the barest inklings of a plan. I would wait. I would grow strong. Then I'd escape.

"Good," Sotera said, noticing. "That hatred is good. You'll need it."

"For what?"

"For all we still have to do." She gestured up, to the roof of their world and the ground of mine. "We will bring everything above down below. Now rest. We start tomorrow."

Once I was sure she was gone, I flexed my fingers to loosen them up. I found a small piece of crystal with a jagged edge the attendants hadn't picked up. Something I could use as a makeshift knife.

Then I rested, and plotted, and waited for my moment to come.

Shatter their souls. Steal their throne.
Grab book 2 in the Savage Wilds series, ***Savage Wild Souls***.

Get notified about new releases, exclusive ARCs, cover reveals, giveaways, and more by **joining my author newsletter.**

Please Leave a Review

I can't thank you enough for choosing to read my books! Every single review helps me find new readers and continue doing what I love: writing great stories for you to enjoy. If you get a second, could **you click here to leave a review or star rating?** Thank you so much for your help and support!

Get notified about new releases, exclusive ARCs, cover reveals, giveaways, and more by **joining my author newsletter.**

instagram.com/seanfletcherauthor

amazon.com/author/seanfletcher

facebook.com/seannfletcher

bookbub.com/profile/sean-fletcher

goodreads.com/seanfletcher

MORE BOOKS BY SEAN

Savage Wilds Series

Savage Wild Hearts

Savage Wild Souls

Savage Wild Gods

Legacy of Dragon Series

Dragon Born

Dragon Lost

Dragon Unleashed

Dragon Blood

The Heir of Dragons Series:

Dragon's Awakening

Dragon's Curse

Dragon's Bane

Dragon's Fate

Paranormal Outcasts Series:

Elemental Outcast

Elemental Trial

Elemental Queen

The Darkness Within Series:

Called by Darkness

The Cursed One

Enemy of Magic

The Dark Prince

The Mages of New York Trilogy

Mage's Apprentice

Mage's Trial

Mage's End

ACKNOWLEDGEMENTS

This book is actually a Frankenstein of sorts. Years ago, I had the idea for a fantasy story where everyone's magic revolved around stones they carried. I even wrote the entire book (over four-hundred pages!) to its completion. Nothing ever came of it, and in the few times I've flipped through the rough draft, I'm glad it didn't. You should be glad, too.

But the idea of magic stones stuck with me, and in late 2022, during a period of great personal and career growth, and asking "What do I *really* want to write?" the idea popped up again. Only this time, the stones were now heart gems, and they had to be carved from beasts. This idea collided with another two loves of mine: dark fantasy, and Miyazaki movies, namely *Princess Mononoke*.

For those who haven't checked out any of Hayao Miyazaki's movies, I highly suggest you do, even if you don't like animation. You may find yourself pleasantly surprised.

For my next book I wanted to create something that was a little different than what I usually wrote. A jumping off point of sorts toward writing stories that truly, *truly* compelled me, and hopefully, in their inception, equally compelled readers. I wanted to capture that imaginative fun I had when I first started writing. I wanted something both dangerous and beautiful. Something you couldn't help being drawn to, despite knowing how much it could hurt you.

You're holding the result. One of what I pray will be many

great stories to come. I hope it brings you as much joy reading it as I did writing it.

As with any book, the author may have written the words, but it passed through numerous hands to turn into something readable. Many thanks to my wonderful alpha, beta, and *I don't know what stage of the process this is* readers, Marie Reed, Kristen Franzke, Eirini Frikantela, Michelle Elsey-Sargent, Veronica Prowant, and Donna from Hot Tree Editing.

Thanks to my proofreader Tia Bach, who made me realize I have a lot of bad writing habits.

Thanks to the cover designer, James T. Eagen, from BookFly Designs.

Thanks to my family; my mother who may not agree with everything I write, but still reads my books regardless; to my brother and father, who *don't* read anything I write (including this), but at least crack jokes about me being a starving artist. Thanks for keeping it real.

And as always, thanks to my amazing fans, both old and new, who support me and make it possible to keep on going with this whole author thing.

About the Author

Sean Fletcher is an award-winning and bestselling fantasy author across multiple age ranges and subgenres, with over thirty books in more than five different series, many of which have hit #1 in their categories. Since writing and pitching his first book at fifteen, he's forged a path through the publishing industry, continuing to hone his craft and expertise at a premier literary agency before becoming a full-time author, speaker, and editor.

When not jotting down highly enjoyable lies, he's often doing something most people find masochistic, like cycling long distances, hiking high mountains, and indulging in more sweets than is medically advisable.

Stalk him on social media or his author newsletter to learn more about his upcoming releases.

Fletcher, Sean
Savage Wild Hearts (The Savage Wilds Book 1)
Denton, Texas
1. Young Adult Contemporary/Dark Fantasy

ISBN (hardcover): 978-1-7365981-9-1
ISBN (paperback): 9798398462937

First edition published July, 2023

www.ingramcontent.com/pod-product-compliance
Lightning Source LLC
Chambersburg PA
CBHW061112310726
48974CB00002B/500